EXTRAORDINARY PRAISE FOR SARA BLAEDEL AND THE LOUISE RICK SERIES

"Blaedel is one of the best I've come across."
—Michael Connelly

"Crime-writer superstar Sara Blaedel's great skill is in weaving a heartbreaking social history into an edge-of-your-chair thriller while at the same time creating a detective who's as emotionally rich and real as a close friend."   —Oprah.com

"She's a remarkable crime writer who time and again delivers a solid, engaging story that any reader in the world can enjoy."
—Karin Slaughter

"One can count on emotional engagement, spine-tingling suspense, and taut storytelling from Sara Blaedel. Her smart and sensitive character, investigator Louise Rick, will leave readers enthralled and entertained."   —Sandra Brown

"I loved spending time with the tough, smart, and all-too-human heroine Louise Rick—and I can't wait to see her again."   —Lisa Unger

"If you like crime fiction that is genuinely scary, then Sara Blaedel should be the next writer you read."
—Mark Billingham

"Sara Blaedel is at the top of her game. Louise Rick is a character who will have readers coming back for more."
—Camilla Läckberg

THE RUNNING GIRL

THE NIGHT WOMEN

leave you wanting more... This is an intense read, totally engrossing and fast-paced." —*Always With a Book*

THE STOLEN ANGEL

"Blaedel keeps everything well-oiled and moving with nary a squeak as she leads the reader through the book to a series of startling and satisfying conclusions." —BookReporter.com

"This book really takes you on quite a ride. It's dark and twisted, and I was floored when I realized just who the crazy sociopath was behind the evil acts... I never saw that coming! I have to say that one of my favorite aspects of this series is the character development we get. This is an addicting, thrilling read. I was glued to the pages, wondering just what was going to happen next and if Louise and her team were going to figure it all out before it was too late. The mix of police procedural and compelling characters really makes this book (and series!) one you don't want to miss." —*Always with a Book*

THE LOST WOMAN

"Leads to... that gray territory where compassion can become a crime and kindness can lead to coldblooded murder." —*New York Times Book Review*

"Engrossing." —*Toronto Star*

"Blaedel solidifies once more why her novels are as much finely drawn character studies as tightly plotted procedurals, always landing with a punch to the gut and the heart." —*Library Journal* (starred review)

"Long-held secrets and surprising connections rock Inspector Louise Rick's world in Blaedel's latest crime thriller. Confused and hurt, Louise persists in investigating a complex murder despite the mounting personal ramifications. The limits of loyalty and trust, and the complexities of grief, are central to this taut thriller's resolution. A rich cast of supporting characters balances the bleakness of the crimes."

—*RT Book Reviews* (4 stars)

"Sara Blaedel is a literary force of nature...Blaedel strikes a fine and delicate balance between the personal and the professional in *The Lost Woman*, as she has done with the other books in this wonderful series...Those who can't get enough of finely tuned mysteries...will find this book and this author particularly riveting." —BookReporter.com

"Blaedel, Denmark's most popular author, is known for her dark mysteries, and she examines the controversial social issue at the heart of this novel, but ends on a surprisingly light note. Another winner from Blaedel." —*Booklist*

THE KILLING FOREST

"Another suspenseful, skillfully wrought entry from Denmark's Queen of Crime." —*Booklist*

"Engrossing...Blaedel nicely balances the twisted relationships of the cult members with the true friendships of Louise, Camilla, and their circle." —*Publishers Weekly*

"Blaedel delivers another thrilling novel...Twists and turns will have readers on the edge of their seats waiting to see what happens next." —*RT Book Reviews*

"Will push you to the edge of your seat [then] knock you right off...A smashing success."   —BookReporter.com

"Blaedel excels at portraying the darkest side of Denmark."
     —*Library Journal*

THE FORGOTTEN GIRLS

WINNER OF THE 2015 RT REVIEWER'S CHOICE AWARD

"Crackling with suspense, atmosphere, and drama, *The Forgotten Girls* is simply stellar crime fiction."   —Lisa Unger

"Chilling...[a] swiftly moving plot and engaging core characters."   —*Publishers Weekly*

"This is a standout book that will only solidify the author's well-respected standing in crime fiction. Blaedel drops clues that will leave readers guessing right up to the reveal. Each new lead opens an array of possibilities, and putting the book down became a feat this reviewer was unable to achieve. Based on the history of treating the disabled, the story is both horrifying and all-too-real. Even the villains have nuanced and sympathetic motives."
     —*RT Times* Top Pick, Reviewer's Choice Award Winner

"Already an international bestseller, this outing by Denmark's Queen of Crime offers trademark Scandinavian crime fiction with a tough detective and a very grim mystery. Blaedel is incredibly talented at keeping one reading... Recommend to fans of Camilla Läckberg and Liza Marklund."   —*Library Journal*

THE RUNNING GIRL

BOOKS BY SARA BLAEDEL

THE LOUISE RICK SERIES

The Missing Persons Trilogy

The Forgotten Girls

The Killing Forest

The Lost Woman

The Camilla Trilogy

The Night Women

The Running Girl

The Stolen Angel

The Homicide Trilogy

The Midnight Witness

The Silent Women

The Drowned Girl

THE FAMILY SECRETS SERIES

The Daughter

THE RUNNING GIRL

SARA BLAEDEL

Translated by Thom Satterlee

GRAND CENTRAL
PUBLISHING
New York Boston

Grand Central Publishing
Hachette Book Group
1290 Avenue of the Americas
New York, NY 10104
grandcentralpublishing.com
twitter.com/grandcentralpub

First published in Denmark as *Haevnens gudinde* in 2009
First published in America: January 2018
First mass market edition: October 2018

Grand Central Publishing is a division of Hachette Book Group, Inc.
The Grand Central Publishing name and logo is a trademark of Hachette Book
Group, Inc.

The Hachette Speakers Bureau provides a wide range of authors for speaking events.
To find out more, go to www.hachettespeakersbureau.com or call (866) 376-6591.

The publisher is not responsible for websites (or their content) that are not owned by
the publisher.

ISBNs: 978-1-5387-5974-5 (mass market), 978-1-5387-5972-1 (ebook)

Printed in the United States of America

OPM

10 9 8 7 6 5 4 3 2 1

For Gitte and Bo

Prologue

The first blow lands on the homeless man's cheekbone, just as the door to the basement slams shut behind them. They keep coming, the blows. They hammer down on him, incessantly. Neither daylight nor sound reaches in here where a group of youths has circled around their victim, but two glaring lightbulbs hanging down from the ceiling reveal that the tormenters are wearing masks. Like bank robbers; only their eyes show.

The terrified man holds his hands desperately in front of his face in a futile attempt to keep the punches away. He turns, trying feebly to defend himself with his thin forearms, until two of the masked assailants step forward on either side of him and twist his arms behind his back. Then, a boot strikes him in the pit of his stomach with a force that takes all the air out of him. He crumples over.

The masked faces blur together as the violence intensifies. No one reacts to the stillness that has crept invisibly into the shabby and unkempt man on the cellar floor. Only a weak moan comes from him as yet another boot rams into the back of his head. Otherwise, nothing.

The man is no longer conscious when one of the masked youths makes sure that his body is visible in the footage. A quick nod is made to the corner, where still another black-masked figure pulls out an iron pipe wrapped in tape and slowly moves closer. He positions himself beside the now lifeless victim.

Step-by-step, the masked attackers move forward in a tightening circle. At first their voices hum low, like an insistent chanting, but eventually the sound grows stronger and finally explodes into a rhythmical cry of celebration, as the iron strikes the man's head and crushes his skull.

Blow after blow. Nobody counts. Their focus is poured into the intense battle cry that increases and approaches ecstasy, while the blood spreads across the cellar floor.

Nobody seems to notice that the angel of death has come and taken the soul of the destitute man with it.

As the film ends, a heavy silence falls on the five boys who sit completely still around the computer screen.

There are small beads of sweat on the upper lip of one; the knuckles of a second have turned white. A third shakes it off and stands up to grab a handful of beers from the boathouse's well-stocked fridge.

Nobody says anything as the bottle caps pop off. But then, suddenly, they speak. All at the same time, excited and eager. The release rolls through them like an orgasm, and then gets washed down with strong beer.

Over the course of the evening, they remain drunk on violence, watching more "Faces of Death," films which feature real people being killed, their murders recorded live. They're saved as downloads on the computer in the primitive clubhouse. Tomorrow night there will be a private party in one of the sailing clubs farther down the harbor. A kid's party. Thrilled with themselves, the boys clink their bottle necks together and toast.

Ah, finally, it's the weekend.

1

I don't respect people who give in to stress, or men who take maternity leave. There you have it! And I don't give a shit what the HR people say about it. If you don't have the interest or energy to do your job in my investigation group, then you're out. There are lots of people who want in and know what it takes to do a job like ours."

The late September sun showed that the windows in the Homicide Department at Copenhagen's Police Headquarters were in serious need of a good washing. The dirt had put a dusty film over the glass, highlighting dead insects and bird splatterings.

Louise Rick closed her eyes for a moment, while Detective Superintendent Willumsen thundered on. Sooner or later he'd get to his favorite line.

"I think I've said it before." Here it came. "When you work with me, it's 'Yes,' 'No,' or 'Up yours.' I want clear responses. This place isn't a rest home for pregnant nuns. There are gang wars in the city and shootings on the streets. And as you all know, late last night, the father of a family was shot in his home outside of Amager. There's no end to our workload. The damned shootings suck up our resources. The police chief's Task Force Group recruits people from all departments, and for the rest of us it'll continue to mean hours of overtime. So, if you have problems on the home front or a hard time balancing family life with work life, then go look for a desk job! It's sure as hell a decision one would expect grown adults to be capable of..."

Willumsen left the last part hanging, while he sighed deeply and wiped the side of his mouth.

In a way, Louise couldn't have agreed more. No one could make those sorts of decisions for you but yourself. She looked at her coworkers. Toft seemed a bit tired, and it struck her that maybe he regretted receiving the offer to come back to Homicide. As the result of a reorganization, he'd been sent out to Bellahøj Station a year and a half ago, and given a position that was later eliminated again.

Michael Stig had pointedly tipped back his chair. His eyes were half shut, while he gazed out of the dirty window panes. He was obviously irritated over being made to attend the detective superintendent's tongue lashing, when it wasn't even aimed at any of the officers Willumsen had called together into his office that late Friday afternoon.

The fit of rage was aimed at Louise's partner, Lars Jørgensen, who earlier in the day had handed in a sick notice, initially for a month's time. According to the doctor, stress was the reason for the long period of absence. Those in the know understood that the real reason was Willumsen's cruel behavior toward Lars Jørgensen, who needed fewer hours after his wife had moved out to her sister's in Vangede, leaving him with the eight-year-old twins and a broken heart.

In the good month and a half since his wife had left her husband and children to find herself, Lars Jørgensen had made a virtue out of leaving on time so he was there when his kids came home from day care. He begged off from extra work on the weekends, and every single time Willumsen went after him.

The lead investigator had always been rude and arrogant. It was like he got a certain pleasure out of wiping the floor with people. Louise studied Willumsen. He was in his late fifties. His hair was still black, and he had sharp facial features. He was holding up well, but the tension had plowed two deep lines across his forehead, which made him look fierce. Her thoughts slipped back to Jørgensen.

A couple of days earlier, as she arrived back to the office after lunch, she'd found her partner sitting with his face hidden in his hands. At first, he tried to let on like it was nothing, as if she hadn't just caught him at a vulnerable moment. But after a couple of minutes of awkward silence, he stood up and closed the door.

"I don't give a damn that he keeps riding me," he said when he was back in his chair. His eyes were sad, and he looked pale and tired. "But the way things are, how the hell do I know if things will ever be different? Maybe she'll never come back. I can't give a date for when everything'll be wonderful again!"

Louise hadn't answered him. There wasn't much to say.

He gave her a blank look, and she could see that he was at least as frustrated over the situation as the superintendent was. Lars Jørgensen wasn't normally the sort to shut down his computer at four o'clock to go pick up the kids and shop at Føtex. On the other hand, she also knew he'd never dream of giving up time with his kids. The idea of seeing the twins every other week wasn't for him, so when his wife announced that she needed time alone without husband or children while she thought about her life, he'd taken on the extra responsibility himself.

"How about you, Rick?" Willumsen continued in the

same tone, snatching her back from her thoughts. "Are you about to hand in your sick notice, too?"

Louise observed the lead investigator for a moment, weighing whether it was worth the trouble to answer him. Instead, she just shook her head. They'd already talked till they were blue in the face about the responsibility she'd taken on when she'd agreed to adopt a twelve-year-old foster son. Still, not once in all the months since Jonas Holm moved into her apartment had the detective superintendent gone after her anywhere close to the way he went after Lars Jørgensen. Maybe it was because the lead investigator himself was moved by the boy's case. Jonas had become an orphan when his father was killed before his very eyes, shot in the back of the head on the family's vacation property in Sweden. At any rate, Willumsen often asked after the boy with something approaching genuine concern.

"Could we maybe wrap this meeting up and move on?"

Toft pushed back his chair to capitalize on the silence that had fallen over the room.

"I need to take care of an interrogation before the weekend."

Willumsen gave a quick nod, but called them back before they'd made it out to the hallway.

"There's just Amager," he said and looked around. "We need to question the suspect who's being held after the shooting last night in the duplex apartment out on Dyvekes Allé. But some of these biker types have gotten so refined over time that they're not happy with just a public defender. They have their own. Right now, he's sitting and waiting for his lawyer to come back from a trial on Jutland. But she should be here around six o'clock."

He looked at Louise.

"Rick, will you take it?"

She stood for a moment with her back to him before turning to the lead investigator.

"Hmmm...I'm sorry. Jonas is going to a party for one of his classmates tomorrow, and I have to go home and buy ingredients to make the meatballs. And I need to drop off some extra chairs for the party, so I'd better slip out now."

She left without waiting for his response, but heard Michael Stig take on the late interrogation with the shooting suspect. On the way down the hall, her colleague caught up with her. For a moment, Louise thought maybe he was expecting her to say thanks, but instead he asked about Camilla Lind.

"Has she left?"

Louise nodded.

"We drove them to the airport this morning. They fly into Chicago first, then on to Seattle, where they're staying until Wednesday. From there, they're renting a car and driving down the West Coast."

"How long will they be away?" he asked.

She still hadn't gotten used to how Michael Stig, who'd never really been her cup of tea, had apparently developed a genuine interest in her closest friend.

It had started up in Sweden, at the Holm family's vacation property, the day Jonas saw his father killed. Michael Stig and Louise had had Camilla in the car with them as they'd literally raced with death—but arrived too late. Afterward her colleague and her friend had kept in touch. He'd also visited her in the hospital.

Louise still had a hard time understanding how the case against two Eastern European sex traffickers could have had such a tragic end. The experience had left deep marks, and she was a long way from coming to terms with the violent conclusion that had caused Camilla to take a leave of absence from her job.

"For two months, so they'll have plenty of time to drive down to San Diego," she answered. "But you can e-mail or text her. She promised me she'd be checking. But they won't be spending any time on Facebook."

Michael Stig nodded. She started to leave, but he stood there.

"How's she doing?" he asked.

Louise stood a while thinking it over before deciding on the honest version.

"She's going through hell. Between us, I really don't think it's responsible of her to take Markus along on such a long trip. Psychologically, she's still broken to bits, and so she's pretty unbalanced. The way I see it, she seems to think it'll help to run away. Because that's exactly what she's doing, even though she likes to call it quality time with her son. Camilla is turning her back on everything that happened, so she can escape a confrontation with anything or anyone who reminds her of it, because she's still not up to it. I just don't know if she's strong enough to put a lid on it. It might have been better to spend the time and money on a good psychiatrist."

Louise thought about all the money Camilla had borrowed from her father in order to go away for so long. Then she added, "She blames herself for everything that happened, and in truth she can't live with herself... or her life, because of it."

She noticed that her voice became a little ambiguous with that last sentence, and so she quickly changed the subject.

"What about the shooting victim from Amager? Will he make it?"

Michael Stig shrugged his shoulders.

"If not, you'll definitely hear from Willumsen before Monday."

2

Do you know how many are coming to the party?" Louise yelled to Jonas. She was trying to figure out whether six pounds of ground meat would be enough for the number of meatballs she had to make. It was a new world for her. Never before had she given any thought to sausage rolls, mini-pizzas, and other junk foods, so she had no idea how much a class of seventh graders would go through, considering there'd be other things on the buffet, too.

And it had been ridiculously bold of her to tell Signe's mother she'd bring the meatballs, Louise thought irritably. It was a private going-away party for a girl who was changing schools, not a class get-together, and no one had asked her to bring anything.

"About twenty-five, I think," Jonas answered. He had a hoarse voice that made him sound like he was on the verge of tonsillitis. In reality, he suffered from a condition that Louise eventually learned was called multiple papilloma larynx, where small nodules had developed on his vocal cords. Over time they'd disappear, but till then they gave his voice a characteristically rough and rusty tone. "It's our class, and probably some others from the music school," he added.

"What about adults?"

Louise walked over and stood in the door to what had once been her guest room, but was now turned into Jonas's bedroom. He lay on the bed and read, his dark hair falling over his eyes. She could see that he had a hard time tearing himself from the book, but out of politeness he sat up and looked at her attentively.

"Just her mom, I think. Do you want me to go down and buy the meatball mix?"

Louise felt a prick and quickly shook her head. Politeness and uncertainty always lay just below the surface, as if he were a well-raised boy over for a visit. If he'd been her own son, he'd no doubt have remained lying on the bed with his nose in the book and only reluctantly have allowed himself to be disturbed. It was heart-wrenching how transparent his vulnerability was.

Jonas's mother had died of a congenital blood disease when he was four, and at the age of eleven, he'd lost his father, too. There was no family, distant relatives, or other relations left when tragedy struck. He'd only known Louise for a brief time, but since he'd expressed his own desire to live with her, she had given the matter careful thought and decided that if she was the safest base he could find, then he was welcome to stay with her. At least until he got some distance from his traumatic experience. At that point, they'd have to find a more permanent solution. But for now, she was his substitute mother, and for as long as she was, she'd do her best to live up to the role.

"We'd better see about getting those chairs out," she said and looked at her watch.

Jonas promptly snapped his book shut and got to his feet.

12   SARA BLAEDEL

Louise had folded down the back seat of her old Saab 9000, and between the two of them they'd managed to cram eight folding chairs in the back, plus the two step stools she'd found in the loft. Once they made it out past Svanemøllen, she turned right down Strandvænget and parked in front of his classmate's white garden gate. On the mailbox, it said "Fasting-Thomsen."

"Signe wrote on Facebook that we're going out sailing."

Jonas smiled and looked out at Svanemølle Harbor.

"It'll be awesome. Then afterward we'll eat."

The garden path smelled of late summer roses. Louise stopped for a moment, and Jonas ran ahead. Classical music from inside the house poured through the front door and reached them all the way out at the storm porch, where Jonas already had his finger on the doorbell.

It was Signe's father who opened the door. He stood with his coat on but smiled and offered his hand, introducing himself as Ulrik. As they stepped into the entryway, he apologized for the loud music and called through the living room door for Signe to turn it down.

Louise had only met Signe and her mother, Britt, when Jonas had gone to their house once after school and needed to be picked up in the evening. But she knew that his classmate played the cello and was a talented musician—like her mother, incidentally, who was a pianist and had played chamber music for many years. But as Louise understood it, Britt Fasting-Thomsen had had to end her career when she suffered something that Jonas thought was called *writer's cramp*. Now she taught at the Music Conservatory.

"Signe is still over the moon about getting in," Ulrik said. "So now she and her mother have started relistening to everything in our classical music collection. And that's not so few."

He smiled and shook his head.

Less than a week earlier, Jonas had come home from school and told Louise that Signe had been accepted into Saint Anne's School of Song and Music. She'd taken the entrance exam for the first time when she was in the third grade, but hadn't gotten in. Nor did it work out for her in subsequent years. But now, finally, they'd gotten lucky.

Louise had had difficulty hiding her smile when Jonas chattered on about how Signe's parents were called by the school, which suddenly found itself with a vacancy and wanted to know if Signe was still interested.

"She's crazy talented, and when she starts going there, she's sure to wind up being famous and getting to play a whole bunch of concerts all over the place."

He'd looked earnestly at Louise, then told her about the going-away party.

"It's on Saturday, so we can say good-bye to her before she starts at her new school. May I go?"

They'd been planning on driving out to the country that weekend, down to Louise's parents' in Hvalsø. But now she didn't have the heart to insist on it. It was the day after that she offered to make the meatballs.

"Everything's happened so fast this past week," said Ulrik. He ran his hands through his dark hair, which had a touch of gray at the temples. There was something in his facial features that made Louise think of a younger and somewhat taller version of Robert De Niro.

"Unfortunately, I can't be at the party tomorrow," he said with annoyance. "I'm an investment consultant, and my firm's strategy weekend starts tonight at Dragsholm Castle up in Odsherred."

Jonas listened politely, but she could tell he was impatient to go inside and say hi to Signe. Ulrik went on about how, six months ago, he'd hired an investment strategist from Switzerland to come and give a motivational speech to the staff, so it was impossible to reschedule the seminar on such short notice.

"Those kind of people are booked solid."

He shrugged his shoulders and nodded to the piles of tablecloths and stacks of dishware lying on the floor.

"But I'm skipping out on the welcome dinner, so we can get all that over to the sailing club. Britt thinks she can manage the rest—and if I know her, she can."

He smiled and said that it was a stroke of luck that they'd been able to rent the sailing club's party room so late.

"It's just been completed, and they don't even have tables or chairs. But they're coming up with the tables and we're bringing the chairs we need. I think it would have been easier to hold the party here, but Signe wouldn't hear of it. She's planning on everyone going sailing before the meal's set out."

"Is your wife taking care of the sailing, too?" Louise asked, remembering how slight Britt was.

"No, no!" he laughed and shook his head. "I've joined forces with a sailor we know. He keeps a big wooden boat in the harbor. Our sailboat is pretty big, but we can't cram twenty-five children on board."

The classical music continued playing loudly, and Jonas peeked impatiently into the living room.

"They're probably out in the kitchen," said Ulrik, and led the way. "They just must not have heard you come."

Louise looked around as they were led through the dining room. It was spacious and light, with modern art on the walls, and a dining table long enough to seat ten people on each side. There were two or three more rooms that all looked out on the harbor. In one of them stood Britt's beautiful grand piano, and behind it Louise saw Signe's cello.

The kitchen was easily the size of Louise's living room. At first glance, it didn't look like much had been done to it over the years, except for an addition of an exclusive French stove with double ovens, which stood along one wall. The rest was kept in the original classical style of the 1920s with tall doors and glass cupboards. If you looked closely, though, you could tell that all the cupboards had been restored to look that way.

"Hi!" Signe shouted happily. When she gave Jonas a hug, her red curls fell over her face. Her green eyes shined. Louise got a quick hug, too, before the girl dashed off into the living room and turned down the music so they could talk without shouting.

"Should I unload the chairs here, or drive them up to the sailing club?" Louise asked.

Britt finished rinsing dough off her fingers and greeted her guests properly.

"No, you don't need to bother with that," Ulrik said, standing behind them. "I have to take all the other stuff there, then afterward I can come back for the chairs."

"If you have to go there anyway, I might as well follow you. Then we won't have to keep loading and unloading them."

"Can I stay here while you're gone?" asked Jonas.

Louise looked over at Britt, leaving it up to her.

"Absolutely," she said.

"OK, great. I'll come back and pick him up after we've unloaded the chairs."

Signe pulled Jonas into her room so they could pick out CDs for the party.

"There won't be all that much classical," her mother said

as they left. "That's mostly for when she's home and can get absorbed in it."

A little blob of dough landed in Britt's pageboy hair as she tucked some loose strands behind her ears. Now it sat there distracting Louise. Signe's mother was short and slender, elegant without being too delicate, and when she talked about her daughter she exuded warmth.

"I hope she can settle in at the new school," Britt said. "It's a hard decision when you're perfectly happy with your current school and all your friends. But the music environment at Saint Anne's is on a whole different level from where she goes now. Out there, she'll be trained in the fundamentals of musical structure and become a strong reader of music. And then there's the chorus, which she's looking forward to being part of."

Louise nodded. Her knowledge of Saint Anne's School for Song and Music was severely limited, just that the school was for children with exceptional musical talents. In fact, she hadn't even realized that they had regular school classes on top of the music ones.

Britt walked over to the windowsill and blew out two pillar candles, so their wax wouldn't drip on the expensive kitchen floor. She checked the bread in the oven and put the next batch of dough into a bowl to rise.

"I ordered sushi for tomorrow. The ones who aren't into that kind of fare can have the meatballs you're bringing. And I'm roasting chicken drumsticks. And then there'll be bread. Do you think that covers it?"

Louise shrugged her shoulders in apology. She confessed that she really didn't have much experience in that area.

Britt smiled and shook her head.

"Jonas seems very happy with you. We were so worried

that he wouldn't recover after what happened to him. He's such a nice boy, but very sensitive. He's come here a lot over the years since he and Signe get along so well. And, clearly, they've got their music."

Louise nodded. Jonas played guitar and had taken lessons since he was nine. But not classical, and he was nowhere near the level Signe was at with her cello. She had been fed music with her mother's milk. Ever since she was very little, she'd gone with her mother whenever the ensemble played.

"It's really sweet of you to take care of the meatballs. I think we're starting to get a handle on it now. The soft drinks and sushi are being delivered down there. Signe and I will have plenty of time to set the tables and decorate, and then I'll have a little time, too, when they're out sailing."

"I'll get the meatballs there in plenty of time," Louise said.

Ulrik came out and said he was ready to go. Louise zipped her jacket.

"Jonas can spend the night here, if it's OK with you," said Britt. "He can go home on Bus 14 or the train from Svanemøllen. If he wants to."

Louise thought it over. It was only a little past seven, so she could easily fit in a trip to Holbæk, if Mik didn't have plans. That was another thing she had to get used to now that she "had a kid." Weekends weren't free for that sort of thing anymore.

Although Louise sometimes longed for her lanky colleague from the Holbæk Police, she wouldn't go so far as to call what they had a relationship. Mik called it an unstable long-distance relationship that they were trying to normalize, but she was happy just to call it casual sex and confessed that she was fine with it. Still, she had to admit she missed him sometimes, and right now she yearned to see him. Maybe, if they didn't sleep in too late tomorrow, they could even take the sea kayaks out on the fjord.

"YES!" screamed Signe when she was presented with the idea of Jonas spending the night.

When she smiled, her freckles smushed together over her nose.

"Then you can help me with the place cards," she told Jonas. "You write so neatly."

"They'll be busy," Britt said with a smile.

She and Louise joined Ulrik, who'd already packed the car.

"And it's also fabulous for her to have something to do," said Britt. "Because she's so happy she can barely stand it."

3

The stall door on the wing where Mik kept his workshop stood open. Louise drove up and parked in front of the farmhouse, then walked across the yard. She was joined by an overenthusiastic wirehaired pointer that herded her in.

"Hello!" she hollered as pebbles crunched underfoot.

"Hi!" she heard from the workshop.

Soon after, Mik stepped out in torn jeans and a long-sleeved shirt with a stain on it.

"Pardon me," he said, pointing to himself. "I had to fix the kayak so it's ready for tomorrow. Pretty soon, it'll be too cold to go out. I've talked with some of the others about going out this weekend since the weather looks to be nice. You're welcome to join us."

Louise smiled at him. She'd already told him she had to drive back to the city before noon tomorrow.

Mik came over and pushed her long, unruly black curls out of her face. He put his arms around her tightly, and she felt the muscles in his arms and back, an added bonus of kayaking. He kissed her. Louise smiled and slipped her hands along his bare back, lifting his shirt.

"Should we go inside, or do you want to undress here?"

He pulled away from her and looked over at the workshop.

"I just need to take care of that kayak," he said.

She let her hands fall.

"I pulled it a little too hard onto a stony beach, and a little stone got lodged under the drop keel. I tried to wiggle it out, but then the cable fell off. Now the kayak's a bitch to steer."

"Can't you fix it tomorrow? We could get up early."

She followed him over to the stall door.

"I just want to finish it up."

He walked over to the kayak, which he'd set across two sawhorses. He found a Phillips screwdriver on his work table and started turning a screw.

The pointer had settled in a corner. It looked at Louise as if it couldn't understand why she was taking so long to come over and pet it.

"Why don't you go inside and make us a pot of coffee or open a bottle of wine?" Mik said.

He smiled at her.

"I'm sanding out some scratches on the bottom side, too," he said. "Since it's already up on the sawhorses."

Louise sighed. She didn't want coffee. She wanted him and hadn't counted on all this screwing and sanding before it was her turn.

She edged past the kayak and walked over to the workbench, which stood along the wall and had the only fairly clean surface in the workshop.

"You're also welcome to go into the living room."

Mik tore a piece of sandpaper from a roll he had on the table.

"I came here to be with you," she said and sat on the workbench.

"And that's terrific."

He smiled at her, and the sight of his crooked front tooth made her feel warm inside.

"And if I'd known you were coming, I would have taken care of this first."

She nodded; she knew. He was always very considerate. At the beginning of the week he'd asked her if they'd be seeing each other that weekend, but she'd said no because Jonas was going to Signe's party. So, she couldn't really blame him for having things to do when she popped in on short notice. Still, she was a little irritated about being put on hold.

She studied him as he went to work, sliding the sandpaper over the bottom of the kayak. He'd rolled up his sleeves, so she saw the bulge of his tendons and muscles every time he passed over small, uneven places. He was so meticulous his movements sent a shiver down her spine.

Suddenly, she was flooded with a memory. She was seventeen or eighteen, and hanging out in a workshop with a bunch of boys messing around with mini-bikes and motorcycles. She had gotten together with the boy whose parents owned the farm where the workshop was. Her Suzuki had been the most souped-up, drilled, and chopped in the entire district. And it was also thanks to that boy she got her motorcycle license at the age of nineteen.

Louise smiled to herself, and Mik gave her a questioning look.

She shook her head.

"Nothing."

"Yes," he said and tossed the sandpaper on the floor. "What is it?"

"I just started thinking about how it often pays to have patience when having to wait in a workshop. Especially if you have designs on the person you're waiting on."

Mik raised an eyebrow.

"Is that your experience?"

He looked at her inquisitively.

Louise nodded and smiled as he walked over to her. He dried his hands on his blue jeans, then pulled her to the edge of the workbench. His hands slid up under her blouse. It tickled her ear when he bent over her and whispered, "Why don't you go inside and make us a couple of Irish coffees?"

4

Camilla's leg fell asleep. The airplane blanket had slid down to the floor, and the little pillow had given her a crick in her neck.

The flight attendants were going through the cabin collecting the passengers' U.S. arrival papers. The info-screen on the headrest in front of her showed one hour and fourteen minutes until landing in Chicago. She still hadn't set her watch back the nine hours for West Coast time, couldn't bear the thought of going through the hours of the day all over again.

Markus kept his eyes glued to a Disney film and hadn't said much during the flight. His blond hair stuck straight up, and his sweatpants scrunched up around his small hips. He had one leg tucked up under him, and he'd stuffed his blanket and pillow behind his back so he sat in an uncomfortable position with his elbows resting on the tray table and his head in his hands.

Camilla stroked his cheek, but he pulled away, didn't want to be disturbed. She dropped her hand. The mood between them had been silent and a bit gloomy ever since they'd hugged and waved good-bye to Louise under the escalator in Terminal 3. She'd tried to talk with him about it, but he'd refused. Shrugged his shoulders, averted his eyes.

She thought it might be the uncertainty. The vagueness of being away for two months without really knowing what they'd spend their time doing. Except traveling that route they'd traced on the big map of America while sitting together at the dining table.

But more likely, she thought, her son was having a hard time being away from his father for such a long time.

Camilla had agreed wholeheartedly with Markus staying with Tobias for the entire week leading up to the trip. Markus, for his part, had been terribly upset when his father hadn't driven them to the airport. But Tobias had had a business meeting on Funen starting early in the morning. Instead of driving them, he'd gotten the bad idea of calling the night before and telling Markus how much he was going to miss him while he was away, which naturally led to the boy crying and losing interest in the trip.

And as if that weren't enough, Tobias had supplied Markus with gift-wrapped presents and told him that during the flight he should open one an hour, knowing full well that his feelings of missing his father would flare up every thirty minutes. The first was to be opened when they'd been in the air for an hour, followed by the others—a Donald Duck comic book, a deck of playing cards, and a packet of Haribo candy.

Camilla brushed back her blond hair and gathered it in a ponytail, straightening the elastic band so it wouldn't sit and press up against her headrest. She'd tried to read, but had given up and stuffed the Danish newspapers down in her bag.

Now a running text scrolled across the little screen. Markus shook his head a bit, trying to return to reality, and asked for juice when the stewardess came by with her cart. He squirmed around on his pillow and tossed his blanket on the floor, then leaned up against her with his head on her shoulder.

For a moment, she just sat there and enjoyed him. Then she straightened up enough to get her arm around him. She put the armrest between them back up and pulled him closer to her.

"I really wanted to go to Signe's party," he mumbled.

He let Camilla run her fingers through his hair without moving away.

Maybe it was his friends, too, that he was sorry to be leaving. She'd noticed a lump in her own throat when she'd said good-bye to Louise in Departures. It was hard to imagine being away for such a long time.

She closed her eyes and tried to sleep a little before they landed and had to go through Immigration and Customs, fingerprinting and passport stamping.

5

It took longer than Louise had expected to fry the many small meatballs that were generated from seven pounds of meat. She was working on the last batch when Willumsen called.

"So, he died," the lead investigator began.

The shooting victim from Amager, he said, had been declared dead an hour and a half ago.

"You're going out and talking with the widow. They have a little newborn daughter. Right now, the family's all together at National Hospital, so you might as well wait until tonight."

The interview with Nick Hartmann's young wife, he added, should be on his desk before noon on Sunday. She could find him at Headquarters.

"I've just read the report from our colleagues at Amager Station," he said. "It seems a little odd that neither his wife nor the baby was harmed in the shooting. The victim took eleven shots, fired through the kitchen and living room windows of their duplex apartment. They have the ground floor on a corner lot in one of the popular residential neighborhoods behind Amagerbrogade."

Louise listened to him as she took the pan of meatballs off the burner. She was still a little groggy from a night with too little sleep but, on the other hand, there had been a fair amount of sex. Toward the end, she'd almost given up hope and started to think the whole night would pass by with them just holding each other and watching movies. But around oneish, she pulled Mik into the bedroom and he finally woke up.

"The crime techs found bullets from four different weapons and bullet holes in the walls and woodwork of all the rooms," Willumsen continued.

"I'll drive down there after I drop Jonas off at the party."

He sounded content.

"Since the shooting, we've put extra patrols on the street," he said. "If this is related to the gang wars, we need to watch out for a swift attack in revenge."

"Was the deceased mixed up in that sort of thing?" Louise asked.

She distributed the meatballs from the pan to the bowls that were going to the party.

"Not unlikely," said Willumsen.

Narcotics. Money. Power and territory. She sighed and asked him for the address.

"Get it from Toft. And now that Lars Jørgensen's staying home, you'll have to drive out there alone. The rest of us will take care of the three we've already arrested."

Louise hadn't known they'd arrested several, but then she'd been the first one to close up shop and head home for the weekend.

"How did the interrogation go?" she asked.

Willumsen snorted.

"Entirely predictable. Naturally, he refused to say a word. And his attorney was an hour late and didn't land at

Headquarters until a little past seven. After which, she had to speak with her client before we could get started. It ended up being a midnight show without much at all coming out of it," he said, adding that he was starting to see the advantage of rival gangs wiping each other out. "Then it'd be done and over with, and we could get a little peace on the street and not have to throw all our energy in their direction."

※

Louise turned at Svanemøllen and drove all the way down to the harbor. The sailing clubs and the cozy, unpretentious restaurants with roast pork and Skipper stew still brought people in, even though the high season was drawing to a close. In the distance, she saw candles lining the wooden pier down to the sailing club's little terrace. The first classmates had already arrived.

"We're having a welcome toast out on the boat," said Jonas.

He was wearing a new Björkvin jersey and had a little extra gel in his hair to keep it out of his eyes.

"After we eat, we're going to dance, and then the bar opens with cocktails and soft drinks."

"Hopefully alcohol-free!" said Louise.

Jonas looked at her with his eyebrows raised.

"What do you think?" he said.

She'd talked it over with Camilla, and so far, the subject of booze wasn't on the boys' radar screens. So, parties were still harmless.

Her whole Saab stank of meatballs. Louise edged the bowls out of the back seat, where Jonas had wedged them in amid her kayak gear. Each carrying a bowl, they walked over and greeted Signe and her mother, who stood and received the guests.

Signe was in a lilac dress. Her long red hair fell in soft curls, and a little bit of makeup brought out the green in her eyes. Britt was dressed more classically in a smart silk pantsuit and short jacket. Both Louise and Jonas got hugs and embraces, before Signe's mother pointed down a short hallway and said they could set the bowls in the kitchen.

"Have a great party," Louise said. "I'll be back to pick him up at ten thirty."

"Then I hope you'll stay and have a glass of wine with us," said Britt. She explained that the parents usually relaxed together when their kids had a party. "It's good for class morale, and it gives us a chance to talk a little with one another."

Louise could see the sense in that, so she said she'd look forward to it. She'd definitely be there, even though she had some work to take care of first.

Jonas stood chatting with a couple of boys. Louise waved to him. No hugging good-bye when his friends were watching. By and large, she was a little reticent about intruding on his private boundaries; didn't want to force her caresses on him. Sometimes he'd put his arms around her and give her a hug. Other times, it was clear he'd rather be left alone.

On her way back to her car, she absently greeted several of the children and their parents. Her thoughts were already focusing around Mie Hartmann, who less than three hours ago had sat beside her husband while he'd died from his wounds.

Louise sighed deeply and punched the address into her GPS.

6

The duplex was on a corner lot with a hedge around it all the way out to the road. There were cars parked along the sidewalk. In the first-floor apartment where the Hartmanns lived, the entryway and kitchen looked dark, but Louise knew they were home. She'd phoned ahead to see if six thirty were too early, but Mie's mother thought they'd be home from the hospital by then. They had to pack some things because afterward she was taking her daughter and granddaughter back home with her and setting them up in her guest room.

Up at the house, Louise saw a dim light spilling through grayish plastic attached to the south-facing windows. There was no trace of the police technicians, who'd left the residence earlier in the day. The cordon tape had been removed and all evidence secured.

It was the grandmother who answered the door when Louise rang. She was middle-aged, with short blond hair and dark rings under her eyes.

"Come on in," she said. She sounded exhausted, as if someone had taken all the strength out of her voice. She stepped aside before locking the door and fastening the security chain. "We don't really like being here after what happened," she said and pointed Louise through the entryway. "My daughter is in the bedroom with the little one."

With her jacket over her arm, Louise followed behind her past hooks with hats and coats and a wardrobe that was stripped of its paint and took up most of the space in the small entry. In the kitchen, which was just beyond the living room, she felt a draft from the two windows that had been shot out.

"You can't step anywhere," the grandmother said. She pointed at all the tiny bits of glass. "The insurance company is sending over a glazier tomorrow."

It was a mess in the kitchen, which had a modern island counter and a flat-screen TV on the wall. Obviously, no one had bothered to tidy up.

"We really haven't done anything to the house. We just got back from the hospital, so no one except the police has been here since my son-in-law was shot. My daughter, of course, went to the hospital when the ambulance arrived."

She seemed absent for a moment.

"It's unbelievable how someone can do that kind of thing. To come and shoot, when a little family lives here."

Louise noticed how quiet the house was. No radio playing or TV on. No sign of the baby or voices. The house contained absolutely no sound, except for a little street noise that drifted in through the plastic-covered window frames.

"Unbelievable," the grandmother repeated. "It's always someone else. You need to put a stop to all these shootings, soon. It's one thing that you can barely walk down the street, but now you can't even feel safe in your own house. And then there are the home robberies, too."

The living room was chilly and lit by a single floor lamp

in the corner facing the kitchen. Where the light did reach, however, it was easy to see traces of the shooting. The technicians' labels were still on the walls and doorframes, and there were several small chalk circles. More than Louise could count as she was shown to the bedroom.

The grandmother knocked softly. She waited a moment, then opened the door and told her daughter the police had arrived.

"The little one's just fallen asleep," she whispered to Louise and then introduced her to her daughter. Mie Hartmann sat in a high-backed wicker chair beside the window and looked out at the trees in the yard.

The bedroom was light and airy. There was a dresser with mirrors from floor to ceiling. A bow of braided silk held the French-lace curtains away from the window.

"You don't have to whisper," said Mie.

She nodded to the crib next to an unmade double bed.

"Our talking won't wake her up."

Louise had learned that Mie Hartmann was twenty-four years old. She looked even younger, sitting there with her long blond hair flowing down her back and appearing to be more in shock than grief. She had a vacant expression on her pale face. It was red around her nose, as if she'd blown it far too often over the last two days.

A tiny sound came from the child's bed, and Mie moved her eyes toward it, but then let them slip back to the trees in the yard. She wore a soft velour dress with a hood, and next to her was an Eastpak suitcase with wheels, ready to be packed. But that must be her mother's doing, Louise guessed, since it didn't look like the young widow had the energy for anything more than sitting in the chair and looking out the window.

Louise walked over and offered her hand, receiving a

limp handshake. She gave her condolences, then asked if they shouldn't go into the living room to talk.

"Can't we stay here?" asked Mie. She pointed to the double bed.

Louise moved some of the clothes that were spread out on the bed, then took out her pad. It was understood that Mie Hartmann wanted to stay here so she could avoid the room where her husband had been killed.

"How many were there?" Louise asked.

"Do you mean in the afternoon, or when they came back at night?" said Mie, her eyes still fixed on the yard as if she found herself on a different frequency.

"I didn't know you'd had more than one visit," Louise said. "I'm talking about the night before yesterday, when your husband was shot. Thursday the twenty-fifth of September. I have here that the shooting occurred at 10:37 p.m."

Mie Hartmann nodded.

"There were some who came earlier in the day, too, but it was just me and the dog at home. Well, and Cecilie."

She nodded to the crib.

"OK, so let's start there," said Louise. "Who came in the afternoon, and at about what time?"

"I don't know exactly who they were. But they were a couple of psychopaths who should thank God Nick wasn't here, because then he would have killed them, and it never would have ended like this."

No, then her husband would have ended up in a jail cell, thought Louise.

But that didn't seem to figure into the young widow's thinking. Louise could find no trace of feeling in her face, which seemed to have shut itself off. The shock kept reality at a distance, and perhaps that was a mercy.

"They came a little past three."

Her eyes met Louise's.

"I'd just been shopping at Brugsen, and took a little walk around the neighborhood with the dog. I was standing in the kitchen taking Cecilie's coat off. I don't know why the dog didn't react, but she didn't bark until they were right outside the door."

Louise hadn't noticed any dog. She looked around.

"Zato was hit with a bullet when the men came back at night," the grandmother explained from the door.

"Won't you sit down?"

Louise pointed to the other side of the bed.

The grandmother hesitated a little before coming over and sitting down. As if she didn't want to join them, but still wanted to be there for her daughter.

"The bullet entered just behind her front leg, and she died almost immediately," said Mie. Her eyes went blank.

"Nick was trying to get her away when he was shot."

Louise brought the conversation back to the first visit in the afternoon.

"Did they leave when you told them Nick wasn't at home?" she asked.

Mie Hartmann shook her head and uttered a sound that lay somewhere between a sob and a brief laugh.

"I wouldn't let them in, right? But then they pushed past me and came in anyhow. One of them walked over to Zato and opened her mouth. He grabbed hold of her jaws and twisted until she yelped. Then he asked me what kind of laughable watchdog we'd gotten ourselves, when you can stick your hand in its mouth and it doesn't even bite you."

She took a deep breath, holding back the tears.

"Even though she was half Labrador and half Rottweiler, she'd never do anything to anyone."

Her mother shook her head, agreeing with her daughter.

"They trampled all over the place and pointed at a bunch of things they said Nick owed them. They acted like they were in a self-service store."

Mie Hartmann kept fighting back her tears.

"Did your husband owe them money?"

She twisted her hair with her index finger and held Louise's gaze, as if that would do the job of convincing the police that someone must have gotten it wrong and mistaken her husband for someone else.

Louise had a hard time taking Mie Hartmann's look seriously. According to the information Toft had given her before she drove Jonas to the party, Nick Hartmann was known to have had dealings with a Copenhagen biker gang. Several times he'd been observed in and around their headquarters, and during a raid in the biker stronghold he'd been among those arrested. If he'd been involved in the gang wars that were dividing up the city into gang districts, then it was natural to expect him to be fighting for the bikers.

At the moment, the bikers' territory was under heavy pressure from both the Folehaven area in Valby and the Vestegn, where a rather aggressive gang was trying to intrude on the city. Besides these there were both Chinese and Pakistani mafias, who showed themselves to be steadily more and more brutal in the fight for power in inner Copenhagen and the big money they could make in whatever fell under the heading of serious crime.

Nick Hartmann could easily have had enemies in several camps, too, but after his arrest in the biker stronghold the police had had to let him go. They didn't have anything on him, and during the interrogation he claimed that he'd just been visiting. He wouldn't say who he knew, and he refused to speak about his connection to the bikers.

That's why Louise ignored Mie's look. There could be several reasons why Nick Hartmann had been sought out, and why it had ended as it did. Right now, the investigation pointed to the gang from Folehaven as being behind the shooting. A witness had noticed a yellow box van parked on Englandsvej late Thursday evening, and the Folehaven guys were known for using run-down postal vehicles for transportation. Toft had told her that their colleagues from Amager Station had made a search of their hangout the day before and seized a considerable number of firearms of various makes and calibers, and these were now out at Slotsherrensvej waiting to be compared with the crime technicians' evidence from the duplex.

And it was three of their guys who sat in holding cells at Police Headquarters awaiting trial. Louise wouldn't be surprised if at least one of them confessed before the week was up. First and foremost, for the sake of their group's prestige, but also because the personal status of having shot down someone from a rival group far outweighed going to jail.

"I honestly don't know what it could have been about," said Mie. "They seemed to want the TV and all the rest. The computer and a couple of the paintings we have hanging in the living room. They were also out in the garage, where Nick keeps his Mercedes and our summer car is parked."

Louise looked at her.

"What kind is it?" she asked.

"A BMW convertible. Brand-new, but we only use it when it's sunny out."

"Did they take anything when they were here?"

Mie Hartmann shook her head.

Louise stood up and asked to see the things they'd mentioned, and the widow reluctantly stood up and followed her.

In the half-dark living room, Louise hadn't noticed at

first how the room was sprinkled with Bang & Olufsen electronics and high-end designer floor and ceiling lamps from Piet Hein and Verner Panton. The fact that the paintings weren't bought at Ikea was something even Louise, who didn't know much about art, could see. Her first impression was that there'd been a lot of money that needed to be put into things that held their value.

The living room was also much larger than she'd first realized. It kept going around a brick fireplace in the corner.

"They must have thought he owed them a lot if they wanted to empty the entire house of its valuables," Louise said.

She took the cup of coffee that Mie's mother handed her and let her eyes wander around again.

"What happened when they came back at night?" she asked, looking over at Mie.

The widow had sat down on the edge of the sofa. Her back was straight and she sat completely still, until her face cracked and the tears rushed out.

The grandmother came flying in from the kitchen carrying a coffee Thermos and a plate of cookies. She quickly put them down on the sofa table and sat next to her daughter to comfort her.

Mie wiped her tears away and took a sip of the coffee her mother poured for her.

"It must have been a little past eleven when they came," she said. "I was lying on the bed in the bedroom with Cecilie. She'd finally fallen asleep, and the door was open, so I could see in to Nick. He was lying here on the sofa and watching TV."

She patted the sofa cushions.

"We didn't hear anything before the shots suddenly burst through the windows. It sounded like an explosion. Nick ran out to the utility room, where he keeps his own weapon."

The tears fell again, and she apparently didn't notice it when Louise made a note that the deceased had been in possession of a weapon in his home.

"Cecilie woke up and started crying. I took her and sat on the floor, so we wouldn't get hit if they went behind the house and started shooting in that way."

She pointed into the bedroom, where Louise estimated there was about three feet on either side of the bed. Even with a night stand on either side of the double bed, there was still enough room to sit in both corners and see into the living room.

"They must have seen him run, because all of a sudden they fired into the kitchen."

She covered her ears with her hands, as if she were reliving it and heard every gunshot.

"It just went on and on."

Mie Hartmann rocked back and forth, her hands still covering her ears.

"It was like an attack from a whole bunch of soldiers. The shots sounded like they were coming from every direction, both here and out in the kitchen. I don't know how many there were, but there was definitely more than one."

She dropped her hands into her lap, as if the gunfire had settled down.

"It looked like Nick jumped over the dining table to come hide with us, but then Zato was lying there and…"

Louise gave her plenty of time. While she waited, her eyes took in all the details of the living room.

"I'd already called the police when I was sitting on the floor," Mie said through her tears. "And they could hear shots being fired."

That agreed with the emergency call at 10:37, Louise thought. She circled the time on her pad.

"And it wasn't long before I heard the sirens. But by then they'd stopped shooting, and I think I heard them driving away. At any rate, I heard a car start up and drive off," she corrected herself and said that she didn't dare get up until the police had arrived.

She hid her face in her hands.

"And Nick was on the floor. If I'd come out sooner, maybe I could have helped him."

"I think it was good you looked after your little daughter," Louise said.

Just then, her cell phone rang. It was Jonas. She looked at the wall clock hanging beside the Bang & Olufsen flat-screen TV; it was barely nine o'clock. For a second she'd been afraid she'd lost track of time, but then realized there was still an hour and a half before she needed to pick him up.

"Hi," she said calmly and stepped away from Mie and her mother.

The tone of Jonas's voice yanked her out of her calm state.

"Hurry up and get here! Quick!" he said.

7

His voice was shrill, and Louise could tell he was scared.

"Some big kids came and wanted to be let into the party. One of them twisted Lasse's arm around, and now they're standing over by Signe's presents."

Louise heard noise, and a boy's rough voice said, "Shut your ass up!"

"Her mother told them to leave. But they won't."

"Jonas, stay away from them. Don't provoke them or say anything. Just grab your coat and I'll come pick you up."

"They're breaking everything!"

He was on the verge of tears.

"I'm going now."

She stood with her bag over her shoulder. The noise in the background had increased. She heard glass shatter and a girl scream.

"Jonas, hang on. I just have to say good-bye."

In the living room, she hurriedly excused herself and took down the address to the grandmother's house, out behind Damhusengen. She promised to keep them informed and said that there was no problem with Mie and her daughter moving out of the house for a bit, as long as the police could get in touch with them.

The grandmother followed her out through the kitchen. Louise heard the door carefully being locked behind her as she hurried to her car.

✶

Her GPS said she was eleven minutes from her destination. Louise plugged her headset into her cell phone and asked Jonas to tell her what had happened.

"Start at the beginning," she said.

"They came while we were dancing. We'd eaten, and afterward we moved the tables out to the side so we'd have a dance floor."

"How many are there?" she asked. "Are there any from your school?"

She heard a girl crying and a noise like something being thrown against a wall.

"Four. No, there are five. I don't know any of them, and they're breaking everything."

His voice had grown thin, and before he could get anything else out he was drowned out by a terrified scream.

Louise sped up and drove too fast. Way too fast.

"Two of them have gone behind the bar. They want Signe's mother to give them beer and booze, but we don't have any of that down here."

His voice rose.

Louise thought she could hear Britt in the middle of the commotion.

"One of them's emptying out the cabinets, and they're tossing everything on the floor. They think there's cigarettes."

Jonas was silent for a moment, but then she heard his voice again.

"Now one of them's got Britt's bag. He's taking her purse."

Jonas stopped talking.

"Has anyone called the police?" Louise yelled.

Several children cried in the background.

He still didn't answer, and over the sound of crying children she suddenly heard a deeper laughter.

"Jonas!" she screamed. "What's happening there?"

"Two of them are taking Signe's mother outside," he whispered so quietly she almost couldn't hear him. "They're hitting her."

He started to cry.

"You need to get away. I'll be there soon."

Louise could hear that he'd gone outside. She could also hear the blows and the cries of frightened children.

"Her mother's lying on the ground, but they keep hitting her."

Suddenly, Signe's voice cut through the noise.

"Stop it! You better stop it. Get out of here. Leave my mother alone!" she shouted at the top of her lungs.

Her voice sounded more angry than scared, and Louise heard her yelling desperately to try to rescue her mother.

The scene painted itself so clearly before Louise's mind that she practically felt the children's fear physically through their voices slicing toward her in the dark. Her adrenaline pumped, but at the same time, her feeling of powerlessness rose.

She stepped harder on the accelerator.

"Now one of them's standing and kicking Britt in the head," Jonas cried into the receiver.

Signe had stopped yelling. Only the sounds of blows and crying made their way through to Louise.

"I'll call the police. But you need to get hold of some more of the adults," she ordered loudly, so he could hear her.

"The other one's run after Signe," Jonas screamed desperately through his tears.

Louise's heart hammered against her chest as she told Jonas to hold on while she called 112. When she got through to the emergency center, she quickly told about the assault and explained where the sailing club was on Svanemølle Harbor.

"We already have cars on the way," said the dispatcher. "We've had five or six calls from out there over the last few minutes."

"They can't drive all the way down there," said Louise.

She waited impatiently at a red light near Svanemøllen Station.

"Park the cars at the Port Harbor office," she said. "The sailing club is at the end of the pier."

The light finally turned, and she tossed her cell phone on the passenger seat.

❧

She tore off on the last short stretch, and just when she'd made it down to where Strandvænget turned, she saw a moving van stopped in the middle of the road. Its hazard lights were on and both front doors were open. Two people stood bent over a figure lying in the road.

Louise turned on her hazards, too. She swung in over the bike lane and left her car. As she ran toward the accident scene, she heard sirens in the distance coming closer.

She was almost right beside her before Louise saw the lilac fabric of the dress, and the strength ebbed out of her

legs. She sank down beside Signe's seemingly lifeless body
and looked up at the man she assumed was the van driver.

He was around sixty and obviously in shock. Behind
him, his wife walked around and around in small circles
with her face in her hands.

"We called for an ambulance," he said.

Blood ran from a dark wound in the back of Signe's
head.

Louise felt completely empty inside.

"I didn't see her," the man said. "Out of nowhere, she
was there, like a flash in the dark, and then I noticed the
bump."

A police car arrived, and Louise quickly stood up. Introduced herself and directed them to the parking lot, then to
the pier, and on out to the sailing club. When the next police
car came, she directed it behind her Saab on the bike lane
and said, as calmly as she could, that she knew who the girl
was.

"Her name's Signe. She and her mother are holding
a party at the sailing club. You need to get hold of the
father. His name's Ulrik Fasting-Thomsen, and he's staying
at Dragsholm Castle, where his firm's holding some seminar, but I don't have his phone number."

The van driver squatted down next to Signe. With two
fingers, he felt for a pulse in her neck.

Louise wanted to go down to Jonas, but instead walked
up closer and sank to her knees beside the older man. She
couldn't see if Signe was breathing. The darkness put her
in shadow, even though her light skin stood out against the
asphalt.

The man removed his hand. For a moment, he hid his
face in his hands despairingly, as if he were trying to control
his thoughts.

"She's alive," he got out.

With a blank stare, he turned to Louise and told her he was a doctor in private practice in Søborg.

"We were helping our youngest one move. The van's rented."

Louise leaned over Signe. Her eyes were closed, and the blood made her curls stick together.

"She has swelling on both sides of her head, and there's bleeding from both ears," said the doctor. "I'm afraid she may have suffered a serious skull fracture."

He shook his head and stood up with difficulty to give room to the rescuers, who'd stepped in.

"We need to stabilize her," one of them said and went back to the ambulance for a neck brace. "It looks serious."

The doctor's wife sat down on the curb with her arms around her legs and her face hidden against her knees.

8

As Signe was being lifted onto the stretcher, Louise saw Jonas in her mind; and while the rescuers carefully rolled the girl to the ambulance, she started running to the sailing club.

The fear in his voice had been like a thick coating, and everything in Louise wanted to protect him from more pain after what he'd just gone through with his father. She felt so bad for him that it made her chest ache. She pictured his thick bangs and his dark, serious eyes.

As she ran, a feeling of claustrophobia tightened around her. Suddenly she couldn't take any more bad news after everything else that had happened recently, and she felt an uncontrollable need to turn and run away. Away from all of it. But as she crossed the parking lot to the marina, she sped up and continued down the pier.

When she reached the sailing club, two officers leaned over Britt, who lay on the flagstones outside the little terrace. Blood ran from her eye and cheek, and the entire right side of her face looked like an open wound. The two officers tried to calm her. One of them tried to press a towel against her face to stop the blood flow, but she was trying to get up.

"Where's Signe?" she cried.

She pushed the towel away so she could turn her head.

More responders arrived. The high, shrill siren went quiet when the ambulance stopped on the road above, but its vehement blue lights flashed on through the evening darkness and cast a glow out across the water.

Louise introduced herself and told them she knew about the party being held inside the sailing club. One of the officers stood up. He was young and seemed unsure of himself when he pulled her off to the side and out of earshot.

"What do you know about what happened in there?" he asked.

He took out his pad from an inside pocket.

"I have a foster son who's in the same class as the girl who was hosting the party," she said. "He called me about twenty minutes ago and told me that some bigger boys had shown up and destroyed everything, and they wouldn't leave. When Britt"—she nodded toward the woman on the ground—"told them to go, two of them went after her. And as far as I understood it, he also saw one of the boys run after her daughter, Signe, when she went for help. I arrived just before you did, which must be when the accident had just happened."

The officer nodded and wrote it down. Louise scanned the door to the sailing club's party room. She hadn't laid eyes on Jonas and was listening with only half an ear when the officer said that it was a little difficult to find out exactly what had happened.

"Some of the kids are saying that the older boys went outside, and two of them allegedly threw themselves on the mother while their companions tried to get them to stop. Others are saying she was attacked by the whole group that crashed the party. The uninvited guests were obviously long gone before we got here."

She placed her hand on his arm, trying to slow him down.

"We'll get to that later," she said. "I need to find Jonas."

She kept her eyes on the sailing club and the group of children who stood in a tight clump. Several cried, some just stood completely still, and others held on to each other. They looked as if shock had been cast over them like a fishing net. She didn't spot Jonas in the crowd.

The atmosphere was chaotic, and when she asked after Jonas, no one had seen him. Louise could feel her blood pumping as she ran into the abandoned party room, calling for him. But there was no one inside; everyone had gathered out on the wharf. She ran around the clubhouse and first caught sight of him a long way off, over by the bulwark.

She slowed her pace and tried to control her panic.

"Was it Signe who got hurt up on the road?" he asked.

He was hoarse from crying.

Louise sat down next to him. She nodded and put her arm around him.

"She ran out in front of a van," Louise said quietly. "The driver couldn't avoid hitting her."

Jonas sat completely stiff.

"Did anything happen to her?"

Louise took a deep breath.

"Yes," she said. "I'm afraid she's been badly hurt."

She pulled him in to her. She smelled the harbor and heard the waves splashing while Jonas struggled not to cry.

Up on the road, a rescue team headed off toward the National Hospital.

"We need to go over and tell the police what you've seen. It's important that they know someone ran after Signe up on the road."

Jonas nodded and dried his nose on his hoodie before standing up.

⚛

The terrace and landing suddenly seemed too small for all the police who'd shown up, Louise thought as they came around to the front of the sailing club. She put a soothing hand on Jonas's shoulder when she sensed him stiffening up at the sight of Signe's mother, who lay on the ground with the officer beside her.

Louise stood on the landing among the voices, the crying, and the chaos and thought this must be what it's like to find yourself in the aftermath of a natural disaster. Everything was in disarray, broken, abandoned, and no one yet knew the extent of the damage.

Two uniformed officers started gathering the children together and directing them into the sailing club's party room.

The children who hadn't gotten hold of their parents were asked to call again, so they'd have an adult with them when the police recorded the names of everyone who'd been at the party.

The young officer from before came over and stood beside Louise. He nodded toward Britt.

"We can't really get anything coherent out of her, but for now we're trying first and foremost to get her to lie still until the rescue workers show up. Several of the children are saying that, yes, the assailants hit her and kicked her in the head. It looks bad, especially around her cheek and right eye, so she may have suffered a skull fracture or a serious concussion."

"Signe!" Britt called out in the darkness.

Louise sensed her once again trying to get to her feet.

"Help me, help me."

"Do you know the mother's name, other than Britt?" the officer asked.

Louise nodded and moistened her lips.

"Her name's Britt Fasting-Thomsen. They live up on Strandvænget," she said, then took a deep breath. "It was a party for her daughter's class and some students from the music school. They're sixth graders."

The officer listened while keeping an eye on Britt, who'd now made it up onto her elbows.

"Isn't there anyone who'll tell me if something's happened to my daughter?" she whimpered. "I don't know where she is. Why won't anyone say anything?"

Behind the Port Harbor Office, Louise saw the blue flashing lights of yet another ambulance. It had arrived without its siren on and swung in behind the trees in the parking lot. A second later, two ambulance attendants came rolling a stretcher over the uneven wooden landing. After them, frightened parents began to pour in.

"Why don't you tell her that her daughter's been involved in an accident and is on her way to the hospital?" Louise asked angrily. "She has a right to know."

The young officer evaded her eyes. Obviously, he hadn't imagined that Britt should be told about the accident before she arrived at the hospital herself.

"There's really no reason to say anything before we know how badly the girl's been hurt."

"No reason!" Louise exclaimed, outraged.

"She'll find out anyway," he said in his own defense. "And right now, we're focusing on finding out what happened before that."

"What the hell are you thinking? Is she supposed to lie there in ignorance while her daughter may be in critical condition?"

"It would be nice if we could track down the ones who came here and made mischief."

She wanted to throttle him. A woman's twelve-year-old daughter was unconscious, placed in a neck brace, and being driven to the hospital, and this idiot called it "mischief." Even though it wasn't Louise's place, nor did she want it to be, she turned around and walked over to Britt to tell her that her daughter was currently in an ambulance on her way to the National Hospital.

"I came immediately after the accident," she said.

She held Britt's hand and stroked the back of it.

The ambulance attendants had set the stretcher on the ground and were ready to lift Britt up and push her away.

Britt turned to the officer, who stood with his pad.

"Why didn't you say anything, so I could be with her?" she screamed through her tears.

"Britt," said Louise, trying to settle her down. "They didn't say anything because you're badly hurt yourself. Something's happened to your eye, and you may have had a concussion, or in the worst case a lesion inside your head. To begin with, they had to think of your health. Once you've gotten to the hospital and a doctor's seen you, you'll find out all there is to know about Signe and how she's doing. But for right now it's about tending to the injuries you've each received and getting treatment to you as quickly as possible."

Louise stood up and nodded to the rescue workers that they could take her away.

"Why don't you go along with her?" the officer suggested.

Louise turned to him and shook her head.

"I have a boy who's sitting in there and waiting for me," she said. She nodded toward the lit-up party room. "Have you gotten hold of Ulrik Fasting-Thomsen?"

He shook his head.

"Not yet. He turned his cell phone off."

"Then you should try reception or the restaurant. They must be able to find him," she said, irritated that he hadn't thought of that himself.

The officer turned, but had his cell phone to his ear while he followed the others over to the ambulance.

In the party room, on the tables that weren't knocked over, there were still soft drinks and candy bowls. The music had stopped playing, but the light display continued and there were heart-shaped strings of lights along the counter of the bar. Everything else was in chaos—shattered glass and bottles on the floor.

Children cried, others stood petrified with glazed looks in their eyes, following from a distance the scene that played out before them. Several girls hugged each other, while the boys sat with expressionless faces and looked much younger than they had when Louise saw them arrive at the party earlier in the evening.

Jonas sat on a chair over by the wall and had saved an empty place for her.

It was completely silent when a uniformed officer cleared his throat and began.

"I am sorry to have to tell you that a short while ago there was a tragic accident. When Signe ran from the party, she ran out on the road right in front of a van. The driver was not able to avoid her."

At that moment, a pin could be heard dropping.

"We are very interested in hearing whether any of you know any of the boys who barged into the party."

None of them had seen any of the older boys before.

"Not even from school or afterschool?" the officer asked.

No, they shook their heads, even though a couple of parents whispered to their children to see if they were really sure. Several of the children still cried. Their tears flowed freely as they sat there pale and frightened and pressed themselves into their parents. Others sat completely passively, as if they'd gone into shock.

"Don't be afraid to say something," one of the fathers said encouragingly. Then he looked around at the children.

It was maybe a bit too much to ask of them, after two people had just been driven away in ambulances and they'd all had every reason to be frightened, thought Louise.

"If we're to have any chance of finding the one who ran after Signe, it's important that you tell us what he or they looked like," said another officer.

It was soon apparent that none of the children could really remember what the big boys had looked like. They could easily recall the beginning of the party, the sailing trip, the mountain of sushi and all of Louise's meatballs. They could also clearly remember helping Britt clear the tables and take the food out to the kitchen, and how they'd just turned on the music when the big kids suddenly burst in. But after that, things faded into a foggy haze that none of the children could quite find their way through.

Nor was anyone entirely sure they'd seen someone running after Signe; maybe they'd just thought they had because Jonas had seen someone. He, on the other hand, was quite sure. A single boy had chased her. He was tall and had his hair in a ponytail.

"Black hair and black clothes, but he had white tennis shoes on," Jonas elaborated when the officer asked him for a description. He said he remembered the shoes because he saw them disappear in the dark.

"Signe ran when two of them started kicking her

mother," he said. "At first, she wanted to make them stop, but when they kept on, she wanted to get help. That's when the one with the ponytail suddenly ran after her. She was probably scared and was trying to get away from him."

"Can you remember what the others looked like?"

"They looked more normal."

"Two of them had those big tattoos that go all the way up the neck," said a boy sitting over by the door.

"Yeah, and one of the tattoos went like this out of the side of his neck," said Jonas and demonstrated with his hand. "The other had one on his neck, a big tattoo that sorta disappeared up under his hair. He's the one who kicked Signe's mom in the head."

The officers looked around until they were sure no one else had anything more to add. Then they asked everyone to give their name, address, and telephone number before leaving the sailing club.

Most of the children were deathly pale and quiet, while several of the parents expressed their outrage over such a brutal attack happening at a party where the children were only in the sixth grade.

"I have just one more thing," the young officer said before the excited voices could grow too loud. "We've called in two of the National Hospital's crisis counselors, and we recommend that you speak with them before you drive home. It would be a healthy thing for all of you after what's happened here tonight, and there will also be opportunities for follow-up sessions."

It was mostly the mothers who nodded gratefully and stood up to take advantage of the offer. The fathers still seemed more taken up with their discussion of how the older boys could even conceive of attacking a woman right before the eyes of a whole group of children. Soon the majority of parents were standing and talking in small groups, while the children were left to themselves; most of them looked like they just wanted to go home.

Louise heard a couple of the mothers start shutting everything down in the party room. They'd come back the next day and clean up, once they'd talked it over with Ulrik.

She was beginning to slip over to the door, didn't really know any of the others, and suddenly she remembered Britt's invitation to stay and drink a glass of wine with the parents when their children were being picked up. Only a few hours ago her plans had looked quite different.

She stood in the dark on the pier, feeling the fresh air and watching the sailboats bob. The light from the sailing club's windows glimmered on the water. She decided she'd better push up Jonas's appointment with Jakobsen, the crisis counselor who was connected to the Homicide Department. Since his father's death he'd had regular sessions with him.

"Can I go home with Lasse?" he asked when he came out to her in the dark.

Louise looked at him in surprise.

"Are you sure you wouldn't rather the two of us go home and talk a little about what you've just gone through down here?"

He shook his head quickly.

"I want to go with him, because then you can go to the hospital and find out how Signe and her mom are doing," he said. He paused briefly. "Otherwise, nobody's with them."

"There are others here who know them much better than I do," said Louise.

"Yeah, but they're not in the police," he pointed out. "So, they're not as good as you are at finding things out."

Louise thought it over. She put her arm around him and turned him so they faced each other.

"Jonas," she said quietly. "Signe wasn't conscious when the ambulance picked her up. You need to prepare yourself that this could be very serious. That's why I think it's better if we go home together."

He already knew it was bad. She could see it on him.

"Won't you please go down there anyway," he begged. "You know something about that stuff and they'll let you stay there till her dad comes."

She could tell that he was holding his breath, trying to keep himself from crying. Then Lasse came over and asked if he was going with them.

Jonas hurried a nod, but Louise waited until the friend's father came out so she could ask him whether he thought it was a good idea.

"I understand if you're worried, but my wife's a psychologist," he said. "I'm positive she won't let the boys go to bed before they've talked it all through."

"Fine," said Louise. "Then I'll go to the National Hospital and stay until Ulrik gets there. I have my cell phone on, so call if there's anything. Or if you'd like me to come and get Jonas."

"What kind of delinquents are they anyhow who'd do something like this?" asked Lasse's father. He shook his head sadly as they walked along the landing.

In the parking lot, she gave Jonas a long hug, and he promised to call if he wanted to go home after all.

"And you'll call, too, when you know something, right?" he said, looking at her earnestly. "Even if I'm sleeping."

She brushed her hand through his hair.

"Of course. I'll call," she promised. "But we might not find anything out tonight. So, don't you stay up, either."

9

The hotel room was dark and cool, the air conditioner hummed, and Camilla cursed her luck for having been too tired to remember to turn it off before she and Markus went to bed. But when they finally hit the sack in their Seattle hotel, they'd been awake for the better part of thirty-six hours. By that point, she'd barely been able to spell their names for the hotel receptionist.

She rested a bit with her eyes closed. When she swallowed, she felt a sharp pain in her throat. Her nose was stuffed up.

Over in the bed beside the thick window curtains, Markus lay with his mouth slightly open and snored quietly. It warmed her heart, but the rest of her body was cold and tired, as if a flu had snuck in and was invading all her muscles.

Her twelve-year-old son had been so terrific for the rest of the trip. The sad and sulky boy had disappeared. He even kept a stiff upper lip when Camilla very nearly lost her patience after a loudspeaker in the Chicago airport announced that their flight to Seattle had a two-hour delay. At that point, they'd already waited for three.

Camilla had immediately stood up to go find someone

to complain to, but Markus took hold of her arm. Shouldn't they just play cards? he asked. Then he dove into his bag and rummaged through the books, empty candy bags, and magazines he'd gotten from his father until he found the playing cards and some more candy. He cleared off a seat so they'd have a chair between them.

Fuming with anger and feeling exhausted, she collapsed back into her seat while he shuffled the cards and asked if she wanted to deal. Then they spent hours playing rummy and eating all the candy Tobias had sent with his son.

Camilla rested a little and looked up at the ceiling. The more exhausted she'd gotten on the trip, the more she'd started to doubt. The uncertainty ate away at her. No definite plans—just a car to pick up and a return flight from Los Angeles at the end of November.

Two months was a lot of time to kill. Maybe too long for her and Markus to be alone together. But at the same time, it felt like a relief to get away. A solace for the soul to be free from all the disturbing memories and all the well-meaning words that constantly reminded her that she was on the brink of a breakdown. As if she'd forget that.

Her recent past had been hellish, and the one thing she wouldn't have was for her state of mind to affect Markus. And since her son had been the hardest hit by seeing his mother go to bits and pieces, the decision hadn't been so difficult. Because there hadn't really been any alternative. Camilla knew she had to mentally extend herself over a cliff's edge in order to move on and get some distance from Kaj Antonsen, the drunk from down in Halmtorvet for whose death she was indirectly to blame.

It was mostly the guilt that had taken hold of her like some insidious virus. She hadn't known Kaj for more than an afternoon and an evening, but even so he'd wormed his way into her heart. She'd fallen for him and his self-exile in the world of alcohol, with Johnny Cash coming through the speakers and a bottle of beer or something stronger in his hand. She'd even been tempted to try his brand of oblivion, but knew that shortcut wouldn't work for her.

Her thoughts found their way back to Stenhøj Church and Henrik Holm's tragic death. She'd always been a couple of steps behind. Now, whenever she was too weak to fight off the thoughts and feelings, the guilt got to her.

Her mother had rushed over from Jutland when the crisis counselor from the National Hospital decided to move Camilla to the open ward of the psychiatric unit, where he was head physician. She'd been there a month before he'd finally seen fit to release her. And that only came about because her mother promised to live with her daughter and take care of her grandchild for the next fourteen days. That way, they'd be in a calm place and could decide whether Camilla had the strength and wherewithal to live alone with the boy.

Then, when she did come home, e-mails, texts, and Facebook messages poured in. It had nearly made her sick. She didn't have a single moment to distance herself from her breakdown.

Her editor, Terkel Høyer, had been nice enough to send good, old-fashioned snail mail because he knew it took a little more effort to make it to the wastepaper basket than to hit delete. She knew he meant well. In fact, he was the one who suggested she get away for a while—although, he was probably thinking more like a week or two.

But it got her thinking. Then one morning after lying in bed most of the night as she did now—gazing at the ceiling with her hands folded behind her neck—she decided that's what she had to do, if she didn't want to lose Markus.

Camilla pulled a thick sweater from her suitcase, then walked over to the window and opened the curtains a smidge. A wedge of sunlight cut through the room's darkness and fell on the bed and her sleeping son.

Straight ahead of her was the Space Needle, the city's landmark where she'd promised Markus they'd eat at the very top in a restaurant that revolved 360 degrees, giving panoramic views of the city.

It looked nice out there, with the water and the harbor. A bunch of boats were out sailing.

One could always just jump, she suddenly thought and leaned her forehead against the window pane. Their room was on the twenty-second floor, and the miniature life down on the street gave her an odd sinking feeling in her stomach and sent shivers down her spine.

"Are you up?" Markus asked from the bed.

Camilla quickly stepped away from the window. She stood for a moment, until she felt ready to turn around and smile.

"Not really. I just got out of bed and was looking around for a room service menu, so we could order breakfast. Doesn't that sound good?"

"Do you think they have pancakes or waffles?"

He was already out of bed and stood next to her with his mouth slightly open. His gaze took in everything innocently.

Camilla tousled his hair and drew him close. She squeezed his boy's body and felt peaceful standing there with him and looking out over a foreign city in a foreign country. It didn't make sense that a twelve-year-old boy should be her pillar of strength. It ought to be the other way around.

10

Eggs, bacon, toast, English muffins, bagels, scones, pancakes, Danishes—Camilla couldn't get herself to order the pastry that had made Danes famous *over there*, even though it bore little resemblance to what you'd get at a real bakery in Denmark. There was also fruit, hot cocoa, and a pot of Earl Grey with warm milk beside it. When the whole thing was rolled in on a table, Camilla could tell she'd overdone it. She hurried to get a handful of dollar bills, so she'd be ready with the tip when everything was in place.

They managed about half of it before they had to give up and stack the plates in a tall pile on the tray, which Camilla set out in the hall. Then she put a DO NOT DISTURB sign on the door and crawled back into bed.

She took out the newspapers she'd grabbed on the SAS flight. *Morgenavisen* and *Berlingske* both teemed with the Sachs-Smith scandal. The old and well-reputed family dynasty that owned Termo-Lux had built up an enormous fortune with thermal windows. The family was on the list of the country's richest people, and now they'd been hit with a messy and salacious scandal that was rocking the media world.

Camilla turned the pages with interest.

It had been a couple of weeks since the flag at the dynasty's headquarters in Roskilde was set at half-mast and the news outlet Ritzau had reported the sad news that Inger Sachs-Smith, married to the head of the family, Walther Sachs-Smith, had taken her own life. She'd been found in her bed with two empty bottles of sleeping pills on the nightstand.

All the papers had cleared their front page. It became the tragic top story for many days, because in the wake of the suicide it leaked out that there was a coup, or a family takeover of power, at Termo-Lux. In the meantime, neither board members, sources in the firm, nor even their press secretary had been willing to comment. That left it with the conjectures and analyses from industry experts, who believed that the two youngest children—Carl Emil, thirty-eight, and Rebekka, two years younger—along with the family's attorney had convinced Walther Sachs-Smith that he should pass on power to the next generation, even though he was still joint owner of the family business, founded sixty years earlier by his grandparents in a rather humble area on the outskirts of Roskilde.

Now she read that Walther Sachs-Smith had disappeared and had been gone for at least three days. A few days after his wife's burial, he was reported missing, and now the vast majority of the press guessed that he'd chosen to follow his wife in death.

Business reporters interviewed experts about the consequences of a power takeover, given that the two siblings were the only family members left on the board and the attorney had only recently been appointed. Gossip columnists were more interested in digging up everything they could on Carl Emil and Rebekka, not least their associations with the royal family's younger generation.

Camilla didn't have the energy for that part of the story. She had a hard time imagining anything more trivial, after what the children had done to their parents. She'd always had a good impression of the Sachs-Smith family, not that she knew them personally, but she'd grown up in Roskilde. The parents always struck her as sympathetic and straightforward, despite their being loaded with money. The father often had to step in and smooth things out when his two youngest children got a little too carried away with their jet-set lifestyle.

Markus had turned on the TV and was surfing through the channels, deeply impressed with the selection. For the moment, he was watching *America's Funniest Home Videos*.

She took up the second newspaper, sighing over how they could spend two whole pages repeating the story of Inger Sachs-Smith's suicide and the domestic worker who'd found her in her bedroom.

SHE DIED IN HER SLEEP

In the caption, it said that Fru Inger had emptied two bottles of potent sleeping pills, so she hadn't been in any doubt over what she was doing. She wanted to die.

More gossip about Carl Emil's numerous lovers and his alleged fondness for kinky sex, and the same old stuff about Rebekka's ex-husband and the child they'd had together. The girl was in kindergarten, and the picture of her was big enough that all of her classmates would easily recognize her—if anyone still needed to be told that it was her mother who'd apparently driven her grandparents to their deaths.

How awful, thought Camilla.

She flipped through.

On the next page, she paused over a picture of the some-what lesser known big brother. The eldest of the children.

Frederik Sachs-Smith hadn't lived in Denmark for the last fifteen years. As a twenty-seven-year-old, he'd moved to the U.S.A. and had never been part of the jet-set inner circle. Still, she recognized his face because she'd written about him when his first American film premiered in Holly-wood.

He was the outsider who'd turned his back on the family dynasty to follow his dream. Before he moved to the U.S.A., he'd gone to the Copenhagen Film School and writ-ten screenplays for two Danish feature films, neither of which met with noteworthy success. After that, he applied to and was accepted at a well-known film school in New York and, as far as Camilla recalled, by then he'd already pulled up stakes for good. She thought of him as a mixture of upper-class bohemian and cool businessman. It cost him absolutely nothing if his projects succeeded or failed, be-cause he had so much money in his checkbook that he really didn't need to earn anything. Along with his film work, he was also a financier and investor and had evidently used his inheritance from his grandparents and the money from his parents wisely. At any rate, he'd made himself a con-siderable fortune and obviously wouldn't be affected by the shockwaves that hit the family's economy.

Camilla knew the stuff about the money only because Markus was in the same class as Signe and she was good friends with Britt Fasting-Thomsen. Ulrik, Signe's father, was Frederik Sachs-Smith's investment consultant and fi-nancial advisor. The previous year Ulrik had been so in-volved in his work for Sachs-Smith that it had cost him his summer vacation with Britt and Signe.

While Ulrik was away in the U.S.A., Camilla and

Markus joined Britt and Signe at their summer house up in Skagen. They'd had some marvelous weeks together, with chilled white wine in the garden and steaks from Munch's Butcher Shop.

She looked at the photo. Frederik Sachs-Smith. Forty-two years old, unmarried, and with an arrogant but somewhat charming smile. His medium-length blond hair blew in the breeze as he stood in bare feet on the edge of his pool at his house in Santa Barbara where, she read, he'd lived for the last eight years after several in New York and L.A.

Camilla folded the newspapers and tossed them on the floor, then crawled over to Markus in the big queen-size bed. He lay there laughing at people who fell on their asses or got hit in the head with a surfboard. The worse they got hurt, the more the audience laughed at them. Pretty tasteless.

Even so, Camilla couldn't help laughing herself when a severely overweight man tried to drive his lawn tractor up a slope and was furious when it stopped halfway to the top. Finally, he backed up, got a good running start, and came at it full throttle. The result was that the little tractor and the large man both went end-over. It had to hurt like hell, but it looked outrageously funny when he hung there suspended between the slope and his lawn tractor.

"What time is it in Denmark?" asked Markus, looking at the clock radio's digital numbers.

"They're nine hours ahead of us, so it's ten thirty at night."

"Then Signe's party's over now."

She nodded. She'd hoped he'd forgotten it. Understood perfectly well that he was sorry to miss it.

"Oh, no!" he yelled and sat straight up in the bed. "I forgot to give Jonas her gift from me. Now she hasn't gotten it, and she must think I didn't give her anything just because I didn't go to the party."

Tears began to swell.

"What did you buy her?" asked Camilla.

She ran her fingers through his hair.

"The new Beyoncé CD, and now it's lying at home on my desk."

For a moment, he sat staring blankly at Camilla, and she started to get the feeling it was all her fault.

"We'll buy something over here and send it back to her. Don't you think she'd like to have a gift from here?"

He sat a while with his eyes on the commercials flashing across the screen, then he nodded and leaned back.

11

Louise recognized the chief physician from a distance. He stood outside Reception and talked with a nurse and one of the trauma center's other doctors, whom she also knew from the night when Jonas and Camilla were admitted after the shooting in Sweden. In the days that followed, he'd come to her department daily to hear how it was going with them.

Louise greeted them and apologized for breaking into their conversation. She ignored the nurse, who was obviously irritated by the interruption.

"I've just come from Svanemølle Harbor," she said and told them how she'd arrived at the accident immediately after Signe was run over. "Jonas was at the party. He's in the same class as the girl."

That last comment was addressed to the two doctors, who knew the boy.

The chief physician nodded to the others and asked Louise to follow him down the hall to his office.

When they got there, the door stood open. They stepped inside, and he closed the door behind them.

"How bad is it?" asked Louise. "I promised her mother I'd come in."

He pointed to the guest chair and pulled his own chair back from the crowded desk. His eyes were bright gray under his blond hair, which hung down across his forehead. A deep wrinkle was etched across the bridge of his nose.

"Signe Fasting-Thomsen has just been declared dead," he said with a sad look.

Louise leaned back, folded her hands behind her neck, and closed her eyes.

"Oh, no. That can't be!"

The happy, red-haired girl smiled in Louise's memory of her, standing outside the sailing club as guests arrived. It was only a few hours ago.

"Her mother's been wheeled into ICU. One of our doctors is examining her now to determine the extent of her injuries. We're waiting to take her into X-ray, so we can see if any facial bones are broken. That could easily be the case. It looks like she was kicked in both the face and the back. At any rate, she has intense bruising over her lower back, which couldn't have come from just a fall."

Louise dropped her hands.

"Does she know that her daughter died?" she asked.

The chief physician shook his head. They sat a while in silence.

When he stood up and walked to the door, Louise followed him.

"What about the father?" she asked. "Has he come?"

"He's on his way. Drove as soon as he heard what had happened."

"It's quite a distance from Odsherred. Are you waiting for him before you talk with Britt?"

The doctor nodded.

"Yes, I think they should be together when they find out.

He doesn't know anything yet, either, only that his daughter's condition was critical when she was brought in."

They walked down the hall toward the ICU.

Louise felt her cell phone vibrate and read the brief text that Jonas had sent her.

"Anything new?" it said.

"Not yet. Sleep well, sweetheart. Good night," she texted him back.

She couldn't have been more evasive, and her conscience gnawed at her.

It was nearly midnight. In the sofa lounge outside the unit where Britt lay and waited to be taken to X-ray, the young officer from the harbor sat with a health magazine in his lap. His eyes drifted across its pages. On the table in front of him, there was a plastic cup with a drop of coffee in the bottom.

"The father's on his way," he said when he saw Louise.

"How much have you told him?" she asked.

He tossed the magazine aside.

"That it looks serious. We didn't know anything more at that point. But I'll stay till he comes."

Louise's body felt heavy as she settled down next to him. Signe's face began to stand out in her mind. For a while she sat slouched over, trying to get her feelings in check so she could focus on the accident.

"Have any witnesses shown up? Anyone who saw what happened down at the harbor?"

"Not yet."

"What about the guy with the ponytail who ran after Signe? Anyone see him?"

"Nope. And the married couple in the moving van didn't see anyone. Only the girl, when she was suddenly in front of their vehicle."

"Jonas saw him running after her."

The officer nodded.

Louise gave him her card, even though Jonas had already given his name and number to the officers down at the sailing club.

"We'll continue with the interviews tomorrow," he said and stuck her card in his pocket. "Wouldn't a lot of people go down to a harbor like that on a Sunday morning? Maybe we'll luck out and find that some of them were there last night and noticed the boys before they reached the sailing club."

Just then the double doors clicked open and the nurse Louise had seen when she'd arrived now escorted Ulrik in. He looked shocked and pale, as if his face were frozen, his eyes blank. For a second, it looked like he was going to stop when he caught sight of Louise, but then with a long stride he followed the nurse, who held the door for him, and disappeared down a long hallway.

Louise fought down the lump that had gathered in her throat. Then she stood up.

"I'd appreciate it if you kept me informed," she told the officer. "Mostly so I know what to say to the children in the class, when they ask."

Feeling cold inside, she walked down the brightly lit hallway. Nurses and doctors came in and out of the rooms. It was the week's busiest shift: Saturday night.

Louise walked with her hands in her jacket pockets and her eyes on the floor, thoughts wrestling in her head.

Meaningless. Utterly pointless. How could a children's party end like that?

She wasn't sure how she'd manage to tell Jonas that Signe was dead. Let alone how she'd explain to him that the police presumably wouldn't punish the guilty party. If it turned out there weren't any witnesses to the accident, then charges for involuntary manslaughter would never be brought. And what would that do anyhow, she thought as she pushed the door open. It still wouldn't change the fact that it had been a tragic accident.

12

The next days were interminable. After Louise dropped off the report of her interview with Mie Hartmann late Sunday morning, she drove to Lasse's parents' house to pick up Jonas. The boys were still in their pajamas, their faces frozen as she told them as gently as she could the unvarnished version of the tragedy, as they all sat around the kitchen table with a basket of rolls and morning papers spread out in sections.

There was nothing encouraging she could soften it with. No hope that it would end well or get better with time. Signe was dead. She'd never get to go to Saint Anne's, and at the beginning that's what occupied Jonas and Lasse the most.

"She'd been looking forward to it so much!" they said with voices full of sadness.

And after that the questions came tumbling out: Was she dead at the scene? Did it hurt her? Was she afraid? Was there a lot of blood? What about the guy who ran after her? Did the driver see him?

The two adults asked more discreetly after Signe's parents. Namely Britt, but also Ulrik, who'd received the terrifying call that all parents dread.

Louise wasn't sure how long she'd been answering questions when suddenly they ebbed away.

Words were replaced with silence, which gave her the opportunity to excuse herself and to thank Lasse's parents for taking care of Jonas.

⚓

The weather was good as they walked out onto the sidewalk and looked up at the Planetarium. Lasse's parents had an apartment on Peblinge Dosseringen, and the sun threw a golden glare across the lake that made Jonas squint his eyes.

They walked home. The shops along Gammel Kongevej were closed like they would be on any other lazy Sunday morning. As they neared the Frederiksberg Town Hall, Louise suggested a cup of hot chocolate at Belis Kitchen, but Jonas wanted to go home.

The hours dragged on for the rest of the day. After he'd hung up his jacket on a hanger in the entryway, Jonas had taken his box set of The Olsen Gang movies down from the shelf and plopped on the sofa, barricading himself with Egon, Benny, and Kjeld.

Louise walked around in the kitchen, not really knowing what she should do. Talk or shut up?

The mood between them was forced as their sadness gnawed deep inside their bones. It took away their appetites, and dinner was left cold on their plates.

At night, he cried.

She heard him first through his door. Then she crept in quietly and sat down on the edge of his bed, stroked his hair. Since he'd moved in with her, she'd sat that way with him many times before. But until now it had always been his father he'd cried over.

Finally, he fell asleep.

As she was getting ready for bed, Mik called several times, but each time she'd declined the call. She didn't feel up to more explaining. She turned her cell phone off.

❧

On Monday, the class observed a one-minute silence. The school's flag flew at half-mast, and the principal gave a talk.

The next day, Jonas sat in the living room with a vacant look on his face, watching one Olsen Gang film after another. Whenever Louise tried to break through his armor, she was rebuffed.

"Want to go to see a movie?" she asked.

It was Wednesday afternoon and she'd just gotten home from work.

"No thanks," he said.

There was a hint of irritation in his voice, and he didn't take his eyes off Egon Olsen and the 1944 model Franz Jäger safe that needed to be blown up.

She got the picture, understood that it was her own sense of inadequacy looking for a way out. But she didn't know how to help him. They hadn't grown close enough yet for him to completely let her in.

She turned to go back into the kitchen.

"When do you think the police will catch the boys who came and ruined the party?" he asked.

He looked at her as the film rolled on.

"I think they're doing all they can to find them."

Louise sat down on the sofa beside him.

"But, Jonas," she said softly, "it won't make any difference. If they're found, they'll be charged with unlawful trespass on private property and for attacking Signe's mom.

But those aren't things that would give them just punishment for what happened to Signe."

"You're in the police, so you can explain how it was their fault. How they broke in and destroyed everything."

Anger and desperation were there, but it was obvious he was holding himself back.

"To begin with, the matter isn't up to us. It's up to the local police in Bellahøj—they're the ones who need to find the boys and uncover what really happened. And as far as that goes, it doesn't help if I go to them and say there was a boy who ran after Signe if we can't find witnesses who saw it."

"I saw it!"

His eyes went back to the screen, just in time to see Kjeld detonate the explosives.

You saw him run after her, but not whether he chased her out in front of the van—so it's not good enough, thought Louise, but she said nothing. Instead, she got up to go turn on the oven so she could start making dinner.

❦

While they were still sitting at the kitchen table having dinner, Ulrik Fasting-Thomsen called. In a faint voice, he said that Signe's funeral would be held in Hellerup Church on Saturday at 1:00 p.m.

"We're so sorry for your loss," said Louise as she wrote down the address. "We feel terrible."

He thanked her, sounding completely worn out. Louise guessed he hadn't gotten much sleep since the accident.

"How's Britt?" she asked.

When Jonas realized who she was talking with, he set his silverware aside and looked down at the table.

"You'll have to excuse me if this sounds a little intrusive," Ulrik said. In a sad voice, he told her how his wife had, understandably given the circumstances, taken a downward turn. "But I'd like to ask if you'd do me a favor and come visit her. She could use someone to talk to."

His voice sounded urgent.

"It might help her, since you were out there and experienced some of it," he said in a tone that revealed his utter despair. He'd tried to hide it with details about the funeral, but now she sensed how the catastrophe loomed large and powerful behind all the practical things that needed to be taken care of. "It's like she hasn't entirely grasped yet that this terrible thing really has happened. I'm sure it would help if she heard it from an eye witness."

Louise looked over at Jonas.

Would it be a good idea to take him with her on a hospital visit? Maybe the visit would pull him out of the shell he'd crawled into. Even though Jonas had already been to see Jakobsen, and Louise didn't claim to know a lot about child psychology herself, she still quickly decided that it would be better if he started coming to terms with the grief that sat and wore away at him instead of barricading himself off from it. And maybe it would move things along if he went with her to see Signe's mom.

"I'd be happy to," she said.

She looked up at the clock. It was six thirty. They'd have to get out the door now if they didn't want to be too late.

"I'm bringing Jonas with me," she said and explained that he'd been the one who'd seen Signe running.

"You should prepare yourselves. Britt doesn't look so good," Ulrik warned. "She has a large blood clot around her eye and a smaller one inside the eye itself, and her cheekbone's broken in two places and caved in."

There were flowers everywhere. The profusion of fresh colors seemed like an insult to the condition Britt Fasting-Thomsen was in.

It wasn't so much her physical injuries, which the doctors had carefully tended to, as the dull look in her one healthy eye. Where there'd once been a glimmer, there was now only pain and desperation.

Even at a distance, Louise saw that Ulrik had been wrong. Britt understood perfectly well that the worst *had* happened, but that was a far cry from saying she accepted that her daughter had been taken from her.

And it was that desperation that Louise read in her face when they walked into the private room.

"Did she cry as she lay on the road after being hit?" Britt asked.

She looked directly at Louise, as if Jonas weren't there.

Louise shook her head.

"What did she look like?"

Why do you want to know that? Louise thought, putting her arm around Jonas. Only then did Britt move her gaze to him and nod at him politely, but immediately she returned her focus to Louise. It was obvious that the questions were struggling to come out, but she forced them back and slumped over. She folded her hands together over the duvet and played with her wedding ring, turning it round.

"I thought they were leaving," she said.

She closed her eye without waiting for an answer. God knows how many times she'd relived the scene.

"I should have called the police as soon as they stood there and wanted to come in. But it didn't even occur to me. Took it for granted they'd leave when I told them to."

She smoothed a fold in the duvet, then slammed her fists down on the bedsheets and exclaimed, "They were just kids, damn it. Not much older than you are!"

Now she looked over at Jonas and shook her head.

He looked away shyly and kept behind Louise.

"I keep imagining how Signe had to stand there and watch it all, without anyone able to do anything. She must have been terrified."

Silence.

"No, she wasn't," Jonas said suddenly and looked over at Britt. "She wasn't scared. She was mad and she wanted to help you and make them stop. But she wasn't scared."

Suddenly it was as though a shadow of Britt's old self appeared and reminded her that she had guests, and that she owed them a bit of good manners. With difficulty, she retrieved a large box of chocolates from the side table and passed them around. She told Louise and Jonas they could get coffee and soft drinks from a cart in the hallway.

Louise shook her head and pulled a couple of chairs over to the bed. She prepared to tell Britt what she could about her daughter's death.

From experience, she knew that one of the worst things for parents who lose a child—or any relative—was uncertainty. All the things they didn't know for certain, but imagined again and again. Uncertainty has a tendency to be a monster that grows bigger and bigger, and it can only be stopped by knowing what actually happened.

Starting with the moment Jonas called her, Louise told the story in detail. She explained how she'd grasped through the telephone that the situation with the boys had gotten out of hand.

Britt nodded and offered more chocolates.

"They killed Signe," she said quietly. Then she placed the box back on the side table.

"Yes," Louise conceded, "but that's not what they came to do. Boys don't go out on the town to beat up a woman they don't know and chase her daughter out in front of a van. When they crash a party, they're after booze and valuables. Maybe they go out to beat up other boys or maybe even a man. But not a woman. There's something unnatural in it."

Britt seemed to have stopped listening. She lay and stared straight ahead.

"I'll never forgive them, no matter what their intentions were."

She gave Louise a hard look to emphasize that she was completely within her rights to fill herself with anger.

"There were only two of them who went nuts," said Jonas. "And then when Signe ran for help, one of the ones who kicked you ran after her."

"If only she'd been the quiet and frightened kind of girl who would crawl under a table and hide," Britt said and suddenly began to smile. "But she wasn't like that. My daughter was strong. But the van...why wasn't I allowed to go up and be there with her when I could tell in my gut that something had happened to her?"

Louise stepped in closer.

"It wouldn't have made any difference for Signe whether you'd been there or not," she said, knowing that it sounded cruel. "She wasn't conscious, and it was important for the rescuers to have calm and room to work. They did what they could to save your daughter's life."

She told her about the van driver and his wife, how they hadn't seen Signe coming until she was right in front of them, and how the girl was already lying on the road unconscious by the time Louise got there.

Jonas listened attentively, and Louise started to think that perhaps he, too, was starting to work through what had happened. Of course, he'd felt plenty of difficult emotions. He, too, had been struck with feelings of guilt and ideas of how he should have helped Signe or should have run with her. She should have told him everything she knew about the accident, even though he hadn't asked her to. She should have helped him control the images he'd doubtless created in his mind.

Britt's eyes began to close. The combination of her fatigue and the medicine she'd been given made her listless and sleepy. Louise signaled to Jonas that it was probably time for them to say good-bye.

After they'd gotten home and Louise had started cleaning up the kitchen, Jonas yelled from his bedroom, "There's an e-mail from Markus and Camilla."

A few minutes passed while he read it, then she heard the printer start up. Soon after he came out into the kitchen.

Louise took the paper from him and watched him walk to the bathroom with his eyes aimed at the floor. She heard him brushing his teeth as she began to read.

Hi you guys!

So, we're here. Seattle is pretty. I had no idea there was so much water around the city. The trip was a rough one. First to Chicago, where we waited for five hours for our connection, but Markus took it like a champ.

Our hotel's nice, sits right in the middle of the city with a view of the Space Needle. We're gradually getting used to the time difference, although it's fine with me if I can avoid being awake for too many hours in the day!

We've just been down to Pike's Market. Have you ever heard of it? That's where the fish merchants throw the fish! We watched when an elderly lady came to buy a piece of salmon, and a second later a huge fish was tossed through the air! Then it got weighed and tossed back again. Could you imagine the fish merchants down on Gammel Kongevej doing that?

On Wednesday, we pick up our car at the airport, and then the road trip begins. First, we're going to a national park called Mount Rainier—it's mostly me who wants to do that, and I only succeeded in persuading Markus by tempting him with black bears and mountain lions!!!

We hope Signe had a nice party. Markus still hasn't forgiven me for not postponing our trip a few days so he could go. But he's bought a really nice present, which we're sending home to her.

We'll keep you posted.

Warm hugs,
Camilla and Markus

Louise set the e-mail on the kitchen table. She needed more space and energy before she wrote back.

For now, she simply turned off the kitchen light and went to bed.

13

On Friday afternoon, Louise sat in her office rereading the interviews taken with the three Folehaven gang members who'd been arrested.

They hadn't gotten any closer on the Nick Hartmann murder. No one spilled the beans or said anything. She was ready to throw up over these biker assholes and drug pushers, and her bold prediction that at least one of them would take credit for the Amager shooting didn't come true. Earlier that morning, the lieutenant had released them, because the investigation had found nothing new that would make a judge extend the custody.

Suhr had gotten the investigation group together just before lunch. Willumsen was furious because the lieutenant hadn't fought to keep the suspects, but Hans Suhr had in his usual manner smiled forbearingly at his lead investigator. A smile that over the years had become a disarming tool that he used when Willumsen got worked up and threatened to go it alone.

The lieutenant's gray hair was combed back in stylish waves, and the furrows on his cheeks were smoothed out for as long as his smile lasted. When it disappeared, the vertical wrinkles returned and highlighted his cheekbones, his face regained its sharp features, and the tone of his voice bordered on irritation.

"I've held them a week, and you haven't found anything useful. Nothing indicates that these three had anything to do with the murder."

Willumsen cleared his throat, but Suhr raised his hand to stop him.

"The crime techs are finished with their report. None of the bullets that were found out on Dyvekes Allé matches the firearms our colleagues seized in the raid. We've released these three guys, but, without question, they'll be charged with unlawful possession of weapons. And, we won't be giving up on finding the weapons that were used in this latest shooting. But as things stand, I had to let them go. And now the folks out in Bellahøj are keeping a close eye on them. You can get on with the investigation."

And that had been about it. Just, get on with it.

It was all still eating away at Louise when she went for lunch. Way too loudly, she'd scoffed at the police higher-ups for not having the balls to put an end to the shooting sprees. It was only after she stood up that she saw the chief inspector of police, who sat at a table behind her with an open-faced sandwich and a small bowl of salad on his plate.

But he'd only smiled and said he agreed with her. They just needed to get the justice minister on board so there'd be money for more resources. He was pretty cool, she thought. Understood, fortunately, that frustration sometimes took the wind out of his people.

Once back, with her feet on her desk, she tossed the last report aside. She took her mug of tea between her hands and tipped back her chair. She'd untied her long, dark hair, and the curls hung down heavily over her shoulders. As long as Lars Jørgensen was home on sick leave, she didn't need to worry about looking decent when she sat behind her closed door and copied over reports. Gradually, though, it occurred to her how boring a private office was and how much she looked forward to her partner having enough energy to come back and take up the battle with Willumsen.

Hearing a knock on her office door, Louise quickly fixed her hair and took her feet down off the desk. In stepped Toft with a case file in his hand, his pullover over his shoulder, and his glasses pushed absentmindedly on his forehead so they sat crooked.

"Now I've gotten hold of all the relevant sources that, as I see it, would prove or disprove whether Nick Hartmann had any connection to the drug trade tied to the bikers' inner circle."

Louise emptied her mug of tea while he talked.

"But I no longer believe that's how they were connected. None of my contacts knows anything about him, whether he dealt in hash or narcotics. No one has any idea who he is or recognizes him from his picture."

Nick Hartmann should be fairly easy to remember if you've seen him, thought Louise. Around six five, he had Greenlandic ancestry that gave him striking eyes and coal-black hair.

"No one," repeated Toft, and tossed the file aside as he sat down at Lars Jørgensen's empty spot. "Now Michael Stig's taken a trip down to see Mikkelsen to get him to check if the shooting victim had any connection to the bikers' brothels."

Mikkelsen from Station City on Halmtorvet was the policeman with indisputably the most insight into Copenhagen's prostitution scene. He was the one who could get hold of information unavailable to other police members, because he'd had his team in the area for so many years and had won people's trust. But he was also very careful about who he passed information on to and what their goal was.

Evil tongues accused him of being more on the side of the whores than the police. Still, the higher-ups had made him the lead investigator of a group that had just been formed to combat the sex trade that, until recently, hadn't been taken seriously enough.

"Maybe Hartmann worked as a stooge between the brothels and the bikers?"

Toft seemed to be thinking out loud. He looked over at Louise and added, "They want to shovel money in, but they're too damned smart to get mixed up with the brothels."

"You're right," Louise allowed. "That may be exactly how they're connected. Because then there'd be a reason for him to pop in now and then at their headquarters."

Toft nodded and straightened his glasses, which had started to slip.

"If it turns out he's connected to the bikers' activities in prostitution, then at the same time we can rule out the guys from Folehaven," he concluded. "Pimping is way too complicated for them."

Louise agreed with him, and said she'd asked the bank for copies of Nick Hartmann's bank statements.

"I've also talked with SKAT, and they're sending his tax returns for the last four years."

Toft's cell phone rang in his shirt pocket. He straightened up and took it. He mumbled more than talked, and afterward he shook his head.

"Mikkelsen doesn't know anything about the deceased, has never heard of him, doesn't recognize him from the photo, but now he'll show it to his contacts. There are apparently five brothels that are of interest.

But as Michael Stig understands it, Mikkelsen's already named the people behind them. All the ones who are on the bikers' payroll."

Another thing that Louise was nearly sick over, was the net the bikers had spun over the city, and how it was so extensive that it had threads going in every direction.

"What did Nick Hartmann spend his time doing? Was he some kind of shipping agent?"

Louise nodded and said he worked in a big shipping company down on Havnegade.

"What the hell was he doing running around in the bikers' headquarters?"

She shrugged her shoulders and suggested they drive out there and ask the members themselves.

"Let's just do that," said Toft. He pulled his sweater over his head and offered to drop Louise off in Frederiksberg afterward.

The fortification was extremely impressive. The fence was so high you couldn't tell there was a three-story house behind it, and above the gate two security cameras looked out over the entryway and the sidewalk for several yards in both directions. It was like an impregnable fortress, lacking only a drawbridge and moat. It even had a high-tech intercom system on the door, with a little camera lens that was activated as soon as you rang up.

Toft called in and asked if they could find out if anyone knew Nick Hartmann.

"No," the voice said simply.

"Come on," said Toft.

He looked directly into the little camera.

"Just let us in."

"Thanks for stopping by," the speaker said in a friendly tone.

You couldn't call them impolite, Louise thought, but at the same time they were irritating as hell. She took a step forward.

"If we can't come in, won't you be nice enough to come out here, or send someone else we can just talk with? We know that the person we're interested in has visited you several times, and now we'd like to hear what his association was."

Louise had barely finished speaking when a door to the gate opened and a tall, short-haired man in a vest with an insignia on the back stepped forward.

Tønnes was his name. Louise recognized him from TV, where he had been recently interviewed after another round of rioting that had sent two high-profile bikers behind bars. He served as the bikers' spokesperson and spin doctor, and if you ignored his rather fierce and provocative appearance, he was as well-spoken as any businessman and certainly seemed as though he'd be perfectly comfortable in a boardroom. But his fashion choices definitely made it clear where he belonged.

It wasn't news to the police that the bikers had found someone with an unusually sharp mind to represent them. Because, clearly, they could use someone who was media savvy, especially now with the rising attention focused on the bikers.

"Don't know him," said Tønnes.

"He's come here to the house," Toft shot back.

"I'm afraid I can't help you."

The peak of politeness.

"He was arrested during a raid a few months back."

The biker shrugged his shoulders and shook his head apologetically.

"That doesn't mean anything to me."

"Now come on," said Louise. "We know he's been here, and you don't let just anyone come and go as they please."

He looked at her.

"What was the name?" he asked.

"Nick Hartmann."

"Not his name. Yours?"

Toft was about to come to her rescue, but she stopped him.

"Louise Rick, Homicide Department at Copenhagen's Police Headquarters."

She wouldn't let herself be provoked, and again asked him to tell her what the deceased's association to the biker club had been.

She couldn't read anything in his face as he once again shook his head. But his gaze was intense as his dark eyes studied her with a hint of curiosity. He was clearly taking stock of what he saw. Then his look turned dismissive again, and he stepped back in the door.

"Thanks for stopping by," he said.

Toft tried to make another effort, but the door was closed in their faces.

"Damn are they irritating!" Louise exclaimed.

Still, she found herself laughing and shaking her head as she followed Toft to the car.

They'd gotten nothing out of it. They'd been completely, categorically shut out in a friendly and utterly un-bikerly manner, and the scary thing was that someplace deep down, past all sense and reason, she felt herself attracted to the brute strength the man had shown.

They're sexy, Camilla had said one summer day as two

of the bikers came riding down Gammel Kongevej on their Harleys, no helmets on and their bare tattooed arms under their leather vests.

That same power had hovered like an aura around the man at the door, Louise thought as she sat down in the front seat of her colleague's Polo.

14

Dear L & Jonas

Packwood is the world's most hopeless and over-hyped little town. I haven't seen anything like it.

When we were out in Mount Rainier, the national park I wrote about—where, naturally, we saw neither hide nor hair of any mountain lions or black bears!—we couldn't agree on where to stay. I was just tired and wanted to sleep, but Markus convinced me to keep driving. Here it's just woods and woods and more woods and then a campground. And that's how it looked too as we got closer to Packwood, a long straight country road—a little bit like out in Osted, the town's just much smaller.

They've got two hotels. We drove past the first, and when we were coming up on the second, which looked like an overgrown wooden hut, Markus yelled, "Stop!"

I yelled, "No way in hell can we stay there." But then the damned kid tells me I'm the one who says you have to take the plunge if you want to experience anything!

Did I say that???

Packwood sells itself on charm and comfort. There

are shops, restaurants, hotels, and an airport. And that's not really a lie. The airport turns out to be a meadow with two run-down two-passenger prop planes AND in the same field there are wild elk walking around loose!

The restaurant was a saloon where they were having taco night, and it was lucky for us because you got two tacos for the equivalent of twelve kroner, and then we sat with a bunch of bikers who could have been extras back when they filmed Easy Rider. Very interesting!

When we got back after our taco night, we met the hotel owner's grown-up daughter who, natural as could be, wore a rifle over her shoulder. She explained that it was both for protecting herself against animals in the woods (read: black bears, mountain lions, et al.) and for keeping her family and the hotel's guests safe.

What the hell! is all I can say. Markus got a supersize Snickers bar for insisting that we stay here. This place is exotic in a way you never even knew was interesting.

And for the first time in a long while, I actually slept for seven hours straight.

Now it's morning and we're sitting in a little cafe... without doubt the most civilized place for miles around— they even have an Internet connection. Markus is working on his second muffin. We've tried to get hold of Signe and Britt to hear about how it's going at the new school, but neither of them calls back. But tell them we said hi. We'll try calling again when it's morning where you are.

Warmest,
C—and Markus

Dear Camilla and Markus,

I'm terribly sorry to have to tell you that Signe died this weekend. She was killed in a car accident the night she had her party. Some troublemakers barged in and trashed the place, and when Britt asked them to leave they attacked her. She's been in the National Hospital with a rather complicated fracture on one of her cheek-bones.

Signe went for help, and one of the boys ran after her. Whether it was from panic or because he chased her we still don't know, but she ran into the road right in front of a car. The driver didn't even have time to swerve. Her funeral is later today.

I would have called you, but couldn't find the courage. Jonas has shut himself up inside, and I don't know what to do for him. Or myself for that matter. I'm really sorry. I know you and Britt spend time together. But anyway, that's why they haven't returned your calls.

It's so sad and painful, and the entire class is affected; that goes without saying. I ordered a wreath and put your name on it too.

Warm hugs,
Louise

15

Steam rose from her tea as Camilla sat with her eyes fixed on the computer screen. As soon as she read the first sentence in Louise's e-mail, she felt her body going tense. She held her breath instinctively and heard her heart beat louder. An odd, empty feeling shut out all other sounds.

Word by word the catastrophe slid inside her as she sat with her shoulders scrunched up and her heart hammering away in her chest, which felt cold and hard.

Markus was engrossed with his Game Boy and didn't notice his mother going quiet.

Camilla clasped her hands over her mouth and started to cry.

"Damn it all to hell!"

Frightened, Markus looked up at her and watched her stand up and turn to the wall in the little café, where three older men in lumberjack shirts sat drinking espresso from tiny, brightly colored cups.

She pressed her hand to her mouth and bit the loose skin between her thumb and forefinger. The tears ran down as Markus looked on in confusion.

"What happened?" he whispered.

The men at the table looked at them, then averted their eyes.

Camilla struggled to regain control. She felt the ground collapsing beneath her. In a few seconds, she'd have to pass on the news to her son, take his hand, and comfort him. She felt like she was sitting on an enormous block of ice just before it broke away from the iceberg and floated out to sea. It made her shake so much her teeth rattled.

She swallowed. Stood a moment getting her breathing under control, dried her tears with her fingertips, and turned to him.

Scared. His eyes were scared, and he stood with his mouth partly open and waited.

"Did something happen to Dad?" he whispered.

She shook her head and watched his shoulders relax.

Then she gently took hold of him. Feeling heavy and miserable, she told him that Signe had been in a terrible accident.

Markus wanted to know everything. Asked and asked, but Camilla couldn't answer very much of it. He read Louise's e-mail until he knew it by heart, but it wasn't until she let him go onto Facebook, where he found the memorial page his classmates had put up for Signe, that Markus quieted down. Looking pale, he read all the sweet and loving things Signe's friends had written to her. And then he began to cry.

He sat quietly with his face in his hands as the tears ran down.

Camilla packed up her laptop and paid at the counter. They'd already checked out of Hotel Packwood, but as the only guests it wasn't any problem getting their room back.

As she opened the hatch to take their bags out again, she felt deep inside herself a powerful gratitude that Markus had been prevented from attending the party he'd wanted so much to go to.

16

The cars were parked tightly along the sidewalk and in front of Hellerup Church. The flag hung limp, and the gray cloud shelf pulled the sky downward so it lay heavily over the roof and the pointed steeple.

Ulrik Fasting-Thomsen stood with the church warden and greeted everyone. His eyes were full of sorrow, but he smiled and shook each person's hand. Even though Louise and Markus had gotten there early, most of the seats were already taken. In the very front sat Britt with her head bowed, not up to greeting all the people who'd come to say farewell to her daughter. She'd just been released from the National Hospital, and the bandage over the left side of her face was smaller, covering only the incision where the surgeons had put her cheekbone back together. Fragile and disconsolate, she sat on the church pew as a pale reflection of the mother who'd smiled happily and received guests at her daughter's party.

With her arm around Jonas, Louise walked up the aisle to the pew behind the family, where there were two empty places, as if the other funeral guests hadn't had the courage to sit so close to the relatives' grief. But Louise had long ago put aside her fear of other people's grief, not least because she knew how lonely and cold that distance could feel to them when the world had caved in. She put her hand lightly on Britt's shoulder as they sat down behind her.

Jonas had walked up the aisle with his head lowered, past the parade of flowers that started all the way back in the entryway. He didn't make eye contact with his classmates, who sat spread around with their parents or with one another, holding on to handkerchiefs. He'd also avoided looking at the white coffin. Until now, when his eyes sought out the dark red roses arranged in a wide bow on the lid of the coffin.

Louise looked at him anxiously, and pulled back her hand.

At the breakfast table, he hadn't touched the rolls that Louise had toasted. He hadn't eaten or drunk anything, and in the end, she couldn't take it anymore. There was a lump in her throat, and the powerlessness of not knowing what she should do was about to drive her crazy. She pushed her coffee cup away and decided to let it all come out, realizing immediately that that was what she'd been going around waiting for him to do. Give in and let the feelings and thoughts come out. Instead, she was the one who started.

"I don't know what to do," she began. "I want so much to help you, to say the right thing. It's all so unbearable, and I want to be there for you. I just don't know how."

He looked at her. He seemed surprised and a little frightened.

"There's been so much misfortune in the short time we've known each other," she said. "And now we're going to another funeral."

The tears were there before she could get hold of herself. Louise took a deep breath, blinked her tears away, and regained her composure while she tried to find the right words. But they weren't there, so she just blurted the first thing that came to mind.

"I don't know the best way to be there for you. What should I do? You need to help me. Damn it, I've never tried to be someone's foster mother before!"

His dark eyes were deep, intense, but not standoffish.

"It's as if I can't cry anymore," he said and looked away. "And it really bothers me. As if Signe weren't important enough for me to cry about her dying."

Louise felt empty inside. Speechless. She understood it: Jonas thought he wasn't grieving enough over his classmate's death; he was sorry he couldn't put as much energy into his grief as he had when his father was shot. He blamed himself for not having any tears left.

She stood up and walked around the table. Held him close and ran her fingers through his hair.

"That's not how grief is measured," she whispered. "You can't compare one to another. You would never think of it that way if you hadn't just experienced a death so recently."

She cursed the fact that he'd had to have all these strong feelings so close together. It wasn't fair. Not fair at all.

"Are you sure you want to go to the funeral? Is it too soon?"

She thought of the psychologist.

"What does Jakobsen say?"

"I want to go. And he says the same thing as you, that I

shouldn't try to live up to anything, that we all respond in
our own way."

Louise looked down at him.

"Don't be so hard on yourself. Right now, you're the one
I feel sorry as hell for. Remember that," she said.

She saw a smile in his eyes.

"You can yell, scream, cry, or just sit and stare at the wall
if that's what you feel like doing. I just want to hear how
you're doing," she said.

Even that was probably asking too much, she thought,
considering how reluctant most preteens were to let their
parents into their lives, especially the emotional side.

⚒

The organ started to play, and the choir led the opening
of "In the East the Sun Is Rising." Soon, the sanctuary
filled with song. Louise held out the hymnal so they could
both follow along, but being the son of a pastor Jonas knew
this hymn down in his bones. He must have heard it sung
countless times when his father served as pastor in Stenhøj
Church. He sang in a clear and pure voice.

In front of them, Ulrik sat beside Britt, who sat erect
with her hands folded and sang toward the coffin. Louise
saw tears running down his cheeks; his jaw was clenched as
he listened to others singing.

Louise knew that Ulrik and Britt had decided not to
speak beside their daughter's coffin. Instead, after the pastor's talk, one of the country's finest solo cellists from the
Royal Chapel would play.

Jonas sat with his eyes closed, carried away by the music. When the pastor had spoken about Signe's meaningless
and all-too-early death, tears had run down the boy's

cheeks. Louise had squeezed his hand and passed him a pack of tissues.

When the cellist's last notes faded away, the church filled with a heavy silence. The silence remained until the pastor stood up from his chair beside the altar and walked over to toss dirt on the coffin. The dirt settled on the lid, and his words filled the room again.

The choir began the next hymn, and the voices in the church quickly followed along. But this time it was harder to focus on the words in the hymnal—the sound of sniffles and the children's deep sobs took the place of the words and blended in with the song.

Louise stopped trying to sing. She cried quietly and was deeply moved. Swept away by the atmosphere and Britt, who cried despairingly and stretched her arms pitifully toward Signe's white coffin. Ulrik put his arm around his wife's shoulder. The parents sat close together, and Louise thought that for at least a moment they ought to have the church and coffin to themselves.

After the pastor spoke the final words, a string quartet came forward. Two violins, a viola, and a cello. As the musicians readied themselves, Britt's tense body relaxed a little. Her dark pageboy hair fell to the side as she laid her head against Ulrik's shoulder; she closed her eyes to the notes of Bach's "Air on the G String."

After that, the strings glided over Mozart's "Ave Verum Corpus" and the organ followed along. Halfway through the piece, Ulrik stood up and signaled to the pallbearers. Trailed by classical music, they bore Signe's coffin out to the hearse.

"God, that music was beautiful," Jonas said as they walked to the car.

Louise looked at him. Jonas was so different from what

she was used to with Camilla's son, who was the same age.
While Markus was mostly into rap, hip-hop, and computer
games, Jonas was absorbed in books, listened to instrumen-
tal music, and played the guitar. He was more introverted
than Markus, and he focused on the things that interested
him, didn't jump restlessly from one thing to the other. He
loved, for instance, lying on his bed and reading books—
could do it for hours.

"Do you want to drive over there? Or would you rather
go home?"

Britt and Ulrik had invited family and friends to a reception at their house.

"The others are going," said Jonas. Louise decided they
should drive out to Strandvænget.

Candles lined the entire length of the garden path, and an
older woman in a dark blue dress stood receiving guests and
taking their coats as they arrived. In the sitting rooms, all the
candlesticks were lit, and two hostesses went around pointing
everyone to the glasses and drinks that had been set out.

The same dark red roses that had lain on the coffin were
used for decoration, only in smaller numbers, like a little
thread still tied to Signe, whose body was on its way to the
crematorium.

Louise and Jonas went into the living room.

"Thank you so much for coming," Britt said.

She smiled sadly, but her eyes were clear and she'd
touched up her makeup.

The house was beginning to fill with people. Their
voices sounded muffled, as if they'd been wrapped in a
blanket.

"There's wine and water, and sandwiches are coming soon," said Britt.

She smiled at a young couple as they came through the door.

"This is Signe's cousin," she said, introducing the girl. Then she showed them to the drinks table.

Louise was beginning to turn, but Britt reached out her hand and stopped her.

"Do you know if they've found the boys?"

Louise shook her head.

"Not yet. At least, I haven't heard anything."

She understood Britt's disappointment. A week ago, she and her daughter were putting the finishing touches on the party. Today they were holding a funeral. Britt needed to put the pieces together before she could even begin to deal with what had happened.

In the music room, the string quartet from the church was starting to unpack their instruments and set up next to Britt's beautiful grand piano. There was an empty space where Signe's cello had stood the last time Louise was here.

"I carried it up to her bedroom. I couldn't bear to look at it every time I walk by," Britt whispered.

A tear fell as she stood watching the instrumentalists, who were ready to start.

"When Signe was little, she'd lie on the floor under the piano while I practiced. And she started playing herself when she was only four."

She grasped Louise's arm and leaned into her.

"I just can't understand it. When I came home from the hospital and was getting dressed for church, I thought I heard her cello. I hadn't been home since we'd left for the sailing club, and the whole time I thought, she's still here. Her sounds, her smell. Her presence. I can feel her, and her room's the way it was when we left on Saturday afternoon. By the way, Jonas forgot his sweater. It's on her bed."

Louise took her hand, which was still holding her arm. Britt shook her head despondently.

"It's driving me crazy. My body aches for her, and at the same time I know she's never coming back. I feel completely empty. It's as if missing her has taken the place of what used to be in my body. It's true what they say, that a mother feels it physically when she loses her child. The most important part of me has been amputated."

Louise nodded and gave her a look of sympathy. Even though she'd never given birth to a child or lost one, she understood what Britt meant.

From the living room came the sound of a glass being clinked. Ulrik stood between two tall glass doors that went out to the terrace. His shirt was untucked on one side. He looked out over his guests and waited until he had everyone's attention.

"It is so terribly sad for us to be gathered here today," he began.

Tears swelled in his eyes. He took a deep breath and held it for a moment.

"But we are very happy and grateful to you for being with us as we say good-bye to our dear, sweet Signe."

Britt walked up and stood beside her husband.

"Sometimes there is no justice," he said as he took his wife's hand. "Unbearable things happen, and the world falls to pieces. That happened to us last Saturday. But Signe will always be in our hearts. Let's toast to her, and to the joy of life and the energy she was so full of. It will help us to remember her and all the good times we were able to have with her. Thank you so much, dear friends, for coming. Now we'll have some music, and in a moment a little food will be brought in."

Around the room, people nodded to one another as the musicians began to play.

The lovely sounds made the small hairs on the back of Louise's arm stand up.

17

Louise nearly lost her patience on Monday afternoon as she sat waiting to see how long five minutes could take. It had already been close to twenty since Hans Suhr had said he'd be back in five. She closed her eyes and leaned her head against the wall. Her shoulders ached from sitting at her desk all day.

After lunch, Mikkelsen had called and said that no one in the prostitution racket knew of Nick Hartmann. She didn't really believe that. At any rate, not in the part controlled by the bikers, and they ran more than a few brothels in Copenhagen. By reading between the lines, she'd figured out that it must be the women themselves—at least one woman at each location—whose trust Mikkelsen had won. Because, of course, it was obvious the men behind the scenes wouldn't talk with the police, nor would they let their women.

She started to think of Camilla and Markus, who were driving along the Oregon coastline in torrential rains.

Camilla had sent an e-mail the day before, saying she'd written a little with Britt.

"She told me about the funeral. I just can't believe that

sweet little Signe is gone. But I'm glad that Ulrik sees that this is a time he needs to be there for his wife. If they can just support each other, then they'll make it through the grief. Britt and Signe were very close. She lived for her daughter, so she must be feeling unbelievably empty suddenly. Poor, poor them. Damn, it's killing me."

She'd also written how she and Markus had gone out to scream at the ocean.

We pulled into a rest area on the edge of the coast. I had no idea how big the waves were—they roiled and roared, and we had to yell to hear each other. Markus can't quite wrap his head around the fact that Signe really won't be there when we come back home. It's almost too much for him. It's as if he can't completely understand that a child could die that way. He knows how Jonas lost his dad, but I don't think he can explain to himself how a child can die before her parents. And maybe it's both healthy and natural to think that way. But it's gotten inside of him and become hard for him to manage, and I understand it. Feel sort of the same way myself. It's so completely meaningless.

Yesterday when we pulled off to the side to stretch our legs, I walked all the way out to the edge of a cliff and looked straight down at the chasm, and it was so engrossing that for a moment I wanted to lean forward and take off. Take a bungee jump without a harness. Then, out of nowhere, I heard Markus yell. He yelled at the waves with a voice and a force I'd never heard before.

Afterward he smiled and claimed that it helped with what was hurting him inside. So, every time we come to a scenic overlook, we drive off to the side and

yell at the waves. Last time we nearly scared the life
out of a pair of motorcyclists.

"Tell me, are you sitting there taking a nap on my sofa?"
Hans Suhr laughed from his door, and Louise tried to
hide how he'd both given her a shock and caught her dozing
in his office.

She got up and pulled a chair over to his desk.

"I've gone through Nick Hartmann's bank statements
and looked over the tax returns that SKAT sent over, and
none of that really fits together. At least the way I read it,"
she said.

The autumn sun was right in Louise's eyes. She had to
keep adjusting her position in her chair until Suhr went over
and closed the blinds, casting darkness over the office.

He sat back down.

"And?" he asked.

"There's an imbalance between his earnings and his expenses."

Louise passed the tax papers across the desk to him.

"His income doesn't square with his high standard of
living."

"What did he do for a living?"

"He was a shipping agent at a company down on Havnegade. Shipping Link International. He'd been with them for
eight years in the same position. Never took advantage of
extra training or internal hiring."

Hans Suhr took hold of the papers and reached around
for his glasses. He turned on his desk lamp and took a closer
look at the numbers.

"400,000 kroner in annual income," he read and did
some figuring. "That's almost 34,000 a month. Well, that's
not too bad, is it?"

Louise shook her head. That wasn't bad at all. In fact, it rounded up to ten thousand more than she brought home, without adjusting for the unequal hours.

"No, but it's all relative," she said.

She pointed to the bank statement.

"If you have yearly expenses of a million kroner for two cars and a duplex in Amager, then 400,000 before taxes is like a snowball in hell."

Suhr nodded.

"What about his wife? Does she have capital?" he asked and lifted his eyes from the paper.

"Mie has a freelance position at a drawing office, but right now she's on maternity leave and doesn't make any money. In the periods when she was working, her income was around 20,000, so that's still not enough to get them up to the level they're living at. Other than that, she doesn't have any income."

Suhr reached for the bank statement and passed his eyes over the figures.

"Have you talked with Business Affairs? Do we know if he had a company on the side?"

Louise shook her head.

"From his statement, you can see there's been a pretty large amount going into his account on a regular basis. 40,000 to 60,000, sometimes more. It seems like they're making up for the negative balance that keeps growing all the time."

As Louise talked, the lieutenant drew boxes on the back of an envelope. At the very top he'd written "Nick Hartmann," and above the boxes he'd written "Income" and "Expenses."

"And where did that money come from?"

"From one of his other accounts."

She gave that some thought before continuing.

"And some of the money was deposited in cash in smaller amounts, so no one in the bank would be suspicious."

"Absolutely," Suhr exclaimed, irritated.

He tossed his pen on the desk.

"It's obvious he was up to something," Louise said. "But it doesn't appear to be either drugs or prostitution. He dealt with the bikers, but we still haven't found out what the connection was."

"We damned well better find out what he's been up to. That is, if we want to have any hope of finding the motive behind the shooting."

Louise nodded.

She'd just about gotten the lieutenant pointed in the direction she wanted.

"Don't you think we should ask Fraud to take a look at this?" she asked.

Her own training in financial crime, she admitted, didn't go much past debit card fraud.

"Yes," Suhr said. "And I know just who to ask."

When Louise came back to her office, she had a message.

"Call Bellahøj Station —ext. 11-118."

A younger woman answered, and it took a moment before the officer remembered why Louise Rick had been asked to contact the station.

"Are you the mother of one of the children from the party at the sailing club?"

"Foster mother," Louise corrected.

Then she asked if anything had happened, if they'd found the boys.

"What's your name?" the woman asked, still a bit puzzled.

"Louise Rick. I'm related to Jonas Holm, who attended the party."

Related, what a damned strange way of distancing herself.

"OK," the woman finally said.

She made a sound like she was getting her papers in order.

"We would like to come by and talk with your son sometime in the afternoon. Will you be home?"

"Have you found out who they are?" Louise asked.

When the woman evaded her question, saying that unfortunately she couldn't speak to that, Louise became irate.

"Yes, by God you can speak to that. Jonas was at the party, and one of his best friends died out there. What the hell do you mean, you can't speak to that?"

The young woman suddenly became shrill.

"We are holding a police investigation..."

"Forget it," Louise exclaimed.

She was suddenly very aware of what it was like to be sitting on the other side of the desk. The side where the witnesses usually sit.

"Just come. We're home by five o'clock."

"We have some photos we'd like Jonas Holm to look through."

"That's fine. We'll be there," she said.

She looked at her watch. All of a sudden, she was busy.

18

"I'm telling you, Egon!"

Louise heard Yvonne's voice from the TV in the living room. She tossed her bag in the entryway and went in to say hi.

Jonas sat on the sofa with his legs tucked up underneath him and his eyes on the TV screen. *The Olsen Gang Goes Berserk.* Louise remembered the scene where Dynamite Harry sat in the back of a beer truck in high spirits after having blown a hole through a wall into a cold storage room.

Jonas reached for the remote and was about to turn it off.

"Go ahead and keep watching," she said quickly. "But I got a call from Bellahøj. They want to come by and show you some photos. It sounds like they've found the boys."

A worried looked passed over his face.

"What if I can't recognize them?"

"Then just say so. And if you're in doubt, there's nothing wrong with that, either. You should only point out the people you're sure of."

Louise smiled at him. She could tell how nervous he was.

He shut off the film and looked at her seriously.

"Jonas, there's no reason to get worked up. We don't know if the police have found the right people. But if it's not them, then they'll keep looking and come by again when they've found them."

He nodded, but just then the intercom buzzed and a twitch went through his body.

They stood out on the landing and waited patiently for the officer to make it up to the fourth floor. Louise recognized him. It was the same one who'd been with Britt in the ambulance. She smiled at him as he rounded the last set of stairs, and nodded admiringly when it was clear he wasn't out of breath from the climb. He offered her his hand and introduced himself as Kent.

She suggested they sit in the kitchen.

"I'd like you to look at some pictures with me," the officer told Jonas after they'd sat down.

Jonas nodded and leaned forward in his chair as Kent took an envelope out of his inside pocket.

"How did you find them?" Louise asked.

She'd gone over to the kitchen counter and started cutting up root vegetables.

"We've been in touch with several of the boat owners who have docks down at the harbor. They told us about a boathouse out on South Pier, where a bunch of older boys hang out. There'd been a lot of trouble from them several times over the summer, and they'd been accused of stealing beer and liquor from boats—which they certainly did. But they were never reported for the thefts."

The officer laid the photos out on the table, and immediately Louise saw that Jonas recognized several of the faces. Without hesitation, he pointed out five of the eight portraits. One of them he placed in front of the officer.

"He's the one who hit and kicked Signe's mom," he said.

He turned his eyes away from the photo, which showed a big guy with closely trimmed blond hair and a big tattoo on one side of his neck.

"Thomas Jørgensen is nineteen," her police colleague said. He nodded and looked over at Louise. "You can go into Headquarters and look him up. And believe me, he's been violent before. He lives in a youth home on Gammel Kalkbrænderivej."

"What's he done?" Louise asked, making use of the way he spoke to her as a colleague.

"Some vandalism. There's an ongoing case against him where the damage claim has gone up to around 250,000 kroner. He spent his early teenage years in Sønderbro and several other locked facilities for juveniles, and he'd just barely arrived in Copenhagen when he and a pal were put in jail for a brutal attack on a father who was on his way into McDonald's with his seven-year-old daughter. The father was in a coma for a week, then died of his injuries. That was four years ago, but Thomas Jørgensen is back again."

Louise went over to the table and sat down. She wanted to pull Jonas close to her, but didn't while the officer was there.

"How old are these guys?" she asked.

She was having a hard time judging from their buttoned-up faces. She guessed the photos were taken during the interrogation at the police station—maybe some of them were from an earlier date, if they'd been in trouble with the police before.

"Between seventeen and nineteen. As I said, they're already in our database with various sentences on the record. They're a bunch of asshole punks trying to be as bad as bikers, but not quite making it."

"What do they say?"

"Nothing."

No, of course, they didn't say anything, a bunch of biker wannabes, Louise thought. It made her feel irritated.

A dark-haired kid stared out of one of the photos, his wispy hair tied up in a ponytail that came to the collar of his sweatshirt. His left ear was pierced and he had a jagged birthmark on his cheek.

"Peter Nymann is in our books for violent assault and for breaking and entering. From earlier cases, we know he runs errands for the bikers. That is, when he's not wasted on pot and beer. I think mostly he works for them for the money, but he's definitely dreaming about rising in their ranks. As of now, I don't think he's qualified, not when it comes to brains or the power to keep his emotions in check."

"He's the one who ran after Signe," Jonas whispered.

Kent nodded and pushed the last three photos farther up the table.

"Sebastian Styhne," he said.

He pointed to a blond-haired kid who looked as hardened as the first two.

"His father owns a café down in New Harbor and is pretty flush with cash."

He looked slightly younger than the others, his hair was medium length and wavy, and the only thing that kept him from looking like the boy next door was a large spiderweb tattooed all the way around his neck.

"We don't have any violent offense priors on him, but he's been in several times for selling pot and speed, both of which he also uses."

Kent told her the boy had tattoos all over his body.

"Like a wetsuit he stepped into," he said.

"You didn't make him take his clothes off, did you?" Louise asked.

"No way," the young officer laughed. "I saw the ones on his arms—those go all the way to his wrists like sweater cuffs—and then he pulled up his pant legs to show me it was the same thing there. I didn't see the rest, but I trust him when says they're *full body*."

"Maybe one of the tattoo artists down in New Harbor gets free meals at his dad's café in exchange for the artwork," Louise said.

She thought it had to be damned awful for a mother to give birth to such a lovely boy, who then chooses to cover his whole body in permanent ink.

Jonas kept his eyes on the last two pictures.

"Jón Vigdísarson is seventeen and lives with his mother on Strand Boulevard."

The boy had thick, dark hair, nice facial features, and black eyes that were standoffish and hard in an almost unnatural manner given his age.

"Car theft and break-ins."

"And he's seventeen," exclaimed Louise.

The officer nodded.

"Last time he was taken in he had stolen goods in a stolen car—booze and cigarettes from a Spar convenience store that had been broken into."

The officer said that the Icelandic boy was the only one who'd confessed to being at the party.

"But he claims they were invited. By Signe!"

"That's a lie," Jonas blurted.

The officer nodded. The others, he said, wouldn't say a word.

"But they were there!"

Jonas stared at the officer.

"I recognize them."

"That's what several of your classmates say, too."

The officer pushed the photo aside and introduced the last one.

He was a big, strong guy heavily tattooed on his very muscular arms. Steroid-type who probably has a permanent address at one of the fitness centers, thought Louise.

"Kenneth Thim is studying to be a mechanic, and several nights a week he works as a bouncer at a nightclub in the inner city. We have him in our books, too, for just about everything—violence, assault, breaking and entering. He's also hoping to cut his teeth with the bikers, and he's ice cold. He doesn't give a shit what gets in his way. But it doesn't look like he was violent at the party."

Jonas shook his head, and Kent cleared his throat.

"Where's the boathouse in relation to the sailing club?" Louise asked.

She watched Jonas stand up, a blank stare on his face. He walked into his room and closed the door behind him.

"Could those boys see that there was a party going on?"

Her colleague shook his head.

"The boathouse where they hang out is farther down in Svanemølle Harbor. In by the warehouses where the big ships come in. But we think they might have gone out looking for booze or cigarettes. By that point at night, many people had gone home from their boats, so maybe they noticed the party."

She nodded while he talked, thinking it sounded likely.

"Have you spoken with Signe's parents?" she asked.

"Not yet. I'm heading out there when we're finished here. I just want to be sure we've identified the boys correctly before I show them the photos."

Considerate, thought Louise, a little more favorably disposed to the young officer.

Root vegetables in the oven. When Louise was a girl, she'd hated it when her mother made that kind of dinner, and especially when she'd sprinkle on a thick layer of parsley from the garden without asking if anyone would rather not have that on theirs. Now she loved slow-roasted celery, beets, parsnips, and carrots, but every time she set them on the table, she saw a little of her mother in herself and didn't like it. The way she saw herself, there was still a fair distance between her parents out in the country and her, living in her own apartment in Frederiksberg.

Her mother was a potter and spent all her waking hours in an apron with clay in her hair. She was opinionated and flighty compared to Louise's father, who sat quietly absorbed in his books or concentrating on typing. He was a well-known ornithologist, and for most of her upbringing his focus had been somewhere other than on Louise and her little brother. Most of his free time he spent with binoculars around his neck. His work hours were with the Danish Ornithology Society, where his duties included bird conservation and protection, as well as editing the society's journal.

Tired, tired, tired—she'd gotten so tired of her parents not having normal jobs with normal work hours. It had been an absolute pain in the neck when her father would pull his kids out of bed at four in the morning because they needed to hustle off for bird-watching in the family's old Simca, without it ever occurring to him that his children didn't share his enthusiasm. Neither her mother nor her father ever felt the need to keep up with the neighbors or friends when it came to new cars or home renovations. They kept their car until it had worn out its service and didn't have any life left in it, and Louise had preferred to bike rather than be driven to school, just to avoid the grins from her classmates.

Since Jonas had moved in, she'd been thrown back to her childhood many times. She drove him to parties in her old worn-out Saab; as long as it started up and got her between points A and B, there was no reason to replace it. And now, here she was roasting root vegetables in her oven. The only mitigating factor was that, unlike her mother, she hadn't drowned everything in parsley.

Damn, she thought, and put hot pads on the table. But she sure as hell wasn't the boy's mother, and Jonas certainly didn't seem ashamed of her. She just hadn't figured out how the change had happened—when, precisely, had she started to be like her parents?

She shook her head and called for Jonas.

"Dinner's ready!"

She used two pot holders to pull the dish out of the oven.

After they'd eaten, she wanted to drive out to Strand-vænget to see how Britt and Ulrik were doing, now that the police had identified the boys. Maybe there were some questions they hadn't asked when the officers from Bellahøj had been there. Not that she thought she could answer them, but maybe she could help prepare them for what would happen now and which charges the police would be able to make.

Jonas had planned a sleepover at Lasse's, and she'd promised to drive him down to Peblinge Dosseringen. She could keep going to Svanemølle from there.

19

The Golf was there. The other spot, where Ulrik parked his big Audi, was empty, but there was a light on in the living room. Louise parked along the sidewalk and called from her cell phone. She didn't want to show up completely unannounced.

"If you can stand me in casual clothes and looking like a mess, then you're more than welcome," said Britt, clearly surprised when Louise invited herself in for coffee.

The outdoor candles were still lined up along the garden path—no one had picked them up after the funeral. The roses seemed overpowering now that the rooms were empty, and their scent was stronger and constantly reminded one of their presence.

"I love roses," Britt confessed when they sat down. "Especially the ones I have out in the garden."

The enormous dining table overflowed with photographs. Small and big, from the time when pictures had to be developed and were delivered on paper in an envelope. Signe as a baby, as a toddler taking her first step, and as a four-year-old sitting on a bench with her long red hair braided down both sides of her head and holding a small cello.

"Memory Lane," Britt said sadly.

She gestured with her hand.

"I'm preparing myself for several trips down it."

Music played softly in the background, classical notes that gently filled the room and made it feel pleasant and secure.

Louise nodded to the offer of a cup of green tea. While Britt was out in the kitchen putting the water on, she let her eyes scan the living room.

"Ulrik is down at Møn's Cliff. I convinced him to go," Britt said with a little smile. "He's absolutely smitten with hang gliding and paragliding. He even teaches it. He claims it's like meditation. He wasn't much into going away—he's been home pretty much the whole time since the accident. But I don't have anything against being alone; I'm used to it. And it's so good for him to be out in the fresh air. It usually relaxes him a little when he's stressed. Do you know anything about paragliding?"

"Not the least, I don't even know the difference between the two," said Louise.

They settled into easy chairs in the sitting room in the back.

Britt shook her head.

"No, it doesn't mean much to me, either. When you paraglide, you're in a harness under a kind of parachute, and when you hang glide you're lying practically in the air under the parachute. It's not for me, but he loves it."

Louise smiled at her.

"Back when Ulrik and I were dating, almost twenty years ago, he'd just started parachute diving, and he was one of the first to try bungee jumping off bridges. Then one thing followed the other, and if I'd have known how it was going to turn into a passion I probably would have reconsidered a time or two. But he's bitten by it, not least of all by the adrenaline rush he gets when he free-falls."

She pretended to shudder and said that her husband had a glider plane parked up in Allerød.

"But I forbade him from taking Signe up with him. I'd heard about how they're always crashing, and the thought of it made me sick. I have no idea how it happened, but apparently, airplanes are the phobia I'll have to go through life with."

Louise didn't know much about Ulrik Fasting-Thomsen, other than what she'd read in the papers every time he'd been involved in a big financial takeover. As she remembered it, he was also an investment consultant to Frederik Sachs-Smith, the eldest of the three siblings from the family dynasty the media were currently spewing about in glowing hot bits and pieces, like lava from an erupting volcano. The scandal had affected business life, not least the Danish exchange market. Throughout the gossip world, it drew as much attention as if the family who owned Lego had hung its dirty laundry out for public view, or a political family who had started to strip in public.

But Frederik Sachs-Smith had apparently been smart enough to get himself out of the family enterprise, long before his siblings started their greedy vendetta against their parents. In that way, he'd avoided being fodder for the papers' front pages or contributing to all the gossip that filled workplace lunchrooms everywhere, and Ulrik had avoided being pulled down in the fall.

The tea was set on the table in a heavy stoneware pot, which Britt carried with both hands. She still had a bandage over her cheekbone and said that later in the week she was going down to her own doctor to have the stitches removed.

She poured them each a cup.

"The police were here today," she said.

Louise nodded.

"I thought I recognized several of them in the pictures, but then suddenly I wasn't so sure. It's all a bit blurry to me. I can remember when you all arrived. And the sailing trip. I can remember sitting down and eating, and that the students from the music school played for Signe."

Her jaw protruded when she clenched her teeth, trying to keep from crying. Just then, the room became quiet. The CD was over.

"After the food, she opened her presents and was so happy. Everyone helped clean up and push the tables to the side so they could dance."

For a short-lived moment, a smile played in Britt's eyes. But then, like a heavy lily, she suddenly bowed her head to her chest.

"I was out in the kitchen getting chips when they came. When I came in, they were standing there. One of them was heading around behind the bar, where we had our soft drinks. At first, I thought they were some kids Signe knew and said hi to them!"

Britt closed her eyes a moment.

"But then I could tell that the children were unsettled, and no one said anything. So, I asked the boys what they wanted. 'Party!' one of them yelled and wanted to know where we kept our booze. But there wasn't any. A couple of the others walked over to the gift table, and that's when I asked them to leave."

"Were they behaving in a threatening way at that point?" asked Louise.

Britt shook her head.

"No, and it still hadn't occurred to me that they could be unpleasant. I thought they'd go once they'd seen we didn't have any beer or alcohol. Two of them came in with some

of the sushi we'd taken out to the kitchen, and I told them
they were welcome to it. But suddenly I saw that the one
behind the bar had taken my bag and stood with my purse
in his hand, and I heard Signe tell them to leave her presents
alone. It was at that moment that I yelled for them to leave,
or else I'd call the police. After that I can't really remember
any more."

Louise let her cry. She thought it must have been at that
point that Jonas had called her.

As they sat, Louise's eyes rested on a tea candle that was
about to burn out. There was artwork hanging on the walls,
and in one of the corners of the room stood a tall, slender
sculpture in bronze. The door to the music room was open,
and there were candles beside the grand piano.

"Tell me about your music career," Louise said.

She poured more tea into their mugs.

"What should I say?" asked Britt, suddenly embarrassed.

"Did you know Ulrik when you started to play?"

A fleeting smile passed across her lips.

"I'm a Suzuki child, just as Signe was. In fact, I was
one of the first to be trained at The Danish Suzuki Institute,
where it has a lot to do with parents going to the lessons
with their children and supporting them. It's a special
method that was introduced in this country in 1972, when I
was four. I can remember my classmates calling me 'Classical pig.' That's more than twenty-five years ago."

She told her that Signe had also started as a four-year-
old.

"You learn to perform, and playing by memory becomes
a natural part of your education. But it all happens on the
child's own terms. It's not like parents standing on the side-
lines and pushing them. They have to play because they
want to. Signe was accepted into their chamber orchestra.

But when I went there, I played the piano so I was placed with a smaller ensemble."

She stood up and went over to the sound system that hung on the wall. A moment later they heard the classical notes again. She turned it down a little.

"Brahms Trio in B major," she said and sat down.

"How did you meet Ulrik? Was he interested in music, too?"

Her laughter sounded surprised and lighthearted.

"Are you insane? He can't tell the difference between a violin and a bass! It was completely banal how we met— in a bar in the city. It was the summer I started at the Conservatory. I was nineteen and had just finished high school music training. And Ulrik is three years older than me and had studied economics at the University of Copenhagen. He was working on his graduate degree at that point."

"So, you were together a pretty long time before you had Signe."

Britt nodded.

"We didn't think we could have children, but in a way, it turned out really well. I started with the introductory courses, which at that time was two years, and after that I had to go through another four years before I took my degree exam. Only then did I go into the soloist program. At that point I was in my midtwenties, and I couldn't have played with a little child in my arms. It's also very common for women to give up at that point. But I was completely focused on music and was so privileged to play my debut concert in Tivoli's concert hall. We had Signe when I was twenty-nine, and that worked out well. I had energy for her and could take her with me when I played abroad. When I was on stage, she was looked after in the dressing room."

She sank into herself for a few seconds.

"I've been lucky, been able to play concerts in Paris and in the golden hall in Vienna, even on a gorgeous Bösendorfer concert piano. And when I practiced here at home, Signe lay on her lamb's wool blanket and listened."

"But you don't play anymore?"

She shook her head.

"My hands won't let me. It crept up slowly, and finally I had to stop. Now I teach as an associate professor at The Royal Danish Music Conservatory, and I have my private students on the side. They come here," she said and nodded toward the music room.

Louise glanced at the wall clock beside the sound system, and Britt quickly apologized for talking so much.

"Don't be silly," said Louise, "I'm the one who asked you to."

She stood up to help carry the tea cups out to the kitchen. But something seemed to have changed with Britt.

She stayed seated in her easy chair, sapped of energy, her gaze fastened to a spot behind the wall, far off.

"Would you like more tea, or should I take the Thermos out with me?" Louise asked.

Britt didn't respond.

Louise walked over and kneeled beside her chair.

"Are you OK?"

"I want to go to bed," Britt said without shifting her gaze.

Louise helped her stand up and walked with her arm in arm, unsure of what to do. It occurred to her that maybe Britt was taking sedatives, and now they'd worn off. But she had no idea whether the doctor had prescribed something like that when he released her, and she wasn't going to intrude on her private affairs.

"When is Ulrik coming home?" she asked.

"He'll be here soon. But I'm fine on my own until he comes."

She gripped Louise's arm tightly and spoke while looking straight ahead. Her voice seemed strangely deep and dry, as if it emerged from someplace hidden behind her frail and feeble exterior.

"They're the ones who took her from me. Do you understand that?" she said. "If they hadn't come and ruined everything, Signe would still be here."

She paused briefly.

"But I'm the one who held a party for her. I could have done a lot of other things to celebrate, and then it never would have happened. I get that."

Louise was going to object, but Britt continued in her monotone voice.

"I'll never forgive them, and every single day I'll hate them so much that I'm sure they'll feel it, no matter how far away from me they are."

Suddenly her expression softened, turned apologetic, as if she'd frightened herself by how strongly the hatred had raged inside her.

She smiled and shook her head. Then she thanked Louise for taking the time to look in on her.

Louise gave her a quick hug and slipped her coat off the hanger. On her way out to the car, she took out her cell phone. She had just enough time to call Jonas and say good night before it was too late.

Her phone showed a missed call and a message.

She started the Saab and turned on the heat. Then she called her voice mail and pressed 1 for new messages.

"Hi Louise. It's Ulrik, Signe's dad. I just heard that the police have found the boys and located the place where they hang out on the South Pier. You need to know that that boathouse belongs to a warehouse I own."

20

The rain blasted the windshield, and the wipers ran on max. Markus sat with the big road map unfolded in front of him. His shoulders slouched, he was car sick, had a headache, but still he seemed to be commanding the car. They stopped at a thirteen-foot-high statue of the horrifyingly huge Big Foot. It was carved in wood and painted all ugly and clumsy, so any kid under five would burst into hysterical sobs at the sight of it.

Camilla took out her camera.

"Stand next to it so I can get your picture," she yelled.

"Mom, really. It's pissing down rain, and I feel crappy. Can't we just skip it?"

"It's just one picture, and it'll only take a second. Then we can get something to drink, or ice cream if you'd rather have that."

Camilla had barely finished speaking when Markus turned his back to her and bent over to throw up. He stood with his hands on his knees and his head hanging down. Then his thin shoulders quivered with another wave of sickness.

The rain was thick and heavy and drenched them. With

one hand Camilla fished paper napkins out of her bag, and with the other she held his forehead.

"Oh, sweetie, is it that bad?"

When she asked him whether they should stop looking for the drive-through tree and concentrate on finding someplace to sleep, he looked at her morosely and nodded.

Camilla got her thick sweater out of the back of the car and helped Markus take off his soaking sweatshirt. She set up water and napkins in the back seat of their Toyota, and after he crawled in she rolled up his jacket and tucked it under his head.

She was suddenly aware of how mechanical their routine had become over the last two mornings. They ate breakfast and got out to the car, as if there was an appointment they had to make it to. It was hard to know what had happened to the happy, relaxed vacationers they'd imagined themselves being back when they planned their road trip down the West Coast of the U.S.A. Everything had become hectic and strained as they tried to find one sight after another.

Now her son was sick and feeling shitty, and she hadn't even noticed it. Because she'd been so eager to get Big Foot crossed off the list of things that their thick guide book told them they must see.

She backed out slowly from the deserted parking lot, where they were the only tourists who braved the pouring rain. The souvenir shops were deserted, and they practically had the winding road through the woods to themselves.

She sighed deeply and put the car's automatic transmission into drive.

✄

Turn left and then turn right, said the GPS, which she'd set to find a hotel in a city called Eureka. It was out on the coast, and Camilla knew nothing about it or its possible accommodations, so she followed the GPS-lady's directions.

Markus had fallen asleep in the back seat, pale and wet-haired.

Lost and completely wrong. That's what it felt like when she turned left and looked for the road that was supposed to go to the right. They'd landed in the middle of a worn-down residential neighborhood, and none of the little houses here made her think of a hotel or for that matter any kind of lodging.

Dead end, no way to turn right—the GPS had gotten it wrong.

She pulled off to the side of the road.

Suddenly everything had started being about getting to the next point. That wasn't at all what Camilla had had in mind when she dreamed of being on the road and seeing where it would take them.

Everything they'd done over the last days had been damned unimportant, she thought and turned the car down the residential street. She'd put herself on autopilot so she could tune out. She'd simply followed the guide book's sights and recommendations so she didn't have to think of Signe and her poor parents.

Now she was hunting around for a place to spend the night. Markus was sick, and for the first time, it actually was important to get to a hotel so he could go to bed.

"Shit," she yelled and banged her hand on the steering wheel. She braked so hard that Markus nearly slid off the back seat.

"Are we there?" he asked. He got up on his elbows and tried to look out the car windows, but a curtain of rain poured down.

"Not yet. I can't find the damned hotel," she said.

She started to laugh. She shut her eyes and took it all in.

The rain thrashed the windshield, and suddenly the absurdity was perfectly clear. How she ran around trying pathetically to find inner peace, while everything around her crumbled. Trying to be whole and normal like before was a forced and useless effort, and right now it was about to keel over with her on board.

There was no damned possible way to get away from the grief over Signe.

She turned off the GPS and let the car coast forward. Markus lay back down again, not having the energy to contribute to her plans other than to say he wanted her to find them a bed and some peace and quiet soon so the pain in his head would go away.

She drove back to the main road that ran through downtown, turned right toward the water, and came up to an old Victorian colossus that made her think of Harry Potter and the wizards' school, Hogwarts. It had the same towers and spires. On a big sign, she read that lodging was available here. Lodging for men only. On the opposite side, there was smaller Victorian script in pink, but she sped up and drove past without reading it.

One-way and back around and not a hotel in sight. She felt done in, and noticed how her blond hair fell in wisps around her face. For the last few days, she'd skipped makeup and really didn't care. It had been one of her trademarks, but over here it didn't really seem to matter. Day after day they sat in the car between five and six hours.

Camilla was ready to give up when she finally saw a sign that looked promising. It said CARTER HOUSE on the three-story corner building, but she couldn't see if it was a restaurant or if they also had rooms.

A few minutes earlier, Markus had sat up and made it clear that she was to stop at the next place they came to. No matter what. He didn't care if it was Packwood II or a big swanky Hilton. He just didn't want to be in the car any longer.

It *was* a hotel, and while they waited to be checked in the receptionist, Kevin, pointed to a little buffet that was set up in the middle of the foyer. There was a fire in the room's big fireplace, and the guests sat around small tables sipping and chatting.

Plush sofas and refinished furniture in cool, luxurious styles.

"Tea or wine?" asked a waiter wearing a white jacket and a cook's apron tied around his waist. "Help yourself, it's included."

Afternoon tea, thought Camilla, smiling as she followed Markus over to a sofa. How decadent—and how idiotic to come to such a nice, quiet place looking like something the cat dragged in.

Fruit, cheese, cold cuts, pâté, and little sandwich breads.

"Do you want anything?" she asked, offering to get it for him.

He was still a bit pale, and he looked exhausted, but the prospect of a few little delicacies got him to follow her up to the table. Before Camilla had had a look around, he'd already heaped a plate for himself and was walking over to the waiter in white to ask for a soft drink.

She smiled at him when he came back to the sofa and sat down.

"I think we need to start over again," she said.

He raised an eyebrow, the same face he made when he wanted to make it clear he didn't find one of his mother's jokes to be funny.

"Drive back?" he asked.

She shook her head.

The waiter came by with her tea. She selected a tea bag from a fancy box with a wide assortment and plunged the bag into the hot water.

"No, I just mean we should enjoy ourselves. Relax, do a bunch of things we want to do. We can start by staying here a few days. That's what I'd really like to do. Maybe they've got a movie theater in town, and we can watch films and eat popcorn."

"Supersize?" he asked.

Apparently, his nausea had passed.

"Pardon me," she said and took the first bite. She felt hungry. They'd mostly had burgers the last couple of days. Not that they'd been bad, just a little monotonous.

"Do you think they have movies in the room?" he asked.

He got up to get more strawberries.

"This place is great. I want to stay here, too," he said.

Camilla smiled at him. She walked up to the reception desk to ask if it were possible to book two extra nights, and whether there was Internet in their room.

21

The sad, tired light of an October morning spread over Gammel Kongevej as Louise biked into Police Headquarters. As usual, the bike lane was packed and moved slowly at that hour. People jostled to get ahead.

She thought about Britt and how her whole life had been filled with music and instruments. After she could no longer play, she'd supported and followed her daughter. Either the music would help her through the grief, or it would tie her to it—and then the slender little woman would fall apart.

She'd been so full of hate standing there in her living room. What was even worse, Louise thought as she made it to Otto Mønsteds Gade and parked her bike in back of Headquarters, was that Britt's own feelings of guilt were starting to eat away at her.

A little after eight o'clock, Louise walked through the side entrance and continued up the stairs to the second floor. She had her office key in her hand, but her thoughts were still on Britt out in Svanemølle.

At first, she didn't react to her office door being unlocked. It was only after she'd put her key away and pushed open the door that she was torn from her thoughts.

Both blinds were rolled down and closed. The ceiling light was off, and only a single lamp on the desk was lit. In Lars Jørgensen's place there was a guy with chalk-white hair buried behind two computer screens. Louise had never seen him before. He had on a big pair of head-phones that sent a throbbing bass spilling through the clunky headset.

Speechless, she stopped and took a step back. If it hadn't been for her own things and the electric kettle, she would have jumped to the conclusion that she'd made a mistake. But everything was there—the tea bags, her files, the draw-ings that Markus had made for her over the years pinned to her bulletin board.

"And who are you?" she asked.

She tossed her bag down, unsure if he'd even noticed her come in.

He stood up.

At first she thought he was a teenager because of his hip hooded sweatshirt and army pants, but she'd gotten that wrong.

He wasn't very tall, a little shorter than her, maybe five foot five. And nowhere near as young as she'd first thought—maybe midforties.

Louise had also guessed that his hair was bleached, but now that he came toward her she saw that everything about him was bleached out. His eyes were piercingly light blue, as if the irises had filled out too much, and his eyebrows were hard to make out against the pale skin of his face.

"Gylling," he said and quickly offered his hand to her, music still blaring from the headphones. "And my first name's Sejr."

Louise just nodded. It was almost more than she could grasp so early in the morning. Behind him she saw a little refrigerator that had been hidden by the office chair. Her eyes then took in a half liter of cola sitting on the desk.

Finally, he whipped off the headphones so they hung like a collar around his neck.

"*Guitar Gangsters and Cadillac Blood.*"

He fished an iPod out of his pants pocket and turned it down.

"Good. You've met each other," Suhr said from the door. "Gylling is one of the top men down in Fraud."

The lieutenant walked over and shook his hand, then sat down on a short bench along the wall.

"But he also has years of experience in the various special departments," he said, on the verge of sounding impressed. "Financial Crimes, International Criminal Cases," he listed off. "And then he was, as far as I recall, also with PET for a longer period."

Suhr talked about the man as if he weren't there in the room. And, as a matter of fact, he wasn't. Louise's new colleague had put his headphones on again and entrenched himself behind his screens.

She went over to pull her blinds up.

"Rather you didn't," he said from behind the screens. "And no light from the ceiling, either, if you don't mind."

She raised her eyebrows and looked at her boss.

"We could in theory have received his expertise from the Fraud Department, and then he could have stayed sitting down there on Store Kongensgade."

"Yes, we could. But that wouldn't have solved the problem of finding you a new partner until we know whether Lars Jørgensen is coming back."

Louise stared incredulously at Suhr, and then over at the other side of the desk.

"Of course, Lars Jørgensen is coming back. It'll be at

most a couple of weeks. And I can easily manage it with Toft and Michael Stig. There's no reason to do anything rash."

"Bingo! Nick Hartmann is registered with Business Affairs. He has a company."

"Now look at that!" Suhr exclaimed with satisfaction and stood up.

Louise followed him out into the hall.

"Now, you stop it," she said.

She planted herself in front of him.

"I haven't even glanced at the central business registry yet. Hell, it was only yesterday we got his bank statements and discovered that there was something that needed to be looked into."

"Sejr is one of the best investigators of money swindling. He has many years of experience," said Suhr, "and we need to get somewhere with this case. So far nothing's come of it, even though you've had three people detained for a week."

Now all of a sudden it was "you" and not "we."

"What the hell's going on with the blinds rolled down and the refrigerator? It looks like he's moved in for good."

"Albinism, it's called. Albinos are very sensitive to light, so we should be considerate of that," the lieutenant said.

Louise could tell that he was starting to get irritated.

Inside the office her phone rang. It was a guard from the entry gate saying that Ulrik Fasting-Thomsen wanted to talk with her.

"Will you come get him?"

"Yes," she said.

She walked out to the kitchen to see if there was any coffee made.

"I bought the building five years ago as an investment," Ulrik said.

He took a cup from Louise. She pushed an extra chair over to her desk and asked him to have a seat.

Sejr gave her guest a brief nod, but kept his eyes glued on his computer screen. He said no thank you to Louise's offer of coffee, and pulled a fresh cola out of his fridge.

"It's a big warehouse. Some of it's rented out, but the rest is empty," Ulrik explained, adding that an attendant down at the harbor worked for him as a sort of vice-landlord. "It caught me completely by surprise that anyone was using the boathouse. I hadn't been informed of it."

Louise looked at Ulrik and leaned forward slightly.

"Does Britt know that the boys hung out on your property?"

He nodded.

"Yes, now she does. But she also knows that I have no idea who they were or how long they've hung out down there. It's just today that I started working again, and I only have one meeting to go to here in the city. After that I'm driving out and talking with the attendant to find out what's been happening, and then he'll have to toss them out."

They sat for a bit.

"I've also made arrangements for the police to go by there. On my way over here, I called Bellahøj and informed the officer on the case. I just thought you should know how it's connected."

Louise nodded and again thought of Britt.

"Is there anything new? Are the boys saying anything?" she asked.

He shook his head.

"No, not as far as I know. At least, we haven't heard anything new."

She could see he was shaken. Understandably. It was completely absurd that the family themselves had given the hooligans a roof over their heads—even if unwillingly.

"How did Britt take it?"

A tinge of sadness came over his face, and he rubbed his forehead.

"She's finally sleeping after spending most of the night crying. She thinks we could have prevented it, either by not having had the party at all or by both of us being there together. And I'm inclined to agree with her. But Britt feels she was irresponsible for having taken it on herself to be there alone, and I think it's unreasonably hard for her to take all the blame, which is just as much my own. I should have been with my family when all of this happened."

Louise watched him as he sat and fell to pieces.

"She's hit even harder now that we know that the suspects stayed in my building," he said. Then he added, "And I really don't know how I'll tell her that these youths may get by with a charge of unlawful trespass and assault on her. At least that's what the young officer I spoke with this morning predicts. She wants them sentenced for driving Signe to her death."

"Let's see what they get when they have a proper talk with the boys and clear up the events of the evening," said Louise. "I'll call the officer, Kent, and hear what comes out of the interrogations."

Ulrik Fasting-Thomsen thanked her, and when they parted Louise stood and watched him as he walked down the stairs. His shoulders were slouched, and he seemed smaller than the first time she'd met him.

"Now we'll unpack these bank statements move by move," Sejr informed Louise when she came back into the office.

He'd put on his headphones.

"Volbeat," he said, nodding along. "I don't like to stop in the middle of an album."

She said no to a cola and sat down. He'd taken copies of the bank statements and put a set on her desk.

"If you go through his private accounts, then I'll look at his business account. He's registered as HartmannImport/Export."

He passed a printout from Business Affairs across the table.

Louise was about to protest when the door burst open and Willumsen yanked Suhr with him into the office, telling the lieutenant to explain what was happening to his investigation group. He flipped on the fluorescent ceiling lights and scowled at Sejr, who sat with his hood pulled up over his head.

"Who the hell's that, and what's all this computer gear set up in here?"

Without looking at Willumsen, Sejr Gylling stood up and went over to turn off the light.

"My eyes can't take strong light," he told Louise, ignoring the argument that was heating up.

"I'm the one who's in charge of staffing in this department," Suhr said.

He looked Willumsen straight in the eyes.

Louise leaned back and looked at her two bosses. She knew Willumsen well enough to know that he wouldn't willingly hand over his cases to others. In his investigation group, he was the one who made decisions. He scavenged extra people when he needed them, but on the other hand he'd give some of his own investigators to other lead investigators when necessary. It would also go against his grain to admit that his own people weren't capable of managing a case. But given that this case apparently involved a financial crime, she was glad that Suhr had agreed with her about asking Fraud for help.

"I'm not in favor of this," yelled Willumsen.

Suhr had to pull him out in the hall and close the office door.

Louise felt like she'd had her hair blown back by a hurricane.

On the other side of the desk, the man from Fraud sat unfazed, his eyes on columns of figures.

Something about Willumsen has changed, she thought. He'd always been boastful and ill-tempered, but ever since last summer when he learned that his wife Annelise had stomach cancer and had to have a large tumor removed, there were days when he was intolerable. Given the circumstances, the ones who knew him could bear with him, but it was worse for outsiders.

A little while later Suhr opened the door.

"I'm so damned sorry about that," he said.

Sejr Gylling looked up and shrugged his shoulders.

To Louise it seemed like his pale blue eyes fixed on Suhr, holding him at a distance with a kind of reverse magnetic force. It wasn't until Sejr turned his eyes back to his papers that the lieutenant came into the office.

"It's not always so easy with Willumsen," he said.

He seemed a little sheepish being brushed off by the new man on the team.

"I'm concentrating on clearing things up now," said Sejr. "When Louise Rick and I have sorted out what happened we can listen to what that man has to say. OK?"

Again, he fixed his eyes on the lieutenant, until Suhr stepped back, clearly satisfied with the decision.

When the door closed, they sat for a while and silence settled around them.

Louise hated numbers. She took the pile of papers with
printouts from Hartmann's private bank account, intending
to get it over with quickly so she could be out the door. Nevertheless, she got absorbed in the bank statements, looking
through them for connections that might help them clear
things up.

Before she knew it, it was already past six o'clock. The
time had gotten away from her, and she hurriedly packed
her things up to rush home to Jonas, feeling a tinge of guilt.
On her way down the stairs, she decided she'd stop and buy
Thai takeout. Chicken satay was one of Jonas's favorites.

But when she unlocked the door and came in with the
takeout bag in her hand, the apartment was empty and dark,
and there was no note on the kitchen table.

Louise set the bag aside and sank into a kitchen chair.
She tried to collect her thoughts. Had they agreed to something and she'd forgotten it? It was Wednesdays when Jonas
went to guitar.

She tried his cell phone and heard it buzzing on his desk.
Now she noticed that his book bag was in the hall, and that
the computer in his room was on. So, he had been home.

Louise started to set the table. Figured he'd gone to the
convenience store or over to the library. But when it got to
be eight o'clock, she started to worry in earnest.

She went into his room and checked his cell phone for
texts. Maybe he'd made plans and just forgotten to tell her
about it, even though that wouldn't be like him. But his in-
box only had messages she'd sent him and a couple from
his schoolmates, but they were several days old.

The Thai food was still in its paper bag when she sat down and called Lasse's parents.

"No," Lasse's mother said in an apologetic tone. "He's not here, but let me just ask Lasse if he knows anything."

Louise waited patiently.

"No," she said when she came back on. "Sorry."

For a moment, Louise closed her eyes and sat completely still, trying to bring some calm to her thoughts.

The library was the most likely possibility, she decided. She grabbed her coat and hurried down the stairs. She ran across Falkoner Allé and was out of breath when she reached the main entrance of the library, which had just closed.

She knocked several times on the glass window, and finally succeeded in getting a librarian to come over and push the door ajar.

"Are you positive no one else is inside?"

The man nodded and didn't remember seeing a dark-haired boy sitting by himself.

"There's hardly been anyone in here tonight. There must be handball on TV."

As Louise walked back, she had her hands in her pockets and her eyes on the ground. She made a determined effort to tamp down the unnerving fear that came from thinking of the many possible explanations for why Jonas wasn't at home. The most reasonable one still was that he'd made plans impulsively. But without his cell?

And then a thought struck her. Could he have gotten it into his head to go out to the boathouse, now that he knew where the older boys stayed?

Louise ran the last stretch up to the entrance, and the door slammed behind her as she took the stairs in leaps to get to her car keys so she could drive out there.

She'd just put the key in the keyhole when the door down on the third floor opened up and she heard Jonas call her.

She stepped over to the landing and looked down.

On the third floor to the left lived Melvin Pehrsson. Jonas stood in his doorway. When she'd gotten down, she peered over his head into a darkened entryway that smelled of old man and cigars.

"Have you been here the whole time?"

Her anger was uncontrollable and rising faster than she could rein it in.

He nodded.

"What the hell were you thinking? I've been running around looking for you."

She'd never raised her voice at him, but now she stood in the middle of the hallway and yelled.

Melvin Pehrsson showed up behind Jonas. Louise had never spoken to him before, just greeted him when they met on the stairs. A musty old homosexual, is what she thought he was, without having proof that it was true. Only that he looked to be somewhere in his midseventies.

"What are you doing down here?" she asked, her voice still raised.

"Maybe we should go into the living room," the man suggested and put his hand on Jonas's shoulder.

Louise wanted to slap it away, but collected herself and instead pulled the boy out of the doorway and with her up the stairs.

"How could you even think of going in there with a strange man you don't even know?" she asked when they'd gotten into their apartment. "He's odd, one of those people who keeps to himself. No one here in our section knows anything about him, and he never goes to the general meetings or garden parties."

They sat down in the kitchen. Jonas kept his eyes on the floor, but then he looked up with those dark eyes under his thick bangs.

"I know him."

Louise scooted back in her chair.

"You know him? You've only lived here for three months, so there's no way you know him well enough to go down into his apartment without letting me know first."

"It was my dad who buried Nancy when she died four years ago. Ever since then he's gone to the cemetery two times a week with fresh flowers."

"Who the hell's Nancy?"

"His wife."

"Honey, Jonas—he's never had a wife."

"Yes," he said and nodded. "He has, but she's been in a home for the past thirteen years, without being conscious. She was Australian, and when they lived there she was given some medicine that damaged her brain. But she was still his wife, and he arranged for her to come back with him to Denmark and stay in a decent place where they took good care of her."

"Why haven't you ever told me that you know our down-stairs neighbor?"

He shrugged his shoulders.

"And why did you suddenly decide to go down to him today?"

"It's not something I suddenly did today," he said.

His defiance was gone, but he didn't look to be plagued by guilty feelings, either.

"We're friends. I often go down to him."

"Friends?"

"I visit him when I come home from school. He's helped me with my homework. I didn't know you'd be so angry.

He likes me to visit, and we have a good time together. He's a research historian and has written for some of the big periodicals, but he stopped when Nancy got sick."

Louise listened in surprise.

"Of course you can visit him," she said quietly. "And I'm sorry for yelling at you. I just panicked because I didn't know where you were. What do you two do?"

"Right now, we're starting to go through a bunch of material from the time when Mylius-Erichsen led the Danmark Expedition through Northeast Greenland in 1906 to 08."

"Let's go down and say hi to him," she suggested. "Do you think he's eaten, or have you been too absorbed in the sled rides?"

"He doesn't usually make food for himself. He mostly eats sandwiches."

Louise unpacked the Thai food and gave it a zap in the microwave, then divided it onto three plates.

❧

"Heavenly," exclaimed Melvin Pehrsson when Louise asked, a little sheepishly, whether it was all right to bring food on a first visit.

Surprisingly clean, she noted, even though the cigar smell hung over the whole apartment. But it was nice, and there were fresh flowers in the vases.

"I buy some for myself, too, when I go over and visit her grave," he said when he caught her looking. He pointed at the dining table and asked them to sit down, then he disappeared into the kitchen for three soft drinks.

The pictures on the wall were paintings in thickly gilded frames, and most of the furniture was dark wood. There was something about the living room that made her think of her own grandmother and the little apartment she'd lived in out on Toftegårds Allé. Safe and pleasant—Louise had loved to go there.

"Thank you," she said.

She looked for the words that would get her started on an apology.

"I owe you an explanation," the elderly man said, pre-empting her.

His hair was more white than gray. His face hung a little on the left side—maybe a stroke had left its mark—but other than that, her downstairs neighbor seemed energetic and in good shape. Now that she was with him up close there wasn't much musty about him.

"I've never really done anything to socialize with the others in the building. When my wife was still alive, I spent almost all my time out with her, and now that she's not here anymore, I'm pretty bad about getting lost in my memories. Thankfully, we were able to spend many good years together. And then, I was lucky enough to meet this young man here."

Jonas smiled, and Louise said she'd already heard how they'd gotten to know each other.

"You've become friends, I understand."

Melvin Pehrsson nodded.

"His father was a great support for me when Nancy died. The time that followed that was hard to get through. So, I know all about what it's like to lose the one who's the ab-solute closest to you, and there are times when it helps to talk about the ones who aren't with us anymore."

Louise understood that only too well, and even though his words might have concealed a slight reproach—that she hadn't been there for Jonas when he missed his father—she was sure that wasn't what the man had meant.

"We just seem to have found each other," he said and gave Jonas's arm a little squeeze. "But we have a damned hard time forgiving the man upstairs for not preventing what happened to the boy's father."

Louise had only known Henrik Holm a very short time before he was killed in the tragic culmination of a case that, without his knowing it, had threads leading out to his church in Frederiksberg.

"What's it been, three or four years we've known each other? Doesn't that sound right?" Melvin Pehrsson asked.

He looked over at Jonas, but nodded himself and continued talking.

"I used to attend the presentations over in the rectory, and then I'd do a little here and there when the steward was on vacation."

How bizarre, thought Louise, to find out that her neighbor shared a history with Jonas. She'd tried several times to establish a relationship with the adults who'd been friends with Henrik Holm, so the boy would have someone to talk with who knew his father, but every time Jonas was brushed off. But what the hell would that matter when he already had Pehrsson right underneath him.

"Now I hope I can give back a little of what I received when I was the one who'd lost someone. The boy's father was so good about coming to the nursing home when Nancy was still there. Then we'd have us a good talk, and he'd hear all my wonderful memories. That's how I know it's important to have someone to talk with when you're trying to get through it. But fortunately, it seems we have many other things to talk about together."

He pointed over to the dining table, where a big map of Greenland covered the whole surface.

"The boy has an interest in history. So now we're starting

on the great Danmark Expedition from the beginning of the last century."

Jonas stood up and walked over to the windowsill, which was piled high with books.

"He's letting me borrow these," he said and came back with a real doorstopper.

"Achton Friis," he said.

Louise had no idea whether he was someone she should remember from her history class at Hvalsø School.

"He's the one who was picked to write about the journey after Mylius-Erichsen died midway," explained Jonas.

She smiled at him. The book didn't look like anything she'd have the courage to tackle, but maybe she should try it. If only to get an idea of what interested him.

"It was a big surprise, that day we ran into each other on the stairwell. It was just after summer vacation," Melvin Pehrsson said. "I'd often thought of what came of the boy, and wondered whether there was some way I could get to know him. And then suddenly, there he stood holding the door for me."

Jonas and the old man smiled at each other.

"I am so pleased he wants to come down and see me, and I hope you don't have anything against it?"

"Oh goodness, no," exclaimed Louise. "It sounds like you're enjoying yourselves."

She started collecting the plates.

"He's also very welcome down here if you ever need a babysitter, or whatever it's called these days."

"Can I sleep here?" Jonas asked eagerly.

Where, thought Louise, is the damned switch to turn off the tears when they swell in your eyes?

She hurried out to the kitchen with the plates.

22

For a day and a half, Louise and Sejr had been buried in figures, calculations, and copies of bank statements when suddenly, from behind his sunglasses, headphones, and hoodie he yelled, "Yessss!"

Louise had gradually gotten used to sitting in the dark and had even drunk a couple of the colas her temporary partner had generously pulled out of the little fridge he'd brought with him. She no longer noticed his headset so much, or the heavy metal beat that spilled out of the massive headphones. Nor even the funky sunglasses with gold lenses or the red hoodie and leather pants that had prompted her to ask if he rode a motorcycle. He didn't.

"There's an old money laundering report on him."

She smiled at him and thought how Sejr Gylling was such a perfect nerd that he'd think of digging way down into the details and sniffing out that kind of case, even though the information was hidden far away and no one had ever pursued it.

That kind of report popped up several times a day from banks across the country. A large amount of cash withdrawn or deposited, or noteworthy transfers, always ran the risk of the bank notifying the secretariat about money laundering.

Sejr already had the telephone to his ear. His headphones were tossed on the desk. Apparently, they could be removed in the middle of an album, if something was important enough.

Nice to know, thought Louise, and leaned back waiting for him to get through.

"Busy," he mouthed over the desk and drummed impatiently on his keyboard.

Finally, he got through.

He gave the account number and asked them to search several years back.

"It has to do with a transfer of 250,000 kroner into an account in Hong Kong," he told her when he hung up. "That was two years ago. On top of that, there's another report from the airport saying that just over a year ago he tried to leave the country with 15,000 euro in cash."

"Do they get you for something like that?"

Louise thought that monitoring had gradually relaxed.

"You can only take 10,000 euro out of the country, and I'm guessing they caught him in a completely random routine check. She'll find the money transfer and e-mail it to us. Then I'll try to track down the recipient."

Louise thought about it.

"Could it be pirated goods or parallel importing?" she asked. It occurred to her that pirating had been at its height when Nick Hartmann had sent the large sum to China.

Sejr nodded.

"It's gotten to where it can be anything from Global knives to pirated medicines. There can be a shitload of money in that crap," he said.

That was true, thought Louise. More and more bizarre

cases popped up, and it was far from just exclusive bags and designer jeans that were being pirated and manufactured for peanuts.

In the office next door, Toft and Michael Stig were still digging like moles to find the threads that connected Nick Hartmann with Copenhagen's criminal underworld. They'd already taken a trip to the bikers' headquarters, but this time they'd secured a meeting beforehand with the club's spokesman, Tønnes. Michael Stig had red blotches on his neck when they'd come back.

They'd been offered coffee, and both the president and the spokesman had been friendliness itself. Polite and obliging, they'd love to help. They just couldn't. They hadn't denied that Nick Hartmann had been allowed into the club, which was smart since the police had hold of the evidence. They just couldn't think of who might have invited him, and refused point-blank that they had the least relation to him.

Toft and Michael Stig had also visited Mie Hartmann at home with her mother out behind Damhusengen, but she hadn't even known her husband had registered an import/export business. So, there hadn't been anything to get from her, either.

Louise smiled as she told Sejr that Mie had had a really hard time explaining to Toft and Michael Stig how they'd managed, on Nick's moderate income and her own quite modest one, to afford living in a big duplex in one of the city's coveted neighborhoods, and besides that drive two expensive cars.

"That's the kind of thing that makes Michael Stig mad as hell," said Louise.

But she thought that Mie Hartmann was possibly being honest when she said she didn't know. There were still a lot of women who didn't concern themselves with finances, and if her husband had made ends meet then maybe she hadn't thought twice about it. There was no reason to ask questions as long as you had what you needed.

Sejr had systematically examined every single transaction in the deceased's account. By far the majority had been made between Nick Hartmann's own accounts but, as Louise had seen earlier, large sums of cash also figured into it.

Willumsen had cooled down. By the next afternoon, he'd come slinking in to introduce himself to Sejr, who for his part hadn't been too interested in the lead investigator's attempts to smooth things over. Several times over the course of the day he'd stuck his head in, but every time Sejr had sat there with his headphones on and his eyes glued to the columns of numbers.

It could easily turn into a dead end if they didn't find something that showed what kind of import/export Nick Hartmann's company was operating with Hong Kong, or who he'd done business with, thought Louise. She closed her eyes for a moment. So far, what they'd uncovered was minimal.

"What about business files? Did they find any?" asked Sejr.

She shook her head.

"Nothing. They've also been over to his work place on Havnegade, but there were no ring binders with private company papers or accounting."

Sejr put his headphones back on before she'd even finished talking.

She sighed. Suddenly, she'd had enough of him. The darkened office made her feel so claustrophobic that she stood up with an acute need for light and air.

She took the stairs in bounds and came out on the Police Headquarters' circular courtyard, where it was mostly smokers out on their breaks. She stood with her back against one of the broad columns of the rotunda, leaned her head back, and looked up at the sky.

Deep and autumnal blue, it made her think of water and Mik and the untenable thing they had going with each other. Although she yearned for him now and then, it still wasn't working. They each wanted something different.

Her next birthday, she'd turn forty. There wasn't much girlish about her anymore. Not that that bothered her, but maybe it was time to take stock and put some effort into thinking about her future.

Her brother, Mikkel, had recently overhauled his otherwise very staid life when his wife, Trine, had taken both children and moved into an apartment out in Havdrup. That had left him with the house and a stack of bills and made him take a second job as a freight carrier.

"Well, shit. Of course!" Louise suddenly shouted.

With her long legs, she bounded back up the stairs to the darkened office on the second floor.

Freight and hauling companies around Free Harbor, North Harbor, and South Harbor. Louise had no damned idea where the big container ships docked.

She held the phone to her ear and waited to be transferred to the first company that came up on Krak's Business Directory when she searched under "Harbor Area."

"Can you check your freight records and see if you've

ever received a delivery for HartmannImport/Export?"

She hadn't noticed when Sejr had taken off his head-phones and shoved the hood off his head. But now she saw him sitting and looking at her with his light, intense blue eyes as she patiently waited.

"No, I don't have another delivery address," Louise told the woman when she was finally back on the line. "But if you've shipped for him, I'd very much like to know where you were asked to ship the freight to."

When she hung up the phone, Sejr nodded at her in ap-preciation.

"Smart thinking."

Louise was about to thank him, but let it go. In fact, it was one of the investigation tactics she handled really well, as opposed to all that stuff with numbers and financial in-formation.

She picked up the phone again. "Hartmann Import/Ex-port," she said and waited.

He still sat listening in. He offered to help her by calling around to the other companies on her list.

She shook her head and gestured that the woman had found something.

"Lautrupvej," Louise repeated and wrote it down.

The woman brought up the freight documents so she'd have the exact dates for the shipping the company had done for HartmannImport/Export.

"They've carried something for him twice this year," she told Sejr. "The last time it was two containers that arrived on a freighter from Hong Kong. That was back in the begin-ning of August."

Louise pulled Krak's up on her screen again and searched for Lautrupvej. She zoomed in, then went in even closer until she was in the immediate area.

She still had Sejr's undivided attention.

"The address is out on South Pier, next to the Svanemølle Power Station," she said as she stood up.

It was Ulrik Fasting-Thomsen's warehouse. The one with the boathouse.

23

Dear Louise

Britt's doing shitty. I just got a text from Susanna—Julie's mom from the class. She'd made plans with Britt to stop by yesterday. No one came to the door, and she was about to give up, but she spotted her inside in the living room. She only managed to get her attention by going around the garden and banging on the big terrace door. Britt had apparently forgotten all about their plans, and Susanna wrote that she seemed odd and woozy.

I think she's taking sedatives, but evidently, she's said no to counseling, even though Ulrik has tried to persuade her. She doesn't think anyone can help her. It's completely idiotic.

I'm afraid she's about to go to pieces. I also gathered from Susanna that Ulrik is trying to be home with her as much as possible, but obviously, he can't be there the whole time.

Keep an eye on her. If it were me who lost Markus like that, there's no doubt I'd be a serious danger to myself.

Warmest C

P.S. We drove through an area with those great big redwood trees yesterday. Holy shit was that nuts. Really, really huge, and you feel tiny and utterly insignificant when you stand and look up.

The trunks are reddish and the smell of wood was so strong it stayed in my nose for the rest of the day. We stood there a long time and looked up at their crowns imagining we were birds and could fly up to the highest branches. Think of sitting up there and contemplating the world. Then maybe you could start to be fond of it again!

24

L ouise sat with her cell phone in her hand, having just
sent a text to Camilla. She reassured her by saying that
she'd be heading out to the house on Strandvænget to talk
with Ulrik, and at the same time she'd certainly see how
things were going with Britt.

"Why didn't he mention Nick Hartmann when he said he
owned the boathouse?"

She looked across the desk at Sejr, who was wearing a red
Coca-Cola baseball cap. It smushed his white hair down over
his ears.

Sejr pressed his fingertips together and looked at her
speculatively.

"It's possible he didn't know about it," he said and
dropped his hands.

He offered her a cola and grabbed two from the fridge.

"If Nick Hartmann had registered himself as just
HartmannImport/Export, it's not for certain that he'd have
noticed the connection to the murder. And besides, Fasting-
Thomsen has had other things to think about lately."

He passed the half-liter bottle across the desk.

Louise thought he was right, and dialed Willumsen's extension to tell the lead investigator that they'd tracked down Hartmann's storage site.

❧

"Two people to the warehouse," Willumsen commanded.

He pulled Toft and Michael Stig into Louise's office.

"You're driving down to Svanemølle Harbor," he said and pointed to them.

He was about to point at Sejr, but thought better of it. Instead he nodded in his direction.

"Maybe you could look a little into Ulrik Fasting-Thomsen? See if there's anything on his businesses? Have we gotten into it at all?"

He looked around at them, but Louise reminded him that until now they'd had no reason to be interested in the investment consultant.

"And strictly speaking, there isn't necessarily any connection between them, other than he owns a warehouse that the deceased's company rented space in," she said. "It was Fasting-Thomsen himself who made us aware that he owns the building down on South Pier, so it's not exactly something he's trying to hide from us."

Then she told them about Signe and the reason why Ulrik had stopped by the department.

"Will you get hold of him and ask him what he knows about his renter?" asked Willumsen.

Louise nodded.

"Then the rest of us will dig into the warehouse and try to find out what kind of a connection there is between the two of them," he said.

Louise remained standing behind her desk as Willumsen and her two colleagues left the office. She reached for her cell phone and found Ulrik Fasting-Thomsen's business card in a drawer where she'd tossed it when he left.

When his phone went to voice mail, she left a message explaining that she was interested in talking with him about his warehouse and the man he'd rented some of the space to.

She waved across the desk to get Sejr's attention.

"I'm heading out to Strandvænget to see if he's back home," she said.

He nodded from his sound bubble.

She shook her head at him and smiled. Then she put her empty cola bottle in the box behind him and took her jacket off the peg.

Just then her cell phone started to vibrate on the desk.

"Louise Rick," she said, adding in the same sentence, "Ulrik, hi!"

Then she realized it wasn't Ulrik Fasting-Thomsen promptly returning her call.

"Hey there, when did you get home?" she said, surprised to be hearing Flemming Larsen's voice on the other end.

It had been a month since she'd last spoken with the medical examiner, even though they'd started going out regularly for coffee or a drink. In the beginning of September, he'd traveled to Thailand with his children. Neither his ex-wife nor the children's teacher had been thrilled about the trip being planned outside of a school break. But it was the only time he could get away from the Department of Forensic Medicine for three weeks in a row, so they'd finally worked it out.

After it had come to shared custody, he often had a ridiculously hard time making things work out, and his ex would sometimes use it against him. So, it had meant a lot to him that the trip actually went off.

"Coffee?" he asked.

Louise gave it a quick thought.

"Love to, but I'm heading out to Svanemølle."

"I could drive you, if it doesn't take too long. I'll just wait in the car, and then we could have coffee afterward—or, what about Jonas?"

"He's down with his new best friend, Melvin. He's our downstairs neighbor, and those two have just started tackling the Danmark Expedition and sit around absorbed in history books. I promised to have food on the table by seven. Then they'll both come up and eat."

"Fine. When should I pick you up?"

Louise could hear that he was already sitting in his car.

"How about now?" she said, grabbing her bag off the floor.

She and Flemming Larsen had gotten to know each other over the years, but it was only in the last three or four that they'd seen each other privately. Otherwise they mostly met in the autopsy bay, when they ran into each other on a case. But their friendship had grown after that day when Louise had come home from work and her boyfriend, Peter, sat in her living room drinking up the courage to tell her he was leaving her for a colleague. In the evening, Flemming had shown up with a bottle of Calvados and cigarettes. He knew perfectly well that neither of them smoked, but that night he thought they might like to start.

Later, Louise had seen that Peter's decision hadn't come completely out of the blue. For years, he hadn't hidden the fact that he wanted a family life with kids and their own place. She, on the other hand, didn't want that at all. It was a relief to be rid of the pressure he'd put on her.

✄

Only the Golf was parked in the double carport when Louise and Flemming Larsen made it out to Strandvænget. But it wasn't much past four thirty, so maybe she'd been a little too optimistic to think Ulrik Fasting-Thomsen would already be home. She looked up at the large house, where someone had left the light over the front door on. Otherwise, the house looked abandoned.

Flemming Larsen turned off the engine and gave the impression that he'd just sit there.

"Please; you should come in with me," she said.

On the drive there, she'd told him about Signe and the party down at the sailing club, and it turned out Flemming already knew about the accident and had read the autopsy report. It was lying on his desk when he got back from his vacation.

"I'm sure Britt would want to know how her daughter died. Right now, she's imagining all kinds of things. So, come on in with me," she said.

She opened the car door and nodded up to the house.

The afternoon had turned gray and damp, and a pungent smell of seaweed rose from Svanemølle Harbor, where the Power Station sent heavy columns of smoke into the air, climbing high up in the sky before they were carried away and dissolved in the wind.

The gate stood open, and the garden path was littered with brown and yellow leaves that clung to each other and got stuck on the soles of their shoes as Louise and Flemming walked up to the house. The outdoor candles were full of water, and several of the roses hung with their petals withered at the edges and their leaves turned brown and curled.

Britt answered the door in a dove-blue house dress, her hair held back in a wide gold barrette with embroidered roses. She looked curiously at Flemming Larsen and held the nearly six foot five medical examiner's hands between hers, while Louise introduced them to each other.

"How nice of you to come," she told him.

She stepped to the side and found a couple of hangers for their coats.

"I've begged everyone I could think of to tell me what happened to my daughter the night she died. But no one could tell me anything more than that she died of her injuries. I'd be glad to have it cleared up," she said, leading them through the living room and on out to the kitchen.

"Would you like something? Tea or coffee?"

The dining room was in partial darkness. Neither the candles nor the lamps had been lit, and on the long dining table there was a stack of newspapers in a lopsided pile, as if they were on their way to the recycling bin but got stranded along the way. The double doors into the music room and the other rooms were closed and the stereo system was shut off.

"I mostly stay upstairs," Britt said.

She pointed them to the table along the kitchen wall, then found a pack of matches in a drawer and lit the pillar candles on the windowsill.

"Actually, what I'd like is something cold," Flemming Larsen said and pulled out a chair. He nodded his approval when Britt took a bottle of mineral water out of the refrigerator and asked if he'd drink something like that.

When he settled into his chair, Louise noticed how his hair had started to go thin on top. His medium-length blond hair had gotten bleached during the three weeks in Thailand with sun and seawater, and it was cut so short that you really didn't see the bald spot that was starting to appear on the top of his head. But normally, you wouldn't have a chance to see it anyway because he was so tall. He had friendly wrinkles that ran down his cheeks when he smiled, and there was a convincing warmth and confidence in his green eyes, which were edged with brown around the irises. They always made Louise feel like she was in competent hands when she worked on a case with Flemming Larsen.

Now his pleasant look was turned toward Britt Fasting-Thomsen, who'd filled up their glasses.

"For Ulrik and me it is indescribable that our daughter isn't here anymore," she said and sank down into the last chair. "It seems like my life's come to a halt. When I was out doing some shopping this morning, it felt like an insult that cars and buses still drove around. Everything just goes on and on, as if nothing happened. The newspapers are still full of that Sachs-Smith scandal. They ran that even before Signe died. But none of the papers have written more than a little paragraph about the accident that took her life. A paragraph. And then the obituary that we submitted ourselves."

She shook her head and rubbed her hand over her eyes, which were sad and tired. Their brilliance was gone. Britt Fasting-Thomsen was withering away.

"What happened to her? Well, I know that she ran in front of a moving van. But how much did she know about it? Did she feel anything?"

Her thin arms rested on the table, and her look was unguarded and vulnerable. She wasn't hiding behind any notions she had of how her daughter had died.

Louise saw Flemming Larsen thinking it over. He delayed by emptying his glass of water.

"They say she died immediately. But she didn't, did she?"

Britt's sea-blue eyes stared at him until he leaned forward in his chair and folded his hands in front of him.

He shook his head.

"Your daughter did not die immediately. No. But she was never conscious, so she didn't feel anything. Didn't suffer," he assured her.

Britt nodded.

"If Signe had been hit by a passenger car, she would very likely have been thrown into the air at impact," he said. "But when someone's hit head-on by a moving van, as in your daughter's case, then most of the body is hit. Besides that, her head was seriously injured when she was flung down on the asphalt."

Britt didn't move and barely took a breath.

"When the rescue workers got to her, she didn't have any visible injuries on her face, just a few skin abrasions, but she had swelling on both sides of her head, with bleeding from her ears, and that raised the suspicion of a fracture in the bottom part of her neurocranium. Sometimes a blow to the head will produce injuries to the cerebral cortex and hemorrhages between the soft membranes of the brain."

"Why hasn't anyone told me this?" Britt interrupted. She looked at Flemming in confusion.

He shrugged his shoulders and couldn't answer.

"The scan showed that there was a large blood clot under the hard membranes of her brain and widespread injuries on her neurocranium. They were about to drill a small hole in her brain to release the pressure on her skull when she died."

He laid his hand over Britt's limp arm.

"I'm sorry," he said.

"All of this happened while I was in the hospital. Why didn't anyone tell me, so I could have been with her?"

Louise put her arm around Britt's shoulder.

"At that point, you were on the operating table yourself," she quietly reminded her.

She hadn't known any of what Flemming said, either. She'd been satisfied with the news that Signe had died shortly after arriving at the hospital.

"What did they do then, after she died?" Britt whispered.

"She was brought into the six-hours room," said Flemming. "Everyone who's pronounced dead is. We wait for there to be positive signs of death, and then the hospital porters come and push the deceased into the cooler. After that, we make a legal medical inspection of the body, and in this case, followed that with an autopsy. The doctors did everything they could to save your daughter."

He gave Britt's arm a soft squeeze then straightened back up.

Louise looked away. Thought he'd told her too much, was too detailed. She hoped Ulrik was on his way. To her surprise, Britt stood up and went over and put her arms around Flemming.

"Thank you so very much," she said and gave him a hug.

"I actually need to talk with Ulrik, but I can't get hold of him. When do you expect him home?" Louise asked.

She stood up to take their water glasses to the sink.

"Not till Sunday. He's on his way to Iceland. There are a bunch of his clients up there who aren't having an easy time with their investments at the moment. But you should be able to reach him at the hotel this evening. He lands at eight o'clock, and so he should be at the hotel an hour later."

Britt no longer seemed so vulnerable, although she still looked tired.

Flemming Larsen stood up, and Britt followed them out. She stood at the front door as they walked back to the medical examiner's silver-gray Passat.

25

Louise's cell phone had vibrated in her pocket when they were sitting in Britt's kitchen. Now she saw that it was a message from Mik, who was in Copenhagen and wanted to know if she and Jonas would like to go out to eat with him before he drove back to Holbæk.

She wrote back quickly, saying she was out on a case with Flemming, so it wasn't a good time, but she was looking forward to seeing him during fall break. She and Jonas were spending a few days at her parents' in Hvalsø, but several weeks back they'd made plans to go up to Mik's and see the latest litter of puppies before they were delivered to their new families.

"I can drop by with sushi, if that's better?" he suggested in his next text.

"Sounds good, but another time," she wrote back and stuck her cell phone in her pocket.

"Do you have the kids this week?" she asked as they drove up toward Svanemøllen Station.

She couldn't help laughing when he grimaced.

"Three weeks, Flemming!" he parodied in a falsetto

voice. "That's how long they're gonna be with me before we go back to the regular schedule!"

Louise shook her head. She'd never met the medical examiner's ex-wife and had a hard time understanding how grown people could keep their children from each other after they'd gotten divorced.

"But she must think it's great that her boys got to go on such a wonderful trip."

"I think she does. It just should have been with her. But in three weeks we'll hopefully be back on level terms, and I'll get to see them."

"When can children decide for themselves where they'd like to be?" Louise asked.

She kept her eye on a cyclist who was attempting a hazardous passing maneuver around a Christiania cargo bike. For a second she thought he was going to hit the Passat's side-view mirror, but he managed to straighten out.

"When they're around twelve, I think. The boys are nine and eleven, but I'm not allowed to have them more often than I do. It would just be nice if things could be a little more flexible."

Louise nodded. It suddenly occurred to her what a great gift it was for Jonas to have Melvin Pehrsson living just below them.

"Why don't you come up and eat with us?" she asked as they got closer to Frederiksberg. "I've got everything prepped, it just needs to be cooked. Then you can meet our downstairs neighbor. You'd like him."

Flemming accepted at once, even though he was on call until seven o'clock the next morning.

"I'll just have to take off if I get a call," he said and insisted that she let him buy wine to go with the dinner.

He glanced in his rearview mirror before merging into

the middle lane. Instead of turning onto Gammel Kongevej, he kept going straight toward Frederiksberg Allé, where he swung in and parked illegally in front of a wine store that was about to take up its sidewalk signs and close for the day.

Louise stayed in the car.

He came back with the wine wrapped up in tissue paper.

"Fancy what a bottle of wine does for a weekday," he said. "However, it is a nice one."

Louise didn't doubt it, maybe a bit of an overkill to go with her meat sauce. But she'd pegged Flemming Larsen for a wine connoisseur long ago.

They'd just parked in front of her entrance when Michael Stig called on her cell phone.

Flemming held the door for her. She gave him the keys and lagged as they climbed up to the fourth floor.

"Designer furniture. Fake, the whole shit-lot of it," said Michael Stig.

He and Toft had just gotten back from the warehouse out on South Pier.

"There was the Egg Chair and the Swan, a great number of them. And furniture from several of the other big-name furniture designers: Kjærholm, Wegner, Eames, Le Corbusier."

It didn't surprise Louise that her style-conscious colleague knew all the names.

"Nothing but classic furniture and lamps, which are easy to get rid of," he said.

She stopped and leaned against the grayish wall of the entryway as he spoke.

"At any rate, we're guessing they're fakes," Michael Stig said. "They were wrapped in plastic, but there wasn't any original packaging or other distinguishing marks. Toft is getting hold of an expert from Bruun Rasmussen or someone in the know at Danish Furniture Industry who can hopefully tell us if we're looking at fakes or the genuine article. But those people have probably gone home for the day."

"So, it was pirated furniture he was up to," she said, surprised.

As she walked up the stairs, she told him that Hartmann's own home was decked out with Piet Hein and Panton lamps, designer furniture, and a Bang & Olufsen stereo system.

"But maybe they were fakes, too," she added, well aware that she couldn't necessarily tell the difference.

"The furniture is being seized and picked up tomorrow, so we can do an inventory of what he had on hand," said Michael Stig.

Louise could hear that Flemming had already let himself in. She suggested to her colleague that he call Mikkelsen down at City Station and tell him what Nick Hartmann had been busy with. They'd troubled their colleague with a trip around the brothels, but now he could get that out of his head.

"I don't understand how people can be so vulgar," Michael Stig said in a tone of outrage. "How tasteless to go and buy a fake Arne Jacobsen and have a replica of the Egg Chair sitting in your living room when you know it was made by little Juan, who made at most a half-krone an hour."

"People don't give a shit!" exclaimed Louise and laughed at his indignation. "Most people take what they can get. Especially if it'll save them money."

But Michael Stig kept on with his sarcasm. Although she'd never seen where her colleague lived, she had a feeling that it was probably a little more stylish than her place.

Some of his good taste could be in jeopardy if he'd taken home too many of the bowling trophies he and Toft shoveled in from the many tournaments they'd won for the Police Sports Association.

"Is there anything we should do tonight, because I could make it in," she said.

She stopped on the third floor to let Jonas and Melvin know they'd be eating in half an hour.

"No, we'll carry on tomorrow," said Michael Stig. "There's really not much we can do now. I've called Sejr. In his department, they've had lots of cases like this, and as far as I could tell they have a good relationship with the tax authorities at SKAT and the leader of the task force set up to fight pirating. We'll just have a hard time sloughing the case off on them, as long as we have an ongoing murder investigation."

❧

A half hour later, steam rose as Louise poured spaghetti into the colander. Flemming found hot pads and called in Jonas and Melvin from Jonas's room, where they sat in front of the computer. The boy was in the process of demonstrating how Alliance and Horde fought each other in *World of Warcraft*. It was apparently his turn to be the teacher.

"It's incredible what young people know," exclaimed Melvin, impressed as he came into the kitchen and accepted the glass of wine from Flemming Larsen. "When I was a kid, we had some little tin soldiers that we set up in rows and shot down with wooden cannons."

He laughed and pulled out his chair carefully, so it wouldn't scrape the floor. The tips of his shirt collar were arranged neatly over the outside of his knitted vest, and he smiled a little sheepishly when he unfolded the paper napkin and tucked it under his neck like a bib.

"I've gotten so bad about spilling," he apologized, and Louise suddenly remembered how she'd met him several times rolling a little wheelie bag from the Laundromat up on Gammel Kongevej.

When the pasta was eaten up, the three generations of men talked so eagerly over the table that Louise had a hard time taking part in the conversation, which was currently centered on a small village in southeast Greenland where both Melvin and Flemming had been several times. The same town was the setting for an essay Jonas had just turned in about a whaler from Kulusuk—strongly inspired by Melvin's stories.

They spoke on top of each other. Described and held forth.

Smiling, she stood and started to clean up.

⌗

Late in the evening, the sofa table was littered with chocolate wrappers from the big box of Quality Street, which Melvin Pehrsson had brought to have with coffee, and which they'd nearly emptied while he told them about the years he'd lived in Australia and about his daughter, Jette, who still lived in a city outside Melbourne with her husband and three children. Not that he saw much of them. He'd been there once since Nancy died, and when she was still alive he hadn't wanted to be away from her, so he'd only seen his grandchildren that one time. Jette, however, had been home twice to visit her father, and she'd also flown home for the funeral. But money was tight, so now their contact with each other was down to two phone calls a month.

That made Jonas sit up.

"You should get Skype on your computer," he exclaimed in his hoarse voice and began eagerly explaining how you could use your computer to call anywhere in the world completely free.

Melvin Pehrsson had looked confused until Flemming came to his rescue by drawing two computers, each with its own little webcam, that communicated with each other over the Internet.

"Just like an ordinary chat," said Jonas, then sank back into the cushions when he realized his seventy-five-year-old friend had no idea how that worked, either.

"In reality, it's just a long cordless telephone connection," Louise said.

She shushed Flemming and Jonas, who practically talked over each other to explain how easy-peasy it all was.

"Don't even explain it," she said. "Just make sure you install Skype and that there's a camera on Melvin's computer."

He had one of those. She'd seen it in his living room, and Jonas had told her that he used Google and sent e-mails.

"And then you two can get it up and running, and find out if Jette even has a Skype address."

Suddenly it was long past Jonas's bedtime, and Melvin made his way back, too, after having received instructions to set up Skype the next day.

"He's one hell of a find," exclaimed Flemming as Louise came in with two cups of freshly brewed coffee.

She nodded and handed him a cup.

"Melvin's been living down there the whole time. I just didn't realize he was him. If you know what I mean."

Out in the kitchen, Louise's cell phone started to ring. She glanced at her watch. It was almost twelve thirty, and she had to ask Suhr to speak louder when she realized it was him.

"Fire," said the lieutenant, "and I'd like you to come down here immediately. It's Fasting-Thomsen's boathouse and warehouse out on South Pier, and after they put out the fire they discovered the bodies of two people burned to death."

"Who burned to death?" Louise asked holding her cell phone to her ear and putting on her coat.

Flemming had picked up the chocolate wrappers and coffee cups in the living room and had come out to the entryway, where his jacket hung on a peg.

"We don't know. It's only been an hour since they got the fire under control enough that they could go in. The boathouse was completely consumed with flames, every surface burned, so the firefighters didn't get in on their first attempt. They had to go back to the hoses before they could manage it. Now they've been inside, and in a little room in the very back of the boathouse they found two partly charred corpses."

"I didn't think anyone was allowed in there," said Louise. "Ulrik didn't want them down there and had gotten the attendant to toss them out. How far along are you?"

"I've just been called. It was only after they discovered the victims that Bellahøj decided to hand the case over to our fire department. But you're familiar with the boathouse, and you know who was staying down there, so I want to have you along."

She walked over to the door into Jonas's room and looked in. He lay asleep, so she wrote him a note and laid it on the floor beside his bed. They'd made that arrangement when he moved in, but this was the first in all the time he'd lived with her that she'd been called out at night. Louise hoped she'd make it home again before he got up for school.

"Would you like to ride together, or do you need to use your own car?" asked Flemming.

He'd also been called out for the on-site inspection, which would happen as soon as the head of emergency operations and the crime technicians were ready to let others go inside the burned-out buildings.

"I'd better take the Saab," she said and stuck the car keys in her pocket.

❧

There were hardly any cars on the road. Louise turned down past The Lakes and drove across Little Triangle and farther on toward Kalkbrænderihavnsgade. As she passed Nordhavn Station, she was hit with the smell of burning, sharp and penetrating.

The smoke appeared like clouds against the night sky. She saw the fire trucks from a distance and parked a good stretch off, so she wouldn't be in the way.

The whole great big warehouse reeked of dense soot, and Louise walked hesitantly past the firefighting vehicles that were parked in a long column. An emergency worker conducted her around them, after she'd shown her police badge, then with both his hands up gestured to a cab to get the driver to pull up a little.

There were shouts through the darkness. Louise had difficulty seeing where she walked, and groped along behind the fire trucks.

The fire-damping operations continued in full swing, and between two vehicles she saw several firefighters coming out a side door of the burned warehouse. They walked back to the emergency department's active fire trucks, which still pumped water. The fire hoses droned on, but it seemed like they'd gotten the fire under control. There weren't any more flames.

Everything was heavy and wet. Soot particles struck Louise in the face and stuck there. She'd gathered her hair in a bun and hidden it under a plastic cap. Boots, overalls, and extra jerseys she always had lying in the back of her car.

Louise hadn't been on South Pier before, but from what she could tell through the dark it was a mixture of new and old buildings. In along the quay there were two new properties built of glass and steel. The renovation of the entire waterfront was also beginning to make its way out to the northernmost parts of Copenhagen Harbor.

As she came around the warehouse and walked over to the back end, where the explosive fire had nearly turned the little boathouse into splinters, she greeted Frandsen, chief of the Center for Forensic Services. She let him lead the way through the cordoned-off areas, where his people were at work securing foot and tire prints around the burned-up wooden building.

Here the devastation was clearly much more serious than it was at the warehouse section, where the building didn't look to have taken so much damage before the fire was put out.

"Is Suhr here?" she asked.

"I haven't seen him yet."

The whole area was lit up by the technicians' floodlights. The scene lay in an unreal and deeply contrasting light, where what was dark was coal black, and what was lit up was dazzlingly white. The mist from damping down the last remains of the fire clung to the night air and settled on her skin.

Frandsen put his hand on Louise's elbow and led her forward, steering her around the technician's chalk marks on the asphalt so they wouldn't ruin anything.

"We can't really get started on the technical investigation until tomorrow, when there's decent light," said the chief, who had an unlit pipe in the corner of his mouth and spoke through clenched teeth. "But I'm very eager to secure the outside clues tonight, so we don't risk having everything vanish if it decides to rain tonight."

Louise stepped carefully amid the glass shards, pieces of wood, lathing, and sheets of roofing that were spread around the asphalt quay as if an explosion had blown it all into the air. The smell attacked her nose. She greeted Åse. The lab technician was already at it with her camera, and her overalls were black and sooty.

Again, she had to take out her police badge and show it to two regular officers to be allowed through the last cordon all the way up to the house, even though Frandsen already held the strip of plastic up for her.

She tried to avoid the pools of water the fire hoses had left behind, and felt broken glass crunch under the soles of her feet.

The lieutenant was nowhere to be seen, but she spotted Flemming, who stood ready in overalls with his bag in his hand.

"I'm going in now," the medical examiner said when Louise reached him.

Just then, Suhr came walking around the corner of the boathouse. He had his hands in the pockets of his thick jacket and greeted a couple of his colleagues before joining Louise and the others.

"Do we know what caused the explosion?" she asked.

Suhr shook his head and drew his shoulders up, so the

thick collar of his coat surrounded his ears. It was cold and a little breezy; the wind came in from the sea and had free rein.

"Anything's possible. They're wooden buildings and old as shit. If there was a gas cylinder lying around or fuel cans for the boats, it wouldn't take much. Once it was lit, it'd go quick," he said, gesturing with his hands to the charred boards spread about them. "But we'll see if we can find out who the victims were. It's an odd place to be on such a raw night."

Louise nodded and thought about the boys who'd hung out in the boathouse. Since Homicide hadn't been involved in the case surrounding Signe's party, she didn't assume Suhr knew that their colleagues from Bellahøj had already been in contact with the boys.

Louise told them what had happened two weeks earlier.

"They at least have the names and numbers of the party crashers," she said.

"Then it's not far-fetched to think it may be a couple of them lying in there," Suhr said.

He waved her with him over to the vice commissioner, who led the initial investigation.

Louise greeted him and handed him the business card that the young officer from Bellahøj had stuck in her hand that Saturday when they'd parted ways at the hospital. She'd had it in her pocket ever since.

"He's at least been in touch with several of them," she said, stepping aside for a technician who wanted to take another floodlight into the boathouse. "They've been in for questioning, and there are photos of them."

A gust blew in from the water and the vice commissioner had to yell.

"I'll send duty officers out to the station to get the names right away."

He turned and disappeared behind the building, where it was sheltered and calmer.

"Lucky for us," said Suhr and pulled his collar up. "So at least we have something to go on."

Louise nodded. Fire victims could be nearly impossible to identify unless you had at least a suspicion of who they were.

She followed Suhr back to the boathouse.

26

The walls and ceiling had been wood constructions. The extreme heat had made the wood swell and flake, so it now looked like burned crocodile skin. The beams were blackened, and fallen debris lay everywhere, but the technicians had cleared a useable path through the drenched ash and charred pieces of wood.

The window frames were empty because the glass had been blown out in the explosion. A wire dangled from the ceiling where a lamp had hung. The shade was burned away and the bulb had exploded in the heat. Only the socket and copper wiring, which had been insulated by the plastic outer coating, now remained.

"There are fragments of clothing under the corpses," the medical examiner told them as he finished his examination.

He stood up and pointed to an area on the floor underneath the charred bodies.

"I think those are mattresses. Most of it was burned away, except for right there where the two of them were lying."

He took a step back so the police around him could see the mattress remains.

"Is there anything to suggest violence?" asked the lieutenant and walked a little closer.

"Not immediately," said Flemming Larsen, stretching his back. "I found soot in their nostrils and soot particles in their mouths, which suggests they were alive when the fire broke out. But the fire's done so much to them, it's hard to make out details. I can tell you more after I've autopsied them."

Louise stepped carefully over two chair legs, which were left behind when the rest of the chair burned up. She could see why Flemming shook his head doubtfully. There wasn't much left to see of the two corpses. They were severely burned, their skin blackened, some parts completely charred. And they lay in piles of burned scraps of what remained of the mattresses.

Suhr stepped forward and bent over the corpse that lay farther back, up against the wall. He pointed to a gash that ran across its stomach.

"Could that be a knife stab?"

Flemming Larsen bent over.

"No, that's a burst from the heat," he said and shook his head.

Louise saw how the skin of the two corpses had burst in several places and made long tears.

"They're lying in a classic fencing pose," the medical examiner continued, pointing to their bent arms.

She'd never seen it so clearly before. Exactly like a fencer who's ready to fight, with one arm bent and the sword raised, and the other arm bent to hold his balance for the thrust. Even the slightly bent knees.

"That position sets in when the heated muscles contract," Flemming explained, adding that it occurs after the person is dead.

Louise bent over and studied the charred corpse. Face, hair, clothes: Everything was burned away. The skin was burned and cracked like pieces of wood in a fireplace after the flames had died out. She took a step back and looked at her watch. It was past two o'clock. She was impatient to have the names and addresses of the youths that Bellahøj had been in touch with. The lieutenant had already called and woken up Toft and Michael Stig. One of them was to stay at the site of the fire, while the other had to help track down the youths, so they could get going quickly on an identification.

"So far there's nothing pointing to a crime," Suhr said.

Ash particles fell on his shoulders like drizzling rain.

"It's tragic and sad, but these two were probably lying here smoking—maybe got stoned and forgot to put their ends out properly. And then the mattresses caught fire. And since everything in this shack's made of wood, it didn't take the fire long to spread."

Louise nodded. She knew smoking was the most common cause for fires. Last year, around forty people had lost their lives that way, and it was unlikely that these kids were responsible-minded enough to install smoke detectors in their clubhouse, Louise thought and looked around. The boathouse had been an absolute fire hazard. The two boys hadn't had a chance to get out from where they were sleeping in the back when the whole thing exploded around them.

"We'll know more when Frandsen and his techs find out where and how the fire started," Suhr continued, then turned to Flemming Larsen. "When do you figure the autopsy will be done?"

It wasn't long before Friday's schedule of autopsies, so Monday at the earliest, thought Louise. But she heard Flemming say they'd be autopsied tomorrow at ten.

"Will you go out and be there for the autopsy?" asked Suhr.

Louise nodded and carefully straddled a fallen ceiling beam.

"We may not be talking about a crime here, but it's still something of a coincidence that the fire should happen right after we find out that Nick Hartmann had his goods here in this building," she said.

They left the boathouse and stood looking out over the harbor in the dark of night.

Suhr nodded and they started walking back to their cars.

"Anyway, it doesn't make much sense to put the two things together," he said. "The explosion obviously happened in the boathouse. If someone started the fire on purpose, they couldn't have known beforehand what the wind direction and wind strength would be like. And so, they couldn't have known with certainty that the flames would reach the warehouse."

Louise shook her head. He was right.

"But there'd be a pretty good possibility for it," she said.

The fire trucks were gone, and just two passenger cars from the emergency team remained in the harbor lot.

"Possibly, but having said that," he continued, looking at her, "why would someone kill Hartmann and then wait several weeks before burning down the warehouse with his replica furniture inside?"

Illogical, conceded Louise.

"Looking at it the opposite way, I can maybe see a connection," he said. "The furniture in there must represent a pretty high value, so it would clearly make more sense for someone to kill him and afterward steal the shit and line their pockets."

They'd nearly reached the warehouse before he shook his head and looked at her.

"I doubt there's a connection between the furniture and the fire," he said.

He waved at Toft and Michael Stig, who came walking up to join them.

"But we must find out if the kids who came here knew anything about Nick Hartmann and what he was up to in the building next door. It's certainly possible that they had contact with each other, or saw who's been in and around the warehouse."

"They'd just turn a blind eye to it!" said Michael Stig and shook his head.

His hair was still wet. It didn't surprise Louise that her colleague had managed a quick shower before heading out the door.

Toft, on the other hand, still had flattened-out pillow hair.

"What about all the furniture that was in there?"

Suhr shrugged his shoulders.

"The techs will be looking into that as soon as they have the lamps set up so they can go inside. They've only just finished damping the fire, so we don't know how widespread the damage is in there."

"Which of you wants to stay here and see what we get out of the warehouse, and which of you wants to track down the kids who stayed in the boathouse?" Suhr asked and looked at his three investigators.

Willumsen was noticeably absent, but that was nothing new. It was only in the most extreme circumstances that Suhr chose to wake the lead investigator, and it wasn't in order to spare him that he wasn't hauled out of his bed in the middle of the night. Willumsen wasn't fit to have his night's rest interrupted. He'd be, if possible, even more surly, and most of them would rather not have to deal with that.

"I'm going, and Toft's staying," said Michael Stig after

conferencing with his partner. "But we're going to a bowling tournament tomorrow afternoon in Haderslev, so we'd
like to catch a little sleep before we drive over there."

Louise sighed.

"We'll see about that," Suhr said dismissively.

He nodded to two journalists, then brushed them off by
saying he had no comment on the fire.

"But the ambulances," one of them tried, only to be si-
lenced when the lieutenant raised his hand in the air and
told him to call tomorrow.

Then he turned to the vice commissioner, who'd come
over to them.

"These are the addresses of the five we have in the report," he said and passed some slips of paper to Suhr. He
added that there were also cell phone numbers for most of
them. "We've already called around, but only one of them
answered."

Louise was handed the notes with the five names, and
saw that there was a circle around Kenneth Thim. So, it
wasn't him lying inside there.

"Could he tell you anything?" she asked, looking at the
vice commissioner.

He shook his head.

"He was apparently so drunk there wasn't much the officers could get out of him. Other than that, just that he was
alive."

He offered to have his folks continue with the calls, but
Louise shook her head and said they'd take it from here.

"Are you working together, or going solo?" Suhr asked
and looked from her to Michael Stig.

"Alone," she hurried to say before her colleague could
answer.

She wanted to, as quickly as possible, confirm or deny if

it was some of the five from the party who lay in there. And if it wasn't them, then whether they knew of anyone who would have dared to stay in the boathouse after Fasting-Thomsen had asked to have it cleared out.

"Hell no, we'll work on this together," her colleague said. "If they're some kind of biker wannabes, then you shouldn't stand up to them alone."

27

The car's windshield wipers ran intermittently, sweeping the small raindrops aside as they moved through the night stillness of Østerbro. An S-train pulled into Svanemøllen Station, but otherwise there wasn't much traffic, outside of the lone taxis that drove way too fast down Østerbrogade.

"Two more live here in Østerbro," Louise read off.

To her great irritation, Suhr had agreed with Michael Stig, so she'd left the Saab at the harbor and sat in her colleague's station wagon on their way to the first address.

"Then there's one who lives above his father's café in New Harbor, and Kenneth Thim lives on Møllegade in Nørrebro, but he's crossed off the list. That's Århusgade," she said and pointed.

She saw a taxi queue and people over in front of Park Café, where the nightclub had just closed. The Thursday night crowd was on their way home or deeper into the city, but Århusgade was sleeping. At any rate, it was dark in almost all the windows, including the communal floor where Peter Nymann had his dorm-style room.

Peter Nymann was the one Jonas had seen running after

Signe up to the road. Louise saw his picture in her mind. Thin, long hair tied in a ponytail, and dark eyes that stared hard and dismissive up from the photograph—and then the jagged birthmark on his cheek.

They rang a long time. Louise walked out to the sidewalk and looked up, but the whole strip of windows was dark. While Michael Stig kept ringing the door, she tried calling his cell phone, but that wasn't answered, either. After several minutes, the tired voice of a young woman came through the intercom speaker. Reluctantly, she was persuaded to let the authorities in, since the alternative was for her to knock on Peter Nymann's door herself and get him out of bed.

The entrance was gray, and the dingy basement walls were covered in graffiti. There were beer cans and cigarette butts and a single empty plastic bag in the corner on the white-and-black speckled terrazzo floor—even though there were garbage chutes on every floor, like little portholes in the middle of the wall between the two entry doors.

The communal level was up on the third floor. When they got there, the door to the left was open and a young woman in an oversize sweater and bare legs met them. She edged over toward the other door and asked if it was OK if she went back to bed again.

She pointed down the other hall and said that Peter Nymann lived all the way at the end.

"In The Arsenal."

Michael Stig raised a questioning eyebrow, and the young woman yawned and explained it was just his door, which was plastered with firearms; but still it wasn't very amusing for the rest of the hall residents to have to look at it every time they needed to go to the bathroom.

They walked past the shared kitchen, which was littered

with dishes, then the bathroom with its door ajar, and all the way to the end of the hall to a door that didn't have much wood grain left to show. Most of it was covered in clippings and posters of sleek firearms and heavy automatic weapons of sizes and calibers that would blow a bear's head off, even fired from a good distance.

They knocked a long time, and kept knocking, until a tall guy opened the next door over, stuck out his head, and asked for peace and quiet. He could tell them that his neighbor wasn't in, so they might as well stop their banging and let the students in the hall get their night's rest.

"Are you sure he's not here?" asked Louise.

The tall guy nodded convincingly.

"Absolutely. When he's here his intolerable death metal pounds through the walls, and it's impossible for the rest of us to think straight. But tonight's been completely quiet."

Louise asked if he had any idea where they could get hold of Peter Nymann.

"He's not exactly someone the rest of us hang out with. So, I have no idea. I'm just happy when he has someplace else to stay."

Michael Stig had his card ready and stuck it out before he was able to close his door.

"When you see him, would you please ask him to contact me?"

The tall guy nodded and stepped back inside. They heard his lock click, and Louise got out the slip of paper with the next addresses.

"We'll take Jón Vigdísarson on Strand Boulevard before we drive down to Gammel Kalkbrænderivej," she decided and got in the car. She'd already tried his cell phone, but it went to voice mail, and when a boy's voice asked her to leave a message, she hung up.

❧

He answered on the second ring, and met them on the fourth
floor in his T-shirt and a loose pair of gray sweatpants.

Tired, but alive, he stepped aside and let them come into
a large kitchen/dining room that stretched all the way to the
door, as if the entryway had been deliberately skipped over.
Even though there were coat hooks and a bureau, the open
kitchen and dining room blended into one large room, with
double French doors out to the balcony overlooking the yard.

Over the dining table hung a large brass chandelier with
winding frosted-glass flowers, and in the windowsills, there
were French altar candles and crystal vases with fresh flowers. On the whole, it was very tasteful and cozy. The walls
were hung with Icelandic art and framed black-and-white
photos, which you could tell were taken on an island where
the stark natural landscape varied from grass-covered hills
to lava deserts. Photos of a mother and her son, through the
years, from when he was just little to more recently. In a
couple of them, the boy was with an older man who might
have been his grandfather.

While Michael Stig told him about the fire, Louise
looked into the boy's room, where the duvet hung halfway
to the floor as if he'd jumped out of bed when they rang. His
mother apparently wasn't home, or else she slept soundly.

"We're not supposed to go down there anymore," he
said, clearly uninterested in sharing with the police more information than he found necessary.

He ran his hands through his thick, dark hair, which was
rumpled and sticking up, but when no one said anything he
continued.

"We got kicked out and had three hours to move our
things. The cops had already taken the computer when they

came with all their accusations and shit. But there was the fridge and stereo, and Sebastian picked them up in his car. So, we didn't have anything else down there, just some old crap furniture we'd picked up, and they can move that shit themselves."

"That's not so relevant now," inserted Louise, a little tired of his attitude. Instead she asked whether any of the boys had been back there after moving their things.

He shook his head.

"We don't have a damned thing down there, and he'll report us if he sees us."

"Fasting-Thomsen?"

Jón Vigdísarson looked confused.

"The one who owns the boathouse and warehouse," she clarified.

"No, that psychopath who keeps his eye on the shit."

The boy's eyes were nearly black, but they had a glimmer that made them very intense and lively.

"During the fire," Michael Stig said, taking over again, "two persons died. Two people burned to death in the back of the boathouse, where they'd apparently been lying asleep on two mattresses. If it's not some of the guys you hang out with, then do you have an idea who else might want to use the place?"

His attitude was dismissive.

"No one else goes there. I have no idea who it could be."

He pulled a chair out from the dining table and sat down with his arms crossed.

"When I tell you there're two charred bodies down there, and there're three of your friends we can't get hold of, what do you have to say to that?"

Finally, a reaction. The boy slumped over and something vanished from his face, so he suddenly looked more like a seventeen-year-old.

"I don't know," he answered a little uncertainly.

Louise shot Michael Stig an angry look.

"You live with your mother, right? Is she home?" she asked and glanced at the living room door and a closed door to the left of it.

He shook his head.

"She's spending the weekend with her boyfriend," he said, looking over at Michael Stig as he launched into more questions, less aggressively this time.

"Exactly how many of you stayed down there in the boathouse before you were kicked out?" he asked, sitting down at the table.

"Seven. But Mini is locked up and Thomas is out sailing, so lately we've only been five."

He nodded as if to confirm he'd counted everyone.

"Do you know where the others are tonight?"

Now Louise sat down, too.

"Home, I think. There's some party out in Vanløse tomorrow, but otherwise, the week's been kind of dead, and we haven't seen much of each other after we moved out of the boathouse. We were with Sebbe yesterday. His dad's got a café down in New Harbor, and he sent us up some food from the kitchen."

Louise started to feel impatient about moving things along, and stood up as a sign that she was ready to go.

"Next to the boathouse there's a warehouse. Do you know anything about the man who keeps his things there?" asked Michael Stig, ignoring her signals.

The teenager-look slipped away again, and he shut down. He shook his head, and it was obvious he'd suddenly thought of rule number one: Never tell the police anything. No matter what it is, keep your mouth shut.

"Don't know who that is."

"Where's Peter Nymann, if he's not at home?" Louise asked.

He shrugged his shoulders.

"Try his cell."

"We *have* tried his cell," she said. "Is there a girlfriend he might be with?"

"Bitches aren't something he spends much time on. It's more likely he's hanging out at a pub or over at the club."

"The club?"

The kid shut down again, but Louise could tell he must have meant the biker club, which they already knew Nymann had a connection with.

"Can't you try to get hold of your friends, and if you get through then give us a call so we know they weren't the ones down in the boathouse?" she said and walked over to the door to get Michael Stig to come with her.

The boy stayed seated while they let themselves out.

28

Gammel Kalkbrænderivej. The Youth Home. It was three thirty when they drove back down Strand Boulevard and turned up Nordre Frihavnsgade.

Every time Louise drove down that street, she thought about the first time she'd had to ring on a stranger's door and deliver the sad news of a death.

A young guy had been the victim of a senseless attack, and Louise was sent with a male colleague to inform his young live-in girlfriend of the death. It had been hard for Louise to handle the young woman's grief, and she'd been deeply affected for a long time afterward. So much so that she had to seek help from the department's crisis counselor. But that had been a long time ago, and many years before her appointment to Homicide.

"That must be the Youth Home across from the nursery school," she said as Michael Stig turned right. "It's not exactly the world's sweetest boys who live there."

Michael Stig agreed with her. It was a place the Copenhagen Municipality used for problem children, when they didn't know where else to put them.

"Do we know anything about him?"

"His name's Thomas Jørgensen, he's nineteen, and he's the one who kicked Signe's mother. The officer from Bellahøj found he's got a string of violent offenses in the crime files."

Michael Stig found a spot on the opposite side of the road.

The street door was open, and they walked up to the second floor and pushed open a red-painted door. Outside was written COPENHAGEN MUNICIPAL YOUTH HOME, but "Home" was spray-painted out and replaced with "Jail."

They came to a large entryway with coats, shoes, and clogs piled up along the walls. There were five doors, each leading to a different room, and a little hallway that continued farther on. It lay in darkness and probably led to more common areas farther into the premises, thought Louise.

Michael Stig turned on the light, and they stood a while. There were numbers on each door, but no names. Finally, he went over and knocked on the first one. A few seconds later, a short migrant boy shoved the door open and came out threateningly.

Michael Stig showed his badge and said they were looking for Thomas Jørgensen.

The kid didn't answer, but nodded to the next room over and quickly shut his door.

"Yeah," growled a dark voice after they'd knocked a few times.

They could hear movements in the room, and a little later he opened up.

Thomas Jørgensen was tall and well-built, and his muscles played just underneath the tattoos on his upper arms. The black color ran up over his shoulders and planted a big spider in its web on the one side of his neck.

It was obvious he wanted to deal with them as quickly

as possible, and repeated Jón Vigdísarson's explanation about how they'd been kicked out of the boathouse. He added, however, that the only one who would think of sleeping over there was Peter Nymann, and that was only to get away from the whore-banging psychos he shared a hall with.

Where the others were, or what they'd been up to, he didn't know. He didn't know anything about the warehouse that sat next to the boathouse, either.

"I don't know nothing, and nothing about the guy who goes there," he said, scratching his stomach under the T-shirt he must have thrown over his head when they knocked.

Nothing, other than that he'd seen him and knew he was the one who'd gotten shot a few weeks back. That much came out when Michael Stig pressed him.

He reached for a pack of cigarettes he had lying on a desk next to the door, broke off the filter, and lit up.

"Listen to what I'm telling you," he said. "I don't know shit about any of it, and I don't give a shit, either."

He shook his head when Louise pointed out that they'd only come to eliminate him as one of the charred corpses in the burned-out boathouse.

"Or some of your friends," she added.

It seemed to bounce right off him. He dropped his cigarette in a bottle and yawned loudly.

Thomas Jørgensen was so unsympathetic that Louise considered not even asking him to call if he got in touch with his friends, but she gave him her card anyway, adding that it would save him more visits from the police if he'd go to the trouble of helping them.

The tiredness had gradually gotten to her, and Michael Stig had started yawning. It felt like it had been several days since she said good-bye to Melvin and handed him the empty Quality Street box as he walked down the stairs in his slippers, and just as long since she'd said good night to Jonas.

Nevertheless, it hadn't been more than three hours since she and Flemming had parted on the sidewalk.

◆

The next stop was New Harbor. They drove around King's New Square and turned down past the Sailor's Anchor, where a little group was sitting on the ground with a couple cases of beer in front of them, holding their own private party, too drunk to be bothered by the drizzle that still fell, or the temperature that was at most a degree or two above freezing.

They sat with blankets and heavy jackets around them. Not like in the trendy cafés, where Smirnoff-brand blankets were passed around to the outdoor guests if the wind got a bit too chilly. This was more like the blankets that the homeless collect to withstand the cold of autumn when they sleep on the street.

Michael Stig drove slowly over the cobblestone. Unlike Østerbro, people hadn't completely abandoned this area. There were signs of life outside the pubs and tattoo shops, and many people stumbling around drunk.

Halfway down New Harbor they came to Sebastian Styhne's father's café. It was closed, but the lights were still on. Through the window pane they saw a man sitting at one of the tables with paperwork and a bottle of beer in front of him. Louise knocked on the window, showed her badge, and waved him over to open the door.

"To what do I owe the honor, that the authorities should brave the rain and make a night visit?" he asked with the exaggerated politeness people sometimes used when trying to be on friendly terms with the police.

"We'd like to speak with Sebastian Styhne," said Michael Stig, stifling a yawn.

The man raised an eyebrow, and it was enough to tell Louise that it wasn't the first time the police had turned up wanting to talk to his son. It hadn't been more than two weeks since Bellahøj had last gotten hold of him, but the fact that they'd come in the middle of the night probably made the father a little more nervous.

"That's my son, but he's not at home. He's sleeping over at a friend's in Østerbro."

"Peter Nymann?" asked Louise.

He nodded to her in surprise.

They declined his invitation to sit down, and he stood there a little noncommittally, as if he sensed something unpleasant was on its way.

"There's been a big fire down on South Pier this evening, and the boathouse where your son and his friends stayed has burned down," Louise said.

The father pulled a chair up close and supported himself against the back of it.

"Two people died in the fire," she continued. "But at the present time, we've not been able to identify the deceased."

He slumped a little and sat down heavily.

"We've also been unable to get hold of Peter Nymann," Michael Stig said in a serious tone. "So, we don't know if he and your son are together, but at any rate they're not at his place, because we've just come from there."

The restaurant owner turned pale.

"Have you called them?" he asked and cleared his throat.

Louise nodded and watched the father as he slipped farther down into his chair, put his hands on his knees, and

leaned forward a little, as if it had suddenly become difficult for him to breathe.

"Are there other places your son might be?" Michael
Stig asked, hoping to get the father thinking.

"Nowhere I can think of immediately. He lives here with
me. His mother died of cancer five years ago, and ever since
we've been alone he's always been good about remembering to tell me where he's gone, so I don't have to go and be
too worried."

He shook his head.

"I'm here most of the time watching the shop. We ate together up in the apartment, and when I was coming down to
take over the night shift, he went over to Nymann's—that's
what they call him. He's from Næstved, and the boys met at
a boarding school for vocational studies."

He drank a little of the beer in front of him. He didn't
seem to notice what he was doing, but rather reached for the
bottle as more of a reflex.

"The boarding school is in Haslev. That's also where
they met Jón, and the big one they only call 'Brute-
Thomsen.' His real name is Thomas Jørgensen. He has
quite the temper, and it's not always so easy for him to control it."

He shook his head, as if he knew this was the glorified
version he was serving to the police.

"I often think that maybe it would have been better
if they'd stayed out there in the country instead of coming in here to the city when they finished school," the
restaurant owner continued. "They haven't all turned out
to be God's best children."

He sank a little into himself before adding that the boys
were OK, and that one shouldn't judge anyone by appear-
ances.

Louise held back an eruption. Three of "the boys" had more violent offenses than there are hours in a school day, so no one was talking about judging them based on their tattoos and shaved heads.

The father turned his face up to them.

"You need to find out if one of them is my Sebastian. He has his whole body covered in tattoos, and he's such a beautiful boy. His hair falls in curls, just like his mom's, who is gone."

Words and sentences flowed from him like a drowning man trying to hold himself above water, before inevitably being pulled down into the deep.

"You can see them, they're over his whole body," the father explained.

Louise looked over at her colleague, who took a step forward and placed a hand on the man's shoulder before telling him, as delicately as possible, that there wasn't enough skin left on the burn victims to identify them based on their tattoos, even if it had been a full-body.

A noise came from deep down in the father's throat, like a hollowed-out sigh.

"His hair?"

Michael Stig shook his head.

"On the other hand, we don't know it's your son," Louise said frankly. "But we need to prepare you that it might be. And since we can't get hold of him or his friend, we need to ask you for the name of his dentist, so we can get his dental records. That would help us with a positive identification."

The restaurant owner nodded and pulled the notepad over. Then he grabbed his wallet from his back pocket and found a little white appointment card. He wrote down the name and number of the dentist, whose building was just around the corner on Store Strandstræde.

"Well then, it's like they say: I hope for the best but fear the worst."

He took his last gulp of beer and sat for a moment with his eyes closed.

"I think it's too early to fear the worst," said Michael Stig, reminding him that the boys had been kicked out by the owner of the boathouse and didn't have permission to be there anymore.

The father nodded and said he knew that, since it was his car the boys had used when they went down to pick up their things.

"It's all upstairs in the guest room, until they find a new place they're allowed to be. Or else they're welcome to use my loft. Now we'll just have to see."

"Couldn't you help us try to get hold of your son?" Louise asked.

She asked him whether there might be a girlfriend he would have wanted to spend the night with.

The restaurant owner nodded.

"That's certainly possible," he admitted, brightening up a little. "I can't always keep up with his female acquaintances, but there's always something going on there. And when they haven't come here, he could easily think of going to them."

Suddenly he'd been thrown a lifeline, and he wasn't slow to grab it and hold on fast. Then the glimmer in his eyes went out again.

"But he would have told me."

Michael Stig began walking to the door and Louise followed him, knowing it would be a long night for Sebastian's father.

"If you know anything about the girls he sees, then try to get their numbers. Maybe there's something in his room. If you find him, we'd really like you to call us so we can cross him off the list."

They parted at the door. Through the window, she saw the father watching them as they came up onto the street and walked over to the car.

"Nymann," said Louise. "It would be nice to know his parents' first names before we start calling up everyone in Næstved and asking if it could have been their son who burned to death down at the harbor."

As long as the burn victims weren't identified, they'd have to get hold of his parents and let them know what was happening.

Michael Stig nodded and offered to drive her home. Then he'd drive himself to Bellahøj and find the parents' names in Peter Nymann's case files.

It was nearly six o'clock, only an hour before Jonas had to get up for school. She'd have to pick up the Saab later.

29

Camilla had taken her laptop with her into the four-poster bed at Carter House in Eureka and was looking at the home page of the Danish newspaper *Morgenavisen*.

There hadn't been any trace of Walther Sachs-Smith, she read. The police had augmented the search with specially trained dogs and helicopters. The Home Guard was searching in the woods around Roskilde, and later in the day divers from the Scuba Corps would conduct a search in the fjord by the family's large property, which abutted the water.

She skimmed the rest and clicked on a related link.

THE CHILDREN GRIEVE

Rebekka and Carl Emil Sachs-Smith were photographed in front of their parents' luxurious estate, which made Camilla think of an old English manor house. A magnificently large and beautiful colossus with windows as tall as terrace doors and an entrance with a wide stone staircase that unfolded in front of the main door with elegant flower pots on either side. The yard in front of the house had a round grass lawn with a little fountain in the middle, and the whole drive was covered in pebbles.

In the article's subheading, it said the children had decided that the estate manager would continue the operations and run everything as before, but the main house would be closed down, and the furnishings placed in storage so it would be ready for sale when the estate was eventually put up.

The two grown children no longer believed that their father would show up alive, and now they must live on with the grief of having lost both parents.

"Holy shit!" exclaimed Camilla.

It hadn't even been a month since Inger Sachs-Smith had taken her own life, and their father had disappeared shortly afterward. Now they were already starting to liquidate the valuables. In fact, they didn't want to risk waiting the formal ten years required by Danish law before selling the estate, if Walther Sachs-Smith's body didn't show up.

Markus stirred in the bed, but then rolled over on his side and pulled the duvet up.

She shook her head and was about to close out of the page when the story was updated. A new headline popped up in all caps.

UNREST ON TERMO-LUX BOARD OF DIRECTORS

The newest was that there'd been discord on the board, with the family's two youngest now starting to argue publicly about how Termo-Lux should be run in the future. The family business had been, as was well-known, continuously owned by Walther Sachs-Smith and his three children, but after he had decided to step down, only Rebekka and Carl Emil remained as family members on the board. With so much power divided between so few people, there were beginning to be tears in the fabric.

Camilla was startled and looked at the pictures of the two well-known jet-set faces—dark Rebekka and fair Carl Emil. It was the daughter, in fact, who looked more like their father, she thought. Both from the slightly screwed-up eyes and the sharper nose. The brother was delicate and fair like his mother. And hot, thought Camilla, but caught herself. Fact was, the two siblings were pretty much the most unsympathetic people she could think of, if she limited herself to the category of rich family members and relations.

The eldest brother, Frederik Sachs-Smith, was not in any of the pictures, and he wasn't even mentioned in recent articles.

Even though Camilla was 100 percent on a leave of absence and doubted whether her desire to write would ever return, she felt the start of an itch.

In fact, it itched all the way to her fingertips.

To her great surprise, it occurred to her that she might very damned well think of hearing what Frederik Sachs-Smith had to say about all of this—even though there obviously must be a reason why he still hadn't come forward and contributed to the scandal with his version of events.

But Signe's father knew him, she thought, and if he'd help some with establishing the contact, then Frederik couldn't very well refuse.

※

Their bags were packed, and Markus had strolled into the restaurant's breakfast buffet and found a table by the window.

There'd arisen a new peace between them, thought

Camilla, and she was glad they'd decided to stay in the same place for a few days. Now it had gotten to the point where they were bored with the little town, which didn't have much entertainment to offer them besides the movie theater on the edge of town.

They'd managed to see two movies, and both times they'd supplied themselves with supersize colas and buttered popcorn. But they'd quickly realized that Eureka's Cinema 8 was a far cry from the new theater they had at home in Frederiksberg. The theaters were big enough, but they smelled like the outdoor music festival in Roskilde on a hot summer day: warm, sourish, sweet, and rather a lot like pee. Suddenly Camilla had turned squeamish and insisted that Markus spread his jacket over his seat before sitting down, which, of course, she knew he thought was ridiculous.

But other than that, they hadn't had any clashes. They'd been to Lost Coast, the town's popular diner, where humongous spiders fell on their heads as they walked in the door, and monsters hung down heavily from the ceiling. The waiter had recommended buffalo wings, which made flames shoot out of their mouths.

The next day they'd agreed it was time to move on to Mendocino, which, according to their guide book for Northern California, was supposed to be a lovely, idyllic town farther down along the coast with a fabulous view.

Camilla got hold of the waiter and ordered coffee, then pondered whether it was best to write or call Ulrik about setting up a contact with Frederik Sachs-Smith.

30

It was 9:15, and Louise had just fit in a quick cup of tea at the office before crossing Hambroes Allé to pick up a car from the police garage. From a distance, she waved to Svendsen, the garage manager, as he left the section where the K-9 patrol parked and walked up to her, limping slightly. As usual, he was testy with her for not calling ahead and making a reservation when Willumsen's group already had two of *his* cars.

"Both Toft and Michael Stig are out today," she answered him.

Her colleagues had postponed the Haderslev bowling tournament, but hoped to leave by evening so they could make the rest of the weekend's activities.

"We have two victims that we're having a hard time identifying," she said.

His attitude softened a little when she told him about the big fire out in Svanemølle, and how they'd gone around all night in hopes of finding out who it was who'd lost their lives in the flames.

It had been several years since Svendsen himself had driven patrol or been part of an investigation group. In 1987, he'd been involved in a serious car accident while chasing a bank robber out in Hvidovre. His partner was killed, and he'd lost his right leg at the knee and had had a hard time getting used to his prosthetic, both mentally and physically. Louise figured it was his sad fate that accounted for the harsh tone whenever officers took Svendsen and his work for granted. So, she always tried to express her appreciation for the puzzle he had to work out in painstakingly administering the police force's vehicle fleet.

"It's the weekend soon. Do you have it off?" he asked as he went over to the computer to sign her up for a patrol vehicle.

"You bet. It'll be nice, but I have a couple of autopsies to get through first."

He nodded.

"Do you have any particular preferences for which car?" he asked with his eyes still on the screen.

She shook her head and said she'd be happy with one of the smaller ones. That was easiest when she had to get around in the city.

The garage was as big as the parking basement under Falkoner Plads. The concrete walls produced hollow echoes, there were long rows of parking spots, and bright fluorescent lighting hung from the ceiling.

The patrol vehicles were spread out among the unmarked police cars, and in a row along the middle column there were spots for motorcycles. In the very back of the garage they parked the big vehicles, the armored personnel carriers that were sent into the streets when there were riots. They filled up most of the space.

"You should try the new Mondeo," said Svendsen cheerfully and tossed Louise a set of keys. "It's not quite as fast as the old model, but she's a little angel to ride in."

He said it so affectionately that he almost made it sound
sexual.

Men and cars, thought Louise as she followed his directions over to the fifth parking spot along the wall. A boat,
she realized as she carefully edged the car out past the concrete pillar. Svendsen would probably not be very pleased if
she scratched the little angel's paintwork all the way down
the left side.

In her bag, she had two dental records. One of them
Michael Stig had managed to get with help from the
Næstved Police, and the other one she'd picked up herself
over on Store Strandstræde.

Sebastian Styhne and Peter Nymann.

The café owner's son with the full-body tattoo and the
dark-haired guy with the ponytail who had run after Signe.

They still hadn't managed to contact those two, and
the parents on the farm just outside Næstved hadn't seen
or heard from their son. Now they were at home in their
kitchen, sitting on pins and needles waiting for the news.

The glass doors at the Department of Forensic Medicine
opened, and she looked at her watch. It was ten minutes before they were to start. Louise went up to the floor with the
autopsy bays. She stood and looked out the window while
she shook her hair out of the hairband and gathered her
long, dark curls into a tight bun that was easy to tuck away
under the hat she had to wear, along with the overalls and
the blue plastic booties.

Flemming Larsen was on his way down with two cups of
coffee, but the lab technicians hadn't arrived yet.

She said hello to two forensic techs as they came out of

the elevator from the basement with the burn victims. From the contours of the body bags it was obvious that the bodies still lay in their desperate fencing positions, with arms and legs stiffly bent.

Preparations had been made in two autopsy bays: the homicide room, which was the farthest back and largest and designed so that both lab technicians and investigators could be there while the medical examiner worked; but at the same time, the other body would be autopsied in a smaller bay next door, where space was a little tighter.

"We've just had both bodies scanned to see if there might be bullets inside them, which we hadn't been able to spot because of the state of the corpses. But there was nothing to see. So now it will be interesting to confirm whether they were alive when the fire broke out," said Flemming Larsen.

He passed a plastic cup to Louise.

"Based on the soot particles I found in the nasal cavities, I feel quite confident, but naturally I can't say with certainty before we've had a proper look at them. On the other hand, I'm quite sure we're looking at two young men, and that agrees very well with what you've come up with."

She gestured with her hand to correct him.

"We haven't come up with anything yet, but we have a suspicion of who they might be."

She held out the two dental records.

Just then, four lab technicians came walking toward them. Their voices were loud, and their steps echoed. It was Klein's voice that rose above the others.

"You should just be happy grill season is over for the year," bellowed the experienced, teddy bear–shaped lab tech as he looked at his two male colleagues, who Louise didn't know by name. "It's awfully unappetizing to go home and fire up the Weber after a day with two charred and crispy-fried corpses."

"Now stop it!" Åse said, irritated, and put her hand on the arm of Klein's blue Windbreaker. "We don't need to listen to that stuff."

Even though Åse was petite and slender as a teenage girl, her light voice sliced straight through and put an effective stop to Klein's noisy penchant for morbid similes.

The first time Louise had met Åse, she'd mistaken her for an intern. That happened four years ago, and at that point she'd already been in the same position with colleagues up in Ålborg, so she was far from inexperienced. Besides that, she was only a couple of years younger than Louise, who'd very quickly reevaluated her view of the other woman and had gained great respect for her crime photography, which was thorough down to the minutest detail.

"Let's get started," commanded Flemming Larsen with a smile, as the forensic technicians came out and said the bodies were ready for the external examination.

They walked into the tiny prep hall all at the same time, and suddenly the small space between the white tiles and the row of white rubber coroner boots became quite crowded.

Åse and Louise went into the women's section and got coveralls and hair protection. Through the walls, they could hear Klein starting to talk about grill food again.

Åse shook her head forbearingly. Klein was one of the brightest, and in all the years that Louise had known him he'd been just the same. Same blue Windbreaker, probably replaced a couple of times, but the replacement resembled its predecessor so much that one really didn't notice the change. His humor was also the same, morbid and dark, but it helped put a distance between them and the reality around them. And then he was meticulous in a way that always made her feel that if there were clues in a case, then it was sure to be Klein who'd ferret them out. That in itself was enough to forgive his rotten sense of humor.

⚬

Åse was starting to unpack her camera when Louise came into the autopsy bay. The smell of burned flesh was unmistakable, and she was grateful that Klein had divided it up so that he followed the autopsy next door. Otherwise she wasn't sure her stomach could take it.

With her pad in her lap, Louise sat on a chair she'd pulled a little off to the side so she didn't sit in the way but could still follow along as they got going on the external examination of the corpse.

She called to mind Bellahøj's photos of Sebastian Styhne and Peter Nymann, but there was nothing left of what she might have been able to recall. Before they'd gone into the autopsy bays, she'd told Flemming and his female colleague who conducted the autopsy next door about Sebastian's full-body tattoo, which should be recognizable if it were him and if even a little of the skin remained.

They started the exam by measuring the corpse's length, but because of the constricted muscles in his arms and legs they had to rely on an estimate of how tall the person had been.

"Around five foot nine inches," said Flemming Larsen and looked at Åse for confirmation.

She nodded that it seemed likely.

"There are widespread third-degree burns and charring

in places on the front of the body," dictated Flemming and made sure that Louise had enough time to write it down.

"Livor mortis on the back is very red, which suggests carbon monoxide poisoning," he continued as Åse finished photographing the area where the skin was still visible.

They began to go over the body for intact skin. The front side was completely burned away, but when the corpse was turned over they found small areas around the shoulders, back, and behind the thighs where the skin was preserved.

A large operating lamp hung over the steel table, and the medical examiner pulled it down closer so they could study the skin minutely and look for defining characteristics.

"In this instance, there'll have to be a tattoo on the back or a tongue piercing if we're to have any hope of finding anything," said Flemming.

Every other defining mark would have been burned away.

Louise felt her mind wandering. Fatigue ate away at her, and her body felt heavy. The light in the autopsy bay was bright and reflected off the white tile and cold steel—the beginning of a headache was coming on. She squinted a little and tried to keep some of the light out.

"Nothing," concluded Flemming, who told the techs to go ahead and open the corpse.

Then it wasn't the café owner's son after all, thought Louise, and walked out to the hall. But she stopped when she heard the colleagues in the other bay agreeing with one another that it could very well be the boy with the full-body tattoo lying on their table.

"I've informed our forensics dentist. He's ready to look at the dental records when we've determined the cause of death," said Flemming as he began on the internal examination.

The light outside was gray and dull, and only a little of it came in through the vertical blinds that hung down from the tall windows of the autopsy bay.

"It's amazing how intact the internal organs are," Åse exclaimed and leaned forward.

"Yes," nodded the medical examiner. "They've been affected by the heat, but undamaged. It looks like a healthy young man."

He began going over the corpse from the top down. His eyes passed over the face, neck, and chest, attentive to every detail.

"There is soot far down in the windpipe and in the bronchioles," he concluded after a short time and looked up. "He was alive when the fire broke out."

"I'd like to know if he's inhaled flammable liquids or if he died of carbon monoxide poisoning," asked Louise, who'd come over to the table. "We need to know if the fire was deliberate."

Flemming nodded. With his scalpel, he sliced off a piece of the brain and a piece of the lung, and put each sample in an airtight container, which would be sent to the forensic chemists for further study. Then he gave the word that the corpse could be wheeled down to the forensic dentist's examination room.

"I'm afraid it'll take a good week before we know anything," he said apologetically and looked over at the technician. "By that time, I'm sure you'll have found out what caused the fire."

"I don't think the fire broke out from an accident," said Åse, once Flemming had placed the airtight containers over on the table. "The boathouse was consumed by flames, almost like an explosion, and that does not suggest a fire started by a candle or cigarette."

Louise shrugged her shoulders. The fatigue had seriously gotten hold of her, and her head was way too foggy for guesswork. She preferred to wait for the technical studies. She closed her eyes a moment, while Flemming and Åse talked on. Everyone waited for the forensic dentist to take X-rays of the corpses' teeth to compare them to the two dental records Louise had brought with her.

She didn't know how much time had passed. Ten minutes—fifteen? Maybe she'd dozed off for a moment, but she straightened up when the corpses were wheeled into the bay again.

"Go ahead and close them up," Flemming said, nodding to the technicians who'd come in with the corpses.

A moment later, the dentist came over and stood in the doorway.

"There's a positive ID on both of them," he said.

Louise felt heavy. Saw the restaurant owner before her. Hope for the best, fear the worst, he'd said. Now she'd have to go to him and confirm his worst fears.

She skimmed through her pad and made sure she had what she needed for her report, up to the conclusion of the medical examiner, which wouldn't be available until sometime next week.

In the little dressing room, she washed her hands and pulled her sweater over her head, before taking her jacket down from the hook. Every one of her movements had suddenly shifted to a different frequency, as if her body had gone into slow motion.

It was hard to have to go over to New Harbor on an afternoon like this, with the weekend standing at the door, and what she looked forward to most of all was a Friday night of sitting on her parents' sofa with *Dancing with the Stars* on the TV, candy in the dishes, and a little wine in her glass.

She said good-bye to the lab techs and waved to Klein. He and Åse stood with their bags, equipment, and paper sacks with the little bit of clothing that had been secured from the undersides of the two burn victims. Now it would go out to the Center for Forensic Services for further study.

Flemming came out buttoning up a clean white coat.

"What are you doing this weekend?" he asked.

"Next week's fall break," she reminded him. "I've taken a couple of vacation days at the beginning of the week, so we're heading down to my parents' in Hvalsø."

They walked together down the hall.

"It's the third attempt," she said.

She smiled and told him how the first time had to be cancelled because Jonas wanted to go to Signe's party, and the weekend after that was the funeral.

"But now it looks like it'll work out, although we'll be leaving a little later than I'd hoped to. We must inform the survivors first. The parents in Næstved will have to hear it from the police down there, but I'm going to Sebastian Styhne's father myself. I spoke with him last night, and he's naturally out of his mind with worry."

Flemming nodded and gave her a quick hug before she took the stairs down to the foyer, where she called Willumsen and told him that the two boys had been identified. She said she was driving out to inform the restaurant owner.

"You're coming in here afterward," ordered the lead investigator.

Louise sighed and shut off her cell. She had been hoping that after New Harbor she could drive directly to the garage with the Mondeo and after that take a bus to go pick up her car on South Pier. Now she was beginning to doubt whether they'd make it to her parents' in time for dinner.

31

It was Friday afternoon rush hour in King's New Square, and people swarmed in and out of the popular department store Magasin. Louise watched them as she waited on a red light in front of the Royal Theater. She debated whether she should spend the time looking for a public parking spot behind New Harbor, so the restaurant owner wouldn't have to have a patrol car in front of his café, but when the light changed she decided that it would take too much time to go driving around. She turned right past the Sailor's Anchor, and the group still sat there with their cases of beer. More had joined them, and one lay sleeping on the cobblestone, as if he'd gone out like a light in the middle of a conversation.

She coasted slowly past Hong Kong, Leonora Christine, and The Ship's Well, then parked the car out along the bulwark, ignoring some foul comments from a group of young guys who sat there with a pack of beer and cigarettes.

She saw the restaurant owner through the window. He hadn't seen her yet. Went around putting glasses up on the shelves.

A bell jingled as she opened the door. At night she hadn't

noticed it, but now she felt that it was insultingly high-pitched and piercing. He turned toward her at once, and she read his face and the reaction that came the moment he recognized Louise.

A shadow passed across the wrinkles of his face and stilled his mouth. Fear was in his eyes, but not in the words he spoke as he came around the counter and walked up to her.

"Anything new?"

His tone of voice was unnaturally high, deliberately positive, but his face was stiff. He already knew what was coming.

Louise pulled a chair out for him and sat down across from him.

"I'm sorry to have to tell you...," she began but paused as he quietly began to cry.

The tears ran down his cheeks—he didn't try to wipe them away. He cried openly as he waited to hear the rest.

"Your son was with Peter Nymann, and they died in the flames," she continued, averting her eyes to give him room to grieve.

They sat like that for a while. He cried, and Louise looked away.

"How did it happen?" he whispered.

"I'm afraid we don't know much more just yet, but we're hoping soon to clear up how the fire broke out. Do you have any idea what made your son and his friend sleep in the boathouse after they'd been kicked out of there?"

The father shook his head slowly, followed by a brief, hollow laugh.

"They said that they'd all pissed on the door handle before they drove off with their things. They were hoping it'd be the owner who'd come open up and see if they were out.

But they apparently couldn't keep themselves from going back."

Louise shook her head sympathetically.

"Sebastian, damn it!"

Now the restaurant owner hid his face in his hands and let the sobs roll through his body.

She put her hand on his shoulder, then turned when the door opened at just that moment and a middle-aged couple came down the stairs with a questioning look to find out if the café was open.

"Sorry," said Louise and stood up. "Try the one next door."

She turned the key in the door before asking if the restaurant owner had anyone who could come and be with him.

He sat with his fingertips pressed against his eyes, as if to block the flow of water, then he nodded and dried his wet fingers on his pants.

"Lene's coming in soon. She's the one who helps me on the weekends," he said and stood up. He went over and opened the beer cabinet, looked at Louise, and offered her a cold pilsner.

She shook her head and heard a key being turned out in the back of the shop.

"That's her coming now," he said, nodding in that direction.

A woman around fiftyish with short chestnut-brown hair came in wearing a brightly colored scarf around her neck. She had a serious look in her eyes.

"I saw the car outside," she said and nodded to the street. Then she went over and stood next to Sebastian's father, putting her hands softly on his shoulders.

"We'll keep you informed, as soon as we know anything about the cause of the fire," Louise promised. "But it won't be until the beginning or middle of next week, at the earliest."

She debated for a short while whether to tell him that they were investigating the murder of the person who rented part of the warehouse next to the boathouse, but decided that wasn't information that would be useful right now.

"I'm very sorry," she said and placed her cell number on the bar counter, then began to walk toward the door.

His son had just turned seventeen. Now he didn't have the boy or his wife. Unbearable for a person to lose so much, she thought, as she drove back to drop off Svendsen's little angel in the garage, before hurrying up to the Homicide Department.

32

The jersey was orange and the leather pants still the same shabby black.

Louise shook her head when she met Sejr on the stairs. He lugged a pack of half-liter Coca-Cola in one hand and a briefcase in the other. Today the lenses of his glasses were blue, and his white hair stood straight up. He had his green military jacket over his arm and let it drag on the floor outside the office.

He's compensating, thought Louise. It's a distraction technique to move attention away from his skin's lack of pigmentation and his rather humble height. But the result was the exact opposite. It jumped out at you that he was paler and shorter than most. And older, too, she thought. Older than the kind of people who went around dressed like that. But it was exactly that part of him that she'd now come to like very much.

"Nick Hartmann wasn't alone in importing that fake furniture," he declared once he'd filled up the refrigerator. "That's stone sure."

She said no thank you when he offered her a cola, and instead turned on her electric kettle on the shelf behind her.

Fatigue had reached the stage where she'd become overtired and the thoughts whirled around in her head and wouldn't hang together right.

Sejr Gylling settled in behind his computer screens.

"I've just been down to the harbor with Michael Stig," he said.

Even though he'd tossed his jacket outside, the smell of fire still hung in his hair and on his pants. It was unmistakable and clung to everything that had been near the site of the fire.

"The furniture is damaged, but not burned, and there's a lot of it down there. A whole lot. He also had his business files lying around with shipping and freight papers. Unfortunately, there's nothing about how he channeled his business, but right now it doesn't matter."

Sejr opened the briefcase and took out a ring binder.

"On average, Nick Hartmann paid 660,000 dollars for a container. Depending on the exchange rate, that's about 4 million kroner, and if he sold the furniture as if it was authentic, it would have brought him in three or four times as much. But that much money didn't pass through his hands. Or else he had a Scrooge McDuck money vault hidden someplace, and I don't think so."

Louise listened to him as she poured boiling water over her tea bag.

"It's someone else who scored the profit, and he's only gotten a percentage."

"The bikers?"

"Could be! In those circles, they at least have the means for that kind of investment, and the profit is so considerable that it'd be an attractive business for them to go into. But, in all fairness, it could just as well be others who felt tempted by a quick payoff."

She could see how that made sense.

"But according to the shipping company I talked with the other day, there'd been two containers the last time."

Sejr nodded and emptied his cola.

"That means he had to shell out around 8 million kroner to Hong Kong, and that's also why I don't think he's been alone in this. If he had, his finances would have taken him to a whole different level."

"Is it even possible to dispose of so much fake furniture in that price range?" Louise asked.

Sejr Gylling sat a while thinking about it.

She'd been on the Web to research the cost of classic designer furniture. The Egg, which was the most expensive Arne Jacobsen chair, cost 30,000 kroner when covered in ordinary fabric and almost twice that in leather.

"It might be, actually, if you have your channels set up right. There's high demand in Sweden, Germany, and southern Europe," he said. "But obviously, at some point the market would get flooded, and that's why I don't see the sense in his suddenly doubling his purchase size. But maybe he had to boost his revenues."

He shrugged his shoulders.

"Maybe he got squeezed and needed some quick capital. Who knows? He may have overborrowed the last time he purchased and couldn't pay it back, and so he's gambled?"

Louise had difficulty keeping up. She wasn't well informed about that kind of crime, but then in the middle of her scattered thoughts she remembered an article she'd read a while back. Only now it made even less sense.

"You'd think it would be even harder," she said and told him about the article, which described how several English furniture houses openly sold reproduced classics. "Over there it's apparently legal to reproduce designs that are over twenty-five years old."

"Yes, but here you have to wait seventy years after the designer's death before it's legal," inserted Sejr. "It's true that you can go online and buy The Egg for around 8,000 kroner, and when it comes from an EU country it's not subject to extra taxes. It's also legal to bring it across the border, not so if it comes directly from China."

"Exactly," said Louise. "That's why I don't get how Hartmann could bring home so much money on knock-off furniture when you can buy them for a comparatively lower price without doing anything illegal. It doesn't make sense."

"Right, but I don't think Hartmann sold his furniture as copies. I'm guessing he kept the prices up and sold them on Internet auction sites here and abroad and maybe on eBay. If the copies were good enough, it would be damned hard to tell the difference, even though there'd always be something about the quality. And so, it's also quite possible that he worked with furniture dealers. We regularly see dealers getting into that kind of thing because it increases their own profits."

Louise recognized the footsteps in the hall, and had just turned to the door when Willumsen knocked quickly and stepped inside. Without apologizing for interrupting their conversation, he turned to Louise.

"Sebastian Styhne and Peter Nymann."

He tossed two photos on the table in front of her. Not the same that Bellahøj had had. Two different ones, but she could easily recognize them. Nymann still had his thin hair tied in a ponytail, and the picture of Sebastian was taken in front of the café on a summer day when New Harbor was full of life and crowds of people at the outdoor tables. He was wearing a T-shirt and shorts, and now she understood what Kent from Bellahøj had meant by a one-piece. The tattoos were like a wetsuit. It looked bizarre.

"Do we agree that these were the two men who were burned alive in the boathouse last night?" he asked, looking at her.

Louise nodded.

"Do we also agree that both were present the evening the girl held her party down at the sailing club?"

She nodded again.

"And that it was this bastard with the ponytail who chased the girl out in front of the van?"

He walked all the way up to her desk and stood pointing at the photos, waiting on her answer.

"Strictly speaking, we don't know if he followed her all the way up to the road," she said, but affirmed that he was the one Jonas saw running after Signe from down at the sailing club.

He tossed a plastic folder onto the table beside the photographs.

"The fire was deliberate," he said. "There were clear traces of flammable liquid in the front of the boathouse. I want you to drive out and have a talk with Britt Fasting-Thomsen immediately. We need to know what she was up to last night when the fire broke out."

Louise rolled her chair back a bit and shook her head, but Willumsen brushed her aside with a wave of his hand.

Sejr had withdrawn behind his two computer screens, and the lead investigator still spoke only to her.

"I'm all caught up concerning the accusations the girl's mother has expressed against the young punks. She blames them for her daughter's death."

Louise held out her hand to make him stop.

"Cut it out with all that," she said, irritated.

She rolled her chair toward him.

"It's true that Britt blames the boys for Signe's death, which is understandable enough. But she reproaches herself at least as much for even having the party. She needs to place some blame. It's nothing more than that."

"Exactly, and she's struck by an enormous grief, and that can easily turn into hatred," Willumsen pointed out.

Louise felt her eyes narrow as the anger came on. Everyone knew that once Willumsen got something into his head, he'd steamroll ahead without any concern for what he plowed over.

She raised her voice and stood up.

"Now listen to me for a second," she said. "Britt Fasting-Thomsen is going through hell. She's devastated, she doesn't filter what she says, she doesn't think about it before she says it out loud."

Willumsen nodded, but kept from interrupting.

"Believe me," Louise said, "she isn't capable of something like that. She has a hard enough time getting out of bed in the morning. How the hell could a woman like that plot murder?"

"Vengeance," he answered.

She shook her head, but sat back down.

"You don't understand what she's going through."

"Oh, shut up with all that female touchy-feely bullcrap," her boss exploded on her. "This isn't some social security office we're running here. Should I get one of the men to drive out to her, or do you think you can do your job?"

"Shut up yourself," she said feebly, feeling defeated.

Then she stood up to put her jacket on.

"In fact, maybe you're too personally involved," said Willumsen, more restrained but no less biting.

Louise shook her head. She imagined how he'd drag

Britt through his merciless wringer. So, it was at least better if she were there to manage how the blow landed.

"And what's all this about your taking time off next week?" he asked her when she'd come into the hall.

"I'll be back on Thursday," she said.

A disapproving wrinkle appeared on his face.

"I'd rather you took your vacation at some other point in time," he said.

He started walking back to his office.

"No," she said. "I have enough comp time for it, and I'm taking these days because it's when Jonas has fall break."

Doubtless, the lead investigator thought it was badly planned; and doubtless he was about to get worked up over it.

"Don't you think it's a little improper to go on vacation when the department is swamped with cases?" he asked, giving her a measured look.

"No," Louise said and shook her head. "I don't consider it any more improper than you being the only one allowed to lie in bed sleeping when the lieutenant and the rest of your group are called out on work in the middle of the night. But if you need personnel, you can call Lars Jørgensen and beg him to come in, or call in one of the ones you have on your list of people ready to take his place."

She took her cell phone out of her pocket, picturing in her mind the burned-out boathouse, the two charred corpses, and Britt Fasting-Thomsen's glazed eyes. Then she called Jonas and said that unfortunately it'd be another couple of hours before she could slip away.

What she didn't tell him was that she was on her way out to see if Signe's mother had an alibi that would rule her out as a suspect for arson, and possibly murder.

33

Dear Ulrik

How's it going with you? Thinking lots about you and Britt and hoping with all my heart that you can find a way forward. Not that I have the slightest idea how the hell one bears it when the very worst hits. I wish I were there for you. Thought of coming home when I heard about the accident—I'm sure you already know that from Britt, but obviously, she was right. It's a grief the two of you must work your way through. But my thoughts are with you.

Markus and I have made it to a little town called Mendocino. When we arrived yesterday afternoon, we went into a cafe to ask about hotels, and we almost never got out again. The barista talked our ears off and wanted to know all about Denmark and Scandinavia in general.

Maybe it's so far past high-season that people around here will talk with anyone at all to get their fix of social stimulation, but on the surface, it reminded me more of genuine interest and friendliness. Curiosity over something that's foreign. That sort of thing we're not so used to back home.

And it actually turned out that, although she didn't know everything about us, she did know a bit about our Lilliputian country. She was first and foremost very aware of who Caroline Wozniacki is. Her own son plays tennis and watches the big tournaments on TV, and understandably enough he's very taken by the Danish tennis star's talent, not to mention her good looks. But when the barista, on her own initiative, served my second espresso she surprised me by bringing up the Sachs-Smith family and the Termo-Lux scandal.

As I'm sure you're aware, the story has made its way over here because Frederik Sachs-Smith has currently released his first American feature film, and in that connection, he's been linked to the family business and the scandal back home. When something involves death and millions of dollars, it's just the sort of thing for the American media, and I'd guess the story's running even harder in Denmark?

You know I'm on leave and haven't given any thought to working while I was away—that's the whole damned reason for the trip!

And I know it's maybe asking a bit much of you under the circumstances, but I'm insanely interested in interviewing Frederik Sachs-Smith. I know you two know each other, so if it's not too presumptuous or doesn't seem wrong would you maybe put me in touch with him?

I'll call Britt this weekend once we've made it to Sacramento, where the cell phone coverage is hopefully a little better than here.

Warmest greetings
Camilla

34

Out in front of Central Station, Louise got into a taxi and asked to be driven to Strandvænget.

Cars were lined up bumper to bumper, and it took a long time to get across The Triangle, even though there were turning lanes on the right and the left. Very slowly they crawled to Østerbrogade. Her eyes followed the Friday shoppers, who walked along with Irma bags stuffed with groceries, and children in tow, but her thoughts were elsewhere. She pondered over how she could get the conversation going with Britt Fasting-Thomsen.

The fatal fire was already on the newspapers' online versions, although without the names of the deceased. The local police in Næstved still hadn't informed Peter Nymann's parents.

Then the light turned green and the taxi driver got to it, using a passing lane to swing around the line of cars and picking up speed.

She spotted Britt while she was still paying. Signe's mother was in the garden with a wheelbarrow, sweeping leaves together. Louise could see her stop in mid-movement when she caught sight of the taxi. Stood a little noncommittally and leaned on the broom, but set it aside and waved as Louise came in through the garden gate. She still had dark circles under her eyes and looked sickly, as if she'd lost weight, as if all life had been sapped out of her body.

"Hi," said Louise, stretching out her hand to avoid the hug that Britt spread her arms out for.

"Hey."

Britt took her hand and, straight off, offered her coffee. She didn't ask Louise what had made her stop by on a Friday afternoon—maybe thought she was visiting out of a sense of duty, or that Camilla had sent her.

She should have said from the beginning that she'd come on official business, thought Louise, so it would have been understood, whereas now Britt took her jacket and found a hanger.

"I was so glad to get to talk with your medical examiner friend. It was very thoughtful of you to bring him out here with you. None of the officers from out in Bellahøj had thought of doing that," she said, then asked whether Louise had gotten hold of Ulrik in Iceland.

She shook her head and followed her in through the living room. Hadn't even tried since the other night. After the fire, she hadn't really had a free moment. He hadn't called her back, either, after she'd left a message.

"It was his building that burned down over at the harbor last night," said Britt as she put the water on. "I don't know if you've heard?"

Louise nodded but wasn't quick enough to seize the opportunity.

"The insurance company was by this morning," said Britt. "But I don't know anything about all that, and Ulrik can't get a flight home until tomorrow. I think he's landing around eleven. It must take around three hours to fly home from Reykjavik."

She asked if instant was all right with her, and Louise nodded.

There was dust on the tabletops and on the lamp shade over the dining table. It swirled in the air a bit when Louise unwound her long scarf and set it over the chair.

"It's actually the fire I came to talk to you about," she began.

She nodded when Britt asked if she'd like milk in her coffee.

"Two young people burned to death down in the boathouse next to your husband's warehouse, and our crime technicians recently determined that the fire was set on purpose."

Louise waited a moment.

"Britt, I have to ask you what you were doing last night."

Britt stopped on her way to the table with the coffee cups. Steam rose from the two mugs. They must be burning her fingers, thought Louise, who stood up and took the mugs out of her hands.

"I was here," Britt finally said.

She came over and sat down.

"No one told me that anyone died in the fire."

Louise shook her head and folded her hands around her mug.

"Two boys died in the flames."

They sat a bit.

Louise hoped that Britt might say something, but she was silent and sat unmoving with her eyes on her coffee. A column of steam lazily curled upward and vanished.

Silence enveloped the house. There was neither traffic noise nor clattering from the S-train that passed not far from there.

Louise cleared her throat to break the silence.

"It concerns two of the boys who were present that night down at the sailing club," she said, adding that one of the deceased was the one Jonas saw running after Signe.

Britt still didn't look at her, only shook her head despondently.

"You understand, don't you, why I have to ask you about your activities?"

Britt stopped shaking her head. Just sat.

"What did you do last night?" Louise repeated and felt a queasiness in the pit of her stomach.

"I was home all evening," she finally answered. "You were here. You know I was home."

Now she looked at Louise with eyes empty of sparkle and life.

"I didn't go down and set fire to my husband's property. I went up to bed after you left."

Louise nodded and lifted her mug. Wanted to put a hand on her arm, but didn't.

"Ulrik tossed the boys out the same day he discovered they were staying in his building. He asked them to move all their things and disappear. There wasn't anyone down in his boathouse anymore," she said, raising her voice to make Louise understand.

"There was flammable liquid poured on the floor and over the sofa they left behind, and the techs believe that a piece of firewood was thrown through the window and set off an explosion, which led to the fire."

Britt held Louise's eyes, and a little smile passed across the corner of her mouth.

"And you suspect me of being behind it?" she asked.

"No, you're not a suspect. We just need to rule you out," she corrected. "The lead investigator is right to think that you could harbor a strong desire to do something like this. But we've just begun the investigation and are starting to form some ideas of what might motivate someone to burn down the building with two people inside it. And this is just one of the possibilities that we need to consider."

Britt nodded.

"I can see where I'd be a likely candidate," she conceded and looked straight ahead.

"You do have a motive," said Louise. "But there are other possibilities. The fire might be connected to the part of the warehouse that Ulrik rented out. We're following that trail, too."

"I understand."

"What were you doing between the hours of eleven and twelve last night?"

Britt said nothing, just sat up a little straighter in the chair and closed her eyes.

Louise took her pad out of her bag and a pen from an outside pocket.

"I'm sorry to drag you through this," she said.

"It's completely all right. I understand."

Britt opened her eyes again.

"I just can't remember doing anything."

"It was around five thirty when we left you yesterday," Louise helped. "What did you do the rest of the evening?"

"I was just here. I slept," Britt answered quickly. "I'd taken some pretty strong sleeping pills," she admitted after thinking it over. "I'm only supposed to take one, but I took two. That wasn't very long after you left. I was pretty out of it, and I have no idea what happened around me. Didn't even hear the sirens. I would have, if it was as intense as you say."

Louise nodded. Of course, she would have.

"Is there anyone who can confirm that you stayed in your house the whole evening?"

"No."

She shook her head.

"Ulrik's not home."

"Did you talk with anyone?"

"No."

"Either on your cell phone or landline?"

"No, not as far as I recall."

"Did you drive anywhere?"

"You mean while I was knocked out on sleeping pills? No, I didn't."

Louise smiled at her, stuck her pad back in her bag, and said she'd like to have permission to look over her car on the way out.

"You're welcome to. The keys are on the bureau," Britt said.

She walked with her out to the entryway.

Louise almost forgot her scarf on the back of the chair, and when she came into the hall Britt was already putting on a sweater and sticking her feet into the rubber boots she'd worn as she went around sweeping.

The black Golf was at most a year old and still had that new-car smell as Louise stuck her head in and looked around. On the front seat, there was a Dior lipstick and a little perfume sample. Typical lady's car, she thought. The back seat was empty and clean.

Truthfully, it was mostly for Willumsen's sake that she went through the car. But then it would be over with. Afterward she and Jonas would take off for the country and enjoy the extra vacation days.

She slammed the door shut and opened the trunk. Took a step back and looked at Britt.

"Do you usually drive around with a spare can in your car?"

Britt shook her head.

"By and large, I don't drive around much. I mostly bike. It's only if I have to go on longer trips that I take the car."

"There's a can of gasoline in the back of your car."

She waved Britt over.

No reaction at all. There was nothing to trace on her face or in her eyes, which just stared at Louise uncomprehendingly. But then she slowly walked over to the car and leaned forward a bit to look into the trunk.

"I don't know anything about that," she answered and looked up at Louise. "I don't have one of those."

Louise closed the trunk with the sleeve of her sweater. She felt irritation, and just then the queasiness came back.

"Britt, what the hell?"

They stood together a moment.

"I don't know anything about that can," she repeated then shook her head. "Never seen it before."

Then she turned to the empty spot where the Audi was usually parked and gestured with her hands.

"Maybe it's Ulrik's. His car's at the airport. He may have put the gas can over in my car to have space for his luggage. Otherwise, I don't know where it came from."

Louise walked over and put her arms around her. She was as thin as a baby bird and stood there with her head bowed.

"Were you down at the harbor last night?"

She stepped back a little and looked at Britt.

"How could I know anyone was sleeping down there?" Britt asked sensibly.

Her eyes were blank and she suddenly seemed like a little girl that someone had forgotten to take home with them.

"You couldn't have known, unless you were keeping an eye on the boathouse and saw them go in there."

"I didn't. I haven't even been down to the harbor since the night we held the party, and I probably never will."

"I need to have your car brought in for a closer inspection," Louise said apologetically.

"Absolutely," said Britt quickly and dried her eyes. "That's understandable. I don't have anything to hide from you, and I'll just be glad if you can find out where that gas can came from so I don't get mixed up in all this."

Louise stepped aside and found Frandsen's number in her contacts. Then she turned her back to Britt, while she talked with the chief of the Center for Forensic Services. Not that she needed to be discreet, she discovered when she'd finished speaking. Britt had already walked over to the front door and stood there waiting to go into the warm house.

"Someone is coming to pick up your car within the next hour."

Britt nodded, and Louise went up the steps to the weathered porch and gave her a hug before saying good-bye.

"It's good that Ulrik will be back tomorrow. Call if there's anything. Jonas and I are driving down to my parents' in the country tonight. It's fall break, you know, so we'll be down there till Wednesday, but I'll have my cell phone with me."

Britt nodded and smiled, so that her lips drew a precise, thin line across her mouth.

"I'm terribly sorry if I've created problems for you. But

I wasn't anywhere last night," she said and opened the front door to go inside. "Just here."

As Louise walked down toward Svanemølle Harbor, darkness was beginning to fall. She called Willumsen's cell, and when it went to voice mail, she left a message informing him that she'd asked to have Britt Fasting-Thomsen's car brought in for closer inspection, even though she said she'd been home the entire evening.

Before finishing the message, she reminded him that she wouldn't be back to work again until Thursday. "Have a good weekend," she said before hanging up. Then she called Jonas and told him she was on her way and promised him they'd make it out to the country before eight o'clock, so they could watch *Dancing with the Stars*.

35

On Saturday, Louise lay on the sofa. She was trying to look like she was reading, but most of the time she slept.

Her father had taken Jonas over to Skjoldenæsholm Golf Center in a nearby town. First, they'd eaten lunch at Kudskehuset and after that struggled up Gyldenløveshøj, which her father in his usual school teacher manner taught the boy was the highest point on Zealand. There, to her father's great delight, they'd sat for hours, each with a pair of binoculars, and when they arrived back home in the afternoon practically frozen to death, they were ecstatic over all they'd seen.

Venison was on the evening's menu, and afterward they played Scrabble until Louise was ready to fall out of her seat.

Mik had called to talk about their Sunday plans, and had been mildly disappointed to learn they wouldn't be making it out to Holbæk at the break of dawn. Louise wanted to be allowed to sleep in until she woke up, then start the day easy.

✕

On Sunday morning, the car radio played as Louise and Jonas drove across the Munkholm Bridge. The sun was low and glared in their eyes underneath their sun visors. She'd shown him the place she used to drive to on warm summer nights to have ice cream and visit with friends when she was younger. Even though he didn't come right out and say it, she could tell that Jonas was so much of a city boy that he couldn't imagine having to drive ten miles on a motorbike to hang out and have ice cream.

Louise smiled at him and took in the view over the water. The leaves were beginning to fall off the trees, and the ice cream stand was closed. Still it was pretty, and the light shimmered as they drove through the forest, where the half-naked branches created a filter for the sun's beams.

She swung to the left up toward Dragerup and let her eyes take in the fields. The road was narrow and curvy, small gravel roads pushed the farms back a little from the main road, off toward the water, and Holbæk Fjord glimmered behind the freshly plowed fields.

Mik's red three-winged farmhouse was on the left, idyllic with its thatched roofs and half-timbers, but Louise was most captivated by the view from his yard, where fields stretched off into the distance, all the way to the forest.

The first time she'd visited him, there'd been a bench up against the wall of the house, so they could sit there and take in a panoramic view. The only minus was that the bench was the kind made from split and planed tree trunks, and across its back in fat letters were burned the words, "Dad's Beer Bench."

For his birthday last year, Louise had presented Mik with a more neutral bench with a matching table and two chairs.

That evening, they'd brought the grill from the garden and sat out in his yard and eaten, instead of having their view blocked by tall trees.

As usual, the pointer was the first to come rushing out to greet them as soon as they'd parked and gotten out in the yard. A moment later Mik came out from the kitchen door. He was wearing clogs, a black crewneck sweater, and a new pair of blue jeans. All shaven and nice-smelling, she realized when he came over with a smile and gave her a hug and a warm kiss on the mouth.

The yellow Lab had also come out, even though she was a bit more hesitant.

Jonas was already occupied with the dogs.

"How are the puppies doing?" he asked.

He let himself be embraced by Mik, who obviously liked him and had offered several times to come into the city and stay with Jonas if Louise had something to do. But so far there hadn't been a something.

"They're in the mud room. You're welcome to go see them."

Jonas ran across the yard. Once he'd disappeared, Mik pulled Louise closer and kissed her a bit more seriously. He put his arm around her shoulder, and they walked to the house.

Mik smiled when he saw Jonas sitting on the floor with the five puppies jumping up around him, three black and two yellow. One of the small light-colored ones tried to crawl up on him, but its back legs couldn't make it up, so every time it tried it fell back down. At last Jonas took pity on it and lifted it into his lap.

Louise shook her head and smiled when, in utter bliss, he bent over and put his cheek against the puppy's soft fur.

Mik's puppies had arrived last weekend, and in the coming week they'd be picked up by their new families. Now—standing and looking at such a sweet litter of puppies—was exactly the time when Louise would suddenly have a hard time remembering why she didn't want a dog.

Fortunately, it always came to her mind rather quickly that they needed to be cared for and taken outside on a regular basis, and she knew she couldn't live up to the responsibility. Mik had offered her the pick of the litter, otherwise.

"Have they all been sold?"

He squatted down and petted one of the black ones.

Mik nodded and sent the pointer out in the yard. His hunting dog wasn't as much of an indoors-dog as the others, but it hated to miss out on pats and loving, so it had barged in and was too rough around the little puppies.

"Yes," said Mik. "Except Dina."

He pointed to the puppy that Jonas sat fondling.

"The vet thinks she's deaf, or at least partially deaf. So, she won't make it as a hunting dog, and no one wants to pay that kind of money for a dog that can't hear properly. Other breeders would probably euthanize her, but I don't have the heart for it."

Jonas looked up at Mik.

"You can't even tell she's deaf," he said.

Mik shook his head and explained that it wouldn't be a problem, either, until her owner wanted to start training her.

※

After lunch, they took a long walk in the woods with the pointer zigzagging around them. Strictly speaking, one wasn't supposed to have a dog off leash, but Mik's hunting dogs obeyed him—they'd come even if he whistled for them from a hundred yards away; if he told them to sit, they'd stay sitting until he released them, even if several hours passed and he was out of sight the whole time.

That's why he scorned the rules and let his dog run free. Jonas tried to keep up with it, and tossed sticks for it—in between tree trunks and onto the soft forest floor.

Louise and Mik held hands and lagged behind.

"How are things in the city?" asked Mik. "It can't be so great living there. Gang wars are becoming the daily fare."

Louise smiled at him and shook her head.

"It's not that bad yet."

"Don't you worry about something happening to Jonas?" he asked and gave her a serious look.

"That's no worse, either," she snapped when she saw where he was headed. "And anyhow, the plan isn't for Jonas to stay with me. He's there for now, but sometime in the new year we'll find a more permanent solution."

"He likes being with you," Mik said and squeezed her hand. "You can't go shipping him off to some people he doesn't even know!"

Louise let go of his hand and stuck her hands in her jacket pockets. She kicked a small stone, which skidded across the gravel and disappeared in the tall grass.

"There's no other option," she said. "I really, really like Jonas. I grow more and more attached to him every passing day, and I want the very best for him. And the very best for him is not living with me. I keep letting him down. One day I'm not home at dinner time, another day I'm not home to help him with homework. There's always something that gets in the way of our plans. I can't do it. It's not the way he should grow up. He just needs to get over everything that's happened, then we'll find another solution together."

"You're running from your responsibility," Mik said quietly.

She turned to him.

"I don't have any damned responsibility to be running from. That's exactly how I've chosen to arrange it. I'm putting myself at Jonas's disposal, but I sure as hell haven't forsaken any responsibility."

"The kid's lost both his parents. There's no one but you—so that's plenty of responsibility!"

He shook his head in frustration.

"Why are you being stubborn?" she asked without looking at him.

"Because there is another option. You can move out here. There's plenty of space, and then we could share the responsibility. Just look at him!"

The boy and the dog both panted for air, but still they bounced and ran along. Jonas, who mostly sat in his room absorbed in his books or computer games, had surprisingly red cheeks and glistening eyes. He tossed a stick in a high arc between the trees, and the dog gladly ran after it.

"It's not so simple," she said.

She let Mik fish her hand out of her pocket.

"Yes, if you'll let it be, it's very simple. You could get transferred and work up here."

"I can't leave Frederiksberg. And Jonas goes to school in the city."

"It might be good for him to switch schools. He still seems to be struggling with losing his friend. And he just told me that the boathouse where those teens stayed burned down a few days ago."

Louise nodded. Jonas had heard about it from some friends at school. She wasn't the one who'd told him.

"It seems to be on his mind all the time," he said.

Of course it was, thought Louise, but it was irritating to have Mik remind her of it.

"Could it have been one of the students from school who set fire to the boathouse, to avenge what happened to the girl?"

Louise looked at him in surprise, but shook her head.

"The boys were thrown out from down there right after the attack. No one was staying in the boathouse any longer."

Suddenly a thought started to stir in her, pushing Mik and everything he was saying into the background.

Could it have been one or more of the boys in the boathouse who'd set fire to it themselves, in response to being thrown out? Clearly, they wouldn't have meant to kill their friends, but it seemed none of them knew that Peter Nymann and Sebastian Styhne had spent the night down there. They'd all reacted as if no one went there anymore. It might be worth checking out when she was back, she thought, before Willumsen single-mindedly went after Britt, staring himself blind in her direction.

Louise nodded to herself as she walked and the new bricks fell into place. Mik may have thought he'd given her something to think about regarding Jonas and her own plans for the future. At any rate, he let the subject rest. When they got home he served them coffee and cinnamon pastries from the bakery, then he got started tying rosemary around a large leg of lamb that needed to go in the oven.

❧

"Are you starting to see more of Flemming Larsen?" Mik asked after they'd eaten and were sitting with the rest of their wine.

She'd been waiting for the question to pop up sooner or later, and shook her head.

"We work together, so we see each other occasionally. Same as it's always been."

She could tell that Mik wanted to press the issue, but thought better of it. Instead, he offered to make a pot of coffee.

She shook her head and looked at her watch.

Jonas was on the floor out in the mud room, petting a puppy that lay on his chest as if it had fallen from the ceiling with its legs splayed out in all directions. It nipped at the scarf around his neck.

They needed to be getting back to Hvalsø. She carried the dishes out to the sink.

Mik came over and stood behind her, then put his arms around her and let his cheek rest against hers.

"I'm crazy about you," he whispered.

She closed her eyes.

She turned and put her arms around him and her cheek against his chest. They stood that way until she pulled herself back a little and looked up into his narrow face and warm eyes.

"I can't move up here," she said.

She looked at him seriously, trying to read whether he understood she really meant it. Right now, love wasn't enough to make her leave the place where she had her routine and the life she'd chosen for herself.

"I'm happy where I am," she said.

He nodded and held her close, until she turned her face toward the mud room and called for Jonas to get his things together so they could head out.

Mik kissed her hair before he let go.

They walked out to the mud room, where Jonas carefully

set the puppy back in its temporary enclosure. He stood a while looking at it, then grabbed his bag with his PS2 and the books he'd brought with him, but hadn't had any use for. Then he gave Mik an extra hug and followed Louise out the door to the yard.

Yet another sign of that politeness that broke her heart. With most other children, the parents would first have to go through a long discussion about why they really did have to leave, even if they were having so much fun. That's not how it was with Jonas. When Louise said they were leaving, he came without complaint.

She gave his arm a tender squeeze before closing the car door for him.

Monday morning a brisk wind blew, and it bit at their cheeks as Louise and Jonas biked through the forest out toward Avnsø Lake. The fall foliage turned the forest floor golden, as if a blanket had been thrown over the ground.

They had to brake on their way down the hill to Helvigstruphuset, a lovely thatched cottage with a water pump in the yard. Previously, it had been completely primitive, without electricity or running water, but now it had been fixed up and functioned as a summerhouse. Their bike tires kicked up small stones. Jonas passed her, but waited until he was down the hill before braking hard, so his back wheel slid out and sent gravel spraying up in a great cloud.

Farther on they passed the fir plantation, where the roe deer went around and bit the tops off the trees. Louise caught sight of a large buck before they'd made it all the way there. She got Jonas to stop so they could enjoy him a little before he saw them.

What Louise loved about Bistrup Forest was that you mostly had it to yourself. She knew every forest road, every trail, every shortcut. And when she'd been in the city too long, it was Avnsø Lake she longed for.

Now the buck lifted his head. Sniffed and pointed his ears in their direction, and then he sprang. So elegant. You could see the tensed muscles under his short, grayish brown hair.

When they turned off for the lake, black and deep in between the trees, Louise's cell phone started to ring in her pocket. The lieutenant's name glowed in the display.

"I'm sorry to bother you on vacation," he said quickly. "But I thought you'd want to be kept in the loop. We've just gotten a report from the crime techs concerning the gas can you found in the back of Britt Fasting-Thomsen's Golf."

Louise jumped off her bike. Jonas was already down at the lake throwing stones in the water.

"It's the same color and brand as a matching gas can that was found a few feet away from the fire site. A German brand that Aldi had in their flyer last week. Willumsen is ready to get started on an interrogation and a search of the home out in Svanemølle."

Louise swept her hand through her hair, which was matted and ruffled and blown about her head. Her bike was propped against her right thigh, and she was breathing heavily.

Damn it all to hell, she thought, and heard Jonas call from down at the lake.

"I'm coming in," she said. "There can be lots of reasons why she had a perfectly ordinary gas can that anyone could have gotten hold of over the course of the week. Couldn't you get Willumsen to hold off until I'm back in the city?"

Suhr laughed on the other end.

"You know him! I think he's planning on doing the interrogation himself."

Hmm, yes, he would, thought Louise.

The lieutenant told her that Sejr was about to go through
some old vouchers in Nick Hartmann's papers, and Toft and
Michael Stig were trying to track down the furniture manu-
facturer out in Hong Kong.

"So, it's only Willumsen who's free, and I think he's
looking forward to a chat with Britt Fasting-Thomsen."

Right, Louise could imagine that.

She sighed and tried to collect her thoughts.

Jonas called again, and there was the sound of a large
stone splashing.

"Suggest to Willumsen that he have a talk with Ulrik
Fasting-Thomsen instead, and find out how he knows Nick
Hartmann. He was away when I wanted to talk with him.
Then I'll talk with Britt."

She turned her bike and started heading back up the hill.

"Sounds like I shouldn't have called. I didn't mean to interrupt your vacation!" her boss said with a dry laugh.

Shit yeah, she thought.

"No, you should definitely call," she said.

If Suhr had felt it was a terrific idea to put Britt through
Willumsen's wringer, Louise thought, then he damned well
wouldn't have called and warned her.

The lieutenant had enough empathy and understanding to
want to spare Signe's mother from that fate. At least until it
was certain she was connected to what had happened down at
the harbor.

Louise called Jonas, and while they climbed up the hill, she apologized for having to drive back into the city.

"Do you want to go with me, or would you rather stay here?" she asked and looked at him as he pushed his bike up.

"Couldn't I just go to Mik's by myself?" he asked, apparently very interested in going back and seeing the puppies before they disappeared with their new families.

Best not, she thought, not very eager for those two to form an alliance that would make it even harder for her to keep her decision.

"He has to work, too," she reminded him.

"Yeah, but he usually comes home early," he said.

He's right about that, thought Louise. There weren't nearly as many long days for the police in Holbæk.

"I could take the train, if he'd rather not pick me up," he suggested as they biked home.

"Couldn't you wait, and we'll go up there together some other time?" Louise said.

She hit a big hole in the forest road and she nearly lost her balance.

"Then the puppies wouldn't be there," he said, trying to hide his frustration behind a polite, friendly manner.

❧

"She'll give you the run-around," snarled Willumsen, irritated when Louise reached Police Headquarters.

She'd abandoned her Saab along the curb without taking the time to get a parking sticker for it.

She didn't answer him.

Willumsen closed the door to his office behind them and pointed to a chair over by the window.

"Shouldn't you just take some time off, now that things are heating up," he muttered with his back to her and walked around his desk to sit down.

He picked up some papers and looked at her.

"I want an explanation for why Britt Fasting-Thomsen suddenly has a spare can that's a perfect match to the one we suspect held the flammable liquid that set the fire, when she by her own admission does not keep a spare can in the back of her car, or even own one."

Louise nodded. She agreed that it would be useful to have an explanation on that matter.

"I didn't get the sense she was trying to hide anything when I was there on Friday," she said, adding that Britt didn't, on the other hand, say very much while she was there. "I can drive over to her right now."

The lead investigator nodded and took a deep breath before leaning forward a bit.

"I know perfectly well what Britt Fasting-Thomsen has been through," he said. "But if a thirst for vengeance has made her set fire to the boathouse and burn the two young people in there to death, then we need to get hold of her."

Louise nodded.

"Yes, but the boys were thrown out of that boathouse. How could she know that anyone was lying in there asleep?"

"That's not for me to answer. I just want to know how she suddenly got a spare can in the back of her car, if it's not something she usually drives around with," said Willumsen. "Any deviation from the normal is interesting right now. It's actually the most important thing. And if we get a reasonable explanation, then fine."

Louise stood up and started walking for the door.

"By the way, her husband is on his way in here," he

added as she was reaching for the knob. "I have an appointment with him in a quarter of an hour, and so hopefully we'll learn a little more about Nick Hartmann and that business he had going."

Louise was about to close the door behind her when Willumsen tossed out the news that Lars Jørgensen had just extended his sick leave.

"So, he's not ready for us to start pulling him back yet," he said, referring to her parting comment on Friday.

"How long?" Louise asked out of curiosity and took a couple of steps back into the office.

"To start with, fourteen more days."

Oh, hell, she thought, feeling bad for her partner. She hadn't called him, even though she'd thought of it several times, but something always got in the way. And given the pace at which her days rolled by, she didn't have much energy left for collegial care. She had to get around to calling him, or else he'd end up feeling that the entire Homicide Department had turned their backs on him.

The expression on Willumsen's face turned hard again.

"My recommendation is that he look for another department. He's asked to be put on reduced hours, so he can hold things together at home. But I've denied the request. We can't work with that kind of thing around here."

"We could at least try," suggested Louise and instinctively took a step back.

"Yes, we could indeed. We could also try to push for having a playroom installed in the basement, so all the staff could bring their kids to work with them when they don't have someone to watch them," he said. "Or, maybe, every department should get its own nanny."

She looked at him and felt irritated, but wouldn't be provoked.

"There might be room for a little flexibility without harming anything," she said.

"People should think a little before they apply for a job like this—especially if they have children."

Louise shook her head at him. The lead investigator had always had it easy. His daughter, Helle, was nearly grown up, and it was his wife, Annelise, who'd taken care of her when she was a girl. He had no idea what it was like to have that responsibility and manage a household. Annelise had a part-time job at the Church Mission, where she sold used clothing three days a week, so he ought to shut up, she thought. And then there were the periods when his wife had been sick, hit with several bouts of stomach cancer. During those months, Willumsen had left early to take her to the hospital for her chemo.

But that was obviously something different, she thought, starting to close the door again.

"When you're finished over on Strandvænget," Willumsen continued, "it might be worth looking into whether any of the other three boys feel that they've been harassed by Britt Fasting-Thomsen after the party down at the sailing club."

"Harassed!"

Louise turned to him.

"Maybe you should go out and talk to her yourself," she said. "Listen, she's going through hell. She can't even take care of herself. The whole house is practically covered in dust, and she spends most of her time up in her room in bed."

She paused a moment, then she collected herself enough to say that it would become him to be just a little bit sympathetic.

"Even her husband admits she's changed since their

daughter's death. It's not something I just sat around and came up with," he said. "Hell, I've never met the wife."

No, exactly, Louise thought and left.

"If she can't answer for herself, then I'm sending a team out to search the house," he yelled after her. "Then they could look for that Aldi receipt. And rags like the ones that were wrapped around the firewood and thrown in to ignite the boathouse and warehouse. What do I want? Whatever will get us something more on her."

Louise didn't even stop by her office before leaving the department and driving out to Svanemølle.

36

Once again, they sat in Britt's kitchen. This time without coffee and with dirty dishes in the sink.

"I really don't know where the gas can came from," said Britt.

"What does Ulrik say? Does he know anything about it?"

Louise looked at her patiently. There was no resistance to detect, but no help from her, either.

"He's never seen it before, either. But he says we need to get hold of a lawyer if the police keep thinking that I had something to do with the fire."

"Let's just see," Louise said to calm her. "But it would be an enormous help if you could think of anyone who could confirm that you stayed home all evening. As long as we don't have any other leads, I can't cross you off the list, and I need to have your activities accounted for."

It seemed as though Britt didn't grasp the seriousness. The whole time there was a distance in her tone of voice, as if Louise's questions really didn't have anything to do with her.

Louise had already asked if Britt had spoken with any-one on the telephone. But she hadn't. Otherwise, that would have been enough to confirm that she'd been in her house. It wasn't enough to check the cell tower, because she could have left her cell phone sitting at home.

"Did you send or receive any texts?" Louise asked and looked at her.

"I don't think so, but you're welcome to look."

She stood up and got her cell phone, which was lying on the buffet in the living room.

Louise watched her come back. Despondency weighed so heavily on her that she seemed not to care, leading all of Louise's questions to a dead end.

There were no new messages on her cell phone.

"I didn't do anything other than lie up in my bed," she said.

She sat down on the chair and folded her arms across her chest.

"I don't care to be in touch with anyone. My thoughts were on my daughter, and I had a bunch of images in my head that occupied me. I fell asleep quickly."

Louise knew everything that Flemming had told her must have set a lot of thoughts in motion. She still felt that the medical examiner had been too detailed. It was much too painful for a mother who'd just lost her daughter.

"Did you watch anything on TV? Can you remember any programs from Thursday?"

Britt leaned over the table a bit and looked at Louise.

"I've stopped watching TV," she said with a serious look in her eyes. "You have to understand, for me the world came to a halt three weeks ago. I don't keep up with anything."

Louise struggled to hold back a growing irritation, and instead tried a new approach.

"Should we take a look at your computer? If you, for instance, e-mailed with Camilla or were on Facebook around midnight, then it couldn't have been you down at the harbor, and we could rule you out of the investigation."

Britt nodded slowly and stood up.

"You're welcome to have a look, but I was lying asleep."

Now she was the one who seemed irritated, as if Louise had a hard time understanding what was being said to her.

Louise left her things in the kitchen and followed Britt out through the living room and up the stairs to the second floor. The steps had carpeting held down by thin brass strips. They came up to a wide landing that was furnished with a cabinet and a several-feet-tall mirror with an ornately carved brass frame. The style was elegant and yet modern. In a nook with natural lighting, there was a large, winged armchair in worn cognac-colored leather, and on the table, there was a stack of old business sections from a variety of newspapers.

They walked down to the room at the end. It was a large bedroom with a white-brick balcony beyond the multi-paneled double doors. Before they made it all the way there, they passed Signe's room. Her name was on the door, but it was closed and Britt walked right by without looking at it. Inside her own bedroom, she pointed to a glass desk over by the window, with a view of the water.

"Ulrik has his own office down on the opposite end. That's my computer over there," she said and nodded to a white Mac. "There's no password, so you can just go in."

The room was light, and a pair of large skylights over the bed made Louise look up.

"They're rain-sensing," said Britt. She explained that you could lie and fall asleep under the open sky, and if it started to rain the windows would close by themselves. "I usually lie here in bed and look up at the sky."

Louise walked over and opened the Mac's e-mail folders. She quickly confirmed that there was only spam coming in and nothing going out over the course of that night.

"Can't you think of anything? It doesn't make any difference what, just as long as it shows you were home all evening," she said desperately.

Britt sat on the edge of the bed with her chin on her chest, as if she were about to fall asleep.

"It's awfully nice of you," she said.

She straightened up and leaned back a little, her weight resting on her arms.

"I know you're trying to help me. But I was here all evening and all night. I have no witnesses for it, and there's nothing more to be said. I can't stamp my feet and conjure up someone who doesn't exist, so I'll have to take it from here and be forced to get hold of a lawyer, like Ulrik says."

Louise nodded and closed the Mac.

"That may be a good idea," she conceded as they walked down the stairs together.

When they said good-bye in the entryway, Louise felt a heaviness inside her. There was a striking indifference behind the fine features of Britt's face; the blood vessels at her temples were visible. As if she's tossed in the towel, thought Louise. She felt a little miffed that of the two of them she seemed to be the one more interested in finding an alibi for Britt Fasting-Thomsen, and a plausible explanation for how a gas can ended up in the back of her car.

Willumsen had sent a message that they'd gotten a search warrant, and that Toft was on his way out there with three officers. There wasn't really much more Louise could do to help Signe's mom.

37

She drove down along the harbor and in past the Power Station, her thoughts circling around Britt. She understood perfectly well that it was time to let go of their private relationship, or else make things even more complicated if she was going to stay on the case. But it was hard not to worry about her.

Willumsen called her cell, but she let it lie on the front seat and buzz, didn't have the energy for him.

She turned right and crossed the train tracks on her way up to Strand Boulevard, waited at the light until she could swing to the left, then slowed down and kept her eyes on the house numbers on the opposite side. Before everyone got carried away with their own ideas, she wanted to find some of the boys on her way back and hear whether they knew anything about that green gas can down at the harbor.

She rang for Vigdís Ólafsdóttir and Jón Vigdísarson's apartment, even though he was in school and possibly hadn't even come home yet. A woman's clear voice said hello, and soon after the door buzzed open.

Up on the fourth floor, Jón's mother stood on the stairs and received her. Vigdís Ólafsdóttir was short, with a slightly pinched but pretty face, her lips painted red in contrast to her blond hair and intense, penetratingly blue eyes. There was something about her that made Louise think of the myths about The Hidden People, who meant so much in Icelandic superstition that people literally believed they could bring a halt to building activities that disturbed nature.

There was nothing supernatural about Vigdís Ólafsdóttir; she merely invited Louise into her large kitchen and said that her son and his friends were in his room.

"They're so depressed," she said sadly and told her they were on their way to see Sebastian's father in New Harbor. "He's holding a small gathering for all the friends later in the afternoon."

Loud, thumping rhythms spilled through the boy's door, and Louise heard someone's voice and the clinking of bottles penetrate the solid sound barrier.

She followed the mother, who walked over and knocked on the door.

The room was thick with smoke. Thomas Jørgensen, the boy who'd kicked Britt and broken her cheekbone, sat on the floor. His eyes were red, and it must have been many hours since he was sober.

Slowly he turned his gaze toward Louise, then just stared at her without focusing. His shirt sleeves were pushed up, and black tattoo lines played over his arms when he flexed and unflexed the muscles, like a bad habit he no longer even noticed himself doing.

Jón sat on the bed, and beside him was Kenneth Thim, who Louise hadn't met before. Each of them had a beer bottle in hand and a joint between their fingers. They were more than a little drunk, and the sweet smell of marijuana hung in the air.

Louise couldn't say she blamed them. They'd been clob-
bered and were out of commission. No one should have
been in that damned boathouse, and maybe it crossed their
minds that it could just as easily have been them sleeping it
off down there, even though they'd been forbidden.

Jón's mother looked a little uneasy and shrugged her
shoulders apologetically, but Louise walked in and shut the
door behind her.

Green gas can. None of them knew anything about it.
She sat a bit and let her eyes roam. What had she expected?
That they'd straight away confess to burning down the
boathouse, not knowing that their friends were in there
sleeping?

"Do any of you know Nick Hartmann?" she asked, then
explained that he was the one who rented space in the warehouse next to the boathouse.

Thomas Jørgensen popped open another beer. He leaned
his neck back so his head rested against the wall, then concentrated his look on Louise, as if he'd only realized she
was there when she'd started to talk again.

No one said anything.

"Have you seen anyone come down to the warehouse?"

She looked at them and gauged where she had the best
chance of getting through. At first, Jón seemed to be the
soberest one, but on the other hand he looked to be the most
stoned—his pupils were tiny and his head hung down.

The boys sat in silence, close to what Louise would describe as unreachable. They shook their heads. Didn't know
anything about anything. Hadn't seen anyone and knew
nothing.

"Someone set fire to your clubhouse," she said in a new
effort to get through. "The fire didn't break out on its own—
it was set. And the person who did it will presumably be

charged with double homicide. I take it you're at least as interested in finding out who that person is, so the concerned party can be punished."

"I'll bash the psychopath, if you just find him," said Thomas Jørgensen from down on the floor.

To illustrate what he meant, he reached out for an iron pipe that was in the corner and started beating the air with it. But it was heavy and tumbled from him when he tried to switch hands. When it fell, it made a clanging noise and left a mark in the floor.

Louise didn't doubt he meant what he'd said.

"But there's no damned way for us to find out who it is," she said, "unless you tell us who you've seen come down to the harbor!"

There passed a brief moment while they looked around the circle at each other, as if to decide how much to say. Again, it was Thomas Jørgensen who took the lead.

"Who the hell comes there?" he asked mostly to himself, trying to tune in and order his thoughts. "Well, uh, there's that Arab-looking guy with the slanty eyes," he said. "And now and then some of the ones Nymann knows from The Castle. But they only go to the warehouse, not to us."

The others nodded, and Kenneth Thim leaned forward a little to contribute.

"And then there are the ones who come help with the loading, when they've got trucks down there," he slurred, too drunk to talk straight.

He stopped, as if he'd suddenly forgotten what Louise had asked about, then gathered up the threads again.

"But you gotta understand! We couldn't see shit because of where they pulled up. They went in down at the other end, so there was no way in hell we could see who else might have been there."

He looked around sluggishly at the others, as if he were waiting for their approval for having put the police in their place.

Louise ignored him.

"Arab-looking guy?" she asked. "Who's that?"

"The one who had all his shit in there," Jón blurted.

He looked at his wristwatch and got on his feet unsteadily.

Arab-looking apparently covered anyone with dark, non-white features—even if their ancestors hailed from Greenland.

"So, I take it you also know that he's the one who was shot?"

They nodded curtly, and Jón walked over to his desk where there was a pile of coats hanging over the back of the chair.

"Time to clear out," he said and looked at the others. He turned his eyes to Louise, and there was an undertone of apology when he explained that they were meeting at the café in New Harbor.

He put a jacket on.

"When you say 'The Castle' I take it you mean the bikers' clubhouse? Not Christiansborg," she said and prepared to let them go.

Kenneth Thim gave a little grunt of dry laughter.

"Damned straight. You think the Parliament dummies go to such nice places?"

He sat laughing at himself, until Jón tossed a short leather jacket to him and the sleeve struck him in the face and knocked glowing ash off his joint.

"Watch out, dammit!" he yelled and with hectic arm movements managed to get the ash off the bedcovers and onto the floor, where he stomped it out with his shoe, so it left behind a black burn mark in the parquet. "What the hell are you doing, your usual tricks?"

He looked up angrily.

"Let's just get going," said Jón and got Thomas Jørgensen pulled up off the floor.

Louise looked at Thim and guessed that most of the time he lived in a fog of booze, smoke, and pills. Whatever would keep him in his own little make-believe world, where he staggered around and only played by his own rules.

Thoroughly unsympathetic and unbalanced, thought Louise, as she made room for the boys to squeeze out of the room. She was still standing in the door to the bedroom when the front door slammed behind them, and they made noise stumbling around in the stairwell.

Vigdís Ólafsdóttir came over from the living room and looked at Louise, as if she should excuse their behavior.

"They just can't understand that their friends aren't here anymore. It's about as tragic as it gets," she said and pulled out a chair from the dining table and sat down. "I know it might not look like it, but inside they're just big boys."

Louise refrained from commenting. Instead she pulled a chair out for herself and sat across from the mother.

"Do you think it's possible they set fire to the boathouse themselves, as revenge for not being able to use it anymore? Of course, without knowing their friends were inside."

The Icelandic woman quickly shook her head, making her blond hair flutter.

"They'd never do that. Besides, they've been allowed to set up in the loft in the property where Sebastian's dad has his café. He owns the whole property, and they've been given two or three rooms, so they already have a new place. When they were thrown out, they drove all their things

there. Now they just need to paint and straighten it up a little. They haven't gone out to hurt anyone."

There was hardly anything left of her Icelandic accent,
only a faint tone under the words.

Louise took a deep breath.

"Do you know if your son and his friends associate with
members of a biker club?" she asked and observed the
woman.

Vigdís dropped her eyes and evidently thought about it.
A moment later, she looked up again and with clear blue
eyes nodded.

"Some of them do, I think. At any rate, Nymann, who
died this weekend. He knew several of them and tried to
get the others to function as a kind of support-operation,
or whatever it's called. But Jón wouldn't—thank God he's
smart enough to think about who's worth hanging out with."

Louise thought about it and wondered how much the Icelandic mother knew about her son's friends already being
written up in the police crime registry. Some parents have
an incredible ability to deny that their children are up to
things they'd rather not know about. And it was easiest on
all sides, until it reached a point where it was too late to help
them through loving care and attention.

She herself had been on a murder case involving a young
man who'd been stabbed in the middle of Copenhagen's
main pedestrian street, and it later turned out that one of the
culprits behind the utterly meaningless attack came from
a "well-situated and proper family." However much those
words meant. Lack of attention and responsibility for one's
teenager could, as she saw it, lead to as much shit as a bad
childhood.

Louise thanked her host and picked up her bag from the
floor. She gave the Icelandic woman her card and said she

hoped they'd soon be a little further with their investigation of the fire.

Down on the street, she called Willumsen. He'd left her three messages while she'd been sitting and talking with the friends of the two deceased. He answered after a single ring, but Louise took the lead before he was able to.

"I've just spoken with three of the friends of the deceased, and they say they've seen Nick Hartmann down at the warehouse with several members of the biker club. And that's despite the bikers' spokesman stubbornly insisting that they don't know anything about him."

Louise spoke so rapidly that he couldn't interrupt her.

"They came down to the warehouse with him," she elaborated. "We need to talk with them again."

The second she finished talking, Willumsen's voice thundered in her ear.

"You just see about getting your little-lady ass in here. Forget the bikers. It doesn't make a shit-bit of difference now. Frandsen just called and said his techs are finished with the black Golf from out on Strandvænget, and the tires match to a tee the tire prints that were taken down at Svanemølle Harbor outside the boathouse. We've arrested Britt Fasting-Thomsen, and sometime in the next couple of hours she'll be charged with arson and double homicide."

38

Louise, what in the hell! Britt hasn't killed anyone."
Camilla had driven off to the side and parked on the shoulder. She had the car in neutral and the emergency brake on. It was almost midnight in Denmark, and she could hear that Louise was tired.

Over here it was just past noon. Markus sat in the passenger seat and looked out the side window at a California vineyard, where the vines were allowed to grow taller than the French vintners permitted. The ground was reddish and well-tended with small tilled rows to keep the soil loose and free of weeds.

But Camilla wasn't looking in that direction. The last hour they'd driven through Napa Valley on their trip to San Francisco, but while she kept her eyes on the road, her thoughts were back home in Denmark. It was Ulrik who'd sent the brief text. Just that his wife had been arrested earlier that day, and not until the evening had the police charged her with the boathouse fire that had cost two boys their lives.

She couldn't understand it and had tried to catch Louise on her cell phone, but it was only now that she'd finally answered, and Camilla could feel how the anger was about to replace the frustration that had first blazed up. She got hold of herself so she wouldn't raise her voice.

"Now just listen," she said with a forced and somewhat restrained calm that made her words sound curt. "Britt couldn't kill someone. She doesn't have it in her."

"Her car's been at the harbor," Louise interrupted, and Camilla could hear her yawning, but she didn't care, to put it mildly. Right now, she was so angry that she sat clinging to the steering wheel with her free hand to keep it from shaking.

"She has no alibi. Can't remember what she did, except slept, or as she put it, 'lay and stared up in the air,' after Flemming and I left her around five thirty," Louise continued. "That's not good enough. Not at all when we've found a gas can that's the same kind the technicians found left behind at the fire site. Britt keeps insisting that she doesn't know anything about it, even though it was in the back of her car."

Camilla let her talk, but no longer listened. She could see Signe's mom in her mind, the fine facial features and her neatly trimmed straight hair.

"It's possible," she said when Louise was silent. "But she hasn't been down to the harbor to avenge Signe's death."

She could hear that Louise wanted to interrupt. In the rearview mirror, she saw a gigantic tractor trailer barreling toward her at a high speed with headlights and lamps that made it look like a high-rise apartment building on wheels. The car vibrated when it passed by, making the dust on Highway 80 lift into a dense cloud before settling back down and revealing the long, straight road.

"That's not how she thinks," Camilla said. "I could do it. Actually, I have no doubt I'd consider revenge if it was

Markus. If someone had chased him out in front of a car, and he'd been killed like Signe, then I'm sure I'd find a way to do it. And sorry for saying it, but I wouldn't give a shit about spending sixteen years behind bars in a situation like that. I wouldn't have anything left anyway…except that it might soothe my grief knowing they weren't allowed to continue living, either."

"You wouldn't do that," Louise interrupted, irritated with her. Her voice suddenly came through more clearly.

"Yes, I sure would. But Britt wouldn't. She doesn't have that anger in her, and that's what makes the difference."

"Come on," said Louise, and the distance between them became clearer from the tone of her voice, which had risen to a professional manner. Their friendship was pushed into the background. "I hear what you're saying, and I understand you."

Camilla straightened up in the car's wide leather seat as anger shot through her.

"But you also need to understand that we're conducting a murder investigation," Louise continued before she could say anything, "a double homicide at that, and so it's not enough that you call home from your vacation trip and say that it couldn't be your friend who did it. We need a little more evidence on the table; and for starters, it would be nice if Britt began to help some herself as we try to get a handle on what she was doing the night the fire broke out."

Camilla wanted to say something, but instead she hung up her cell phone. Discouraged, she let it rest in her hand and felt empty and far away. Too far away to do anything for Britt. She came to think of John Bro. The star lawyer she'd run into several times as a journalist for *Morgenavisen*. He was outrageously expensive, but he won his cases. She found Ulrik's last message to her and sent him his name and the address of his firm on Bredgade.

"Did Signe's mom kill someone?" asked Markus, who hadn't said a word during her conversation with Louise. He hadn't even asked her to say hello for him, so she knew he'd sensed that something had happened that wasn't good.

"Of course not, but the police suspect her of setting fire to a place where two of the boys who ruined Signe's party were lying asleep."

She turned and looked at him. There was something far-off in his look, as if everything had happened too close together and was too painful for him to process.

"We might need to go back home," she said and reached out and took his hand.

He sat for a moment without reacting, then turned to her and nodded. It was almost a month early, according to the plans they'd made, but Camilla knew that she wouldn't get anything more out of the trip if Britt was jailed for homicide without her doing something to help her. If they scratched the rest of the trip, at least she'd be able to visit her.

She put the car into drive and swung out. There were still two and a half hours of driving to San Francisco. They should find a place for lunch, and after that she'd have to call home to the travel agency and get their plane tickets changed.

Her cell phone beeped again. It was a text from Ulrik.

"We have a lawyer, but thanks. Have just spoken with Frederik, he'd like to see you, but won't be back until the weekend, sending the address. Best, Ulrik."

❧

Camilla drove and kept her eye out for a diner or gas station, so they could at least get a sandwich and something to drink.

Her thoughts whirled.

It surprised her that Frederik Sachs-Smith had so quickly agreed to a visit, but she was still deeply shaken over the arrest back home, and that fact dampened her enthusiasm for an in-house interview. On the other hand—if she got his version of the family scandal, she could sell it to *Morge-navisen* and cover at least one of the tickets home.

She shook her head. She could also just screw the interview. If she went home now, they wouldn't have to spend money on hotels and food, but she had sublet her apartment and would have to find someplace else to live during the time they'd planned on being away.

"I don't want to go home," Markus said suddenly.

They'd driven for half an hour without finding any place to eat.

"It's all wrong to go to school when Signe's not there. And we said we'd be gone for two months, so it sucks to come home before that."

"We need to go home and be there for Signe's mom, if it will help her," Camilla said quietly, even though she understood him.

Britt had been placed under arrest and would be arraigned by the judge the next morning. If the police had as much to put on the table as Louise claimed, then she'd probably be put in prison and await trial for two to four weeks, Camilla guessed. She hoped Ulrik's lawyer was good.

Finally, they caught sight of a sign—Ruby's Diner was coming up in three miles. They'd driven from the hotel a little after 8:00 a.m., and now she felt hungry. At the same time, she also felt a little bit of doubt down in the pit of her stomach, but it was too early to let it grow into something big. Much too early.

There were three cars in the diner's parking lot, and Camilla drove all the way up to the entrance with the red-and-white sign.

"Can I get a vanilla milkshake and a cheeseburger?" Markus asked Camilla while she held the door for him.

She smiled, knowing he was taking advantage of how out of it she was, with her thoughts everywhere except on him and their agreement not to eat burgers more than twice a week.

God, she really should do that interview with Frederik Sachs-Smith, she decided as a waitress with a ponytail and few clothes on set their tall glasses on the table along with the shiny shaker containing the rest of the vanilla drink.

Frederik still hadn't spoken with any journalists, but he'd agreed to speak with her—also, it meant they could spend three or four days in San Francisco before driving along the coast down Highway 1 to Santa Barbara where, according to Ulrik, he lived in a big house on the water.

39

The coffee was Thermos-dull and far from being as hot as when she'd poured it in the kitchen, shortly after Britt Fasting-Thomsen had been taken from her arraignment to a further interrogation.

The judge had, as expected, ordered her to be held for four weeks.

Britt was wearing the same clothes as the day before. Her face was free of makeup, but that's how it had been for the last weeks. Soon after the funeral, Louise had started to notice the change. Signe's mother wasn't untidy, she'd just stopped doing anything to herself.

She nodded mechanically when Louise offered to fill her cup with the lukewarm coffee. Next to her sat the lawyer Nikolaj Lassen. Ulrik had introduced him as the family attorney, and Louise had understood that they knew him well and got together with him privately, too. He was in the range of forty, blond and well-groomed. His suit was shiny and looked expensive.

It was mostly Nikolaj Lassen who'd done the talking, once they'd come up to the office on the second floor after the arraignment hearing. Britt managed no more than a nod or a shake of her head.

"I wasn't down at the harbor, in the evening or at night," she repeated in a tired voice. She no longer looked at them, kept her eyes on the table, her hands pressed together nervously. She didn't feel comfortable, that was clear. "And I can't explain how my car got down there."

There was a pause, then Louise switched directions.

"And you're sure Ulrik hadn't seen the gas can, either?"

The lawyer scooted forward in his seat.

"It could have been him who bought it and put it in your car, because it's not wise to drive around without a spare can," Louise suggested.

They'd already confirmed that Ulrik knew nothing about the green can, but she wanted to hear Britt's answer.

Louise and Toft had been granted the help of two officers from the Homicide Department's other investigation group, and they'd gone around to various Aldi stores in the Østerbro, Nørrebro, and Frederiksberg neighborhoods. The discount chain didn't have any stores in Hellerup, where the Fasting-Thomsen family shopped. But no one had recognized the photo of Britt, or remembered if anyone had bought more than one can while it was on sale. It was a product on a good sale, and they'd already sold many of the green cans by the beginning of the week when it appeared in their flyer but, their two colleagues told them, truth was that most of the young people behind the cash registers seemed entirely uninterested in what came down the belt and who handed them a credit card.

The officers had also gone through all the credit card payments, but neither Britt's name nor her account number had popped up.

"I don't know anything about it," Britt said faintly and cleared her throat uncertainly.

She'd taken the judge's decision about holding her in jail very collectedly, had just bowed her head and stood obediently when an officer came over and took her by the elbow to escort her out.

Now she looked over at Louise and didn't try to hide the blank stare in her eyes.

"I didn't set fire to that house," she said faintly. "I don't know how the can ended up in the back of my car. But I didn't put it there."

Again, Louise got the feeling that Britt didn't think this really had anything to do with her, and if it weren't for her insistence on her innocence Louise would worry about her falling apart. But she wasn't on the verge of a breakdown. In an odd way, she was calm inside despite the serious charges. She didn't seem afraid or nervous. It was more as if she expected the whole thing to go away again as long as she maintained that she wasn't the one who'd done it.

Toft stood up and walked over to the printer for the transcript of the hearing.

The lawyer reached out his hand and took the three A4-size pages. He wanted to read it over thoroughly before letting his client sign.

Louise leaned back a little and slumped in her chair. Nikolaj Lassen took his time. Britt sat looking out the window, but she didn't seem interested in how the autumn sun made rays of light dance over the windowsill. She appeared to have sunk back into herself and into the thoughts that drew fine wrinkles across her nose.

An abrupt, hard knock came on the door and everyone straightened up quickly as Willumsen stepped into the office and walked over to the desk, where he leaned in toward Britt and her lawyer.

The whole day he'd been buzzing around between offices and the hallway like a fly in a bottle. Anxious to have her held in prison and irritated over her not giving an inch.

"I'd be very interested if you could tell me what kind of firewood you have stored in your woodshed in the garden behind your house," he said and waited on Britt with a look that made her scoot back in her chair and braid her fingers together into a tight fist. A touch of uncertainty flickered across her face and made her eyes seem uneasy.

"The firewood," she repeated, bewildered. "I really don't know about that. That's not something we do ourselves. We order it and then it gets delivered in a tall crate type of thing. Then, of course, my husband stacks it in the woodshed, but it's not something he cuts down and chops himself. It's all finished and ready to use when it comes."

She spoke nervously and explanatorily.

"Do you know what kind of wood you heat with?" asked the lead investigator, still leaning toward her.

Her lawyer moved a little nervously, and Louise waited to see how long before he stepped in. If he'd been the more cut-throat type, it would already have happened, but she bet Nikolaj Lassen would just see where Willumsen was going before he began to interfere.

"I'm not familiar with that," said Britt. "It's always Ulrik who orders, when we start running low."

"Oak, beech, or pine?" Willumsen attempted, but shook his head.

And now the lawyer leaned forward.

"Where are you heading?" he asked and pulled back again to create a little distance from Willumsen's big shadow that spread across the table.

There was nothing timid about the lawyer, and he didn't look particularly nervous from his elegant appearance, but he didn't seem like the aggressive type who tries to pick up points before the game's opening whistle.

Willumsen turned toward him and straightened up, stuck his hands in the pockets of his dark blue gabardine trousers, whose creases gave his pants legs a sharp edge. His glasses were pushed up onto his forehead—they were heavy and dark and blurred together with his black hair.

"I'm heading somewhere where I might get an explanation for the incredible coincidence our crime techs just shared with me."

Again, he turned his gaze on Britt and told her that the criminal technicians had just finished their inspection of the house on Strandvænget.

Louise knew that Michael Stig had been out there, and that the whole house had been searched.

"The wood you have in your shed is oven-dried beech, cut and split to lengths of ten to twelve inches, and would most likely be delivered in a tall crate containing one face cord. The pieces of firewood that were thrown through the window in the boathouse and lit the gasoline that had been poured in the room were, interestingly enough, the same kind. The exact same kind," he highlighted. "It wasn't ash, birch, or mixed hardwood—or any of the other kinds of wood people buy finished and ready for use. Out at the Center for Forensic Services, they've concluded it was oven-dried beech, because unlike firewood that's air-dried, that kind of wood gets a reddish color when treated in an oven."

The lawyer didn't interrupt. Didn't say a word.

"It is an absolutely incredible coincidence, isn't it? Maybe especially considering that none of your neighbors have that same kind of wood in their woodsheds."

He turned on his heels and left the office.

Louise took a deep breath and pushed her cup full of cold coffee off to the side. She looked from Nikolaj Lassen to Britt, waiting for one of them to say something. The lawyer seemed resigned, and he avoided looking over at his client.

Toft reached for the papers that were ready for Britt's signature.

"Should we step out for a moment, so you can have a chance to talk together?" suggested Louise and looked at the lawyer. She suddenly had the feeling that he was ready to leave Britt in the lurch.

He nodded, and they left them alone.

Out in the hall Willumsen stood triumphantly, waiting for them like a chess player who'd long foreseen his opponent's next move. He knew that his news would require a time-out and had waited for Toft and Louise to come out.

"Are we looking at a confession?" he asked, mostly aimed at Toft. He and Louise were still a little on edge with each other after what he'd said the day before, about moving her little-lady ass.

"Possibly," said Toft.

He pulled his V-neck sweater over his head and fished his nicotine gum out of his shirt pocket. After the no-smoking policy hit Police Headquarters, he started sucking on a plastic cigarette that released a measured dose of nicotine, but later he realized how pathetic it looked to have a plastic thingamabob hanging from the corner of his mouth. A couple of months back he'd given in and traded the plastic cigarette for the more discreet chewing gum. The tobacco-substitute only came into play when he was indoors, though. Otherwise, he was happy with his Prince-brand cigarettes. He just didn't want to have to go to the courtyard every time he craved nicotine.

Louise shook her head, but Willumsen ignored her.

"If Britt wanted to confess, she'd already have done it when I went out to talk with her. Then she would have been spared from sitting in there."

She nodded toward the office and could see that Toft was inclined to agree with her.

"She won't confess as long as you keep giving her hope that there's a way out," Willumsen corrected and looked at the clock.

The door behind them opened, and Nikolaj Lassen stuck his head out and said they were ready.

Behind him sat Britt, pale but just as composed as when the judge decided to send her behind bars for four weeks.

After they'd sat down, the lawyer shook his head.

"My client doesn't know anything about the coincidence that seems to have happened. But the firewood on the family's property is accessible to anyone. It's not locked up or hidden from the road."

"But it's not visible to outsiders, either, unless they come into the part of the garden that's behind the house," Louise pointed out and looked over at Britt.

"That's true," she said and nodded to Louise.

"I'd like to ask that we stop for today," the lawyer said, speaking over them. "I need to consider this new information and go through anything else the technicians have found. So, I'd suggest that my client be driven back to Vestre Prison."

"Are you escorting her out there, or should we find transportation?" Louise asked and remained standing in the doorway while the lawyer packed his things together.

"I assume you can see to that," he said without looking up.

"Is it all right with you if I drive her alone?" Louise asked Toft when they stood in the hall.

He nodded and watched the lawyer disappear down the hall.

☙

Louise picked up the keys to the patrol car that Michael Stig had parked down on Otto Mønsteds Gade when he came back from the search at the Fasting-Thomsen home.

She and Britt didn't talk together as they walked down the stairs, and the arrestee kept her eyes on the ground when Louise opened the door to the back seat and asked her to sit inside, then locked the police-secure doors and walked around the car.

Britt had nothing with her besides the clothes she was wearing. No coat, no bag. Only the ice-blue cashmere cardigan, which she pulled a little snugger around herself when a journalist and a press photographer suddenly came running toward the car.

The arson and homicides had been front page stuff in the weekend papers, in which both the restaurant owner in New Harbor and Nymann's parents down in Næstved had spoken about their two big teenage boys who'd died in the flames.

The journalists had also gotten hold of childhood friends and the three others from down at the boathouse. Louise guessed that it was the restaurant owner who volunteered their names. But it hadn't yet gotten out that a forty-two-year-old woman had been arrested and charged in the case, even though it would only be a matter of time before the media found the connection between Signe's death and her mother's arrest. Then the story would explode for real.

Suhr had already brought it up during the morning meeting in the breakfast room, but there wasn't much they could do about it, except try to shelter Britt when she was driven to and from interrogations at Police Headquarters.

While they drove over the Tietgens Bridge and out past DGI-byen, with its bowling alleys and restaurants, and the train yard, Louise decided she'd better warn Ulrik about what would be coming from the press, if he hadn't already thought of it himself. Maybe it would be best if he moved out of the house for a while, she thought and stopped for a red light at Enghave Station, where they could look across and see Vestre Prison.

She saw Britt in the rearview mirror and tried to read the blue eyes and flat expression that vacantly followed the daily life that glided past the right-side window.

They turned off Vigerslev Allé and drove the short stretch up to the prison's gate, which made her think about The Olsen Gang movies and all the times Egon was picked up outside Vridsløselille State Prison by Benny and Kjeld.

Her thoughts turned to Jonas. This morning there'd been a text from Mik, who'd written that he'd taken time off so he and the boy could enjoy themselves, now that it was fall break. He hoped it was OK, now that she herself had to work. He'd drive him home to Copenhagen, so he'd be there around supper time; he'd even offered to take care of the food.

It was not by any means OK, and Louise had already called and made that clear. She couldn't have him pushing his way into her daily life and trying to be part of it. Still, she'd agreed to have him drive to Hvalsø and pick up Jonas so they could be together, because she couldn't come up with a reason for why it was better for the boy to sit around doing nothing at her parents' until his train left for Copenhagen at the end of the afternoon.

What had also played into it was her awareness that

she'd go to great lengths to keep Jonas happy and things light, up until the point where she'd have to tell him that the police had arrested and charged Signe's mother with the murder of two of the kids who'd barged into the party.

Louise drove the patrol car up to the gate and waited for it to slide to the side. In front of them there was yet another gate, but that wouldn't open until she'd talked with the guard in the booth and the door behind them had closed with a heavy click. Under complete security they were let into the prison.

Inside the compound, Louise drove slowly down to the parking lot behind Registration, and when she'd parked and turned off the engine she turned to Britt in the back seat.

"You don't need to tell me if you did it or not. You just need to tell me if it's worthwhile to keep looking. I can't get you out of the charges the police have made against you. They are serious allegations, some of the most serious that can be made, and you're not just facing sixteen years behind bars. You're facing a life sentence in a high-security prison. Deliberate homicide carried out as vengeance is one of the harshest crimes a person can commit. So, forget about telling me whether you're guilty. Just tell me if I'm wasting my time trying to find out who did it, if it wasn't you."

The look in her eyes changed, became present. Dark and intense as if they'd latched on to Louise's eyes. Britt leaned forward, so her upper body was between the two front seats, and put her hand on Louise's arm.

"You shouldn't do anything for my sake," she said in a voice that was deeper than it had been in Police Headquarters.

She let go of Louise's arm and gazed out the window. Then her thoughts made her sit back in the seat again, and her look became distant.

Louise sat a bit and observed her, then she started the car again and drove the last stretch to the door with the intercom.

A uniformed prison officer took Britt by the elbow and escorted her in. Louise waited in the car until the door closed.

40

Louise hammered the steering wheel with both hands in frustration, as she again stopped and waited to drive out onto Vigerslev Allé.

She thought about Camilla, who was bombarding her with messages in which she kept insisting that it was a mistake to arrest Britt and wanted Louise to find evidence that pointed in another direction. After a while, Louise got so irritated that she didn't want to read the texts that kept coming.

Britt would have to take her punishment, if she was guilty of arson and homicide. Louise knew perfectly well what the thirst for vengeance could do to entirely sensible and ordinary people.

It was awoken by the strongest feelings on the whole spectrum—love, hate, jealousy—and it could drive a well-functioning person completely over the edge. That's why it didn't really help her to hear Camilla go on and on about how it wasn't something Britt had in her.

She beeped angrily at a white car that was blocking her way, then squeezed over into the turning lane and swung past Enghave Station. Right now, she was dead tired of Britt

Fasting-Thomsen and how she wouldn't give a fig, all the same to her what the police dished up for evidence.

Louise drove on, following the stream of cars and trying to shake off thoughts of Britt. She sighed and thought of Sejr. While she'd had Britt in interrogation, he'd started looking into whether there were international transfers that could document a connection between Hartmann and the bikers. He'd promised to let her know if he found something, but so far, she hadn't heard from him.

They weren't the least bit closer, even though Sejr had slogged on. After the arrest, her own focus had blurred, but now there was a little calm again. They'd have to see about digging through all the information on HartmannImport/Export in order to find all the connections that were relevant regarding the shooting victim's business.

A group of kindergarteners with backpacks bouncing on their backs passed over the crosswalk on their way to Enghave Park.

Vengeance could also be unleashed by cheating, money, and anger, she thought as she watched the children gather around two benches and unload their backpacks in a big pile. She hoped she could find Tønnes out at the club, and that he was in the mood to talk.

Even though it clearly wasn't on Willumsen's list of priorities, she was still interested in hearing how he'd explain the fact that several of the members knew Nick Hartmann and had gone down to the warehouse at the harbor when, the last time they'd spoken, he'd insisted on something different.

The afternoon traffic was stuck in long caravans across Nørrebro, but cleared up when she zigzagged down the smaller
streets for the last stretch.

Louise parked a long way from the gate and the two security cameras because she didn't think it would be very
fruitful to adorn their main entrance with a patrol car. She
looked directly into the camera over the gate as she introduced herself and asked to speak with Tønnes.

After a moment, she was allowed to come into the
courtyard. To the right of the house there was a big heavy
oak tree. Inside the gate, the courtyard was covered with
asphalt and empty, except for four shiny motorcycles with
newly polished chrome, parked beside each other in a
ruler-straight line along the right side of the building.
There were also a couple of big cars in the courtyard—a
Porsche Cayenne with white plates and an Audi Q7.

She saw recognition in his dark eyes and extended her
hand when he appeared in the door.

"I'd like to trouble you with a couple more questions,"
she led off with politely.

He wore a wide silver ring on the middle finger of his right
hand, and a tattoo crept out under his watchband. His hair was
blond and short, and he had on a black long-sleeved T-shirt
unbuttoned at the neck under his leather vest.

He didn't comment about her coming alone, but she noticed that he registered it and didn't know what he made of it.

"Last time we talked about Nick Hartmann, who was
shot down in his home a month ago," she began. "As you
may remember, we were interested in knowing which of the
members in the club here he knew."

The biker spokesman nodded.

"And as you may remember," he said, "no one knows
anything about him."

"That's not entirely true," Louise corrected. "We've just confirmed that the deceased had connections with several of the members, and that they've frequented the warehouse he rented down on Svanemølle Harbor."

He looked at her expressionlessly. Behind him a broad-shouldered guy came to the door.

"What have we here?" he asked and put his hand on Tønnes's shoulder to signal that he was ready to toss Louise out, if he'd like him to.

Tønnes shook his head and waved him away without turning around, but there were no signs of hospitality—he still didn't let her come into the clubhouse.

"I've asked around, but no one knows anything about him," he said.

"Give it up, will you!" exclaimed Louise, irritated with him. "We know damn well he knew several people here, and that they came down to the harbor."

She held back for a moment and thought it over before appealing to his sense of brotherly understanding, if such a thing existed behind all those muscles and tattoos.

"Nick Hartmann left behind a wife and a practically newborn daughter. On Thursday, his warehouse was burned down, and two young guys died in the flames."

The reaction came in a twitch along his mouth, and the biker spokesman shifted his weight from one foot to the other.

"I've heard about the fire, and the two who died in the flames," he answered without seeming particularly moved. "What happened to the warehouse?"

He was taller than her. Rather a lot, in fact. Louise came up to his shoulders and had to look up.

"Some of the building burned down. He was keeping some import furniture there. In fact, there was a whole lot in there. Two containers with furniture manufactured in China, ready to be sold. But all that's in the police's care now."

He wanted to say something, but Louise beat him to it.

"But if you don't think you know him, then there's not much more to talk about. Might just be you had something to do with the warehouse, since folks from here went down there."

He followed her with his eyes as she prepared to leave.

"I don't know where you got it from that he has connections here. But I'd like to repeat that no one knows anything about him—and besides that, we have no interest in his warehouse."

His language was a strange contrast to his outer appearance, and it obviously cost him nothing to lie straight to her face.

"We got a guy from the Fraud Department to go through all of Hartmann's monetary transactions and telephone conversations, from landline to cell phone," Louise said and took a step back toward him after she'd come out on the sidewalk. "He's also going through all e-mail correspondences and other Internet contacts. We've seized Hartmann's computers, and everything on them has been dumped. That'll get looked through."

It didn't seem to faze him.

"If there's been, at any point in time, a connection between some members of the club here and Nick Hartmann, we'll find it. It would just go a little quicker if you helped."

She could see the muscles playing under his jersey as he folded his arms over his chest and leaned his upper body back a little, so he could look down on her even more.

But he said nothing.

"But you're not prepared to do that, I sense."

She turned and walked over to the gate, knowing his eyes were on her back.

41

"Don't say anything to them. At the most: 'No comment.'"

Camilla fell back in the hotel bed. Ulrik had caught her when she and Markus had come back from breakfast down at Starbucks. Muffins and coffee.

The boy sat over at the desk with her computer. There was free Internet, and she'd let him play a little and check his Facebook profile, where the messages nearly overflowed with greetings from home.

"They were waiting outside when I came home," said Ulrik. "So, I had to just keep driving."

"So where are you now?" asked Camilla, and it suddenly hit her that it had been a while since she'd felt the weight of her own worries. It was as though all that had given way for what had happened to Britt and Ulrik.

"I'm staying in a hotel in the city."

"Smart," she answered. "It'll be at least a few days before they stop holding your house under complete siege. If you can, stay at the hotel until they think you're not coming back."

She shook her head at herself. Who was she to be giving

advice about that sort of thing! If she'd been home and didn't know the family, it could easily be her laying siege to the house out on Strandvænget.

"Couldn't you get hold of John Bro?" she asked, changing subjects.

"I decided to let my own lawyer take the case. He knows our family, and I think that's a big advantage in our situation."

"John Bro is better!"

"Britt's being charged with one of the most serious crimes. Nikolaj Lassen will be more loyal than someone who doesn't know us."

"Possibly," Camilla conceded and sighed. "How's she doing?"

There was silence on the other end for a moment, then he cleared his throat.

"It's hard to say," he said. "I don't really feel like I can get through to her."

"What do we do? What does she say about it? Can she handle sitting in jail?"

"Does she have a choice?" Ulrik asked drily. Then he took a deep breath. "The biggest problem is that she doesn't say anything. She doesn't try to defend herself or talk her way out of it. And that might be exactly what speaks the loudest for her."

A moment passed before Camilla caught what he was saying.

"Ulrik, hell! You know your wife—you know damned well Britt didn't kill anybody. What's happening to you?"

But at the same time, she saw the journalists waiting in their cars for him. She saw newspaper headlines and felt the pressure as if it were tightening up in her own chest.

"Are you able to travel away for a few days, turn your back on everything, and relax a little?"

"That won't make it go away, now, will it?"

"You think it was her?" Camilla said and realized that Markus was looking at her.

"I'm not saying it's her. I'm just not blind to the possibility that it could be. And if that's the case, then it's hard to feel sympathy for her."

42

Mik's car was parked in front of Louise's front door when she arrived home. As she stood and rooted through her bag for her keys, she suddenly heard Jonas calling from farther down the street. She turned and was surprised to see him jogging down the sidewalk with the deaf Labrador retriever on a leash.

"Hey!" she shouted, and a moment later Mik came around the corner.

"He's letting me borrow Dina," Jonas shouted happily. "Mik says I can have her as much as I want because no one else will have her since she can't hear."

Louise felt her smile stiffen, and she stepped a little away from the door when the puppy got ready to jump up.

"We can't have a dog in there. It's a shame to have it live in an apartment."

"It's OK to have a dog. I called and asked Melvin."

Mik had caught up to them.

"It looks like you two are getting along together nicely," he said with a smile and ordered the yellow puppy to lie down, but it ignored him and kept dancing around them.

"She's almost housebroken," Jonas said and squatted

down. He threw his arms around its light-colored head with the brown eyes and nuzzled its fur with his cheek.

Louise could have knocked Mik to the asphalt right there. She was so mad that it was absolutely impossible for her to speak straight.

"Who the hell do you think you are?" she hissed and looked at him.

She noticed how Jonas stiffened and stood up straight again. Louise tossed her keys over to him and said he should go up to the apartment while she finished talking to Mik.

But the boy didn't move, just stood completely still and got that vulnerable and unhappy look on his face, which she didn't know what to do about.

"I'm the one who said I always wanted a dog," he said quickly, defending Mik. He came a little closer and looked up at her. "I couldn't have one at home because my dad was allergic."

"We can't have a dog, either, Jonas."

He remained standing and held Dina by the leash.

"But I can't go on living here with you, right?" he said. "And when I can't stay here anymore, then I can take Dina with me. So I won't be all alone."

Louise walked over and unlocked the front door, sending him and the dog inside. With the same hand, she waved up the stairs and pushed him away.

When the door closed behind them, she turned to Mik.

"Have you gone completely insane? You know damn well I can't have a dog that needs to be fed and walked and the whole nine yards. I'd get reported for cruelty to animals!"

"Well, you're not the one I loaned her to, either. It's Jonas, and I'll just come pick her up if he needs a break."

"You have no damned right to decide that. He lives with me."

Mik studied her a bit. Gone was the warmth and happiness that usually played in his eyes. He took a deep breath.

"Now, you seldom let an opportunity go by for telling us all that Jonas is only living with you until you find a more permanent solution. How do you think a message like that makes him feel after what he's gone through? Do you think it makes him feel secure and wanted?"

"He's the one who wanted to live here, and this is what I had to offer."

Mik inched forward, close to her face.

"You are so goddamned egocentric. One would damned well think you were a man. You take what you want, and leave the rest of the shit behind. No responsibility, no emotional attachment. No consideration. Just you!"

She'd never heard him swear so much at one time—and that fact, more than anything else, is what penetrated the fog that was beginning to settle around her brain.

"If you don't let Jonas be with that dog as much as he wants to, when it makes him so happy, then I'm going up there and telling him he's welcome to come and live on the farm with me, and he can live there for as long as he wants, until he wants to move from home himself."

She was about to say something, but his stream of words didn't give her any room.

"And as for you, I don't want to see you anymore. Period. We end here. You make me feel like your 'friend-with-benefits,' someone you haul out when you're hankering, but otherwise you don't give a thought about. I don't want to be part of that, and I don't think you'll find anyone who will for the long run. Definitely not, if they're like me and want to spend all their time with you. And do you know what that means? That means you'll end up dying lonely—and the sad part is that it's gotten to where I don't even feel sorry for you."

The fog in Louise's head thickened.

She watched him walk over to his car and unlock it.

He stood for a moment beside the sidewalk and observed her.

"Call, if you decide that Jonas and Dina should live in Holbæk."

He got in his car and drove off without looking at her.

⚜

It was a long way up to the fourth floor. She could hear them in the stairwell. Could also hear that Melvin had come out to the stairs.

"Sure is a nice dog," said the elderly man when Louise reached them. He'd crouched down, and Dina stood with her front legs on his thighs and sniffed around at his face. He smiled and scratched her behind the ears.

The fog remained thick inside Louise's head.

Jonas had sat down on the stairs. He was pale, and his hair covered his eyes like a thick curtain he hid behind. He avoided looking at her, but had a little smile on his lips as he reached out and stroked the puppy's coat.

Damn it! Louise thought and mostly wanted to turn around and drive back to Headquarters and help Sejr, who sat with all the stuff they'd dumped from Hartmann's hard drive. But she knew good and well that there was no escape route.

"It's just, with puppies—they can't stay at home alone. They need to be taken out, and have company," she said a bit clumsily.

Jonas looked down at the floor. He had to understand that he couldn't ask the dog to take care of itself for six or seven hours a day when it was so little.

"Right, but that's where I come into the picture," Melvin said cheerfully, obviously not catching the tense mood between Louise and the boy. "I could take her for a walk over in Frederiksberg Gardens. We can have a good time together until you two come home."

Louise felt her cheeks tug back when she tried to smile. She squeezed past Jonas on the stairs and kept walking up.

The anger made her blood pump, and it throbbed in her temples. She had just sat down in the kitchen to clear her head when her cell phone rang in her jacket. She didn't want to get it, thought it was Mik calling to apologize. Her first reaction to his harsh words was more anger than hurt. Still, they stayed on her mind and worked there.

Her cell phone rang again, and Louise saw that she might as well get it over with because Mik had a way of calling and calling until she picked up. But when she took the phone out of her pocket, she didn't recognize the number in the display, nor the voice that cried in her ear.

"Damn it, speak calmly. How else am I supposed to understand what you're saying?"

Right now, Louise had no use for a girl who was completely out of it.

"They were here again. They say Nick's cheated them and owes them so much money that I'll have to sell the duplex. If not, they'll take Cecilie the next time they come."

Nick Hartmann's young widow cried so loudly that Louise had to hold the phone away from her ear.

"When were they there?" she asked, quickly setting aside her grumpy tone.

"Just now. They just left. They came in a big box van

and took a whole bunch of our things. The TV, stereo system…"

Mie cried again, making her words indecipherable.

"I don't want to stay here," she finally got out.

In the background, the baby started to screech.

"Stay there a little longer. I'm on my way out to you."

She didn't need to ask who'd paid her the visit. Louise could imagine. Tønnes had gotten his men to react quickly. She was sure it was learning that the furniture had been confiscated—so the value it represented was now in the possession of the police—that had triggered the reaction. It was foolish of her not to foresee that it might turn out this way. Irresponsible.

She took her jacket and flew out the door again. Melvin and Jonas still sat out on the stairs with Dina. Another neighbor had joined them, and the deaf puppy wagged its tail and lapped up all the attention that was given to it.

Louise pulled Jonas aside.

"I need to head out for about an hour. I put 100 kroner on the kitchen table, so you can get a pizza if you're hungry before I get back, but I won't be later than eight o'clock."

Jonas nodded and stood there sheepishly.

She reached out her hand and laid it on his arm.

"We need to talk together, but it'll have to wait until I come home."

He nodded, and she hurried down the stairs, knowing full well that she'd left him back there with a load of thoughts and uncertainty. It was both mean and unfair, she knew that well, but more than anything else she needed to get control over her own thoughts before they got started on a conversation that would have a great deal of meaning for Jonas's future.

The windows in the duplex on Dyvekes Allé had been re-placed and the police's cordon tape taken away. Through the kitchen window, she could see Mie with her daughter in her arms. She'd stood watching for Louise, and the door was opened before she made it all the way down the front walk. Mie's eyes were gray with blurred mascara and red from crying.

"What happened?" Louise asked as she came in.

"Two of them came. They barged right in and forced me into the living room with them."

"Were they the same ones who came before?"

"Not the ones who were here in the afternoon. But then I didn't see who came at night."

Louise pulled out a kitchen chair for Mie and asked her to sit down. She sat across from her and told her that the police had reason to believe that Nick had gotten himself involved with the bikers, and that their business relations could have led to the shooting.

"Do you know anything about their connection?"

It looked like the woman thought about it, but her eyes were vacant.

"He didn't, at any rate, tell me about it," she answered and shook her head. "But the ones who were just here could be that type."

Louise nodded.

"What do you know about the furniture he kept down at Svanemølle Harbor?"

"Nothing. I already said that."

She started to cry again.

Louise looked at the baby, who'd fallen asleep over her mother's shoulder.

"Couldn't we put her down to sleep?" she suggested, nodding toward the living room and bedroom.

Mie stood up and took her daughter to her crib.

"They said they were filing a claim for between six and ten million kroner. But if I agreed to pay them voluntarily, then they'd make a settlement, so I wouldn't be dragged into court, and that way I could get by with paying them just four million of what Nick owed."

Louise shook her head, impressed by how quickly Tønnes had gotten a lawyer to formulate an agreement. It was well-known to the police that the bikers had lawyers, accountants, and other professional folks on their payroll, to take care of just this sort of thing. The henchmen they sent out to collect the valuables weren't in a position to formulate matters like that on their own.

Interesting, she thought. Four million came pretty close to what Nick Hartmann had paid for one of the two containers with fake designer furniture, and the demand on Mie confirmed that he hadn't pulled the money out of his own pockets. The way the situation had unfolded, the people who'd invested the money now sat back without being able to demand either the money or the furniture, and Louise could easily see how that could make the backers do whatever they had to to get their tab covered.

"I think it's wisest if you move away for the time being. Is there someplace you can stay?"

Mie nodded absently.

"We can stay with my mom. That's where we went the other time."

Louise shook her head.

"That's not good enough, too easy to find you there."

"Do you think they mean it? That they'd come and take Cecilie from me if I don't pay?"

There was a closed-in smell in the kitchen, as if nothing had been opened since they'd moved back in. The candlesticks on the table had burned down, but the stumps were still in their holders. Here, too, a death had put life on hold, exactly as it had for Signe's parents, Louise thought as she looked around. But for Mie it wasn't over with yet—fear was hanging over her head.

"I can't pay them," she exclaimed and made a desperate gesture with her hands. "It's completely nuts with all that money, and I don't even know if I could sell the duplex. Don't you think it's just something they're saying?"

"No," Louise said and shook her head. "I'm afraid there's reason for you to be scared, that they mean it seriously. You need to be out of here by this evening."

"But what about all the furniture he had? Can't they just have it?" she asked, not seeming to understand.

In theory, yes, thought Louise, but it's not that simple.

"To begin with, we don't know if they own any of it. They certainly won't tell us if the furniture was bought with their money. But in this instance, they'll wind up suffering a big economic loss. That's what they don't want to happen. They can't get hold of the furniture that's been seized because it's going next to SKAT, where it'll be confiscated since it's illegal to import copied goods from China. So, you're the only one they can hand the bill to for what they've lost."

"Yeah, but…"

Mie nodded heavily, but didn't seem to understand that there was no way to take her out of the picture. She sat that way a while, then turned her eyes to Louise.

"I just don't understand how it can have anything to do with Nick, and how they can come and demand a bunch of money when he's dead?"

Louise kept herself from smiling.

"I can only guess," she said and asked if she could get herself some water.

Mie nodded and pointed to a kitchen cupboard.

"We don't have any proof of it yet, but we're working on it. My guess is that Nick started a business with someone who was willing to throw a considerable sum of money into the enterprise. Then your darling earned a nice bit for his part of the work, but it was the investor who earned the big money."

"Who?"

"Could be criminals who've been at it for years, and maybe earlier they earned large sums selling drugs. It could be that they no longer think it's so attractive to involve themselves in criminal businesses with high risk. Such as drugs, for example, where sentences are relatively severe. And so, they've switched over to something where the penalty is more lenient, but the earnings are almost just as high. A safer choice, you could say."

"But then it's not the bikers, if they're old?"

"Yes, it easily could be. The ones who've been in it a long time are getting into their midfifties. And they might not want to run the risk of long prison sentences."

"But the ones who came here weren't old."

It looked as though Mie had stopped trying to follow what she was saying and, honestly, Louise didn't care if she understood.

"Are you packing a bag?"

Mie nodded and stood up.

"Have you thought about where you're going?"

"I'm going to a girlfriend's. But what about all the stuff they took with them?"

"First it needs to be reported, and then I'll have a couple

of criminal technicians out here so we can see if they've left fingerprints. How much did they take?"

"You can see in there."

Louise went into the living room. It was easy enough to spot what had vanished. The most expensive and at the same time easiest to sell. She skipped an inspection. Called instead to Frandsen, who was having dinner but took his time and said he'd send someone out there that evening.

Mie had packed and put Cecilie in a carrier with a flowered, baby-soft blanket draped over it. Louise held the door and took the bags.

"Call if you feel in any way threatened," she said as she stood out in front of the house and Mie locked it behind them. With a bag in each hand, Louise followed her to the garage where Nick kept his cars, the convertible with the beige top and the dark blue Mercedes that he usually drove around in. That was the one that Mie carefully set Cecilie in, and Louise thought that before long it might be seized, once they'd gotten a sense of how large her husband's earnings had been from the illegal furniture import.

She remained standing on the sidewalk and watched the widow and her little child, as the dark blue Mercedes drove up toward Englandsvej on its way to northern Zealand, where Mie's girlfriend lived on a farm.

43

I was not down at the harbor on Thursday evening. I have never been in the boathouse; I didn't even know my husband owned anything down there."

Britt had said no to coffee when she was driven in from Vestre Prison to a new interrogation.

She sat, looking pale, but managed to nod when Louise offered her a cup of tea instead.

"The problem is that we have so many things that point to your being down there," Louise said, looking at Britt.

"Circumstantial evidence can't be used for anything," Nikolaj Lassen interrupted loudly.

"We're not talking about circumstantial evidence in this instance," Louise corrected. "We have a handful of very clear and concrete proof and…"

She looked at Britt.

"What we have is enough to find you guilty on the charges we made against you."

Britt nodded.

Before they'd seated themselves in the office, Britt's lawyer had pulled Louise aside and whispered to her.

"My client has asked if you could visit her in prison, off

the record. It's OK with me, if we can agree that you don't discuss the case. And if something does come up that might be relevant, then you'd write that into the report. What do you say about that?"

Louise had nodded. Had earlier made that sort of agreement with lawyers to work together if something came up. And she wanted to go by Vestre Prison and talk a little informally about everything except the fire. She could always hope to leave with something relevant.

"You maintain that you've never been down to the boathouse?"

Louise spoke calmly and in a soft voice. Already at the start of the interrogation, the lawyer had admitted that he wasn't in a position to bring forward anything that proved his client's innocence. In other words, nothing had turned up to confirm she was telling the truth.

"I've never been to that part of the harbor," Britt said. "Only to the sailing clubs."

"Did you notice that your car was missing over the course of Thursday evening, when the fire broke out?"

"No," she said and shook her head patiently. "Most of the time, I slept upstairs, as I explained earlier."

Every answer was vague and circular.

"How would somebody get hold of your keys, if it wasn't you who drove the car to the harbor that evening?"

Britt Fasting-Thomsen shrugged her shoulders and shook her head—she didn't know. Maybe she'd left them in the car.

"Wouldn't you have noticed if someone had gone into your yard and taken firewood?"

Now the lawyer leaned forward.

"Anyone could have gone into the yard without my client noticing it," he said with conviction in his voice. "Damn it, she's taking sleeping pills to shut the world out. Anyone could have taken her car. Anyone could have gone into the house, if they'd wanted to. It's not certain that my client remembered to lock the front door."

He paused briefly and emptied his cup before continuing.

"You need to understand that my client has lost her grip," he said and looked from Louise to Thomas Toft. "She takes sleeping pills and sedatives; she's no longer that attentive. She doesn't notice details and changes. She has enough to do just getting through the great tragedy that's struck her."

His artistic pause was wanton, followed by a theatrical collapse in his chair and a sigh of resignation.

"In fact, someone could have lain in bed beside her without her noticing it," he said. "But that doesn't make her guilty of the charges against her."

"You'll just need to prove that to us," Louise said, irritated at his taking the obvious route.

"No," he suddenly yelled with renewed strength in his voice and banged his hand on the table. "It's damned well you who have to prove that she was at the harbor that night. Not me who needs to disprove it!"

Louise raised an eyebrow and looked over at Toft, who'd stayed quiet during most of the interrogation.

"That's exactly what we've already done," he said and turned his gaze to Britt.

"We'll end up sitting like this many more times in the days to come," he said and nodded pensively. "If you have anything at all to add that would point in some other direction, then it would spare you from having to go through these same motions."

"I have nothing to add," Britt said quietly and stood up when her lawyer nodded toward the door.

44

There was a pool in their hotel in Santa Barbara, and the sun was shining warmly even though it had gotten well into October. On the other side of the street was a wide sandy beach and wavy blue water, but the sea spray was a little too heavy to invite swimming, so Markus had immediately set his sights on the lounge chairs and the swimming pool. There weren't any other guests interested in soaking up sun, and there were clean towels on a little table at the entrance to the pool area.

They had two hours before they had to leave. Camilla had already located Frederik Sachs-Smith's house on a map and punched the address into the car's GPS. Twenty minutes with normal traffic. At the hotel's reception, they'd let her print out all the articles she'd found online in Danish newspapers about the family scandal, and now she took the stack with her to the pool, along with a cup of coffee and a soft drink for Markus.

As she saw it, the family's eldest son had always kept himself out of the jet set. He'd gotten a degree in film studies at the University of Copenhagen, but not much more than that had come up when she'd searched for him. There was a bit in the business sections about his real estate investments.

Each of the three siblings had received 10 million kroner on the day they turned eighteen, and they'd gotten another large monetary gift when they'd turned twenty-five. She hadn't been able to find the amount, but reading between the lines it must have been substantial. Unlike his siblings, who'd lived life in the fast lane with a lot of flair, expensive habits, and luxury cars, Frederik had as far as she could tell managed his millions sensibly by investing in real estate, and at a time when housing prices were low.

In one of the public records she'd found on his Danish enterprise, the worth of his properties totaled just under two hundred million—and on top of that there were the profits from his foreign investments. Frederik Sachs-Smith still owned a portion of Termo-Lux, but he no longer needed the family's fortune. He'd long ago made his own.

An hour later, the coffee was drunk and the papers smelled faintly of her sweaty hands. She'd been in the water twice, but only for short dips. Markus, on the other hand, spent almost the whole time in the water and felt like he hadn't gotten enough swim time when she told him it was time to go.

They drove south along the coast and looked at people who played beach volleyball or skated in the bike lane. The car windows were rolled down, and the wind grabbed hold of Camilla's blond hair and flung it in her face. She pushed her sunglasses onto her forehead to keep it somewhat in place and out of her eyes.

The road twisted and grew smaller. Wind tossed the

palms, and she'd already noticed when they'd arrived in town the previous day that there was a relaxed, vacation-like atmosphere around here. Even though this was precisely the one place on their long travels where she was not on vacation.

After the interview, she'd planned on continuing to Los Angeles, but now she suddenly felt that they deserved a couple of days in Santa Barbara, lounging by the pool, driving around the city and out to the famous pier that stretched like a branch out into the water and oozed with atmosphere from the restaurants and small shops.

"Turn right," droned the mechanical female voice. "Turn right."

The gate was wrought iron, and she had to step out of the car to reach the button on the intercom. But as soon as she introduced herself, the gate slid open.

❧

He stood on the stairs in a white shirt that hung down over his long shorts, which came down to his knees. His medium-length blond hair was held out of his face by a pair of sunglasses pushed onto his forehead. Two small dogs stood beside him yapping, so Camilla decided not to drive all the way up to the front door. Instead, she parked beside a tall flowering hedge that ran along the fence between his and his neighbor's property.

"They're friendly," he yelled from a distance and walked across the pebbles in his bare feet to greet them, the two dogs barking and jumping around him.

Markus stayed behind his mother and wasn't convinced until the dogs lay down affectionately and rolled over on their backs to have their stomachs scratched.

They were led into a large hall with tall wooden panels painted white and double doors into the living room, where there were huge, panoramic windows out to the sea. Their host waved them with him out to the terrace. The pool was somewhat larger than the one Markus had just swum in at the hotel—there were lounge chairs and raised umbrellas all the way around.

It looked like a vacation paradise with waving palms, but Frederik Sachs-Smith did not, however, look like someone who spent much of his time lounging beside the pool. He seemed restless, as if a great deal of energy poured out of him, and he'd normally be making better use of it.

On one of the shaded tables there was a laptop, and beside it was a thick manuscript with a large white stone on top to keep the pages from blowing away.

Staged, thought Camilla.

She guessed he usually sat and worked in his office. There was something about him that came across as more goal-driven professional than what you'd associate with the writer type who sits and writes beside the pool, but she found it in a way sympathetic: that he tried to tone himself down a little and wanted to present himself as a bohemian. When it was obvious to anyone that he was stinking rich.

"I'm sitting and working on some corrections to my film script. Universal starts filming next week, so I'm a little pressed for time."

Camilla smiled and was going to assure him that she'd keep it brief, but stopped herself. He'd agreed to talk with her, so he'd have to deal with his deadline himself.

"First, I'd like to say how sorry I am for your loss," she said.

It was always awkward to have to go through those sort of condolences, but it was also impolite to skip them.

He brushed her words aside and nodded toward the living room, where an older Mexican maid with a tray came into view. Fruit, water, and coffee. They'd have time for that.

The woman served them, and a moment later came back with a child-size bathrobe and a pair of white swimming trunks, which she handed to Markus. She smiled and pointed to the pool.

Markus looked over at Camilla, who nodded and said that if he were allowed to, then it was perfectly all right with her.

"Of course, that's what I have it for. I only use the pool when I swim in the morning."

She'd gotten it right. He wasn't the sort who spent his days loafing.

He lit a cigarette and lazily blew the smoke up into the air. Observed her with curiosity. His eyes were gray and his eyebrows pronounced and dark, unlike the medium-length blond hair.

"So, you're the one who'll satisfy the gossip-hungry Danes with my comments on the drama. Why's it interesting?"

From the pool came the sound of a splash, as Markus jumped off the diving board. Camilla suppressed a sigh. It could turn out to be a long afternoon if that was his attitude toward the interview.

"Because I think it could be fascinating to hear your views about what's happening back home," she said honestly. "My son and I have been traveling around over here for the last month, so during that time I've only followed the write-ups from a distance."

He seemed uninterested in her explanation.

"What are you doing over here?" he asked.

"Traveling around."

"Why?"

Now she sighed so he couldn't miss hearing it.

"Because...to tell you the truth, I'm so damned tired of the Danish press and various other things that I wanted to get away."

The look in his gray eyes changed a bit. He crushed out his cigarette in a glass ashtray on the table.

"Well, what d'ya know," he said in a special Zealander dialect that pegged him as coming from the edge of Roskilde, where the singsong tone wasn't quite as pronounced as it was in people from Holbæk, Ringsted, or Næstved, or anywhere else in the area.

That was something Camilla really liked about him, she decided. He hadn't cultivated an American accent, and he didn't search for words in order to carry on a conversation in his mother tongue. It was so pathetic when Danes ventured out into the world and after five minutes suddenly couldn't remember simple words or spoke Danish with a strong, fake accent.

"I'm curious," she said. "How do you feel about what's happened? Your mother's death and your father's disappearance? And your siblings? It's not being put in the best of lights."

He leaned forward toward her. The two dogs had come out to the terrace, and one of them put its head on his bare feet.

"My mother is one matter. But you're nuts if you're sitting there feeling sorry for how my siblings have been treated by the press. What's come out in the media is only the tip of the iceberg. I sure as hell don't feel sorry for them, and you shouldn't, either."

Camilla raised an eyebrow in surprise, but kept from interrupting.

"They're no sacrificial lambs, those two. They've gotten exactly what they wanted. And now that they have it, they're starting to fight with each other, as expected. Just wait and see," he said and nodded to her. "Up until now they've agreed about going after power in the firm. Now that they have it, I'd lay ten big ones they won't be able to agree on anything anymore."

"I don't quite know what it is they've agreed on," Camilla confessed and looked at him questioningly.

He leaned back and folded his hands behind his neck. The sun hit him in the eyes and made him squint a little.

"A few years back, my father drew up what's called an ongoing generational shift. At that point, I'd already moved away fifteen years earlier, so I wasn't there physically, just on paper."

He paused for a moment when he saw Camilla beginning to write.

"The board consisted of my father, me, and my siblings. Besides us, there were two members and the family attorney."

Camilla looked up from her pad as he leaned toward her.

"But all of this is simply boring, nothing but business talk, and I'm sick to death of hearing about it. Just like sex: It's always more fun when you're part of it."

She kept her eyes on the lined paper and got by with a nod.

"The short version is that the family attorney retired three years ago. His replacement was voted in, and it was quickly apparent that he was disloyal toward my father and the values that Termo-Lux was built on. He was greedy and must have thought there was more money in the youth. I don't know what Rebekka and Carl Emil paid him under the table to get him over to their side, because at that point I announced that after the next general assembly I wouldn't be continuing on the board. I had no need of being involved. I sat over here and looked after my work."

As if he needed to work at all, Camilla thought.

"I didn't want to listen to them, and it had gotten to where I didn't care what happened to the business. I didn't want to take it over, and financially I'm not dependent on it."

He tossed out his hands in a gesture of regret, as if he knew how extreme it was of him to not give a shit about the family enterprise.

"I left the board, and at the last general assembly my father did the same. He couldn't take it anymore. It's disturbing what happens to people when they get both money and power. It's not many who can handle the job. My siblings at any rate can't," he said, and for a moment he looked sad.

"And now my siblings are also the only family members on the board, and they're going on with the firm, and do you know what?" he asked and again leaned toward her.

Camilla, as expected, shook her head.

"The smartest thing is to stay far away..."

He'd apparently known it would turn out like that if his siblings came to power, yet he hadn't intervened to prevent it from happening.

"Was that the reason your mother took her own life?"

Frederik Sachs-Smith stood up and stuck his hands in his pockets. The dogs got up, too, and looked up at him expectantly, sweeping their tails over the tiles.

He shrugged his shoulders and looked out over to the sea, closing off any further questions in that direction.

Camilla studied him as he stood with his side to her, and

wondered how much envy and resentment there was in the relationship between the three siblings.

He started walking over to the living room door, and Camilla stood up to follow him.

"What about your father?" she asked.

He stood with his back to her.

"My father...!" he repeated.

"Do you think he's followed your mother in death, like the newspapers say?"

He still stood with his back turned.

"How do you know Ulrik?" he asked.

Finally, he turned and faced her. His parents were apparently a closed topic.

Camilla waved Markus out of the pool. She sensed that the visit was drawing to an end. She'd gotten less time than she'd hoped for, but wasn't prepared to leave the house before she'd gotten a couple of good quotes.

The story was in the bag; there was enough in what he'd said about his siblings and the whole background for why the renowned family had suddenly landed on the front pages, but she could really use a little about his grief, she thought and called for her son again.

"Markus and Signe have been in the same class since kindergarten," she said and walked with him into the living room.

"It's terrible what happened to her. That sort of thing just isn't bearable." His voice was full of sympathy. "Ulrik and his wife were here last summer. They visited me and stayed here a couple of days before they went on to Hawaii. He was going paragliding or something like that. He's completely possessed with putting his life in danger."

He smiled a bit and shook his head, as if it was a part of life he simply couldn't fathom.

Camilla stopped short and looked out at Markus, who was still drying himself off.

"That's odd," she said. "I've never heard of that."

"I hadn't met his wife before, but I've known Ulrik since my midtwenties. We have some businesses together. He's one of the best, but on the other hand he's got that hobby I'll never understand."

"He couldn't have been over here with Britt. She suffers from a fear of flying, and never travels with him. And she'd never leave without Signe."

Frederik Sachs-Smith blinked at her.

"Trust me, it's amazing what a person can get over for a trip to Hawaii," he said, and laughed. "I have a house on Kauai, and I don't know anyone who couldn't pull himself together and get on a plane if they had a chance of vacationing there."

Markus came in. His wet hair was plastered against his head and dripped down his T-shirt.

"Maybe, but it's not like that for people with aerophobia," Camilla said, not really caring for the arrogant tone he'd suddenly adopted. "If you have that, there's nothing that's attractive enough for you to willingly get on a plane and fly over to the other side of the globe. Not even your house in Hawaii."

He was still smiling, as if he knew a good deal more about what you could get a woman to do if what you were offering her were attractive enough.

"And certainly not if you have the opportunity to have your vacation in Skagen, as Ulrik's wife and I did last summer," she added.

She told Markus to go to the bathroom and dry his hair properly.

"Are there any pictures from their visit?" she asked.

Frederik shook his head and seemed irritated.

"It's not like I go around photo-documenting every time I have visitors."

"Of course not," Camilla said hurriedly. "But can you remember what she looked like?"

"It's hard to remember that sort of thing, but I recall a really nice set of breasts, and then she had blond hair, the way most women get it colored, I think."

"Then it definitely wasn't Ulrik's wife who visited you," Camilla said. "To begin with, she is not in possession of a memorable pair of breasts, and her hair is dark."

He looked like he was starting to be amused by her.

"Tell me, wouldn't you like a glass of wine? We could also have a bite to eat?"

He walked out to the terrace and Camilla followed him.

Frederik Sachs-Smith called for his Mexican house maid and asked her to bring provisions of various kinds.

"Actually, I'd rather you remember who the hell Ulrik had with him when he visited you," she said.

"Does it really matter who he was with? Now you know that he screws around—that should be enough."

She shook her head.

"Yes, it does so matter," she snapped. "I've known their family the last seven years, and I want to know who the woman is. I happen to know that his wife—that is, his real wife, Signe's mother—is sitting in prison at Vestre, charged with double homicide, which could send her to prison for life."

His face turned serious while Camilla spoke.

"That's terrible for them," he said quietly, then suddenly shook his head with obvious regret. "But if it wasn't his wife, then I don't know who it was. She was good-looking— maybe she was someone he paid for."

He paused a while and thought it over.

"When a friend introduces a woman as his wife, you don't ask anything more," he said.

They sat a little.

"I can tell you went to school in Roskilde," Camilla said. "You talk just like the boys I went to school with at the Cathedral School."

"That's where I went. Are you from Roskilde?"

The maid came out carrying a large tray covered with white cloth napkins. He nodded for her to set it on the table.

Camilla couldn't remember ever meeting him, but everyone knew that his family lived just on the edge of town.

"Would you like a cola?" he yelled to Markus, who was coming back from the bathroom.

The boy nodded and sent his mother a questioning look. He'd just gotten the message that they were about to leave, but now apparently, they were staying.

"We might know some of the same people. Do you want to sit in the sun or shade?" asked their host, who suddenly was not so busy with his manuscript, for which Universal was presumably still awaiting his corrections.

"Sun."

"When were you in school?" he asked, positioning the umbrella so the things on the tray wouldn't melt.

"I think I started just after you left," Camilla said and was about to sit down. Instead she looked at her watch and figured out what time it must be in Denmark.

"I just need to make a call first," she said.

45

At half past four, Louise was ready to drive home. She wanted to be sure she and Jonas had plenty of time to sit down together. The night before, when she'd come back from Mie's, he'd closed himself in his room with the puppy. On the kitchen table, he'd laid *Morgenavisen* for her. The front page was splashed with a large photograph of Britt Fasting-Thomsen, and in bold caps it read:

VENGEANCE THIRSTY MOTHER
JAILED FOR ARSON-HOMICIDE

She'd knocked softly on his door and asked if he wanted to talk about it. She wanted to tell him about the investigation, but he'd shaken his head and focused on the puppy. She, for her part, hadn't been ready to talk about that issue yet.

The next morning, he was out walking Dina when Louise got up, and they came back just before he had to leave for school. With her tea cup in hand, she'd stood listening as he grabbed his book bag and went down to drop off the puppy at Melvin's.

It wasn't very grownup of her not to have talked it through with him. Poor of her to delay. She should also have told him about Britt's arrest. Jonas had known Signe's mother much longer than Louise had known her, and it was low of her to make him read about it in the newspaper when she could have prepared him first. But the dog and Mik had gotten in the way, and then she'd had to drive out to Mie and her little baby.

Louise unlocked her bike and tightened her helmet.

They needed to talk about the dog, she thought, and that was the hardest part of the conversation for her to tackle. She needed to be sure that she'd thought it over thoroughly, so she was able to make a lasting decision.

After Louise had driven Britt back to prison following the day's interrogation, she'd taken her coat and gone for a walk down to the harbor. She walked down along the water past The Black Diamond library, while she tried to bring order to her thoughts and make them clear and definite to herself. Went back and forth, tried to look ahead and feel it out. Words like "consequence" and "forever" emerged and filled her thoughts a good deal, but at the same time she felt a heavy load of sadness overshadowing everything.

She kept walking and saw a couple of men sail by in a little motorboat. Mik still hadn't called. Her anger had settled down a bit, but far from enough for her to want to call him.

An hour later she felt ready to walk back. To say that she felt serene was probably going too far, but she felt satisfied. At the office, she'd packed her things and went around to Suhr's office to say she was leaving for the day.

"Is something wrong?" he asked, worried.

She shook her head.

"I was just out to Nick Hartmann's widow last night."

So far nothing had come out of the technicians' inspection, and that made Louise doubt that they'd find anything.

"I'd like to spend some time with Jonas today."

"Understandable enough," her boss said, and nodded. "Michael Stig and the president of Danish Furniture Design are about to go through the furniture in the warehouse, so we'll soon have a general idea of what the fake furniture would bring in if it were sold as authentic."

On her way home, she pulled off at the Irma on Gammel Kongevej and went inside for baking potatoes and veal cutlets.

❦

No one was home when Louise let herself into the apartment on the fourth floor, but in the entryway, there was an opened roll of dog-waste bags. The signals were clear: Jonas wanted that dog. It looked as though he'd gone shopping on his way home from school. In his room, there was a newly purchased dog bed and next to it two bowls for food and water. Everything was there except dog and boy.

On the other hand, there was a sea of messages from Camilla on the answering machine connected to her landline, and she noticed that her cell phone had also been bombarded. She'd put it on silent mode while she walked along the harbor gathering her thoughts, and then she'd forgotten to take it off.

"Skype?" she wrote in a text to Camilla and went in and turned on the computer in her bedroom.

Five minutes later, there appeared a blurry image of her friend, shouting the way you do when a telephone connection is bad and several words get drowned out before they reach their recipient.

"Why the hell haven't you called? Haven't you seen my messages?" Camilla asked on the computer screen.

Louise could see that she'd taken the laptop with her to a corner of the hotel room, where evidently, the wireless connection was better.

"I just got in the door. What's happened that's so important?"

"Earlier today I was out and interviewed Frederik Sachs-Smith," said Camilla. "He said he'd had a visit from Ulrik and his wife."

"Hmm...," Louise said absently and didn't immediately catch what was alarming about the information.

"But Britt's never been to the U.S., and the person Ulrik introduced as his wife in Santa Barbara didn't look like Britt, either. She was blond and buxom. You need to find out who the hell he travels around with and refers to as his wife."

She said that she'd pumped Frederik for more information, once he'd become more talkative, and apparently Ulrik and the blonde spoke about everyday things, experiences, and travels in a way that made their host believe they were married.

"It must be someone he knows pretty well, to be able to convince people they're married. At any rate, it's not Britt because she doesn't fly and besides that she was with me at the summer house when Ulrik was away. But it doesn't fit with the picture I have of him, at all."

"No," Louise conceded and shook her head at Camilla's face on the screen.

Her friend sighed and brushed her blond hair back. She looked tanned and healthy, had on a white shirt open at the neck.

"Have you thought that it might be his secretary or a

business connection?" asked Louise. At the moment, she was more preoccupied by the talk she and Jonas would be having when he came home.

"No, that's what you need to find out. But if he's got something or other going on the side, then he might think it's awfully convenient for his boring wife to be shoved out of the way in the slammer."

"Take it easy," Louise said.

She could see that Camilla had sat down on the floor with her back against the hotel's striped wallpaper. The picture quality was fine now. She could even see the tears in the corner of her friend's eye before they spilled over the edge.

"I just know that Britt didn't set fire to that boathouse," said Camilla, suddenly looking tired.

Louise was going to interrupt. They'd been through this before, and she'd begun to be irritated with Camilla's insistence, especially considering that she was on the other side of the planet. She hadn't even been anywhere near Britt since she lost her daughter.

"What is it you want us to dig up? The name of Ulrik's lover, so you have something to hit him over the head with?" she asked, a bit more condescending than necessary.

"No, that's not it," Camilla answered, cross. "But if he's living some kind of a double life, then there could be other things and other motives you're not getting served up on a silver platter. It's the same with Britt. You've been staring yourselves blind. What I'm trying to say is just that there could easily be others with a motive. What about the boys who stayed down there? What do you know about them?"

"What do they have to do with whoever Ulrik travels around the world with?"

"Nothing, probably, but I'm just saying there's lots of

things you haven't considered at all. You didn't know, for instance, that he had someone besides his wife."

"No, we didn't."

"And you wouldn't have found out about it, either, if I hadn't told you."

"No," Louise confessed and nodded when Camilla said that that was precisely what wasn't good enough if Britt sat in Vestre Prison. "You have to find out every damned thing. Otherwise she'll end up being sentenced."

"I don't really have time for this sort of thing," Louise began.

"Now hold on," said Camilla. "Won't you please go through everything? For my sake and for Britt's. Everything that relates to that boathouse. I could have landed in her situation, and you could have, too. What if we hadn't done it, and there was no one who believed in our innocence?"

She paused briefly.

"You need to try to prove that Britt didn't do it. If you don't find anything that points in another direction, and if she continues to take the blame herself, then that's that. But at the very least we need to try to help her."

Camilla took a deep breath and leaned her head back against the wall.

"You also need to understand something," Louise said calmly. "Even people you believe in and trust are capable of killing. I think anyone can kill another person, if they're driven far enough, and in Britt's case the police are in possession of very strong evidence that she was driven all the way to that point."

"Yes," said Camilla, nodding. "I've thought about that, too, and it's possible that that may be the case. But if no one thinks she's innocent, then it's just stuck there. Then she ends up sitting and waiting in jail until the sentence comes, and every day she'll sit and know she's in jail for something she didn't do. Without having a chance to convince anyone around her about it. That's what'll happen if we don't dig deeper and at the least rule out every imaginable possibility that could point to it not being her."

"And then when the day comes that you have to confess that it damn well was her all along, you can relax with a good conscience because you did everything you could to help her. Is that what you're saying?" asked Louise.

"Yes, that's pretty much it," Camilla admitted. "But we have a long way to go before we can relax."

Louise heard a key in the door and paws jumping up.

"Hi!" she heard from the door as Jonas came in with the puppy in his arms.

"Hi!" Louise said, smiling, and asked if he'd like to Skype a little with Camilla and Markus.

"I'll have a chat with Ulrik, and I'll drive by Vestre tomorrow and talk with Britt," Louise promised.

"Just call. We'll be here a few days before we head out. Frederik has invited us to stay in his annex. After that we're flying to Hawaii, where someone's letting us borrow a house right on the beach."

"Would that someone also be Frederik Sachs-Smith?" Louise asked.

"Yes, he's awfully generous. Don't you remember him? He went to Roskilde Cathedral School just like us, but he left the year we started. His siblings went down to Herlufsholm. It seems a standard high school education wasn't good enough for them."

Louise heard something softer and lighter in her friend's voice when she spoke about her celebrated host, something that hinted at Camilla cozying up to the rich and famous.

Louise didn't know exactly what she thought of it, but considering the state her friend had been in before the trip, anything that brought more lightness and happiness into her voice was more than welcome.

"All right, then, have a nice trip," she said.

Louise had long ago given up interfering in her friend's private life.

"Here come two who want to say hello," she said, scooting over for Jonas.

He lifted Dina affectionately to the web camera and smiled when Camilla and Markus completely melted over what a sweet dog she was.

Louise turned on the oven. She rinsed the roasting potatoes and rubbed them in oil, then laid them in an ovenproof dish with coarse salt on the bottom. After that, she opened a bottle of red wine, poured herself a glass, and called out to Station Bellahøj to get hold of Kent's cell number.

"That computer you seized out at the boathouse, is it with you or has it been sent to NITEC?" she asked when she got him on the line.

"It's in with them, but we didn't ask them to find out what's on it," he apologized. "The boys were let go again, and it'll be a long time before their case comes up."

"That's true. I'll call down there myself and find out if they've even done anything with it," she said.

He asked if there were something new, since she'd become interested in it.

"No," Louise answered. "It just needs to be entered into the investigation. Right now, I'm trying to collect the threads."

She didn't think there was any reason to tell him that she wanted to investigate whether there'd been any correspondence between the boys in the boathouse and Signe's father, or if there might be other relevant information on the computer that showed some other connection between them.

"Hang on while I get you the case number. That'll make it quicker for them to find it for you," he said.

46

At the National Police's IT Crimes Investigation Center, a man answered the phone and hummed in a friendly way as he took down the case number. Then he asked for her local number so they could call when they found the computer and had time to look at it.

"I'm in a bit of a rush," Louise said, hoping he didn't feel pushed.

He promised to do what he could.

From the bedroom, Jonas asked if she needed to talk more with Camilla before he closed the session.

"No, I'm finished. Aren't you coming out here?"

She got a soft drink out of the refrigerator and sat down at the table.

Jonas stood a little hesitantly with Dina in his arms.

"It's OK if she runs around," Louise said and nodded to the floor. "Come have a seat."

He seemed anxious and uncertain and hid his eyes under his bangs. His voice was even more hoarse than usual when he answered, "OK," and took a glass.

They sat a bit in silence before Louise got started.

"Jonas. It's not about my just waiting to have you shipped

off. The only reason I didn't offer, from the beginning, for you to live here for as long as you wanted is that I didn't feel like I was cut out to be anyone's mother. You do everything right, and I can't even fall for a puppy—the way most normal people do. I'm alone because I'm afraid of being forced to commit. And that's just not right."

Louise nodded to the puppy, which was stretched out on the floor, fast asleep with its head on its paws, the way puppies do. All tuckered out from a walk in the park.

Jonas gave her a sideways glance from under his hair, unsure if what she said was good or bad.

"You're welcome to have Dina here as much as you like, but I just can't offer to take care of her if someday you're tired of doing it yourself."

"I won't be," he muttered, and Louise quickly shook her head.

"I don't think you will be, either. And so it won't be a problem, and it doesn't mean I won't go for a walk with her or feed her. I just can't promise you I'll arrange my life around suddenly having a dog. Every boy wants a dog, and every boy—except you—gets tired of taking care of..."

"What about afterward?" he asked, looking up at her with his dark eyes. "When I can't stay here anymore?"

"There won't be any afterward. Not if you want to stay here."

❧

The blast was so powerful that the windows in the living room rattled. Louise jumped up and ordered Jonas to stay in the kitchen while she ran into the living room and looked out at the street. She saw smoke and flames, but couldn't see where they were coming from.

"Stay in here," she yelled to Jonas.

Dina still lay flat on the floor, exactly as deaf as Mik had feared.

Several people along the stairwell had opened their doors and talked together in alarm.

Something about a car that exploded, and huge flames.

Louise bounded down the stairs, already seeing through the windows that it was her Saab on fire.

She took the half flight of stairs down to the cellar, where the fire extinguisher hung on the wall. She tore it out of its holder.

Melvin came down to her in slippers, pulling on his brown cardigan.

"I called 112," he said breathlessly.

He looked at Louise.

"What the hell did you have in there that would make something like this happen?" he asked, shaken, and held the door for her as she came up with the heavy fire extinguisher.

Out on the sidewalk, she ripped the safety off the top so the trigger would depress, and white foam came out as though the extinguisher were a giant-size spray bottle.

"I didn't have anything in there. This is something someone else has done," she yelled to him and waved him away from the front door. "You'd better go back in. When the fire reaches the tank, it'll really start smoking."

The cars were parked tightly on the street, and she wanted to get the flames down before they shifted direction, but she didn't want to get too close because she couldn't see how much of the undercarriage was on fire and how close it had come to the tank.

Sirens blared. The fire truck came down from Allégade, taking up the whole road, and the alarm got people opening their windows. For once Louise was happy to be living so close to the Frederiksberg Fire Station. Usually it was just irritating to always hear the sirens go off.

She looked up at her apartment. Four dormer windows facing the street, and Jonas was at one of them. The fire extinguisher brought down the flames, but the fire had gotten to the seats. The firefighters pushed her back when they were ready with the fire hose, which handled the extinguishing work with a violent force. Countless gallons of water spread over the street and coursed away into the gutter.

She hadn't noticed the police car that joined them, and didn't know the officer who came over to her.

"Is it yours?"

She nodded. The Saab was completely burned out. What remained was a black skeleton: no windows, no lights. Everything had shattered or been burned away.

Louise felt herself shaking when she gave her name and pointed to the entrance.

"I live up on the fourth."

"Is Rick with a *k* or *c-h*?"

"With *c-k*," she answered and looked up to the house, where Jonas was now gone.

"I'd be ready to bet it was blown up," said one of the young men who'd assisted with the extinguishing. "It would look different if it were just set on fire, although there's a good deal of that kind of vandalism, too."

"Yes, but not at six o'clock, right in the middle of when people are eating," Louise said and shot him an angry look.

He shrugged his shoulders and turned away.

"I work over at Police Headquarters in the Homicide Department," she explained and gave the officer her cell number.

"I'm afraid he's right," he said and nodded to the car. "Is there anyone you've riled up or put behind bars?"

He smiled a little, and a moment passed before he reacted to her nod.

"Not put behind bars. But I have a vague idea who the sender might be, if it turns out not to be random vandalism. So, good luck with clearing it up..."

He stood with his pad in his hand and flipped to a new page.

"Nick Hartmann," Louise said, and he was about to write down the name, but stopped when she continued, "was shot."

Now he nodded, remembering the name.

"He had dealings with the bikers, and we suspect that he tried to cheat them out of an outrageously large amount. Yesterday there were serious threats made against his wife and their little newborn daughter, and we've intensified the investigation and are close to establishing a connection between them and the shooting victim. Maybe it isn't too far-fetched to think that this is a message to me to drop things and leave them in peace."

Louise gave him the name of her insurance company and said she'd send an accident report sometime in the next few days. The remains of her car, in the meantime, were wrapped in red-and-white police tape and awaited the crime technicians, who'd pick it up for a closer inspection.

"There's nothing in there you need, is there?" he said with a dry laugh. "When we know how it got started, you'll hear from us. First and foremost, we need to go around and find out if anyone saw or heard anything. You'd think there'd be a good chance someone did, considering the time of day. So, go on back in. We'll keep you informed, and please do contact us if anything happens that's relevant in connection with this."

She nodded.

"You're welcome to tell Frandsen this is my car," she said.

She took a couple of steps back to look over the Saab. The hatch was blown open and looked like a mouth gaping at the street.

She shook her head feeling more sorry than frightened by what had happened. She went over to her building and let herself in the entrance.

On the second floor, she saw Vivian, who had three children and whose husband worked at a bank.

"It's not so pleasant for the rest of us who live in the building to have something like this happen in the middle of our peaceful neighborhood. That's one of the reasons we pay extra to live in a decent place..."

Louise didn't even care to look at her as she walked by.

Up on the third, Melvin stood at his door and met her.

"Jonas and the dog are in here. Come on in."

She was glad to be led into his grandfatherly living room, where she was parked at the dining table. He took out a thin glass and poured her a stiff one.

Jonas didn't say a word. He sat on the sofa with Dina at his feet. She was the only one entirely unscathed by the shock that had turned Jonas pale and made Melvin reach for the shot glasses.

"That was something, huh?" Louise said, trying to smile happily at the boy.

He got up and came over and put his arms around her. He had to bend over, and it turned out to be a little awkward. The lump in his throat made it hard for him to speak.

"Think, if you'd been in it!" he whispered.

Louise pulled back a little, so she could look up at him.

"Then it wouldn't have happened," she said and cleared her throat.

Melvin sat down on a chair across from them.

"It was only to get a scare. There's no reason to be really afraid," she said, shaking off their concern so she wouldn't catch it herself. "But now we're also without a car."

"Can't you just use my dad's? It's still up in Sweden," he said earnestly. "OK, it's not a Saab, but a Citroën."

She smiled at him. Henrik Holm's estate hadn't been settled yet, and she hadn't interested herself in it, just received regular payments from the pastor's lawyer to help cover the extra expenses she'd had after Jonas moved in.

"Is there someone we should notify about this, that is, over at Headquarters where you work?" asked Melvin.

She shrugged her shoulders.

"It might be a good idea if I tell my chief, just for the sake of protocol," she said.

She was suddenly aware that Jonas still held her.

She turned a little and pulled him down onto her lap so she could put her arm around him. His body was warm and rested against her heavily. She could feel his rapid heartbeat against her underarm, and knew that he was in greater shock than he let on. She squeezed him a little tighter and drew him close, then whispered that it was all over with now and the police would find out who did it.

A hackneyed phrase. Unless there'd been a witness, there wasn't a chance in hell they'd find out who did it. And, in reality, it was mostly just what one said to calm other people down. She was fairly certain it was connected to Mie and her daughter being moved from their house. The bikers felt the police breathing down their necks, and they didn't like it.

She nodded gratefully when Melvin offered her another shot, then called Suhr at home, disturbing him in the middle of evening coffee.

When they came up after having taken Dina on an evening walk around the neighborhood, the baked potatoes in the oven were completely dried out. She'd forgotten all about them when she'd offered to take the dog for a walk. But Jonas had wanted to go, too, and now it occurred to her that he didn't want her to go alone. He wanted to be there to rescue her if the strangers came back.

She kissed him on the cheek when they said good night, and refrained from saying anything about the puppy, which had slipped into bed with him.

47

It was 8:45 the next morning when Louise met with Ulrik Fasting-Thomsen at his home on Strandvænget. On her way into Headquarters, she'd called him and asked for ten minutes for what she'd called a brief update.

He was still staying at a hotel in the city to avoid journalists. When Louise caught him on his cell phone, he apologized for his day being filled up with meetings and suggested they meet in the early morning, when he had to run by the house to pick up some papers he had on his desk.

The garden path was covered with yellow leaves, and it was wet from last night's rain. Ulrik had parked his big Audi out on the street instead of driving it to the carport, and everything about the house looked abandoned and darkened when Louise walked up and rang the bell.

His suit was designer and the shirt underneath it white and freshly ironed. Well-groomed, like the first time she'd met him, thought Louise, even though the lines on his face seemed deeper, his chin more pronounced. He's lost weight, she decided and followed him into the entryway, where a big pile of unread newspapers lay just inside the door.

Ulrik pointed to the living room and asked her to follow him.

"Should we make some coffee?" he asked, looking at her.

"Not for my sake," Louise said.

She pulled out a chair from the long dining table and invited him to sit down.

"How did you and Nick Hartmann come into contact with each other? Did you advertise that you had a warehouse for rent?" she asked.

Ulrik shook his head.

"I gave him lessons a few times. He was mostly into parachute diving, but wanted to try paragliding. He went to a couple of my weekend courses, and one of the times we got to talking about his needing space."

Louise took her pad out.

"Did you know what he'd be using the warehouse for?" she asked.

He shrugged his shoulders.

"I'm not interested in that sort of thing, as long as it's not containers with hash or narcotics," he said and smiled. "And I could see that it wasn't."

She nodded.

"You knew what he was storing there?"

"Yes, furniture, but I've only been by a single time since he moved his things in. I pay a man to keep an eye out for me."

"What did you know about Nick and his business?"

Ulrik leaned forward a little toward Louise.

"I didn't know much at all about him. I don't about the renters in the other properties I own, either. I have caretakers and administrators who keep up with the individual leases. There are a couple of friends I've helped into an apartment, but otherwise there's a law firm that's responsible for the rents. The only thing I knew about Nick was that we had the same hobby."

"Did you know that he had connections in the biker scene?"

A shadow passed over Ulrik's face.

"I had an idea, or rather I should say that it doesn't surprise me," he admitted. "He talked a little about it at one point, and the money had to come from somewhere. He had expensive cars and seemed to like to live with a lot of flair."

Louise waited for him to continue.

"But, honestly, I don't get myself mixed up in where people's money comes from, as long as they can pay their rent," he said. "He was a decent and steady guy with a respectable job in a large shipping firm. His circle of friends, and who's in it, didn't interest me."

She nodded a couple of times and changed the subject.

"I've been informed that you have a lover. Is that so?"

Ulrik scooted back in his chair and looked at her in surprise.

"Where did you hear that?"

"Do you have a relationship with another woman?" she repeated.

"Why?" asked Ulrik. "Why are you asking that?"

"Because," Louise said, "I'd like to have a complete picture of everything that relates to you and your family. I want to know everything. Nick Hartmann was shot down, and the motive might be related to the things he was storing in your warehouse. Not long afterward, that same warehouse burned down."

"The boathouse burned down," Ulrik corrected. "And according to the charges you've made against my wife, there is a motive for it."

"Who's the woman you introduced as your wife when you visited Sachs-Smith in July last year?"

His face fell a bit. He sighed and his body slouched.

It was obvious that he was thinking it over before he said anything. Pros and cons were being considered with lightning speed in his mind.

"It's true that I've had a relationship with another woman," he admitted and glanced at Louise with a look that was more sad than ashamed. "I ended it after what happened to Signe. I suddenly couldn't do it anymore, so I no longer see her, and I'd be very grateful if you would refrain from telling this to my wife. It's over, and there's no reason to hurt Britt any more than she already has been."

"No," Louise said, instantly agreeing. "But I need to ask you if it's possible that your lover may have been involved in the fire down at the harbor."

He looked at her in confusion, apparently at a loss for where she was headed.

"If you'd just ended your relationship because of your daughter's death, then couldn't your lover have decided, out of pure jealousy, to set fire to the boathouse and direct suspicion against Britt?"

Louise sat through his violent outburst.

"What in the hell are you saying! God, no, she couldn't do that!"

"And you know that for a fact?" Louise asked and studied him.

He nodded, outraged. Combed his fingers through his hair and suddenly seemed unhappy. The rage left him, and he leaned back in his chair with a look of despair.

"She had nothing to do with it, because she was with me the night the fire broke out," he said and looked straight ahead. "Up in Iceland. It was up there that I ended it between us. So, I can say with certainty that it wasn't her."

"OK, I take it someone can confirm that," Louise said and stood up.

"You can call the hotel. We stayed at 101 in Reykjavik," he told her. "They know us, we've stayed there several times before."

"Are you visiting Britt out in the prison?" she asked when he followed her out to the entryway. She should have gone out there herself, but hadn't gotten around to it yet.

He shook his head a little sheepishly.

"I've only been out there once. I think it's hard. I don't know what the hell to say to her."

"I'm not sure you have to say anything. Maybe it's enough just to be there," Louise said.

He opened the front door and offered her his hand.

"Is it commonly known that you're the one who owns the warehouse down at the harbor?" she asked before stepping out to the weather porch.

"No, but it's listed in Krak's Business Directory if you look it up, isn't it? Or maybe my firm comes up, but it's in my name."

"You should know that the people Nick Hartmann created businesses for have started making very serious threats to his widow, trying to extort the unpaid money from her."

"Did he borrow?"

Louise shook her head.

"It seems like they're going after the value the one container of furniture would have brought in. We don't know how he raised money for the second. But all the furniture is seized now, so that money's lost. A few days ago, two men broke into the widow's house and took all the valuables in the home. Now they're trying to pressure her into selling her duplex apartment and paying 4 million kroner, or else they'll take her daughter from her."

Ulrik stood with one arm against the window frame and listened intently.

"It sounds absolutely insane," he said. "Mafia methods. What if they find out that I'm the one who owns the property down there? Would they think of coming here?"

For the first time he seemed genuinely shaken, Louise thought. She shrugged her shoulders.

"They're not the kind of people you'd want to owe money to. But if you didn't have anything to do with Hartmann, then there's nothing for them to come after."

She walked down the steps.

"Do I have reason to be concerned?" he asked.

She turned to him, a bit annoyed that it should be that kind of worry that would upset him.

"You'd know best yourself," she couldn't resist saying.

48

"He has an account on the Isle of Man, and I'm guessing the money is double-black," Sejr said as soon as Louise came back to the office at Headquarters.

"What the hell is double-black?" she asked and tossed her bag on the floor.

Sejr Gylling had his yellow sunglasses on today, and his hoodie was beige. None of it went very well with his white hair.

"Double-black is money that neither the tax authorities nor your wife knows about," he explained and looked as if he'd just found a big bag of Haribo candy someone had forgotten about.

"He's generated a huge profit by sending the fees from foreign customers directly to his account on the Isle of Man, where he's established a business."

"Slow down!" said Louise and interrupted him. "Bring it down a notch. I have no idea what the hell you're talking about, and you're talking like an Energizer Bunny on full battery."

He leaned back, waiting for her to get it. His headphones were on the desk and looked as if he'd completely forgotten them in his preoccupation with his new find.

"Do you mean Hartmann paid for the extra container with money he had in a hidden account out of the country?" she asked.

"Not Hartmann," Sejr said with a shake of his head. "It's Ulrik Fasting-Thomsen who's using a hidden account."

Louise looked at him with surprise.

"Well, damn. And you know that for a fact?"

"I got an international court order to see if either of those two had a foreign account. Those are sent out by the foreign secretary and Interpol, and then it takes several weeks before the official bank information in question gets delivered to Denmark, but I've received unofficial information from Interpol, so that's good enough. On the other hand, they haven't been able to track down anything on Hartmann."

"That's a hell of a thing for a respected investment consultant to be doing," Louise exclaimed and leaned back in her office chair. "An account on a British island in the Irish Sea without mandatory reporting. Does it work like a tax haven in the same way as the Canary Islands, Gibraltar, and Monaco?"

Sejr nodded.

"What was all that you were saying about generating a profit? From what?" she asked.

"Yeah, at first glance it looks like all the deposits he received from foreign customers were sent directly in there. Plus, the quite considerable sum his foreign investments must have brought in. I found very few foreign deposits in his regular Danish business account, so I didn't think he had many foreign customers. But from his vouchers I could see that there'd been lots of business trips and expenses in connection with meetings held abroad, and, of course, that made me wonder whether anything came out of all those travel days he'd had. So, I got suspicious that the foreign profits might be hidden someplace out there."

Louise smiled at him. It was so Sejr-like, she decided. Compared with her methods, he was more like a book-keeper, but right now he was the one who'd gotten further.

"The authorities on the Isle of Man are sending the bank information to the Ministry of Justice, and they're reason-ably quick compared with a lot of the countries we work with," he said.

Louise's telephone rang, and she shook the image of Ul-rik out of her mind.

"This is Hansen from NITEC. You asked us to look at a computer. Do you have time to come over? I think it's wise that you see the contents for yourself instead of relying on a transcript!"

※

"Cannibal Corpse," said Hansen when he received Louise at the National Police's IT Crimes Investigation Center. He led her into a little room where the head-banging death metal hammered out of the Dell computer that Bellahøj had seized in their search of the boathouse the day they con-nected the boys with the assault on Britt.

"The band gets a higher and higher status whenever one of their songs is banned or someone tries to censor their mu-sic," explained the IT expert, who'd apparently read up on the band's history. "It's not exactly the sort of music you hear played on the popular radio stations," he added, saying the music was downloaded from the Internet.

Louise nodded quickly when he motioned that he'd turn it off.

"Have they used the computer for anything other than

music?" she asked, still standing behind him with her jacket on and her bag over her shoulder, ready to be out the door again quickly.

He pulled a chair over and nodded to her.

She tossed her coat onto the windowsill and sat down in front of the screen.

"Do you know anything about a special genre of movies called 'Faces of Death'?" he asked and looked at her.

She shrugged her shoulders.

"I've heard of it. I think I know what it's about. But I've never felt a strong need to deepen my knowledge by watching one of them."

He looked like he understood her. At the same time, he obviously had a much wider knowledge of films shared online, where no one censored the content. She had to remind herself that the people in IT investigations were also the ones who had the pleasure of looking through all the seized files with child pornography, which had to be at least as disgusting to lay eyes on.

"There's lots of it here. People who die in accidents, recorded on cell phone videos. Traffic victims, suicide, and victims of violence—and it's that last category that seemed to have lit them up the most."

Louise thought about the boys from the boathouse. As for the one who'd beaten a father into a coma, it didn't surprise her that he'd find something like that amusing.

He found a list of the downloaded films and let the cursor pass down it.

"It keeps going," he said. "A homeless man beaten to death in a basement. A young boy who's waiting for the bus attacked by two people wearing hoods, and they only leave him when he's dead."

He mentioned a couple more examples, adding that he

suspected some of the attacks were staged and the victims didn't die, as they appear to in the films. But by far, the majority of the films the boys entertained themselves with looked to be genuine.

"How about e-mail—is there anything to show who the boys corresponded with?"

"There's no e-mail or other correspondence, and they haven't created a Facebook account or used other forums."

"Does the name Ulrik Fasting-Thomsen appear anywhere?"

He shook his head apologetically. It seemed like the computer was used exclusively for music and films.

"There are lots of feature films, and you can pretty much figure they're in the violence genre."

He closed the site with the downloads, and Louise only listened with half an ear to what he was saying. Her eyes caught on a document in the upper right corner: "Unedited."

"What's that?" she asked, pointing.

"It's an AVI file. The things on the desktop are a little mixed. I haven't had a good look through it yet, but it seems to be something that was transferred. Probably with a USB drive. Photos and newspaper articles..."

"See if you can open that one," she asked and pulled her chair closer.

When he clicked, the file opened in Media Player and showed that it was a clip lasting just five minutes.

"Man shot down" was written in green ink on a piece of lined paper. Might be meant as an intro and was filmed by hand.

"September 25" it said in the upper right under Properties.

Louise leaned forward and scooted in so she could be right on top of the screen and follow along.

Play.

The camera must have been on a stand because the picture didn't follow along when the two people in the film moved. Now and then they disappeared from the screen, but then popped back up again. It was hard to get a good look at anything because it was too dark and the people only appeared as vague silhouettes.

Darkness swallowed up most of the action. But then they were there again, and one of them passed a firearm to the other. Several weapons passed in front of the camera's lens; the two people walked away holding four firearms up to the camera, so there was no doubt that they were heavily armed. But it was still too dark to see details, just outlines of the mouths and barrels of guns—one of them was a machine gun.

The pair started moving; one of them carried the camera. You could see that it was being raised, and at one point the lens caught some light that gave Louise the impression that they were moving toward a house with lamps lit behind the windows.

She heard noise, something clattered, and the camera went out. Raised again on another stand, farther up. All the way up to the house, with a clear view of the lit-up windows.

There was a humming sound as it zoomed in and sharpened the focus.

In on the sofa lay Nick Hartmann. You could see perfectly that his eyes were on the TV, which was a little to his right.

There was a yell that sounded like "Clear," and then the first shot.

Behind the window, Hartmann jumped off the sofa. Glass shattered and he ran through the living room out to what Louise knew was the kitchen.

The shots went on and on.

When Hartmann came back, the one carrying the machine gun bounded up to the broken window and carefully positioned the gun barrel in the window frame before firing away.

Louise leaned forward.

The ponytail was perfectly visible, and she recognized the profile from the photos the police had brought to show Jonas.

"How clear can you make these images?" she asked, just as Mie's dog came into view.

Zato stood in an attack position, but soon fell over on his side, hit by a single shot.

It was in the moment he turned to the dog that Nick Hartmann himself was hit.

You could see that he tried to hide, but didn't manage to before a burst from the machine gun reached him. He was blown backward, and at the same time there was a shot from the other end of the living room.

Louise's eyes ached from focusing. The person who shot in through the window farthest to the right, the window that was closest to the kitchen, was taller and seemed more heavily into it. She couldn't say with certainty that it was Kenneth Thim or Thomas Jørgensen, but she was almost positive it was one of them.

"How clear can these images be if you enhance them?" she asked again.

"I can't do much with the part that's taped in the dark, but I'd think we could get very close where it's lit up by the light in the living room."

Suddenly, the camera moved, aimed and zoomed in on Nick Hartmann's bloodied body as a final shot struck him in the chest.

The finale.
All over then. The camera shut off as the feet ran away.

※

The others had gone to lunch when Louise came back with a copy of the film, given to her by a National Police officer on the other side of the street. She'd already called Suhr and told him what they'd found on the computer from down at the boathouse.

She went over to the lunchroom for a cup of coffee, but was too full of disgust to be hungry.

VENGEFUL MOTHER DENIES ALL was on the front page of one of the day's newspapers. There was also a large photo of Britt, taken through the side window of a patrol car. Louise thought she must have been caught as she was being driven back to Vestre after the last interrogation. She took the newspaper with her into the office.

The caption underneath the photo went on about how Britt had set fire to the boathouse with flammable liquid while two young teenage boys lay sleeping inside.

The word choice varied a little, but they either called her "thirsty for vengeance," "vengeful," or "arsonist." Sebastian Styhne's father, the restaurant owner from New Harbor, had been quite generous in telling the public about his son and his friends, and the picture he painted for them was of a bunch of happy boys who hung out together, drank a little beer, and went into the city like all the other young people.

After the film Louise had seen, there was quite some distance between what the father presented and reality. A bit cynical, she thought and pushed the newspaper aside, feeling profoundly disturbed over the way Nick Hartmann had been executed only a few yards from the room where his wife and their little baby were.

Her cell phone rang. It was Michael Stig. He and Toft were in their office with the police's prosecuting attorney and were ready to play the film.

Louise poured the rest of her coffee in the sink. In the hallway she met Suhr, who was also joining them, and Willumsen had rolled an extra chair in.

"If the people in the images are clear and identifiable, we'll get started with the arrests immediately," said the lieutenant.

※

"An ordered killing?" Suhr pondered afterward, walking with her to her office, where Sejr sat behind his screens.

"Presumably," Louise conceded, and added that the youths were also sick enough to make a little entertainment out of it for their film collection.

"Do people sell that kind of film?" asked the lieutenant and looked across the desk.

Sejr Gylling took his headphones off when he sensed that he was being spoken to, and asked Suhr to repeat himself. Then he shrugged his shoulders.

"People either join a group for trading, or they can be bought and sold. It can go either way. But if you don't have any of your own films to trade, you'll have to pay big money for the ones you want to watch."

"Then we'll have to have the folks in IT take a look to see what else is on the computer. Hartmann might not be the only one the boys have tossed into the entertainment collective," the lieutenant said, adding that it would be a nice bonus if they could also track down the people who up-loaded death videos onto the Internet.

"Like to know if they filmed my Saab getting blown up," Louise mumbled drily.

She didn't disagree with Suhr when he concluded that it was the connection between the bikers, or at least people on their periphery, and Nick Hartmann that had led to the mur-der. The boys in the boathouse had been involved; several of them had hopes of making it into the biker ranks, and so they'd run errands for them.

"Shouldn't we get Mie to review the photos of these boys?" she asked. "They might be the ones who were sent to scare the life out of her and empty the valuables from her home."

Suhr nodded and looked at Sejr.

"Can you go through Nymann and the other boys' bank statements so we can see if there's been a large deposit that might be payment for an ordered killing?"

Gylling nodded, but warned the lieutenant that it could be days before he could get access to their bank statements.

Michael Stig and Toft had joined them and stood in the door, but had to move out of the way when Willumsen squeezed through.

"We're picking up all three boys for questioning, and I'll be damned if they're getting out of here before they've given an account for the whole shit. They're going to tell us what they know about Hartmann, and what their connec-tion is to the bikers, and whatever the hell else they've spent their time doing," snarled the lead investigator.

He was clearly torn up over the premeditated and cold-blooded shooting he'd seen, but also over the tastelessness in their cynically filming the whole thing, so they could both amuse themselves and share it afterward.

"And they must not be allowed to talk together when they realize we're after them," he continued and looked at Toft and Michael Stig. "Make sure they don't have a chance to call or write each other."

They nodded. Discussed quickly in which order to pick them up. A sudden intensity took hold like a vibrating tension—an adrenaline kick waiting to be released. Louise had much more respect for Willumsen when he played the role of someone who looked ahead and delegated, instead of going around all pissed-off and spoiling everyone's mood.

He looked at Louise.

"Britt Fasting-Thomsen ought to be grateful she wasn't hurt worse than she was when they attacked her down at the sailing club."

There went a little of her respect for him again.

"Britt couldn't have been hurt worse than she was that night," Louise said and gave him an irritated look.

"Oh yeah, she could have. Now that we know what these boys go around doing," Willumsen said.

"You still don't get it," she said, holding his gaze. "Signe's mother lost everything when she lost her daughter. She's checked out. She didn't even have the energy to set fire to the shitty boathouse and the even shittier boys. She's been lying at home in a world that's stood still. And now she's playing the scapegoat for someone who doesn't give a damn that she's taken the fall. So, to be honest with you, I think it's hard to imagine how she could have been hurt worse."

She exhaled and reminded herself once again that she ought to pay Britt that off-the-record visit.

"And that's something you know?" Toft asked and looked at her with interest. Among her colleagues, he was the one who took her intuitions most seriously.

Louise nodded.

"I feel very convinced that she's innocent. But it'll be us who'll have to prove she didn't do it. Because it's not something we'll get her to say."

Now she looked at Willumsen and elaborated.

"She's still going through so much hell that it doesn't matter to her where she wears out her life. It doesn't matter which side of the wall she finds herself on, because she's already lost everything."

The lieutenant stood up from the short bureau, and the lead investigator stuck his hands in the pockets of his gabardine trousers, his striped sweater creeping up and revealing a paunch that stuck a good distance over his belt buckle.

"Let's go into my office," Suhr said and asked Louise to join him while the others got ready to pick up Kenneth Thim, Thomas Jørgensen, and Jón Vigdísarson for questioning.

❧

"I just don't believe she did it," Louise repeated once the lieutenant had closed the door behind them.

But at the same time, she admitted that she couldn't explain how Britt's car had gotten down to the harbor when she said she hadn't driven it there. Or where the firewood had come from if not from the woodshed behind the house on Strandvænget.

"I have no idea," she said and gestured with her arms. "Someone wanted us to think it was her. That worked at first, but now we need to prove that she wasn't there."

"The evidence is already quite clear," the lieutenant said from his chair behind his desk.

He looked at her, waiting for her to come up with something concrete to strengthen her impression.

"And who else might it be? The boys? Would they burn down their meeting place with two of their friends inside in order to pass the blame onto a woman they don't know?"

He looked doubtfully at her.

"Of course not."

"Then who?"

She took a deep breath.

"Ulrik!"

Suhr raised an eyebrow.

"Her husband?"

Louise nodded.

"Maybe, but I don't think anyone counted on there being someone in the boathouse. The boys were tossed out and had moved their things. No one could know that Sebastian Styhne and Peter Nymann lay sleeping in there. Not even Britt."

He listened, but gave her a skeptical look.

"Do you mean to say it was Ulrik Fasting-Thomsen who set fire to his own buildings and then afterward let his wife sit in prison charged with arson and double homicide?"

"No, that wouldn't fit," Louise had to confess. "But one might imagine that he's the one who kicked in the money for Hartmann's extra container, the one that came from Hong Kong last time. Sejr's found a hidden account in a bank on the Isle of Man."

It seemed like the lieutenant was already informed, because he nodded and asked if they'd looked through transfers and bank statements yet.

"We're getting them from Interpol later today, but it's quite clear that he's knowingly kept money hidden from the tax authorities at SKAT and from his own firm's account-ing," she said.

"Really? A swindle from one of the country's most re-spected investment consultants?" Suhr asked doubtfully.

"It looks that way," she said, nodding. "He could have kicked the money in. He knew Hartmann and knew what was in the warehouse. Once we started looking closer at the things down there, it may have been very convenient for him if it all went up in flames."

Hans Suhr leaned back in his chair and studied her. Then he cleared his throat, and she saw that he hadn't bought it.

"And lose the value of what was in there?" he asked.

"I think he'd damn well rather lose the four million he kicked in than his good name and reputation, which he risked if he was found out," she said.

She reminded her boss that if the episode down in the boathouse hadn't happened, then the police would never have interested themselves in Ulrik's finances.

"Let's just wait and see what that secret account tells us before we go getting carried away," Suhr decided. "It may be there's only pennies in there, and nothing more."

She nodded, then stood up to leave.

"What do you suddenly have against Ulrik Fasting-Thomsen?" he asked.

She stood a bit thinking it over before answering.

"I have something against how we're single-mindedly fol-lowing a track that doesn't make sense to me. Also, I have reason to believe that Ulrik isn't so completely loyal as I first thought. When I spoke with him this morning, I confirmed that over a long period he's had a lover who he's traveled around with and introduced as his wife. To my eyes, it's start-ing to look like he's led a double life next to the nice and presentable one that we know about."

Now she had Suhr's undivided attention. He took off his glasses, folded them, and laid them on his desk between two stacks of paper.

"Where do you have that information from?" he asked and wondered if it was something Britt had told her.

Louise shook her head.

"I'm not even sure that Britt knows anything about it. I haven't spoken with her yet."

She told him about Camilla and her visit in Santa Barbara.

"Camilla Lind," the lieutenant said with a nod. "I thought she was on leave?"

"She is. It was just an interview she wanted to do, and while she was there Sachs-Smith told her he'd had a visit from Ulrik and a wife who turned out not to be Britt."

Suhr chewed on that a bit before he surrendered.

"Well then, we'll have to give him a careful looking over."

He began to nod.

Louise shrugged her shoulders.

There was a knock on the door and Willumsen came in with red splotches along his neck. He was breathing rapidly.

"Someone's been after Mie Hartmann again," he said without apologizing for the interruption.

"Has anything happened to the child?" Louise asked.

He shook his head quickly and looked at Suhr.

"They found her at a friend's up in North Zealand— however the hell they tracked her down," he snarled and ran his hand through his black hair. "She'd been out taking a walk in the woods with her little girl in a baby carriage, and when they came back to the house there was a child's bed out in the yard, with a duvet and the whole shit. Inside it was a photograph of her daughter—the same photograph

Mie had in her living room at home. They'd taken it with them when they paid their visit the other day. But they'd added a detail. In this photograph, the daughter has a rope around her neck."

He put his hands around his neck to illustrate.

"They must have Photoshopped it. I just got it in an e-mail, and it looks a hundred percent real," he said, shaking his head. "Along with the photo, Mie Hartmann found a note that said she should call a cell number when she was ready to pay what her husband owed. If not, the girl would end up like in the picture."

Willumsen had started pacing back and forth in the office. He had his eyes on the floor while he talked, and the furrows that appeared across his brow clearly showed his concern.

"Someone means all this seriously," he said. "Hartmann's widow is, according to what our colleagues are saying, a basket case and doesn't want to be alone. Understandably enough," he added, revealing a side of Willumsen that was softer and more understanding. Because it was there, just buried deep.

"For God's sake," Suhr exclaimed and put his glasses back on.

"Where are she and the child now?" asked Louise.

"They're still up with the friend, but we need to see about getting them moved. There's a team from North Zealand's police up there now."

Willumsen explained that the farm was a good distance from the nearest neighbor.

"No one saw when the child's bed was brought to the farm, and as far as I understand you have to go up a long driveway to get to the house," he said. "We need to get the crime techs up there," Suhr decided and lifted the phone to call Slotsherrensvej, where he was put straight through to Frandsen.

Louise felt a knot in her stomach. She thought about the film and didn't doubt for a second that they'd follow through on their threats if Mie didn't pay. But she couldn't pay. What was she supposed to do about it?

"How far are you with the arrests?" she asked and looked at Willumsen.

If the ones who chased Mie were the same ones who'd shot down her husband in cold blood, they needed to be stopped now.

"Two of the boys have just been arrested. We're missing Thim, but his supervisor tells us he's on the way back to the garage with some parts he went out to Værløse to pick up. He's training to be an auto mechanic."

Willumsen squinted his eyes and stood with a thoughtful expression on his face. He agreed with Louise that the suspect who was with Nymann at the shooting out on Dyvekes Allé looked the most like Thim, and it was obvious that the lead investigator was mentally preparing to question the boys when they arrived at Headquarters, with their rights to think about.

"Toft is ready to meet him at the garage when he gets back," he said and told them that Michael Stig and the officers who'd assisted in the arrests would be coming through the door any minute. "And in an hour, we'll have the images from the film printed out on paper. And then they'll have a goddamned hard time trying to explain themselves."

He slapped his hands together with a satisfied clap and left the office.

Suhr looked at Louise.

"We need to figure out if Fasting-Thomsen was financially involved in what was stored in his warehouse," he said.

Music poured out of the office when Louise opened the door. She stopped dead at the sound of the classical notes that rose to the ceiling in the comparatively shabby space, making the darkened room seem much too small for all that sound.

Surprised, she looked over at Sejr, who smiled and explained that now and then you need to clean out your head so more can go in.

Louise thought of Britt out at Vestre Prison and hoped that someone had taken care of getting a little of her music out there.

"I think Hartmann bungled it," Sejr said and turned down the volume.

He waved her over to his screen, where she could see he'd logged into the Fraud Department's archive.

"I searched for designer furniture, and on August twenty-eighth we received a call from a buyer for a large furniture chain on Jutland. He'd been contacted by a person who offered him a quantity of Arne Jacobsen's Swan chairs. When the buyer asked when they could be delivered, he was told that they'd just arrived from the factory in Asia, and then he realized something was wrong."

"How?" Louise asked and looked at him in confusion.

"It's possible that some of the genuine designer furniture is manufactured out there, but the classic Egg and Swan are only manufactured in Europe, and you always have to account for extra delivery time because they can't be ordered like mass produced goods."

"So, it had to be someone without that knowledge who was trying to get rid of something," she concluded.

"Yeah, pretty clumsy, wouldn't you say?"

She nodded.

"My guess is that Hartmann knew what he was doing when he purchased, but he didn't know how to go about selling replicated furniture. Others must have handled that part. With the large quantities, it's actually not that easy unless you have established channels who'll buy," he explained. "If he, as we're assuming, tried to find private buyers, it's a big job. And with furniture chains and auction houses you risk being exposed if the quality doesn't live up to the authentic product. That's why it's best to stay away from them and go after the gullible and ill-informed private customers, who don't know enough to challenge the seller on details."

"Doesn't it also draw too much attention if a large quantity of expensive furniture suddenly pops up?" Louise asked and emptied the cola Sejr had offered her.

"Yes, there's a natural limit to how much the market can bear. And it could very well be that that's what pissed off his original collaborators. They probably discovered what he was up to."

Things started to whirl for Louise. In her mind, she saw Mie and her little daughter and knew that neither of them would be safe if the sum of money really was so large.

"Could Hartmann have been working for Ulrik the whole time? Are we the ones who've been mistaken in believing in the biker angle?" she asked and screwed the cap on her cola bottle before dropping it into the box beside the fridge.

"No," Sejr decided. "If it had been those two, then Hartmann wouldn't have been killed. You don't slaughter the fatted calf. The capitalist needs someone who can do the work. If neither had felt cheated or squeezed, then it could have been an ongoing business and they would have continued raking it in. There was another party involved, who at some point felt cheated—I'm entirely sure of that."

The telephone on Louise's desk started to ring, and Sejr put his headphones on and turned his gaze toward the screen.

At first, it was difficult for her to hear the words, which were nearly a whisper. For a moment, she thought it was Mie and nervously sat up straight. But when the woman cleared her throat a couple of times and got her voice under control she realized that it was Vigdís Ólafsdóttir on the other end. Jón's mother.

"Would you please come out? I need to talk with you."

And then, the Icelandic woman began to cry.

49

When, a half hour later, Louise stepped into the large open kitchen in the apartment on Strand Boulevard, the doors to the French balcony stood wide open. The wind made the thin, lightly colored curtains flutter so strongly that they struck the radiators with small, heavy snaps. It was cold in the room. Ice-cold. And at the oval dining table sat Vigdís Ólafsdóttir with a white sweater over her shoulders and eyes that were all cried out.

After they'd exchanged greetings, Louise walked over and closed the balcony doors before sitting down at the table. The kitchen was cleaned up, everything was fine and bright, the colors of the flowers in the windowsill matched the Nordic-themed paintings on the wall.

So far, Vigdís hadn't said anything but hello, but she seemed grateful that Louise had come lightning quick.

"They picked up Jón," she said when Louise sat down across from her. "He was driven away in a police car."

Quiet. The room was still so cold that Louise felt goose bumps rising under the sleeves of her blouse.

"It's all so terrible, and I can't understand it anymore," she began but had difficulty going on. Her nose was slender and delicate, and her eyebrows so well formed that they looked as if they were drawn on. Her features were almost doll-like.

"Do you know why your son and his friends were arrested today?" asked Louise.

The Icelandic woman nodded slowly.

"I didn't know the others were picked up, too."

"They killed a man."

Louise tried to catch her eye.

"Not Jón," his mother exclaimed with conviction in her voice.

"No, not your son," she answered with thinly veiled sarcasm.

A bird had landed on the railing out on the balcony.

Vigdís leaned forward again as if to underscore that she meant it seriously. That she knew perfectly well that that's what every mother would say, but there was more weight behind her words.

"I know the sort of shit they sit and watch in there behind the closed door. And I've always feared that Jón's friends might one day cross the line."

"But you didn't think about stepping in?" Louise asked and looked at her. "You never believed your own son was just like his friends?"

There was a shake of the head.

"The night your son's friends shot and killed Nick Hartmann, his young wife became a widow and their two-month-old daughter lost her father."

Vigdís Ólafsdóttir hid her face in her hands and sat a while before she straightened up and looked at Louise.

"If I'd known it were that serious, I would absolutely have stepped in. But the first I was aware of it was when the two officers arrested him a little while ago."

Louise leaned back and listened.

"I called you because I'm scared," Jón's mother said, and her blue eyes suddenly appeared unsure as she looked away. "If it really turns out that his friends have killed a man, then I know my son well enough to know that he'll tell the police everything he knows, and so I'm scared that something may happen to him afterward..."

She stopped short and fought back tears.

"That they'll come after him when he's talked."

Louise sat a while considering. The goose bumps had gone away and her muscles were beginning to relax.

"You don't need to be nervous about that part now," she said. "We know that it wasn't your son who did the shooting that evening, and the evidence we're in possession of is so strong that we have enough to get the suspects convicted without needing his testimony."

Jón's mother listened without looking at Louise. As if it were asking too much of her to be completely present while the police authorities confronted her with things she didn't want to know.

"Of course, we're interested in hearing what your son has to say, and if it turns out that he rode in the car out to Amager that evening, but just didn't participate in the shooting, then that's another matter," said Louise.

Vigdís Ólafsdóttir nodded quietly, as if she was searching for an explanation. She breathed deeply and ran her fingers over her hand.

"Jón's never had a father," she began. "It's my feeling that he's looking for that raw and masculine side in his friends, but he doesn't have it himself. He's soft and sensitive, and he's missing something that I'll never be able to give him."

"And you think he gets it from that crowd?" Louise interrupted.

Vigdís stretched out a hand to stop her.

"No, I don't mean that at all. The fact that he goes around with them I take as more of a rebellion against me. He feels that I've let him down, and maybe I have by being more occupied with my own needs than with a desire to create an integrated family that he could be part of. I just mean he's looking for boundaries. Apparently, I haven't been too good at setting those for him, and there haven't been others to do it. Maybe that's why he's wandered so far off. But he's not violent, he wouldn't harm anyone. It's a battle that's raging inside him."

Louise let her talk.

"If you hadn't picked him up, he would have gone in himself," the mother said pensively. "I could see it in him, but he wasn't willing to talk about it. He has hardly spoken to me at all recently, just lay there in his room. Look, he's been very affected by what happened to his friends in the fire."

"What do you know about the fire?" Louise asked and observed her.

"Nothing. Nothing except that I never believed it was Britt who set fire to the boathouse."

Louise looked at her with surprise.

"Do you know her?" she asked, astonished.

The woman shook her head.

"No. But that's not how you act when you lose someone. You go to pieces and you're devastated. There are other feelings that make people burn houses down. It's not the kind that women have."

"It's happened before," Louise pointed out.

"Maybe from jealousy, but not from sorrow."

Vigdís sat and played with a thread that had come loose on the sleeve of her high-neck sweater, which fit snugly over her chest and accentuated her bosom.

It was quiet between them while their thoughts settled down and became peaceful.

Louise gazed out the window, where the bird was about to fly off.

Then she straightened up a little and turned her eyes back to Vigdís.

"Tell me. It wouldn't have been you who had a relationship with Ulrik Fasting-Thomsen, would it?"

It had suddenly struck her that Jón's mother had been away with her boyfriend on the eve of the fire, when she and Michael Stig came to speak with her son.

Vigdís Ólafsdóttir sat with her eyes blue and bright. They weren't ashamed or frightened; she seemed more relieved that she hadn't had to confess it herself.

"How long have you known each other?" asked Louise.

"Eight years," answered the Icelandic woman and let her eyes rest while she waited for Louise's reaction. "I was twenty-seven when I came back to Copenhagen. Jón was starting third grade."

Eight years was a long time to be somebody's lover, thought Louise, especially when you're the age when it's natural to marry and have a family.

She was apparently easy to read, because Vigdís smiled sadly.

"Ulrik would never leave his family," she said and shook her head. "He made that clear from the beginning. He loved them more than anything on earth, and he never promised me more than what we had. And it was enough for me. We were together several times a week and traveled a lot. I always felt I got a good deal out of it. Everything that people call the whipped cream on a relationship."

"But you don't see each other anymore?" Louise asked, leaning back in her chair.

The blue eyes flooded, and a tear ran over the tip of her slender nose.

"Not after the terrible thing that happened to his daughter down at the sailing club," she said, shaking her head. "When he found out that Jón was with them that evening, he put an end to it. But then that's understandable."

She looked down at the table and dried her cheeks.

"We're also moving," she continued and lifted her eyes again.

Louise looked at her, not understanding.

"This is his apartment we're living in, and he pays. He threw us out when all of that happened."

They sat a while in silence.

"What do you know about the evening down at the sailing club?" Louise said.

"Nothing other than what I've been told. I wasn't home. Ulrik had invited me to go with him to Dragsholm Castle, where his company was holding a seminar."

Louise gawked.

"You were with him up there?"

Vigdís nodded.

"I was almost always with him when there was something. It wasn't any secret among his colleagues and business associates that we saw each other. I also traveled with him on business trips and all the adventure outings—not because I do that sort of thing, but I liked to watch him and he liked to have company."

"Does that mean you were with him when the police got hold of him at Dragsholm Castle?"

Louise felt her heart thumping against her chest. She saw the darkness on the road and the blood from Signe's head, and she remembered the heavy stillness at the National Hospital with the much-too-brightly-lit empty hallways. Meanwhile, Ulrik had been with his lover and covered it up with the poor excuse that he couldn't back out of the scheduled seminar, as much as he'd like to.

The anger knotted in her neck, and she saw that Vigdís had long ago read her thoughts.

"We couldn't keep seeing each other after that. You understand, of course," she said.

"Yes, thank you. I understand," Louise said with a nod.

She also wondered if the Icelandic woman felt she'd put her life on hold during the time she was with Ulrik Fasting-Thomsen. He'd apparently provided for her and paid her rent. Her entire existence had been dependent upon his good will. She'd also lost a good deal the night that Signe died. And if he'd turned his back on her when he found out that her son had been there that evening, then possibly she had reason to feel jealous.

"Were you also with Ulrik in Iceland the night the fire was set at the boathouse and warehouse down by the harbor?"

Vigdís didn't try to pretend as if she didn't know what night they were talking about. She propped her chin on her hands.

Then she nodded. Heavy and sad, without a spark in her blank eyes.

"He ended it the night we went up there, and he wanted us to move out as quickly as possible. It turned out, he'd already found an apartment for us. We were supposed to go see it the next day. He had money with him to pay the deposit in cash, so we could move in the next month."

Efficient, thought Louise.

"He'd also arranged for some of our furniture to be shipped up there, but there's not enough room for all of it, so he'll take the rest himself," Vigdís continued, adding with a little smile that he'd even managed to get her a job as a secretary with one of his Icelandic business associates.

"That's how easily we're swept aside," she exclaimed with a brief, dry laugh.

"What does your son say about it?" Louise asked and suddenly felt sorry for Vigdís, who'd trusted another woman's husband so blindly.

The Icelandic woman shrugged her shoulders.

"He doesn't really say anything. I think he's upset to be leaving his school and friends, but he's never cared for Ulrik. He doesn't think he treated us right when he wouldn't have us full-time. And I don't blame him," she said thoughtfully. "At the same time, I sense that he's glad we're leaving. It's my understanding that it would mean a lot to him to be part of a real family. He's never had that, so he probably hopes I find a new man once we go home to Iceland and everything will be more normal. So maybe he's not so upset about our leaving."

Vigdís sat getting lost in her own thoughts.

"Have you spoken with Ulrik since you were in Iceland?" Louise asked and pushed her chair back so she could stand up.

Vigdís looked up at her under her thick, straight bangs and smiled a little.

"Well, yes. Now that Britt's been arrested and he's left alone, it seems like he's had second thoughts and wants me to stay. He comes around all the time and has even offered to pay for Jón's education, if he stays. He'll also get him an apartment."

She shook her head.

"But it won't work. I don't want to anymore. And now is when he needs to be there for his wife; otherwise he might as well have left her years ago," she said. "What we had together will never come back. It's time for Jón and me to go home and start fresh."

Louise nodded and stood up to get her coat.

"When do you think he'll be allowed to leave?" Vigdís asked as she followed Louise out.

"It's hard to say. It depends a lot on what comes out of the interrogations today."

50

Louise had left the patrol car in a parking spot in front of the Cancer Center. With her cell phone to her ear, she crossed over Strand Boulevard.

First, she called Sejr to hear if he'd received Ulrik's foreign bank statements. When he told her, with more patience than she had, that they hadn't yet come, she called Suhr.

"It's Jón Vigdísarson's mother who's been Ulrik's lover," she yelled into the receiver as she unlocked the car. "While Signe was dying in the National Hospital, he was with her."

The wind caught hold of her hair and whistled into the phone. The lieutenant asked her to repeat herself, and this time she left out that final remark and kept to what was relevant.

"Are you saying that it's the Icelandic mother who's his lover?" he asked calmly.

Louise got in the car and settled into her seat.

"For eight years, they've carried on a relationship on the side. He and Jón have known each other since the boy was nine, so it sounds completely unbelievable that Ulrik didn't know about the boys using his boathouse. He may have given them permission to. How else would they have known about the place?"

Suhr muttered something that Louise couldn't hear. Presumably, it was just the noise that accompanied his thoughts.

"We just gave the kid permission to go," he said. "He wasn't with them the night Nick Hartmann was shot, but he told us what he knew, which happens to be pretty interesting. It was a paid job. Michael Stig and Toft are sitting with Kenneth Thim. He's the one who was out there with Nymann, and he confessed as soon as they started to play the film. Now we just need to find out where the money came from. But that's a little harder, since they won't say anything. We know that it's people who belong to the biker scene, but they won't name names...yet."

"What about Thomas Jørgensen—what does he say?" Louise asked and rolled the window down a bit to get some fresh air in the car.

"He was the driver, but didn't go in with them. But we're charging him with accessory to murder," Suhr said and told her that the boys weren't all that cocky and far from as hardboiled as they'd seemed that night out at Nick Hartmann's house. "We'll get it out of them who ordered the job, even though right now they claim not to know. It was apparently Nymann who was their contact, but Thim has already more than hinted that it was their deceased friend's biker connections, and it seems like we'll have to look in the inner circle. The money was paid out in cash, and they burned through it over a few nights in the city. They got twenty thousand."

"Twenty thousand," said Louise. "It's laughable to kill someone for twenty thousand kroner."

"They didn't do it for the money," Suhr said seriously. "For them, it was about the prestige that comes with it. They considered it a test of their manliness—that's usually how you prove your worth in that circle."

"Yes, and so they can be happy they passed the test when they come out in sixteen years," Louise said, thinking that there wasn't much chance of their landing in better company while doing time. But as far as she was concerned, they could just rot away in a hole in the ground.

Her thoughts drifted back to Britt Fasting-Thomsen in Vestre Prison. She was facing a sentence that was at least as long, if not longer, than the boys' sentences. Boys who'd cynically and as cold as ice shot down another human being, just to show their courage.

"Should we see about getting hold of Jón Vigdísarson again?" Suhr asked, interrupting her thoughts. "It's been about fifteen minutes since he left. You could wait on him out there?"

"I'd actually rather drive out to Vestre and talk with Britt, if that's OK with you. I think it's Ulrik who's looking the most interesting," she said and, to her surprise, Suhr agreed.

"Do that. Then we'll look at his bank statements tomorrow."

She started the car. Svendsen had again decked her out with the big Mondeo, and she had to give him credit—it was a pleasure to drive, but damned hard to park.

"What about Mie and her daughter? Have they gotten away from the farm?"

Louise had difficulty letting go of the young mother and the unfair emotional pressure that was being put on her.

"She's safe," Suhr said calmly. "Nothing is going to happen to them."

"You sound certain."

"Willumsen has lodged her and her child at his home in a guest room."

"Well, my goodness. Has he gotten Annelise to stand guard?"

"No, that he hasn't. That cushy job he's given to Lars Jørgensen, who's keeping an eye on the house when Willumsen can't be there himself."

"Lars Jørgensen! Isn't he on sick leave?" Louise exclaimed.

"Not anymore. He's back on reduced time, and he comes into the investigation group without weekend and on-call duties."

"When was that decided?" Louise asked happily.

"When it occurred to Willumsen that we didn't have anyone who could look after Mie and her little daughter. He wouldn't risk having anything happen to them. He thought a bit about putting Sejr Gylling on the assignment, but dropped the idea himself before he got around to asking."

Louise smiled. She was glad that a solution had been found so Lars Jørgensen could come back to the department.

"I'll see you tomorrow. I'll call after I've talked with Britt. But I'll be driving home afterward—there's a dog that needs a walk and a boy that needs to do his homework."

"Sounds reasonable," her chief conceded.

Before Louise left the parking spot, she called out to Vestre Prison to announce her arrival. She also left a message with Britt's attorney, saying she'd like to visit his client and was on the way out there.

❧

The leaves on the trees were turning yellow, and the wind made a pair of them fall to the earth as Louise turned down

Vigerslev Allé and crossed over the little street that led down the last stretch to the prison's main entrance.

"Britt Fasting-Thomsen," she told the guard when he asked her who she wanted to talk with. Then she waited patiently for the gate behind her to close completely, so the one in front could slowly begin to slide open.

Over in the visitors' section, she had to show her badge and hand over her weapon before she was led to the check-in, where all visitors were registered. The set security routines took time, but once through them she was pointed to a little visitation room at the end of the hall.

On the way, she stopped at a vending machine and bought two soft drinks and a bag of candy. Then she went in and took off her jacket. It would be a while before Britt made it over from her cell block.

The room reminded her of a little waiting room, with a reproduction on the wall. Beside the door was a table and two chairs. Like a private nook, thought Louise, and was extremely glad they hadn't been given one of the family visitation rooms, where besides the table and chairs there was also a bunk with stains on the mattress for the hurried lovemaking that had to be completed before the end of the visit time.

She tossed her bag on the floor and had just pulled out a chair when Britt was led in. She quickly offered her hand, so the prison officer wouldn't get the impression that she and Louise had a private relationship.

Britt sat down and accepted the soft drink Louise placed before her, but said no thanks to the candy, her pageboy hair swinging over her slender shoulders. Up at the part, her hair had grown out and revealed that the roots were more gray than dark. But her hair was recently washed and styled.

"How are you getting along in here?" Louise asked when they sat across from each other.

Britt smiled without irony.

"I think I can get used to it," she said, quietly adding that it was better than she'd hoped.

There was a new calm about Britt. The sorrow was still there, surrounding her like an aura, but the new thing was that she seemed serene.

Louise leaned back in her chair.

"Camilla wanted me to give you her love. Lots of it, and a hug and a kiss on the forehead."

Britt smiled and thanked her.

"She's just visited Frederik Sachs-Smith in Santa Barbara. She had an interview with him about that whole family drama."

"Yes, isn't that incredible," Britt said. "That topic still fills the papers."

Louise let her talk, but thought how bizarre it was that she'd end up talking about that subject. Especially now when she herself had been front page news and on everyone's lips since the arrest, and the journalists still tried to dig up anything they could on her and her family. There was no sparing of harsh words when they described how mercilessly she'd burned two young men to avenge her daughter.

"Haven't you ever run into Sachs-Smith? Hasn't he had a lot to do with your husband?"

Britt shook her head indifferently.

"I've never met him. He lives so far away."

"But isn't he in Denmark regularly?"

She shrugged her shoulders.

"To tell you the truth, I'm not that interested in my husband's business associates, and when Ulrik had a meeting or luncheon with one of them I was the one who stayed home with Signe. And he's always been so considerate not to invite them home for dinner, because then Signe and I wouldn't be able to practice so well in the rooms."

Louise understood.

"Last summer, as I understand it, Ulrik visited Sachs-Smith at his home in the U.S."

Britt thought about it.

"In July," she said with a nod. "During summer vacation."

Louise folded her hands and leaned in over the table, letting her eyes rest seriously on Britt's face and her dull blue eyes.

"Camilla is convinced that you're innocent and that it would be a travesty of justice if the police succeeded in having you sentenced."

Britt looked away and slowly began to shake her head.

"And," Louise continued without letting herself be distracted, "maybe I'm starting to think she's right. I have nothing to base it on. Except that I actually don't think you know anything about what happened down at the warehouse."

Britt kept shaking her head, but said nothing.

Louise sat thinking and observing her before she got started.

"It seems that your husband has had a lover for quite some time," she said. "Did you ever get a feeling that Ulrik was having an affair?"

A moment passed before Britt answered.

"Maybe," she said, then nodded, as if it didn't matter that much. "Maybe I did, but I always knew that he'd never leave Signe and me."

"Do you know who he was seeing?" Louise asked and looked at her intently.

Britt shook her head.

Louise took a deep breath and said that the lover's name was Vigdís Ólafsdóttir.

First silence, then the outburst.

"What are you saying?"

Now her face fractured. Fell apart piece by piece like a jigsaw puzzle shaken loose.

"That can't be," she cried. "He couldn't have known anything about the boys who chased Signe to her death. He would have said. He would have reported them."

She began to shake violently.

Louise stood up quickly and went over to her. Pulled her up from her chair. Her body was slender like Jonas's, but the sobbing inside of it was as violent as a storm that tore at every branch.

They stood a long time before she helped Britt down into her chair. Blinded by tears and wet in the face, Signe's mother dried her eyes with the sleeve of her blouse. She sat as still as a mouse and stared straight ahead. Into the wall. Into herself most of all, thought Louise and left her in peace.

"How long did he know her?" Britt asked after a long pause.

Something contracted inside Louise.

"Eight years. Since her son started third grade. I don't know more than that."

She didn't have the heart to tell the rest, needed to let Britt digest.

"This information is new to us," she said. "And then, it's interesting that there could have been a connection between your husband and one of the boys who were charged for the attack. Especially since I never got the sense that Ulrik knew anything about the group that stayed down in the boathouse."

Britt shook her head and sat up a little.

"No, me neither. But that doesn't change anything about my being here," she noted.

"That's true," Louise conceded. "In a way, it doesn't. But it does change some aspects of the case, now that I'm trying to prove that you weren't the one who set the fire."

Her laughter was dry and sounded more like a cough. Her eyes seemed even bigger in her pale face.

"You shouldn't even get started on that," Britt said quickly, her voice still covered with a thin layer of sobbing. "Honestly, it would only be a relief for me to be allowed to stay here. Everything I had out there is gone."

She looked down at her hands, fiddled a bit, and folded them together.

"They've ended their relationship and no longer see each other. So maybe it's not so bad," Louise attempted.

Britt stared at her with a look that cut.

"It is bad," she said. "Every bit as bad. If my husband is having or has had a relationship with a woman whose son was there the night my daughter died, then that's serious enough that I never want to see him. Then that's it. Then there's nothing that would give me reason or desire to speak with him again."

Her eyes looked away and the tears began to run.

"I don't understand it," she cried. "How could he have known about the boys and not said anything to me?"

Louise let her be. When they had sat a while, her crying died down. Louise took Britt's hand from across the table and looked at her seriously.

"I'm not supposed to ask you about this here, without your lawyer present. But I'm going to anyway, and it means that your answer won't be recorded anywhere and therefore can't be used in the case."

Britt looked at her with eyes red from crying, but she listened.

"Did you drive down to the harbor and set fire to the boathouse to avenge your daughter's death?" Louise asked quietly.

Signe's mother looked down at the table, her expression blank again, as if the thought of her daughter's death suddenly stood out clearly.

"No," she said and looked up. "I did not."

There was nothing to trace in her eyes. They looked directly at Louise without trying to seem convincing.

"I could have done it," she admitted. "Would even wish that I had, and that's at least as bad as if it had been me who was behind it. But it wasn't me. I didn't even think of avenging what they did to Signe, didn't have the energy for it. But maybe there's a goddess of vengeance, and maybe she's been on my side since it turned out the way it did."

She took a deep breath and sat a while.

"I even allow myself to feel gratitude over the fact that it happened," she admitted and straightened up a little in her chair. "And I'm more than willing to take my punishment for feeling this way."

She squeezed the soda bottle and looked down at the table as if she'd just bared her darkest thoughts and was ashamed of it.

"That's all I wanted to know," Louise said and stood up.

She gave Britt a hug and went over and pushed the bell to signal that they were ready to be let out.

When the prison officer came and opened the door, Louise remained standing over by the table; she watched Britt being led away.

51

"Fucking 87 million kroner," Sejr said with a big smile when Louise came into the office the next morning. "I got the information about Ulrik Fasting-Thomsen's foreign accounts from Interpol just before I went home yesterday."

After her visit with Britt, Louise had forgotten how impatient she'd been to have a look at the hidden account on the Isle of Man. On the way in, she'd followed Jonas to school. They'd biked together along Gammel Kongevej, and afterward she'd had time to stop in at a bakery.

Now her adrenaline was rising.

"Son of a bitch!" she exclaimed and was about to turn on her desk lamp but stopped herself. Instead, she turned on her electric kettle and found a tea bag for her mug.

Sejr Gylling pointed to the lamp.

"You can turn it on. As long as you aim it toward yourself."

Louise pushed a bakery bag across the desk.

"There are a whole lot of bank statements we need to look through. If you have time, I'd suggest we go through the printouts from the foreign account."

Louise nodded.

"That's a helluva lot of money!" she exclaimed in a broad mid-Zealand dialect and tipped her chair back while she waited for the water to boil. "How in the hell did he earn so much on the side? Weren't his businesses at home doing terrific, too?"

Sejr nodded.

"Yes, they look pretty healthy. It's like we guessed: profits from foreign customers and investments that were made abroad. Buy and sell, and then he found it attractive to go into the fast-cash business that Hartmann had going, where he could double his investment in no time. It gives you quite a high to haul in that kind of profit."

Louise nodded and mumbled that you could certainly say that.

"And that kind of gambling fits very well with his interest in extreme sports. Isn't it paragliding and that sort of thing you said he does?"

She nodded again.

"That type of person is attracted to the thrill of pushing himself all the way over the edge, and you can do that in several ways," he added and straightened his cap a bit so the light from Louise's desk lamp wouldn't shine in his eyes.

"Have you found anything that ties Ulrik with Hartmann or the boys in the boathouse?"

"Not directly. There haven't been any money transfers between Nick Hartmann and Ulrik Fasting-Thomsen except for the rent, which was paid every month," he said. "And that went into the completely normal business account."

He held back a little before his smile grew bigger and he added, "But in the beginning of July there was a transfer of 660,000 dollars to Yang, Inc. in Hong Kong from the account on the Isle of Man."

"Holy shit!" exclaimed Louise and leaned forward excitedly.

The water boiled, but she ignored it.

She saw clearly the contours of the double life Ulrik had going, and that he seemed to be more of a smooth operator than she'd been capable of seeing at first.

"With that transfer, can we be sure that it was him who paid for the second container?" she asked dubiously, suddenly nervous that everything could fall apart again.

"I think so," Sejr said, warding off her worries. "I have Hartmann's business folders and papers here, but there's nothing for the extra container. Only for the one he had delivered last time, and the earlier deliveries he received. But on the freight paper both containers are entered with numbers, so I've written to the office in Hong Kong to have them pull the invoices. We need to confirm that the money that was transferred from the British bank was payment for the specific container number. And when we have that, then the trap's closed."

The picture was now quite clear. Ulrik and Hartmann had known each other from Ulrik's courses. Hartmann had presumably gotten greedy and wanted to run import alongside the business he had going with the bikers. But he didn't have enough capital for investing, and that's when he turned to Ulrik. He had plenty of capital and was more than happy to see his money multiply.

There was a knock on the door, and Willumsen came in.

"People are a hell of a lot dumber than you'd think!" he said with a certain enthusiasm and closed the door behind him. "That apprentice-mechanic idiot definitely was out in Værløse getting parts for his supervisor, but he also took a little side trip up to North Zealand with a child's bed."

He sat down on a bureau inside the door and clapped his hands together.

"The fool forgot about the packaging from a set of baby sheets and the receipt from BabySam on Roskildevej. All of it was lying in the back of the garage's box van."

Willumsen slapped himself on the forehead.

"Oh, my God! If the criminal mind is in such rapid decline, then there's some damn hope for us in the future."

Louise grinned and shook her head, then stood up to pour water over her tea bag.

"That's a relief for Mie," she said.

She offered the lead investigator a cup of tea and pointed to the bakery bag.

Willumsen declined the tea, but looked over at the cola Sejr had on the desk.

"You're welcome to take one," the fraud investigator said and pointed to the refrigerator.

"How about the arrestees?" asked Louise. "Are they still not saying who ordered or paid for the job?"

Willumsen shook his head and twisted the cap off his half-liter cola.

"They're saying nothing. And we probably won't get them to, either. That's biker rule number one, and if they break it they'll be targeted the whole time they sit in the slammer. A couple of goons like them know that much."

"Yes," said Louise, knowing he was right.

"The problem with these damned biker assholes is that they never get their hands dirty," he said.

He took a gulp from the bottle and opened the bakery bag, fishing out a pastry.

"They're uncanny about avoiding the fall when one of their businesses goes bad."

The lead investigator took a big bite of his pastry.

THE RUNNING GIRL   383

Louise nodded thoughtfully.

"It probably wasn't all that difficult for the bikers to see what Hartmann was up to when he suddenly went off on his solo ride," she said. "They would have been bat-shit angry, and wouldn't have wanted to be cheated like that. And so, they got their trainees to put a stop to him."

"In a way, that's what Thim and Thomas Jørgensen have already confessed to," the lead investigator said. "They just won't cough up the names of the ones who were behind it. And maybe they don't even know them," he said, brushing crumbs off his pullover. "After all, it was Nymann who was the primary contact and got paid for the killing."

"I'd like to know if a new team's being sent after Mie, now that Thim and Thomas Jørgensen are sitting behind bars," Louise said.

She dove into the bag herself and broke a pastry in two.

Willumsen shook his head.

"Actually, I don't think so. They might make big, bad threats, but usually nothing happens when there are witnesses against the bikers. It's extremely seldom that there are revenge attacks afterward. And they know we're onto them. The bikers got those two to take a test, and they got nothing out of it. Now it's too dangerous to do more."

Louise nodded and thought he was probably right.

"But what the hell are we doing with this stuff?" asked Willumsen. "We need to get the father in, so he and the wife can each have their own cell out at Vestre. They're one hell of a nice married couple."

Sejr pulled his chair over to the corner of the desk, so he sat facing Willumsen.

"What we're doing with this stuff is, Rick and I are going through everything there is on Ulrik Fasting-Thomsen, so we're well-armed when we pull him in," he said.

He gave a rare smile.

"And you can go in to the lieutenant and tell him there's a rather considerable offshoot that's come up in connection with the investigation of the fire and the Hartmann shooting. If these things hadn't fallen together, then Fasting-Thomsen could have kept on living his double life, free and clear, until the day he decided to leave his wife and head out of the country with his lover, or a new one like her."

"Yup, the whole thing's been damned unlucky for him," Willumsen said happily.

He thanked them for the soft drink and pastry.

"If you can make it, then come to the morning meeting. But it's more important that you take care of this stuff, so we can get our claws in him."

He hummed contentedly as he left the office.

52

W hat'll happen to all the money Ulrik has stashed?"
Louise asked when they were alone.

"It'll be seized. He'll be tossed in and do some years in
prison, and he'll pay a big fine. But then he'll be let out and
will probably be fit for fight and start some new business
ventures."

Sejr shook his head as if he had a hard time taking it very
seriously.

"Like all the other financial geniuses who just needed to
test how far they could push the boundaries. They turn up
again and start in where they left off."

He started to sort the new piles of paper in front of him
on his desk.

"Would you start by running through these?"

He pushed a big stack across the desk. Eleven years of
bank statements from Ulrik's foreign account that Sejr had
had unofficially printed out.

"It appears that this is the foreign account he used for
private expenditures whenever he was abroad, so you can
practically follow his movements. And it's a feast of hotels

and restaurant visits that were probably a tad too private to figure into his legal business account."

He smiled.

"And then there are the large deposits and withdrawals, but I haven't gone through any of it very thoroughly yet. Take a look through while I try to see if any of it can be related to his Danish business accounts. If any black money was involved there, then we can get him for it."

Louise stood and walked out to fill the kettle. She prepared for hours with numbers and columns, which wasn't exactly what interested her most. But at the same time, her dislike of Ulrik had risen to the point where she wanted everything on him before they drove out and made the arrest.

"He set his lover up with an apartment he pays for," she said when she came back with a full kettle. "And I think, too, that he's transferred money to her every month. That was part of the idea: that she wouldn't work so she'd be at his disposal."

She thought about Britt, who'd taken care of their daughter at home and formed the secure frame around the family life he hadn't been willing to give up.

Louise snorted, and Sejr tore himself away from his screens for a moment and looked at her.

Louise shook her head. She'd just happened to speak out loud.

He wanted everything, she thought. Completely over the edge, like when he threw himself off a cliff with a parachute tied to his back.

"I think he owns that property out on Strand Boulevard," Sejr said and looked at her again. "So, she was probably living there rent-free. But he may have set up an automatic monthly transfer to her from the account you're sitting with."

He nodded at Louise's papers.

They sat in silence, reading numbers and taking notes. There was only a single time when a $660,000 amount was taken out. Louise checked the dates on the freight papers in Hartmann's files, but there weren't any other transfers from Ulrik's hidden account that matched with the deliveries. Each month, on the other hand, 15,000 kroner was transferred to the same account number.

"Could that be Vigdís Ólafsdóttir?" Louise asked and looked over at Sejr.

He asked her to read the recipient's account number. She heard his fingers on the keys, and shortly after he nodded.

"At any rate, it's an account in Danske Bank down on Østerbrogade, so it very well could be hers."

Louise marked all the payments to the lover's account in red. There was another transfer to the same bank, but to a different account number. On April 29, 50,000 kroner was transferred. But whereas the transfer of fifteen thousand occurred every month and had done so over eight years, the larger sum of fifty thousand was only repeated one time a year.

She got her computer going and waited patiently for her password to be accepted. Then she pulled up the Central Registry of Persons and inserted the code that gave the police direct access to name information and data.

"Vigdís Ólafsdóttir" she wrote in the search field, and a moment later her name and address appeared.

Born October 2, 1975. Then the fifty thousand couldn't have been a birthday present. Vigdís had moved her registered address to Denmark in 2001 and lived on Strand Boulevard ever since.

From the information, Louise could see that she'd also lived in Denmark earlier. For two years. That might be in connection with studies, she thought. Her age certainly fit.

She'd been around eighteen–nineteen at that time, but then she'd gone home again.

At the bottom, it said, "Children: Jón Vigdísarson, born April 29, 1992; Father: unknown."

Louise slammed her hands on the desk, harder than she'd meant to. The palms of her hands sweated, and Sejr looked over at her, startled. He was so occupied by all his numbers that for once he wasn't listening to music.

"What's wrong?"

"It's money he transfers to Jón every year on his birthday. It adds up to 400,000 kroner so far."

"Well, what d'ya know!" Sejr exclaimed, then looked at her speculatively. "Why the hell does he do that? The kid couldn't have been a criminal going so damned far back, could he?"

"I think Ulrik's the boy's father," Louise said.

She heard a knock on her door, and when she looked up she saw Lars Jørgensen sticking his head in.

The morning meeting must be over, and she hadn't even known he'd attended it.

She jumped out of her chair and gave him a hug.

"Do you have time to drive to Østerbro with me?" she asked when she'd let go of him.

He looked at her, caught off guard, then walked over and shook hands with Sejr before checking his watch.

"Yes," he said. "I could manage that. I promised Willumsen I'd take a walk with the widow and her little girl, so we look like a nuclear family out for a stroll. As if that would attract less attention!" he said and added with a smile that it was mostly women who went on afternoon walks with their children when they were home on maternity leave. The men, of course, had to work. "But if it makes them feel more secure to have me with them, then I'm happy to do it."

"Do you have a car down there?" she asked and started walking down the hall, too occupied with leaving to fill him in on things.

❧

It was Lars Jørgensen who drove, and Louise gave him an update on Fasting-Thomsen as they crossed the streets of Copenhagen and turned down past Østerport Station. They drove along the tracks and before they reached the bridge to Langelinje quay, he got over in the left lane and swung onto Strand Boulevard.

"It doesn't sound like he and the boy had a very close relationship," Lars Jørgensen said after she'd told him about her visit with Vigdís.

Louise sat observing him while he drove. The two of them had been partners for the last five years, and she'd gradually started to fear that he wouldn't be coming back to the department. But thank God, she thought, and confessed to herself that she must still be addicted to a sense of security.

"It's not even for certain that the boy knows that Ulrik's his father," she said. "And if he does know it, then I can damn well understand if he feels let down and would rather move back to Iceland with his mother. Because that suggests his father hasn't ever really been there for him."

It made her angry to think that someone could renounce his parental responsibility like that.

"It's only now that Ulrik's been ready to sign on full-time, because now he no longer has his other family," she added. "So now all of a sudden, there's room for Vigdís and her son. Jón's mother said that Ulrik has offered to pay for his education and get him an apartment."

"Think how she's put up with that," Lars Jørgensen mumbled and parked in front of the entrance, a little too close to the corner to avoid getting a ticket if an attendant came by. "There's probably not that many kept women around anymore, now that they'd all rather take care of themselves."

There was a bitter undertone in his words, but Louise didn't have the energy to ask questions.

"Now we'll get Vigdís to tell us all about the man," she said, standing on the sidewalk. "I consider him to be just as twisted and cynical as the boys who shot Nick Hartmann. Ulrik's façade of respectability just makes it all the more terrible."

A paper boy came out, and they went in. On their way up the stairs, Louise told him about Britt, who had never tried to defend herself against the serious charges that had been raised against her, but instead directed her thanks to the goddess of vengeance, who she thought stood by her.

When they reached the fourth floor, the door to the apartment was ajar. Louise put a hand on her partner's arm and stopped him before he got his finger on the doorbell. A faint moan, which sounded more like an animal than a human, had made her react.

They waited a moment before she carefully pushed open the door.

The dining table was straight ahead, and in a chair with her back to them sat Vigdís with her legs tucked up and her head hidden between her knees, slowly rocking back and forth and moaning.

On the floor over by the balcony door, there was shattered glass from the vase in the windowsill, broken flowers in a sea of water. They stepped into the room, and the curtain in front of the French balcony fluttered.

The blood had drawn a path across the shiny parquet floor and still ran from her face, as if her nose bled.

Louise called her name and walked forward.

Vigdís was wearing the same white sweater. She must have lain on the floor, Louise thought, because she was spattered with blood on the left side of her back and her sleeve. She didn't react to the voice behind her, but continued to hug herself and rock back and forth.

Except for the pitiful moaning, everything in the apartment was completely quiet.

Lars Jørgensen had already gone into the living room and now pushed open the door to Jón's room, but shook his head when he saw that it was empty.

It looked like the fight had only taken place in the large kitchen. Several things were on the floor, the table was pushed askew, and chairs toppled. It was like stepping into the aftermath of a drama that had played itself out.

Louise walked over and put her hand on Vigdís's shoulder, then crouched down beside her.

"What happened?" she asked quietly.

The Icelandic woman just kept rocking back and forth. Louise tried to remove her hands so she could see her face. The blood ran, and Lars Jørgensen came over from the kitchen sink with a hand towel that Louise passed her.

It seemed as though Vigdís Ólafsdóttir had gone into shock. The small, wheezing animal noises made Louise's hair stand up as she leaned forward to study the gash over her eyebrow and nose, which looked like it might be broken. But it didn't seem to be the injuries to her face that Jón's mother was whimpering about. It was something else, as if something inside her had fallen apart. As if she'd barricaded herself against reality.

Louise gently shook the Icelandic woman's shoulder.

"Vigdís, you need to tell us what happened," she said, then shook a little harder and raised her voice.

Still no reaction came, except her eyes, which closed yet more tightly.

Louise shook her again, but Vigdís Ólafsdóttir held desperately to her knees and pressed her face against her pant legs like a child trying to hide.

"Where is Jón?"

Louise had stood up.

Lars Jørgensen came over and put his hand on the white sweater and spoke calmly to her.

"This is the police," he said in an authoritative voice. "We need to find out how badly you've been injured, so we can decide whether to call an ambulance."

Something happened with the woman's shoulder—it collapsed a little, like a suit of armor being taken off.

"Help him," Vigdís whispered, and her moaning turned into sobs. She shook and had difficulty speaking. "Be nice and help my boy."

Louise leaned closer.

"Is Ulrik Jón's father?" she asked.

Slowly Vigdís began to nod.

"Ulrik came. He was so angry that I'd told you about our relationship, and that we were together the night his daughter died. He hit me, and while I was lying on the floor Jón suddenly appeared in the door."

She cried so quietly now that Louise's heart constricted.

"It'll end badly, I know it'll end badly," she whispered and kept rocking from side to side.

"Where are they now?"

Louise had straightened up and looked at the kitchen door. That's what was open and made the curtain flap.

She pushed the chairs on the floor aside and ran over to the door and out onto the kitchen stairs.

The sounds rose from the stairway, hollow sounds and blows that landed. Two people in a fight, where one was in control and the other defended himself.

Louise took the stairs in bounds, and Lars Jørgensen was right behind her.

53

Ulrik lay at the bottom of the stairs with his back to the cellar door and his head against the gray concrete floor. Next to him was a cavity under the stairs, and it looked like he'd tried to find shelter there. But Jón held him tightly and pressed him against the floor.

Louise had stopped short at the sight, but slowly took one more step down.

"Stop, stop, stop," begged Ulrik.

She could see his eyes from the light that came in through the window above the door to the yard.

The boy had a heavy lead pipe in his right hand, and he'd raised it up for yet another blow, but was checked by the sound of running footsteps on the stairs.

Louise took one more step and saw the vibration in his shoulder as his muscles tensed. She recognized the iron pipe. It was the one she'd seen up in his room, a fighting weapon that had lain ready to be used.

"Don't do that," she said quietly behind his back. She reached out her hand and laid it on his shoulder, feeling him stiffen.

"Jón," she repeated and gave his shoulder a careful

squeeze. "He's not worth it. Don't make yourself a murderer on his account."

She spoke neutrally and quietly, calm and controlled. Suddenly grateful for the experience she'd had from the time when she was trained as a negotiator. It had been Willumsen's recommendation when, after a case that ended in a dramatic hostage situation, he'd decided that she possessed the necessary abilities and qualities to be part of a negotiations group, and had granted her the extra training.

Down on the floor, Ulrik looked up at her desperately, but Louise only had eyes for the boy, who slowly turned.

"Don't let him make you kill," she repeated when he finally looked at her.

A twitch ran across his face, and something shifted in his dark eyes. Despair that was so abysmal that it didn't at all fit with his young age.

"It's too damned late," he whispered hoarsely, as if his throat had closed. "He's already done that!"

The hatred was so penetrating that for a moment Louise was fixated by the feeling that enveloped the boy. She wasn't able to react before he'd suddenly straightened himself up and hammered the iron pipe across his father's chest. Then he let it drop, so it lay over Ulrik's body. He took a couple of steps back and collapsed on the stairs. With his eyes on Ulrik, he whispered:

"I hate you, you fucking psychopath!" Then it was like something had ended, like the air and anger had gone out of him. The boy hid his face in his hands and cried.

An odd void took over. Ulrik lay unmoving, and there was a dull sound when the iron pipe rolled off his stomach and struck the concrete floor.

Louise nodded to Lars Jørgensen when he signaled that

he wanted to go down to the boy's father. She'd already heard him communicating with the control center at Headquarters, but now he stepped carefully around Jón on the stairs and took the last step down to Ulrik.

A sound came from above, and through the white bars of the stair landing Louise saw Vigdís looking down. She had the hand towel pressed against her forehead, but her eyes were free.

Louise concentrated on the boy. She went a couple of steps down and kneeled in front of him.

"Tell me, how did he already make you kill?" she asked.

He cried like a child who's lost perspective and can only see the darkness and the dangers.

Louise reached her hand out and took hold of his shoulder. Calmly stroked the soft fabric of his sweater.

"It was him," he said and took a deep breath. "It was him who made me burn down the boathouse. I didn't know they were in there, you know?"

Louise had difficulty understanding what he said. The words flowed in between each other, but she'd understood enough to help him up and support him as he walked up the stairs to the apartment.

She registered that Ulrik was stirring, heard his voice from down on the floor. He yelled aggressively up to his son, but she walled him out. Let Lars Jørgensen take over, she thought, and noticed that Vigdís had gone back into the apartment again.

Up on the fourth floor, Louise lifted the chairs that were knocked over, pulled them to the table, and told Jón to sit down.

His face was completely closed, and his eyes saw nothing but the abyss that seemed to have opened underneath him.

"Was it you who set fire to the boathouse?" Louise asked when she'd sat down beside him.

Vigdís kept herself in the background, probably because she couldn't bear to hear more, Louise thought when she saw her standing over by the window behind the kitchen counter.

"I didn't know they were inside," he repeated and shook his head. "No one was supposed to be there. We'd moved everything. No one was supposed to get hurt. He just wanted all the shit burned down, with the warehouse and everything."

Louise nodded.

"Was it also him who wanted to make it look like Britt had done it?"

The boy didn't look at her, didn't answer at first, but stared straight ahead, as if a remnant of the toughness he otherwise hid behind had come back again.

"Was it him?" his mother asked sharply from over by the window and took a couple of steps toward them.

The armor cracked again and with tears and despair he shook his head.

"No, it was me. He didn't say anything about how he wanted it done, just that it should be taken care of while you were in Iceland."

Vigdís crumpled a little and supported herself with both hands against the kitchen counter.

"But why Britt?" Louise asked, although she'd already guessed the answer. If she no longer stood in the way, Ulrik and his mother could get together and be the family the boy longed for.

Jón straightened himself up a bit, so his long body seemed lanky and fragile. He pulled himself together, took a deep breath, and glanced at his mother in the kitchen.

"After what happened with Signe, he suddenly didn't want to see my mother anymore," he began. The anger rose again. "She's arranged her whole damned life around him. We've never been able to do anything ourselves, because he decided for her, but then all of a sudden she's not good enough anymore."

"He found out that you were there that night at the party?" Louise asked, trying to bring him back to the beginning.

"She'd written on Facebook that it was going to be down at the harbor, and I just said to the others that we should drop by and see what was happening."

He started to cry again. His mother had come over, but kept herself at a distance.

"I told the others we should leave. That they should stop it and leave them alone."

He slouched, quickly dried his tears with the back of his hand.

"Did you know that Signe was your half sister?" Louise asked after letting him sit for a moment.

He nodded.

"But I didn't know her."

He tried to get himself together, man up. But right now, he was a little boy of seventeen who was fighting to keep his head above water while his world caved in.

"He tossed us out of his whole fucking life, and still it was me he came and asked for help when the warehouse had to be set on fire."

In those last words, Louise heard so much craving for acceptance that she had to look away. His mother stood still and listened, couldn't say anything. Seemed pale and frozen.

"You used Britt's car and stole firewood from behind the house," Louise concluded.

"He gave me the keys and said I should just take it."

"You're only seventeen!"

Jón nodded.

"I've driven a car since I was fourteen. I learned how in Iceland. We drive out on my grandfather's fields in his old Land Rover."

"What did Ulrik say when he found out that you'd made it look like it was his wife who set the fire?"

Louise scooted forward in her chair and heard voices out on the kitchen stairs. Michael Stig stuck his head in, but kept from interrupting.

The boy shook his head.

"Nothing. He couldn't really say anything, either, because then he'd reveal that it was him who'd ordered me to do it."

Finally, a slight glimmer came into his black eyes.

"He could have denied that he asked you," Louise pointed out. "It would have been your word against his, and you would have been in for it alone."

Jón shook his head as she continued to talk.

"He could easily as anything have turned his back on you and fought to get his wife cleared of the police charges."

The boy kept shaking his head and fished a cell phone out of the pocket of his tight jeans.

"I told him I recorded our conversation."

"Do you have it on your cell phone?"

Louise reached out her hand.

Jón laid his Nokia on the table.

"Nope, but he believed it."

Louise leaned back in annoyance and heard Toft tell Vigdís to grab a coat so she wouldn't end up freezing inside Headquarters.

"But I recorded the conversation where he said there was no reason to confess anything, now that his wife was sitting in prison and the police thought it was her. He wanted to move with us to Iceland when I was finished with school."

54

Dearest Camilla,

I'm sorry, but there's a terribly sad thing I need to tell you. Britt has taken her own life. I'm the one who found her. It is so sad, but at the same time it was beautiful.

After the arrests out on Strand Boulevard, I was given permission to drive out to Vestre Prison and release her. She seemed both glad and relieved, but she was very unhappy to hear that the goddess of vengeance turned out to be a seventeen-year-old boy who'd craved Ulrik's recognition and love so much that he was driven all the way out there where the heart turns cold and reason runs out, as she put it.

It must have been all the classical music that made her think so poetically. Others would probably say that the boy suffered so much hurt that he became a cold and calculating shit. But that's not how he seems now. He's desperately unhappy and thinks a lot about his mother, who he feels he's let down. Now she's alone while he sits in prison.

Vigdís has decided to stay in Denmark, and she'll try to find a place to live close to where Jón will serve

his time, so she can visit him. It'll most likely be on Jutland. That's where most of the high security juvenile
prisons are.

Britt was sorry that Signe was never allowed to meet
her brother. And if she had decided to keep on living,
she would never have been able to forgive him. Ulrik,
that is. Jón she mostly felt bad for, and she was very
sad when I told her that he'd end up serving his sentence for many years to come.

But Ulrik also got his punishment. He's in prison and
already confessed during the first interrogation that
he'd known for several years about Nick Hartmann's
business with replica furniture. He even named the two
people Hartmann entered into a business agreement
with, both full-fledged members of the biker club. One
of them is that Tønnes, who you must know from the
media and who was a complete stone face the times I
talked with him. But that's how they are!

It turned out to be Ulrik himself who suggested
that he and Hartmann get together and split the
profit if he brought an extra container home. But he
got scared when Hartmann was killed, didn't want
to do anything with the goods and was planning
to just let it all sit there until things calmed down
again. But then everything with Signe happened,
and when the police could suddenly connect him to
the warehouse and started looking at what was in
there, he went into a panic. He can't explain how he
could let Britt take the blame. He's completely silent
on that matter.

When Britt and I drove out of Vestre Prison, we
stopped and did some shopping along the way so she
wouldn't come home to an empty fridge. No one had

lived in the house for several weeks. She said she was looking forward to coming home. To her music and garden. She seemed glad and talked about everything she had to do.

She fooled me.

I called her the next morning. Several times. When she didn't answer her phone, I decided to drive out there. But she didn't answer the door either, so I smashed a window pane on the weather porch. She lay up in her bed. She'd plucked the last roses from the garden and tied them in a little bouquet, which she held on her chest along with a picture of Signe. Next to her bed was the cello.

In a letter, she asked that there not be any formal funeral service, just wanted to be placed in the earth next to Signe.

I am terribly sorry to have to write this to you.

Warm greetings,
Your Louise

The sun cast a sheen over the thin leaves of the palms. Camilla sat on the beach and cried. Markus was out in the water on his boogie board and bobbed in the waves. She still hadn't gotten herself together enough to tell him what had happened at home.

The tears rolled even more when, in the middle of feeling powerless over how it had ended, she admitted that it was probably best for Britt to end things that way. She couldn't go on living. Why should she? There was nothing more for her, nothing to live for. Even though her thoughts and grief overwhelmed her, still Camilla understood her decision.

She'd taken a chair from the terrace with her down to the beach and for a long time just sat and looked out over the Pacific Ocean, letting her thoughts rest.

Kauai was so lush and filled with greenery that she'd immediately understood why it was the one out of Hawaii's seven islands to be called Garden Island, and the one Frederik Sachs-Smith had chosen for his vacation paradise.

They'd arrived in the morning on a plane from Honolulu, so she hadn't managed to see much yet, except for what they drove by when they crossed the island from the airport. When she'd unpacked, she borrowed the computer that was in the living room to check her e-mails, and there was the e-mail Louise had sent the previous evening.

※

Camilla wailed like a child, the tears dripping from her cheeks down onto her chest. On the edge of the water, Markus practiced jumping up on the short surfboard and riding along when the waves crashed toward the beach.

She was startled and jumped when she heard a deep, male voice behind her. When she turned around, the sun was in her eyes and she only saw the shadow of the person who came walking toward her from the house.

He seemed concerned, solicitous, and a little puzzled to find an unknown woman sitting in a chair from the house and crying.

Camilla dried her cheeks, embarrassed. Felt herself caught, had thought she was alone with her grief.

"Sorry," she said. "I didn't know anyone else was here.

My son and I arrived this morning, and we have permission to borrow the house."

He looked older and taller than she'd imagined.

"A death," she said in explanation. "I just found out about it."

"I'm sorry to hear that."

Walther Sachs-Smith reached out his hand and said that she really didn't need to apologize.

"I'm the uninvited guest," he said. "My son owns the house, and he doesn't even know that I'm here."

Camilla took a step back, didn't entirely know how she should react or what she should say.

Behind her Markus called for her to look and see that he'd just about gotten it. He was about to put his feet on the waves, but when she turned to see, he was already in the water, patiently preparing himself for yet another attempt.

"I know who you are," she said and smiled as she turned her eyes from her son to the head of the Sachs-Smith family. "But it's a bit of a surprise to meet you here. Aren't you supposed to be dead?"

He smiled at her and laid his hand on her shoulder to get her to walk up to the house with him.

"We can see your son from the terrace," he said and gallantly pulled out a chair for her.

He disappeared into the kitchen and came back with a bottle of white wine and two glasses.

"Right now, I'm happiest letting people think that I'm dead," he said.

"I'm not sure that Frederik believes the story. At any rate, he didn't seem convinced when I visited him."

Camilla extended her hand and introduced herself, which she'd forgotten to do when he'd suddenly appeared on the beach.

"I actually interviewed your son to hear what he thought about the way the story was playing out," she said and took the glass he poured for her.

He was trim and obviously kept himself in good shape. His shorts were light colored and his flaxen shirt hung over them loosely. His eyes were friendly, but nevertheless decisive when he sat back into the cushions of his wide bamboo chair and looked at her.

"Am I wrong in thinking that I recognize your name?" he asked.

She looked away for a moment. Then she shook her head and said that she couldn't deny it.

"But I'm not working as a journalist right now," she added. "Just in this one instance when I visited Frederik."

"It would mean a lot to me if we could keep it between the two of us that you met me out here."

Camilla waited, wasn't much in favor of that kind of agreement if she felt there was something more behind it.

"Why's it so important for you to let people go on believing that you're dead?"

He sat a while studying her, as if he were assessing. Then he leaned forward in his chair and folded his hands.

"Because I'm not ready to turn up yet. I'm not coming home until the day I can prove that my wife was murdered."

He chewed on the words a bit, as if it were the first time he'd said them out loud.

Camilla's thoughts flew to Britt, and she couldn't manage to stop the tears. Quickly, she blinked them away.

From down at the water, Markus came walking up toward them. He'd caught sight of the man and seemed shy, but still curious.

"My wife was killed, and if I'm found I'll also be killed. That's why it's important that I find out what they've done before they find me. But it'll take time because I can't get to the information I have lying at home. So, I hope we can agree that you won't tell anyone that you met me?"

Camilla realized that she'd sat holding her breath while he talked.

"Of course," she promised and nodded. "I'd also like to help you get hold of what you have lying at home. My only condition is that I get exclusive rights on the story."

He thought about it for a moment.

"Agreed," he said, and with a smile, reached out his hand.

ACKNOWLEDGMENTS

The Running Girl is fiction. Everything could actually have happened, and some of it did, because the idea for the story stems from a party that was crashed. There, too, it went badly, but fortunately not as badly as in the novel. Everything else, on the other hand, has sprung up from my imagination. Similarly, the characters in the novel have no resemblance to any existing persons.

The action takes place in areas that have much in common with real places, but I have made use of artistic license to make changes and move things around. For example, in Svanemølle Harbor there are both sailing clubs and the South Pier, but in reality, it looks a little different because the boathouse and warehouse have been built into the story. On the other hand, the bikers and their hangout naturally have nothing to do with existing biker gangs. Also, Termo-Lux is pure invention, and I would like to thank the attorney Lone Brandenburg for insight into the generational shift of a family business and all other knowledge about corporate law and business structures.

In this book, as in my previous ones, it has been crucial for me to do thorough research in order to make my story appear trustworthy and realistic. As usual, thanks also to my friends at Copenhagen's Police Headquarters, without whose help the framework around Louise Rick wouldn't hold.

And a completely, unbelievably huge, thanks to Tom Christensen, Flying Squad, who has been with me from before the first line was written, and generously contributed with talk and details as the book was in progress. Tremendous thanks for your time and your empathy in the story.

Heartfelt thanks go, as always, to my friend, forensics expert Steen Holger Hansen, who is there to help out when a plot needs to be spun together. Without you there would be no book.

Great thanks also go to the journalist Lotte Thorsen, who is amazingly skilled with words.

Also, big thanks to my talented Danish editor, Lisbeth Møller-Madsen, and to my publisher, People's Press. It's a pleasure to work with you.

A million thanks to my savvy, tireless, and wonderful American editor, Lindsey Rose, and to the spectacular team at Grand Central. It is a thrill, an honor, and an enormous joy to work with you all. I appreciate every single effort you've made on my behalf, and being part of this esteemed family. I'm very happy to be with you.

Thank you so very much to my supremely visionary American agent, Victoria Sanders, who has moved heaven and earth for me, and to your fabulous and super-smart associates, the lovely and talented Bernadette Baker-Baughman and Jessica Spivey, whose great work, all around the world, leaves me filled with gratitude and aware of just how fortunate I am.

Thank you to my brilliant translation expert, Benee Knauer, who knows what I am thinking and what I mean, and how to capture it perfectly. It means so much to know you are there, to have you behind and beside me.

I want to express my heartfelt appreciation to the American crime-writing community and to my dear American readers. I cannot sufficiently convey how much your warm welcome has meant to me; you have made my dream come true. I love this country so much that I have made a new home here.

My warmest thanks must go to my son, Adam, whom I love with all my heart, and who has traveled every step of the way with me on this indescribable journey.

—Sara Blaedel

If you enjoy Sara Blaedel's Louise Rick suspense novels, you'll love her new Family Secrets series.

An unexpected inheritance from a father she hasn't seen since childhood pulls a portrait photographer from her quiet life into a web of dark secrets and murder in a small Midwestern town...

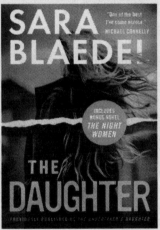

Please see the next page for an excerpt from *THE DAUGHTER.*

Available now.

1

"What do you mean you shouldn't have told me? You should have told me thirty-three years ago."

"What difference would it have made anyway?" Ilka's mother demanded. "You were seven years old. You wouldn't have understood about a liar and a cheat running away with all his winnings; running out on his responsibilities, on his wife and little daughter. He hit the jackpot, Ilka, and then he hit the road. And left me—no, he left *us* with a funeral home too deep in the red to get rid of. And an enormous amount of debt. That he betrayed me is one thing, but abandoning his child?"

Ilka stood at the window, her back to the comfy living room, which was overflowing with books and baskets of yarn. She looked out over the trees in the park across the way. For a moment, the treetops seemed like dizzying black storm waves.

Her mother sat in the glossy Børge Mogensen easy chair in the corner, though now she was worked up from her rant, and her knitting needles clattered twice as fast. Ilka turned to her. "Okay," she said, trying not to sound shrill. "Maybe you're right. Maybe I wouldn't have understood about all that. But you didn't think I was too young to understand that my father was a coward, the way he suddenly left us, and that he didn't love us anymore. That he was an incredible asshole you'd never take back if he ever showed up on our doorstep, begging for forgiveness. As I recall, you had no trouble talking about that, over and over and over."

"Stop it." Her mother had been a grade school teacher for twenty-six years, and now she sounded like one. "But does it make any difference? Think of all the letters you've written him over the years. How often have you reached out to him, asked to see him? Or at least have some form of contact." She sat up and laid her knitting on the small table beside the chair. "He never answered you; he never tried to see you. How long did you save your confirmation money so you could fly over and visit him?"

Ilka knew better than her mother how many letters she had written over the years. What her mother wasn't aware of was that she had kept writing to him, even as an adult. Not as often, but at least a Christmas card and a note on his birthday. Every single year. Which had felt like sending letters into outer space. Yet she'd never stopped.

"You should have told me about the money," Ilka said, unwilling to let it go, even though her mother had a point. Would it really have made a difference? "Why are you telling me now? After all these years. And right when I'm about to leave."

Her mother had called just before eight. Ilka had still been in bed, reading the morning paper on her iPad. "Come over, right now," she'd said. There was something they had to talk about.

Now her mother leaned forward and folded her hands in her lap, her face showing the betrayal and desperation she'd endured. She'd kept her wounds under wraps for half her life, but it was obvious they had never fully healed. "It scares me, you going over there. Your father was a gambler. He bet more money than he had, and the racetrack was a part of our lives for the entire time he lived here. For better and worse. I knew about his habit when we fell in love, but then it got out of control. And almost ruined us several times. In the end, it did ruin us."

"And then he won almost a million kroner and just disappeared." Ilka lifted an eyebrow.

"Well, we do know he went to America." Her mother nodded. "Presumably, he continued gambling over there. And we never heard from him again. That is, until now, of course."

Ilka shook her head. "Right, now that he's dead."

"What I'm trying to say is that we don't know what he's left behind. He could be up to his neck in debt. You're a school photographer, not a millionaire. If you go over there, they might hold you responsible for his debts. And who knows? Maybe they wouldn't allow you to come home. Your father had a dark side he couldn't control. I'll rip his dead body limb from limb if he pulls you down with him, all these years after turning his back on us."

With that, her mother stood and walked down the long hall into the kitchen. Ilka heard muffled voices, and then Hanne appeared in the doorway. "Would you like us to drive you to the airport?" Hanne leaned against the doorframe as Ilka's mother reappeared with a tray of bakery rolls, which she set down on the coffee table.

"No, that's okay," Ilka said.

"How long do you plan on staying?" Hanne asked, moving to the sofa. Ilka's mother curled up in the corner of the sofa, covered herself with a blanket, and put her stockinged feet up on Hanne's lap.

When her mother began living with Hanne fourteen years ago, the last trace of her bitterness finally seemed to evaporate. Now, though, Ilka realized it had only gone into hibernation.

For the first four years after Ilka's father left, her mother had been stuck with Paul Jensen's Funeral Home and its two employees, who cheated her whenever they could get away with it. Throughout Ilka's childhood, her mother had complained constantly about the burden he had dumped on her. Ilka hadn't known until now that her father had also left a sizable gambling debt behind. Apparently, her mother had wanted to spare her, at least to some degree. And, of course, her mother was right. Her father *was* a coward and a selfish jerk. Yet Ilka had never completely accepted his abandonment of her. He had left behind a short letter saying he would come back for them as soon as everything was taken care of, and that an opportunity had come up. In Chicago.

Several years later, after complete silence on his part, he wanted a divorce. And that was the last they'd heard from him. When Ilka was a teenager, she found his address—or at least, an address where he once had lived. She'd kept it all these years in a small red treasure chest in her room.

"Surely it won't take more than a few days," Ilka said. "I'm planning to be back by the weekend. I'm booked up at work, but I found someone to fill in for me the first two days. It would be a great help if you two could keep trying to get hold of Niels from North Sealand Photography. He's in Stockholm, but he's supposed to be back tomorrow. I'm hoping he can cover for me the rest of the week. All the shoots are in and around Copenhagen."

"What exactly are you hoping to accomplish over there?" Hanne asked.

"Well, they say I'm in his will and that I have to be there in person to prove I'm Paul Jensen's daughter."

"I just don't understand why this can't be done by e-mail or fax," her mother said. "You can send them your birth certificate and your passport, or whatever it is they need."

"It seems that copies aren't good enough. If I don't go over there, I'd have to go to an American tax office in Europe, and I think the nearest one is in London. But this way, they'll let me go through his personal things and take what I want. Artie Sorvino from Jensen Funeral Home in Racine has offered to cover my travel expenses if I go now, so they can get started with closing his estate."

Ilka stood in the middle of the living room, too anxious and restless to sit down.

"Racine?" Hanne asked. "Where's that?" She picked up her steaming cup and blew on it.

"A bit north of Chicago. In Wisconsin. I'll be picked up at the airport, and it doesn't look like it'll take long to drive there. Racine is supposedly the city in the United States with the largest community of Danish descendants. A lot of Danes immigrated to the region, so it makes sense that's where he settled."

"He has a hell of a lot of nerve." Her mother's lips barely moved. "He doesn't write so much as a birthday card to you all these years, and now suddenly you have to fly over there and clean up another one of his messes."

"Karin," Hanne said, her voice gentle. "Of course Ilka should go over and sort through her father's things. If you get the opportunity for closure on such an important part of your life's story, you should grab it."

Her mother shook her head. Without looking at Ilka, she

said, "I have a bad feeling about this. Isn't it odd that he stayed in the undertaker business even though he managed to ruin his first shot at it?"

Ilka walked out into the hall and let the two women bicker about the unfairness of it all. How Paul's daughter had tried to reach out to her father all her life, and it was only now that he was gone that he was finally reaching out to her.

2

The first thing Ilka noticed was his Hawaiian shirt and longish brown hair, which was combed back and held in place by sunglasses that would look at home on a surfer. He stood out among the other drivers at Arrivals in O'Hare International Airport who were holding name cards and facing the scattered clumps of exhausted people pulling suitcases out of Customs.

Written on his card was "Ilka Nichols Jensen." Somehow, she managed to walk all the way up to him and stop before he realized she'd found him.

They looked each other over for a moment. He was in his early forties, maybe, she thought. So, her father, who had turned seventy-two in early January, had a younger partner.

She couldn't read his face, but it might have surprised him that the undertaker's daughter was a beanpole: six feet tall without a hint of a feminine form. He scanned her up and down, gaze settling on her hair, which had never been an attention-getter. Straight, flat, and mousy.

He smiled warmly and held out his hand. "Nice to meet you. Welcome to Chicago."

It's going to be a hell of a long trip, Ilka thought, before shaking his hand and saying hello. "Thank you. Nice to meet you too."

He offered to carry her suitcase. It was small, a carry-on, but she gladly handed it over to him. Then he offered her a bottle of water. The car was close by, he said, only a short walk.

Although she was used to being taller than most people, she always felt a bit shy when male strangers had to look up to make eye contact. She was nearly a head taller than Artie Sorvino, but he seemed almost impressed as he grinned up at her while they walked.

Her body ached; she hadn't slept much during the long flight. Since she'd left her apartment in Copenhagen, her nerves had been tingling with excitement. And worry, too. Things had almost gone wrong right off the bat at the Copenhagen airport, because she hadn't taken into account the long line at Passport Control. There had still been two people in front of her when she'd been called to her waiting flight. Then the arrival in the U.S., a hell that the chatty man next to her on the plane had prepared her for. He had missed God knew how many connecting flights at O'Hare because the immigration line had taken several hours to go through. It turned out to be not quite as bad as all that. She had been guided to a machine that requested her fingerprints, passport, and picture. All this information was scanned and saved. Then Ilka had been sent on to the next line, where a surly passport official wanted to know what her business was in the country. She began to sweat but then pulled herself together and explained that she was simply visiting family, which in a way was true. He stamped her passport, and moments later she was standing beside the man wearing the colorful, festive shirt.

"Is this your first trip to the U.S.?" Artie asked now, as they approached the enormous parking lot.

She smiled. "No, I've traveled here a few times. To Miami and New York."

Why had she said that? She'd never been in this part of the world before, but what the hell. It didn't matter. Unless he kept up the conversation. And Miami. Where had that come from?

"Really?" Artie told her he had lived in Key West for many years. Then his father got sick, and Artie, the only other surviving member of the family, moved back to Racine to take care of him. "I hope you made it down to the Keys while you were in Florida."

Ilka shook her head and explained that she unfortunately hadn't had time.

"I had a gallery down there," Artie said. He'd gone to the California School of the Arts in San Francisco and had made his living as an artist.

Ilka listened politely and nodded. In the parking lot, she caught sight of a gigantic black Cadillac with closed white curtains in back, which stood first in the row of parked cars. He'd driven there in the hearse.

"Hope you don't mind." He nodded at the hearse as he opened the rear door and placed her suitcase on the casket table used for rolling coffins in and out of the vehicle.

"No, it's fine." She walked around to the front passenger door. Fine, as long as she wasn't the one being rolled into the back. She felt slightly dizzy, as if she were still up in the air, but was buoyed by the nervous excitement of traveling and the anticipation of what awaited her.

The thought that her father was at the end of her journey bothered her, yet it was something she'd fantasized about nearly her entire life. But would she be able to piece together the life he'd lived without her? And was she even interested in knowing about it? What if she didn't like what she learned?

She shook her head for a moment. These thoughts had been swirling in her head since Artie's first phone call. Her mother thought she shouldn't get involved. At all. But Ilka disagreed. If her father had left anything behind, she wanted to see it. She wanted to uncover whatever she could find, to see if any of it made sense.

"How did he die?" she asked as Artie maneuvered the long hearse out of the parking lot and in between two orange signs warning about roadwork and a detour.

"Just a sec," he muttered, and he swore at the sign before deciding to skirt the roadwork and get back to the road heading north.

For a while they drove in silence; then he explained that one morning her father had simply not woken up. "He was supposed to drive a corpse to Iowa, one of our neighboring states, but he didn't show up. He just died in his sleep. Totally peacefully. He might not even have known it was over."

Ilka watched the Chicago suburbs drifting by along the long, straight bypass, the rows of anonymous stores and cheap restaurants. It seemed so overwhelming, so strange, so different. Most buildings were painted in shades of beige and brown, and enormous billboards stood everywhere, screaming messages about everything from missing children to ultracheap fast food and vanilla coffee for less than a dollar at Dunkin' Donuts.

She turned to Artie. "Was he sick?" The bump on Artie's nose—had it been broken?—made it appear too big for the rest of his face: high cheekbones, slightly squinty eyes, beard stubble definitely due to a relaxed attitude toward shaving, rather than wanting to be in style.

"Not that I know of, no. But there could have been things Paul didn't tell me about, for sure."

His tone told her it wouldn't have been the first secret Paul had kept from him.

"The doctor said his heart just stopped," he continued. "Nothing dramatic happened."

"Did he have a family?" She looked out the side window. The old hearse rode well. Heavy, huge, swaying lightly. A tall pickup drove up beside them; a man with a full beard looked down and nodded at her. She looked away quickly. She didn't care for any sympathetic looks, though he, of course, couldn't know the curtained-off back of the hearse was empty.

"He was married, you know," Artie said. Immediately Ilka sensed he didn't like being the one to fill her in on her father's private affairs. She nodded to herself; of course he didn't. What did she expect?

"And he had two daughters. That was it, apart from Mary Ann's family, but I don't know them. How much do you know about them?"

He knew very well that Ilka hadn't had any contact with her father since he'd left Denmark. Or at least she assumed he knew. "Why has the family not signed what should be signed, so you can finish with his...estate?" She set the empty water bottle on the floor.

"They did sign their part of it. But that's not enough, because you're in the will, too. First the IRS—that's our tax agency—must determine if he owes the government, and you must give them permission to investigate. If you don't sign, they'll freeze all the assets in the estate until everything is cleared up."

Ilka's shoulders slumped at the word "assets." One thing that had kept her awake during the flight was her mother's concern about her being stuck with a debt she could never pay. Maybe she would be detained; maybe she would even be thrown in jail.

"What are his daughters like?" she asked after they had driven for a while in silence.

For a few moments, he kept his eyes on the road; then he glanced at her and shrugged. "They're nice enough, but I don't really know them. It's been a long time since I've seen them. Truth is, I don't think either of them was thrilled about your father's business."

After another silence, Ilka said, "You should have called me when he died. I wish I had been at his funeral."

Was that really true? Did she truly wish that? The last funeral she'd been to was her husband's. He had collapsed from heart failure three years ago, at the age of fifty-two. She didn't like death, didn't like loss. But she'd already lost her father many years ago, so what difference would it have made watching him being lowered into the ground?

"At that time, I didn't know about you," Artie said. "Your name first came up when your father's lawyer mentioned you."

"Where is he buried?"

He stared straight ahead. Again, it was obvious he didn't enjoy talking about her father's private life. Finally, he said, "Mary Ann decided to keep the urn with his ashes at home. A private ceremony was held in the living room when the crematorium delivered the urn, and now it's on the shelf above the fireplace."

After a pause, he said, "You speak English well. Funny accent."

Ilka explained distractedly that she had traveled in Australia for a year after high school.

The billboards along the freeway here advertised hotels,

motels, and drive-ins for the most part. She wondered how there could be enough people to keep all these businesses going, given the countless offers from the clusters of signs on both sides of the road. "What about his new family? Surely they knew he had a daughter in Denmark?" She turned back to him.

"Nope!" He shook his head as he flipped the turn signal.

"He never told them he left his wife and seven-year-old daughter?" She wasn't all that surprised.

Artie didn't answer. *Okay*, Ilka thought. *That takes care of that.*

"I wonder what they think about me coming here."

He shrugged. "I don't really know, but they're not going to lose anything. His wife has an inheritance from her wealthy parents, so she's taken care of. The same goes for the daughters. And none of them have ever shown any interest in the funeral home."

And what about their father? Ilka thought. *Were they uninterested in him, too?* But that was none of her business. She didn't know them, knew nothing about their relationships with one another. And for that matter, she knew nothing about her father. Maybe his new family had asked about his life in Denmark, and maybe he'd given them a line of bullshit. But what the hell, he was thirty-nine when he left. Anyone could figure out he'd had a life before packing his weekend bag and emigrating.

Both sides of the freeway were green now. The landscape was starting to remind her of late summer in Denmark, with its green fields, patches of forest, flat land, large barns with the characteristic bowed roofs, and livestock. With a few exceptions, she felt like she could have been driving down the E45, the road between Copenhagen and Ålborg.

"Do you mind if I turn on the radio?" Artie asked.

She shook her head; it was a relief to have the awkward silence between them broken. And yet, before his hand reached the radio, she blurted out, "What was he like?"

He dropped his hand and smiled at her. "Your father was a decent guy, a really decent guy. In a lot of ways," he added, disarmingly, "he was someone you could count on, and in other ways he was very much his own man. I always enjoyed working with him, but he was also my friend. People liked him; he was interested in their lives. That's also why he was so good at talking to those who had just lost someone. He was empathetic. It feels empty, him not being around any longer."

Ilka had to concentrate to follow along. Despite her year in Australia, it was difficult when people spoke English rapidly. "Was he also a good father?"

Artie turned thoughtfully and looked out his side window. "I really can't say. I didn't know him when the girls were small." He kept glancing at the four lanes to their left. "But if you're asking me if your father was a family man, my answer is, yes and no. He was very much in touch with his family, but he probably put more of himself into Jensen Funeral Home."

"How long did you know him?"

She watched him calculate. "I moved back in 1998. We ran into each other at a local saloon, this place called Oh Dennis!, and we started talking. The victim of a traffic accident had just come in to the funeral home. The family wanted to put the young woman in an open coffin, but nobody would have wanted to see her face. So I offered to help. It's the kind of stuff I'm good at. Creating, shaping. Your father did the embalming, but I reconstructed her face. Her mother supplied us with a photo, and I did a sculpture. And I managed to make the woman look like herself, even though there wasn't much to work with. Later your father offered me a job, and I grabbed the chance. There's not much work for an artist in Racine, so reconstructions of the deceased was as good as anything."

He turned off the freeway. "Later I got a degree, because you have to have a license to work in the undertaker business."

                        ❧

They reached Racine Street and waited to make a left turn. They had driven the last several miles in silence. The streets were deserted, the shops closed. It was getting dark, and Ilka realized she was at the point where exhaustion and jet lag trumped the hunger gnawing inside her. They drove by an empty square and a nearly deserted saloon. Oh Dennis! The place where Artie had met her father. She spotted the lake at the end of the broad streets to the right, and that was it. The town was dead. Abandoned, closed. She was surprised there were no people or life.

"We've booked a room for you at the Harbourwalk Hotel. Tomorrow we can sit down and go through your father's papers. Then you can start looking through his things."

Ilka nodded. All she wanted right now was a warm bath and a bed.

                        ❧

"Sorry, we have no reservations for Miss Jensen. And none for the Jensen Funeral Home, either. We don't have a single room available."

The receptionist drawled apology after apology. It sounded to Ilka as if she had too much saliva in her mouth.

Ilka sat in a plush armchair in the lobby as Artie asked if the room was reserved in his name. "Or try Sister Eileen O'Connor," he suggested.

The receptionist apologized again as her long fingernails danced over the computer keyboard. The sound was unnaturally loud, a bit like Ilka's mother's knitting needles tapping against each other.

Ilka shut down. She could sit there and sleep; it made absolutely no difference to her. Back in Denmark, it was five in the morning, and she hadn't slept in twenty-two hours.

"I'm sorry," Artie said. "You're more than welcome to stay at my place. I can sleep on the sofa. Or we can fix up a place for you to sleep at the office, and we'll find another hotel in the morning."

Ilka sat up in the armchair. "What's that sound?"

Artie looked bewildered. "What do you mean?"

"It's like a phone ringing in the next room."

He listened for a moment before shrugging. "I can't hear anything."

The sound came every ten seconds. It was as if something were hidden behind the reception desk or farther down the hotel foyer. Ilka shook her head and looked at him. "You don't need to sleep on the sofa. I can sleep somewhere at the office."

She needed to be alone, and the thought of a strange man's bedroom didn't appeal to her.

"That's fine." He grabbed her small suitcase. "It's only five minutes away, and I know we can find some food for you too."

The black hearse was parked just outside the main entrance of the hotel, but that clearly wasn't bothering anyone. Though the hotel was apparently fully booked, Ilka hadn't seen a single person since they'd arrived.

Night had fallen, and her eyelids closed as soon as she settled into the car. She jumped when Artie opened the door and poked her with his finger. She hadn't even realized they had arrived. They were parked in a large, empty lot. The white building was an enormous box with several attic windows reflecting the moonlight back into the thick darkness. Tall trees with enormous crowns hovered over Ilka when she got out of the car.

They reached the door, beside which was a sign: JENSEN FUNERAL HOME. WELCOME. Pillars stood all the way across the broad porch, with well-tended flower beds in front of it, but the darkness covered everything else.

Artie led her inside the high-ceilinged hallway and turned the light on. He pointed to a stairway at the other end. Ilka's feet sank deep in the carpet; it smelled dusty, with a hint of plastic and instant coffee.

"Would you like something to drink? Are you hungry? I can make a sandwich."

"No, thank you." She just wanted him to leave.

He led her up the stairs, and when they reached a small landing, he pointed at a door. "Your father had a room in there, and I think we can find some sheets. We have a cot we can fold out and make up for you."

Ilka held her hand up. "If there is a bed in my father's room, I can just sleep in it." She nodded when he asked if she was sure. "What time do you want to meet tomorrow?"

"How about eight thirty? We can have breakfast together."

She had no idea what time it was, but as long as she got some sleep, she guessed she'd be fine. She nodded.

Ilka stayed outside on the landing while Artie opened the door to her father's room and turned on the light. She watched him walk over to a dresser and pull out the bottom drawer. He grabbed some sheets and a towel and tossed them on the bed; then he waved her in.

The room's walls were slanted. An old white bureau stood at the end of the room, and under the window, which must have been one of those she'd noticed from the parking lot, was a desk with drawers on both sides. The bed was just inside the room and to the left. There was also a small coffee table and, at the end of the bed, a narrow built-in closet.

A dark jacket and a tie lay draped over the back of the desk chair. The desk was covered with piles of paper; a briefcase leaned against the closet. But there was nothing but sheets on the bed.

"I'll find a comforter and a pillow," Artie said, accidentally grazing her as he walked by.

Ilka stepped into the room. A room lived in, yet abandoned. A feeling suddenly stirred inside her, and she froze. He was here. The smell. A heavy yet pleasant odor she recognized from somewhere deep inside. She'd had no idea this memory existed. She closed her eyes and let her mind drift back to when she was very young, the feeling of being held. Tobacco. Sundays in the car, driving out to Bellevue. Feeling secure, knowing someone close was taking care of her. Lifting her up on a lap. Making her laugh. The sound of hooves pounding the ground, horses at a racetrack. Her father's concentration as he chain-smoked, captivated by the race. His laughter.

She sat down on the bed, not hearing what Artie said

when he laid the comforter and pillow beside her, then walked out and closed the door.

Her father had been tall; at least that's how she remembered him. She could see to the end of the world when she sat on his shoulders. They did fun things together. He took her to an amusement park and bought her ice cream while he tried out the slot machines, to see if they were any good. Her mother didn't always know when they went there. He also took her out to a centuries-old amusement park in the forest north of Copenhagen. They stopped at Peter Liep's, and she drank soda while he drank beer. They sat outside and watched the riders pass by, smelling horseshit and sweat when the thirsty riders dismounted and draped the reins over the hitching post. He had loved horses. On the other hand, she couldn't remember the times—the many times, according to her mother—when he didn't come home early enough to stick his head in her room and say good night. Not having enough money for food because he had gambled his wages away at the track was something else she didn't recall—but her mother did.

Ilka opened her eyes. Her exhaustion was gone, but she still felt dizzy. She walked over to the desk and reached for a photo in a wide mahogany frame. A trotter, its mane flying out to both sides at the finish line. In another photo, a trotter covered by a red victory blanket stood beside a sulky driver holding a trophy high above his head, smiling for the camera. There were several more horse photos, and a ticket to Lunden hung from a window hasp. She grabbed it. Paul Jensen. Charlottenlund Derby 1982. The year he left them.

Ilka didn't realize at the time that he had left. All she knew was that one morning he wasn't there, and her mother was crying but wouldn't tell her why. When she arrived home from school that afternoon, her mother was still crying. And as she remembered it, her mother didn't stop crying for a long time.

She had been with her father at that derby in 1982. She picked up a photo leaning against the windowsill, then sat down on the bed. "Ilka and Peter Kjærsgaard" was written on the back of the photo. Ilka had been five years old when her father took her to the derby for the first time. Back then, her mother had gone along. She vaguely remembered going to the track and meeting the famous jockey, but suddenly the odors and sounds were crystal clear. She closed her eyes.

"You can give them one if you want," the man had said as he handed her a bucket filled with carrots, many more than her mother had in bags back in their kitchen. The bucket was heavy, but Ilka wanted to show them how big she was, so she hooked the handle with her arm and walked over to one of the stalls.

She smiled proudly at a red-shirted sulky driver passing by as he was fastening his helmet. The track was crowded, but during the races, few people were allowed in the barn. They were, though. She and her father.

She pulled her hand back, frightened, when the horse in the stall whinnied and pulled against the chain. It snorted and pounded its hoof on the floor. The horse was so tall. Carefully she held the carrot out in the palm of her hand, as her father had taught her to do. The horse snatched the sweet treat, gently tickling her.

Her father stood with a group of men at the end of the row of stalls. They laughed loudly, slapping one another's shoulders. A few of them drank beer from a bottle. Ilka sat down on a bale of hay. Her father had promised her a horse when she was a bit older. One of the grooms came over and asked if she would like a ride behind the barn; he was going to walk one of the horses to warm it up. She wanted to, if her father would let her. He did.

"Look at me, Daddy!" Ilka cried. "Look at me." The horse had stopped, clearly preferring to eat grass rather than walk. She kicked gently to get it going, but her legs were too short to do any good.

Her father pulled himself away from the other men and stood at the barn entrance. He waved, and Ilka sat up proudly. The groom asked if he should let go of the reins so she could ride by herself, and though she didn't really love the idea, she nodded. But when he dropped the reins and she turned around to show her father how brave she was, he was back inside with the others.

☙

Ilka stood up and put the photo back. She could almost smell the tar used by the racetrack farrier on horse hooves. She used to sit behind a pane of glass with her mother and follow the races, while her father stood over at the finish line. But then her mother stopped going along.

She picked up another photo from the windowsill. She was standing on a bale of hay, toasting with a sulky driver. Fragments of memories flooded back as she studied herself in the photo. Her father speaking excitedly with the driver, his expression as the horses were hitched to the sulkies. And the way he said, "We-e-e-ell, shall we…?" right before a race. Then he would hold his hand out, and they would walk down to the track.

She wondered why she could remember these things,

when she had forgotten most of what had happened back then.

There was also a photo of two small girls on the desk. She knew these were her younger half sisters, who were smiling broadly at the photographer. Suddenly, deep inside her chest, she felt a sharp twinge—but why? After setting the photo back down, she realized it wasn't from never having met her half sisters. No. It was pure jealousy. They had grown up with her father, while she had been abandoned.

Ilka threw herself down on the bed and pulled the comforter over her, without even bothering to put the sheets on. She lay curled up, staring into space.

3

At some point, Ilka must have fallen asleep, because she gave a start when someone knocked on the door. She recognized Artie's voice.

"Morning in there. Are you awake?"

She sat up, confused. She had been up once in the night to look for a bathroom. The building seemed strangely hushed, as if it were packed in cotton. She'd opened a few doors and finally found a bathroom with shiny tiles and a low bathtub. The toilet had a soft cover on its seat, like the one in her grandmother's flat in Bagsværd. On her way back, she had grabbed her father's jacket, carried it to the bed, and buried her nose in it. Now it lay halfway on the floor.

"Give me half an hour," she said. She hugged the jacket, savoring the odor that had brought her childhood memories to the surface from the moment she'd walked into the room.

Now that it was light outside, the room seemed bigger. Last night she hadn't noticed the storage boxes lining the wall behind both sides of the desk. Clean shirts in clear plastic sacks hung from the hook behind the door.

"Okay, but have a look at these IRS forms," he said, sliding a folder under the door. "And sign on the last page when you've read them. We'll take off whenever you're ready."

Ilka didn't answer. She pulled her knees up to her chest and lay curled up. Without moving. Being shut up inside a room with her father's belongings was enough to make her feel she'd reunited with a part of herself. The big black hole inside her, the one that had appeared every time she sent a letter despite knowing she'd get no answer, was slowly filling up with something she'd failed to find herself.

She had lived about a sixth of her life with her father. *When do we become truly conscious of the people around us?* she wondered. She had just turned forty, and he had deserted them when she was seven. This room here was filled with everything he had left behind, all her memories of him. All the odors and sensations that had made her miss him.

❧

Artie knocked on the door again. She had no idea how long she'd been lying on the bed.

"Ready?" he called out.

"No," she yelled back. She couldn't. She needed to just stay and take in everything here, so it wouldn't disappear again.

"Have you read it?"

"I signed it!"

"Would you rather stay here? Do you want me to go alone?"

"Yes, please."

Silence. She couldn't tell if he was still outside.

"Okay," he finally said. "I'll come back after breakfast." He sounded annoyed. "I'll leave the phone here with you."

Ilka listened to him walk down the stairs. After she'd walked over to the door and signed her name, she hadn't moved a muscle. She hadn't opened any drawers or closets.

She'd brought along a bag of chips, but they were all gone. And she didn't feel like going downstairs for something to drink. Instead, she gave way to exhaustion. The stream of thoughts, the fragments of memories in her head, had slowly settled into a tempo she could follow.

Her father had written her into his will. He had declared her to be his biological daughter. But evidently, he'd never mentioned her to his new family, or to the people closest to him in his new life. Of course, he hadn't been obligated to mention her, she thought. But if her name hadn't come up in his will, they could have liquidated his business without anyone knowing about an adult daughter in Denmark.

The telephone outside the door rang, but she ignored it. What had this Artie guy imagined she should do if the telephone rang? Did he think she would answer it? And say what?

At first, she'd wondered why her father had named her in his will. But after having spent the last twelve hours enveloped in memories of him, she had realized that no matter what had happened in his life, a part of him had still been her father.

She cried, then felt herself dozing off.

Someone knocked on the door. "Not today," she yelled, before Artie could even speak a word. She turned her back to the room, her face to the wall. She closed her eyes until the footsteps disappeared down the stairs.

The telephone rang again, but she didn't react.

Slowly it had all come back. After her father had disappeared, her mother had two jobs: the funeral home business and her teaching. It wasn't long after summer vacation, and school had just begun. Ilka thought he had left in September. A month before she turned eight. Her mother taught Danish and arts and crafts to students in several grades. When she wasn't at school, she was at the funeral home on Brønshøj Square. Also on weekends, picking up flowers and ordering coffins. Working in the office, keeping the books when she wasn't filling out forms.

Ilka had gone along with her to various embassies whenever a mortuary passport was needed to bring a corpse home from outside the country, or when a person died in Denmark and was to be buried elsewhere. It had been fascinating, though frightening. But she had never fully understood how hard her mother worked. Finally, when Ilka was twelve, her mother managed to sell the business and get back her life.

After her father left, they were unable to afford the single-story house Ilka had been born in. They moved into a small apartment on Frederikssundsvej in Copenhagen. Her mother had never been shy about blaming her father for their economic woes, but she'd always said they would be okay. After she sold the funeral home, their situation had improved; Ilka saw it mostly from the color in her mother's cheeks, a more relaxed expression on her face. Also, she was more likely to let Ilka invite friends home for dinner. When she started eighth grade, they moved to Østerbro, a better district in the city, but she stayed in her school in Brønshøj and took the bus.

"You *were* an asshole," she muttered, her face still to the wall. "What you did was just completely inexcusable."

The telephone outside the door finally gave up. She heard soft steps out on the stairs. She sighed. They had paid her airfare; there were limits to what she could get away with. But today was out of the question. And that telephone was their business.

Someone knocked again at the door. This time it sounded different. They knocked again. "Hello." A female voice. The woman called her name and knocked one more time, gently but insistently.

Ilka rose from the bed. She shook her hair and slipped it behind her ears and smoothed her T-shirt. She walked over and opened the door. She couldn't hide her startled expression at the sight of a woman dressed in gray, her hair covered by a veil of the same color. Her broad, demure skirt reached below the knees. Her eyes seemed far too big for her small face and delicate features.

"Who are you?"

"My name is Sister Eileen O'Connor, and you have a meeting in ten minutes."

The woman was already about to turn and walk back down the steps, when Ilka finally got hold of herself. "I have a meeting?"

"Yes, the business is yours now." Ilka heard patience as well as suppressed annoyance in the nun's voice. "Artie has left for the day and has informed me that you have taken over."

"*My* business?" Ilka ran her hand through her hair. A bad habit of hers, when she didn't know what to do with her hands.

"You did read the papers Artie left for you? It's my understanding that you signed them, so you're surely aware of what you have inherited."

"I signed to say I'm his daughter," Ilka said. More than anything, she just wanted to close the door and make everything go away.

"If you had read what was written," the sister said, a bit sharply, "you would know that your father has left the business to you. And by your signature, you have acknowledged your identity and therefore your inheritance."

Ilka was speechless. While she gawked, the sister added, "The Norton family lost their grandmother last night. It wasn't unexpected, but several of them are taking it hard. I've made coffee for four." She stared at Ilka's T-shirt and bare legs. "And it's our custom to receive relatives in attire that is a bit more respectful."

A tiny smile played on her narrow lips, so fleeting that Ilka was in doubt as to whether it had actually appeared. "I can't talk to a family that just lost someone," she protested. "I don't know what to say. I've never—I'm sorry, you have to talk to them."

Sister Eileen stood for a moment before speaking. "Unfortunately, I can't. I don't have the authority to perform such duties. I do the office work, open mail, and laminate the photos of the deceased onto death notices for relatives to use as bookmarks. But you will do fine. Your father was always good at such conversations. All you have to do is allow the family to talk. Listen and find out what's important to them; that's the most vital thing for people who come to us. And these people have a contract for a prepaid ceremony. The contract explains everything they have paid for. Mrs. Norton has been making funeral payments her whole life, so everything should be smooth sailing."

The nun walked soundlessly down the stairs. Ilka stood in the doorway, staring at where she had vanished. Had she seriously inherited a funeral home? In the U.S.? How had her life taken such an unexpected turn? What the hell had her father been thinking?

She pulled herself together. She had seven minutes before the Nortons arrived. "Respectful" attire, the sister had said. Did she even have something like that in her suitcase? She hadn't opened it yet.

But she couldn't do this. They couldn't make her talk

to total strangers who had just lost a relative. Then she remembered she hadn't known the undertaker who helped her
when Erik died, either. But he had been a salvation to her.
A person who had taken care of everything in a professional manner and arranged things precisely as she believed
her husband would have wanted. The funeral home, the
flowers—yellow tulips. The hymns. It was also the undertaker who had said she would regret it if she didn't hire an
organist to play during the funeral. Because even though
it might seem odd, the mere sound of it helped relieve the
somber atmosphere. She had chosen the cheapest coffin, as
the undertaker had suggested, seeing that Erik had wanted
to be cremated. Many minor decisions had been made for
her; that had been an enormous relief. And the funeral had
gone exactly the way she'd wanted. Plus, the undertaker had
helped reserve a room at the restaurant where they gathered
after the ceremony. But those types of details were apparently already taken care of here. It seemed all she had to do
was meet with them. She walked over to her suitcase.

   Ilka dumped everything out onto the bed and pulled a
light blouse and dark pants out of the pile. Along with her
toiletry bag and underwear. Halfway down the stairs, she remembered she needed shoes. She went back up again. All
she had was sneakers.

The family was three adult children—a daughter and two
sons—and a grandchild. The two men seemed essentially
composed, while the woman and the boy were crying. The
woman's face was stiff and pale, as if every ounce of blood
had drained out of her. Her young son stared down at his
hands, looking withdrawn and gloomy.

"Our mother paid for everything in advance," one son said when Ilka walked in. They sat in the arrangement room's comfortable armchairs, around a heavy mahogany table. Dusty paintings in elegant gilded frames hung from the dark green walls. Ilka guessed the paintings were inspired by Lake Michigan. She had no idea what to do with the grieving family, nor what was expected of her.

The son farthest from the door asked, "How does the condolences and tributes page on your website work? Is it like anyone can go in and write on it, or can it only be seen if you have the password? We want everybody to be able to put up a picture of our mother and write about their good times with her."

Ilka nodded to him and walked over to shake his hand. "We will make the page so it's exactly how you want it." Then she repeated their names: Steve—the one farthest from the door—Joe, Helen, and the grandson, Pete. At least she thought that was right, though she wasn't sure because he had mumbled his name.

"And we talked it over and decided we want charms," Helen said. "We'd all like one. But I can't see in the papers whether they're paid for or not, because if not we need to know how much they cost."

Ilka had no idea what charms were, but she'd noticed the green form that had been laid on the table for her, and a folder entitled "Norton," written by hand. The thought struck her that the handwriting must be her father's.

"Service Details" was written on the front of the form. Ilka sat down and reached for the notebook on the table. It had a big red heart on the cover, along with "Helping Hands for Healing Hearts."

She surmised the notebook was probably meant for the relatives. Quickly, she slid it over the table to them; then she opened a drawer and found a sheet of paper. "I'm very sorry," she said. It was difficult for her not to look at the grandson, who appeared crushed. "About your loss. As I understand, everything is already decided. But I wasn't here when things were planned. Maybe we can go through everything together and figure out exactly how you want it done."

What in the world is going on? she thought as she sat there blabbering away at this grieving family, as if she'd been doing it all her life!

"Our mother liked Mr. Jensen a lot," Steve said. "He took charge of the funeral arrangements when our father died, and we'd like things done the same way."

Ilka nodded.

"But not the coffin," Joe said. "We want one that's more upscale, more feminine."

"Is it possible to see the charms?" Helen asked, still tearful. "And we also need to print a death notice, right?"

"Can you arrange it so her dogs can sit up by the coffin during the service?" Steve asked. He looked at Ilka as if this were the most important of all the issues. "That won't be a problem, will it?"

"No, not a problem," she answered quickly, as the questions rained down on her.

"How many people can fit in there? And can we all sit together?"

"The room can hold a lot of people," she said, feeling now as if she'd been fed to the lions. "We can squeeze the chairs together; we can get a lot of people in there. And of course you can sit together."

Ilka had absolutely no idea what room they were talking about. But there had been about twenty people attending her husband's service, and they hadn't even filled a corner of the chapel in Bispebjerg.

"How many do you think are coming?" she asked, just to be on the safe side.

"Probably somewhere between a hundred and a hundred and fifty," Joe guessed. "That's how many showed up at Dad's service. But it could be more this time, so it's good to be prepared. She was very active after her retirement. And the choir would like to sing."

Ilka nodded mechanically and forced a smile. She had heard that it's impossible to vomit while you're smiling, something about reflexes. Not that she was about to vomit; there was nothing inside her to come out. But her insides contracted as if something in there was getting out of control. "How did Mrs. Norton die?" She leaned back in her chair.

She felt their eyes on her, and for a moment everyone was quiet. The adults looked at her as if the question weren't her business. And maybe it was irrelevant for the planning, she thought. But after Erik died, in a way it had been a big relief to talk about him, how she had come home and found him on the kitchen floor. Putting it into words made it all seem more real, like it actually had happened. And it had helped her through the days after his death, which otherwise were foggy.

Helen sat up and looked over at her son, who was still staring at his hands. "Pete's the one who found her. We bought groceries for his grandma three times a week and drove them over to her after school. And there she was, out in the yard. Just lying there."

Now Ilka regretted having asked.

From underneath the hair hanging over his forehead, with his head bowed, the boy scowled at his mother. "Grandma was out cutting flowers to put in vases, and she fell," he muttered.

"There was a lot of blood," his mother said, nodding.

"But the guy who picked her up promised we wouldn't be able to see it when she's in her coffin," Steve said. He looked at Ilka, as if he wanted this confirmed.

Quickly she answered, "No, you won't. She'll look fine. Did she like flowers?"

Helen smiled and nodded. "She lived and breathed for her garden. She loved her flower beds."

"Then maybe it's a good idea to use flowers from her garden to decorate the coffin," Ilka suggested.

Steve sat up. "Decorate the coffin? It's going to be open."

"But it's a good idea," Helen said. "We'll decorate the chapel with flowers from the garden. We can go over and pick them together. It's a beautiful way to say good-bye to the garden she loved, too."

"But if we use hers, will we get the money back we already paid for flowers?" Joe asked.

Ilka nodded. "Yes, of course." Surely it wasn't a question of all that much money.

"Oh God!" Helen said. "I almost forgot to give you this." Out of her bag she pulled a large folder that said "Family Record Guide" and handed it over to Ilka. "It's already filled out."

In many ways, it reminded Ilka of the diaries she'd kept in school. First a page with personal information. The full name of the deceased, the parents' names. Whether she was married, divorced, single, or a widow. Education and job positions. Then a page with familial relations, and on the opposite page there was room to write about the deceased's life and memories. There were sections for writing about a first home, about becoming a parent, about becoming a grandparent. And then a section that caught Ilka's attention, because it had to be of some use. Favorites: colors, flowers, season, songs, poems, books. And on and on it went. Family traditions. Funny memories, role models, hobbies, special talents. Mrs. Norton had filled it all out very thoroughly.

Ilka closed the folder and asked how they would describe their mother and grandmother.

"She was very sociable," Joe said. "Also after Dad died. She was involved in all sorts of things; she was very active in the seniors' club in West Racine."

"And family meant a lot to her," Helen said. She'd stopped crying without Ilka noticing. "She was always the one who made sure we all got together, at least twice a year."

Ilka let them speak, as long as they stayed away from talking about charms and choosing coffins. She had no idea how to wind up the conversation, but she kept listening as they nearly all talked at once, to make sure that everything about the deceased came out. Even gloomy Pete added that his grandmother made the world's best pecan pie.

"And she had the best Southern recipe for macaroni and cheese," he added. The others laughed.

Ilka thought again about Erik. After his funeral, their apartment had felt empty and abandoned. A silence hung that had nothing to do with being alone. It took a few weeks for her to realize the silence was in herself. There was no one to talk to, so everything was spoken inside her head. And at the same time, she felt as if she were in a bubble no sound could penetrate. That had been one of the most difficult things to get used to. Slowly things got better, and at last—she couldn't say precisely when—the silence connected with her loss disappeared.

Meanwhile, she'd had the business to run. What a circus. They'd started working together almost from the time they'd first met. He was the photographer, though occasionally she went out with him to help set up the equipment and direct the students. Otherwise, she was mostly responsible for the office work. But she had done a job or two by herself when they were especially busy; she'd seen how he worked. There was nothing mysterious about it. Classes were lined up with the tallest students in back, and the most attractive were placed in the middle so the focus would be on them. The individual portraits were mostly about adjusting the height of the seat and taking enough pictures to ensure that one of them was good enough. But when Erik suddenly wasn't there, with a full schedule of jobs still booked, she had taken over, without giving it much thought. She did know the school secretaries, and they knew her, so that eased the transition.

"Do we really have to buy a coffin, when Mom is just going to be burned?" Steve said, interrupting her thoughts. "Can't we just borrow one? She won't be lying in there very long."

Shit. Ilka had blanked out for a moment. Where the hell was Artie? Did they have coffins they loaned out? She had to say something. "It would have to be one that's been used."

"We're not putting Mom in a coffin where other dead people have been!" Helen was indignant, while a hint of a smile appeared on her son's face.

Ilka jumped in. "Unfortunately, we can only loan out used coffins." She hoped that would put a lid on this idea.

"We can't do that. Can we?" Helen said to her two brothers. "On the other hand, if we borrow a coffin, we might be able to afford charms instead."

Ilka didn't have the foggiest idea if her suggestion was even possible. But if this really was her business, she could decide, now, couldn't she?

AN EXCERPT FROM THE DAUGHTER

"We *would* save forty-five hundred dollars," Joe said.

Forty-five hundred dollars for a coffin! This could turn out to be disastrous if it ended with them losing money from her ignorant promise.

"Oh, at least. Dad's coffin cost seven thousand dollars."

What is this? Ilka thought. *Are coffins here decorated in gold leaf?*

"But Grandma already paid for her funeral," the grandson said. "You can't save on something she's already paid for. You're not going to get her money back, right?" Finally, he looked up.

"We'll figure this out," Ilka said.

The boy looked over at his mother and began crying.

"Oh, honey!" Helen said.

"You're all talking about this like it isn't even Grandma; like it's someone else who's dead," he said, angry now.

He turned to Ilka. "Like it's all about money, and just getting it over with." He jumped up so fast he knocked his chair over; then he ran out the door.

His mother sent her brothers an apologetic look; they both shook their heads. She turned to Ilka and asked if it were possible for them to return tomorrow. "By then we'll have this business about the coffin sorted out. We also have to order a life board. I brought along some photos of Mom."

Standing now, Ilka told them it was of course fine to come back tomorrow. She knew one thing for certain: Artie was going to meet with them, whether he liked it or not. She grabbed the photos Helen was holding out.

"They're from when she was born, when she graduated from school, when she married Dad, and from their anniversary the year before he died."

"Super," Ilka said. She had no idea what these photos would be used for.

The three siblings stood up and headed for the door. "When would you like to meet?" Ilka asked. They agreed on noon.

Joe stopped and looked up at her. "But can the memorial service be held on Friday?"

"We can talk about that later," Ilka replied at once. She needed time to find out what to do with 150 people and a place for the dogs close to the coffin.

After they left, Ilka walked back to the desk and sank down in the chair. She hadn't even offered them coffee, she realized.

She buried her face in her hands and sat for a moment. She had inherited a funeral home in Racine. And if she were to believe the nun in the reception area laminating death notices, she had accepted the inheritance.

She heard a knock on the doorframe. Sister Eileen stuck her head in the room. Ilka nodded, and the nun walked over and laid a slip of paper on the table. On it was an address.

"We have a pickup."

Ilka stared at the paper. How was this possible? It wasn't just charms, life boards, and a forty-five-hundred-dollar coffin. Now they wanted her to pick up a body, too. She exhaled and stood up.

ABOUT THE AUTHOR

Sara Blaedel's suspense novels have enjoyed incredible success around the world: fantastic acclaim, multiple awards, and runaway #1 bestselling success internationally. In her native Denmark, Sara was voted most popular novelist for the fourth time in 2014. She is also a recipient of the Golden Laurel, Denmark's most prestigious literary award. Her books are published in thirty-seven countries. Her series featuring police detective Louise Rick is adored the world over, and Sara has just launched her new Family Secrets suspense series to fantastic acclaim.

Sara Blaedel's interest in story, writing, and especially crime fiction was nurtured from a young age. The daughter of a renowned Danish journalist and an actress whose career included roles in theater, radio, TV, and movies, Sara grew up surrounded by a constant flow of professional writers and performers visiting the Blaedel home. Despite a struggle with dyslexia, books gave Sara a world in which to escape when her introverted nature demanded an exit from the hustle and bustle of life.

Sara tried a number of careers, from a restaurant apprenticeship to graphic design, before she started a publishing

company called Sara B, where she published Danish trans-
lations of American crime fiction.

Publishing ultimately led Sara to journalism, and she
covered a wide range of stories, from criminal trials to the
premiere of *Star Wars: Episode I*. It was during this time—
and while skiing in Norway—that Sara started brewing the
ideas for her first novel. In 2004 Louise and Camilla were
introduced in Grønt Støv ("Green Dust"), and Sara won the
Danish Academy for Crime Fiction's debut prize.

Originally from Denmark, Sara has lived in New York,
but now spends most of her time in Copenhagen. When she
isn't busy committing brutal murders on the page, she is an
ambassador with Save the Children and serves on the jury
of a documentary film competition.